EQUAL & OPPOSITE

ARCANE CASEBOOK 11

DAN WILLIS

Print Edition – 2024

This version copyright © 2024 by Dan Willis.

All rights reserved. No part of this book may be reproduced or transmitted in any form or by any electronic or mechanical means, including photocopying, recording or by any information storage and retrieval system, without the express written permission of the copyright holder, except where permitted by law.

This novel is a work of fiction. Names, characters, places and incidents are either the product of the author's imagination, or, if real, used fictitiously.

Edited by Stephanie Osborn
Supplemental Edits by Barbara Davis

Cover by Mihaela Voicu

Published by

Runeblade Entertainment
Spanish Fork, Utah.

1

SERVICE

"As you can see, Mr. Moeller," Alex said, handing an open folder to the man on the couch in his front office, "your sister, Lilly, was adopted by a family from Iowa." He indicated a spot on the exposed page inside the folder.

Moeller leaned down a bit to read, then sat back up with a look of wonder on his face. He was a thin, fit man in his mid-twenties with slicked-back hair and a short, neatly manicured beard. He'd come to Alex to locate his sister, whom he hadn't seen for over a decade. Their parents had been killed in a fire and both children had been adopted out of an orphanage, just not together.

"Is she okay?" Moeller asked, his voice catching in his throat.

Alex leaned down and turned the page in the folder.

"More than okay," he said. "She lives in Des Moines, just twenty miles from where she grew up. She works in a millinery shop." Alex moved his finger down the page. "Last year, she married a man named Rhett Grayson, who is an alchemist that everyone calls Red on account of his hair, and she's expecting their first child."

"She's married," Moeller said, his voice sounding like he'd been brained with a shovel. Recovering his wits, the young man looked up at Alex. "Is she happy?"

"I suspect she is," Alex said, putting a reassuring hand on Moeller's shoulder. "I called the local branch of the Office of Magical Oversight. According to them Red Grayson is an upstanding citizen and there have been no complaints laid against him by angry customers."

Young Moeller slumped back against the couch, letting out a pent-up breath.

"This is really her?" he said after a long pause. "You're sure?"

"I guarantee it."

"How..." Moeller managed, shaking his head.

"She requested a copy of her birth certificate," Alex supplied. "Probably so she could get married. I assumed she'd been born in the same town you were, so it wasn't too hard to find."

"And that led you to her," Moeller said, following the chain of events in his mind, "but how did you find the rest of this?"

"That was the easy part," Alex admitted. "Once I knew that the records office had sent the copy of the certificate to Des Moines, I called the registrar's office there and had them search up her name. They didn't have a record of Lilly Moeller, but a Lilly Paxton had applied for a marriage license about the same time as the birth certificate was requested." Alex shrugged. "After I knew her adopted last name, it wasn't hard to figure out the rest."

"Thank you, Mr. Lockerby," Moeller said, closing the folder. "I can't believe it. I never thought I'd see Lilly again."

"Now she's just a train ride away," Alex said, stepping back as Moeller stood up. He had to clutch the silver topped cane tightly to keep from losing his balance and falling over. In his experience, he lost a lot of his prestige when he fell down in front of clients.

If Moeller noticed Alex's balance issues, he gave no sign. He reached into his pocket and withdrew a sealed envelope, offering it to Alex.

"The rest of your fee," he said, "and worth every penny."

Alex accepted the envelope, then bade Mr. Moeller good luck as the younger man headed for the door. A moment later Alex heard the sound of his footsteps retreating down the hall, and he turned and limped over to Sherry's desk. A twinge of pain hit his foot as he shifted his weight to sit down and, since the room was empty, he swore.

Equal & Opposite

"Cursed foot," he growled, then leaned down to the bottom right drawer in Sherry's desk and withdrew the steel strongbox. Alex had been shot in the foot at the end of last year and the wound hadn't fully healed. From the looks of things, it might not heal at all, at least until Alex was able to receive magical healing again.

"It's me," he almost shouted at the box, his frustration getting the better of him. The strong box didn't seem to care and its locking rune glowed purple before the lid popped free.

Alex opened the box, counted the cash Moeller had given him, added it to the cash in the box and wrote the new total on a notepad inside. Without bothering to double check his work, he shut the lid and returned the box to the drawer.

That done, he sat back in his receptionist's chair and tried to relax. Moeller's case involved a lot more calling around and dealing with disinterested bureaucrats than he'd admitted, and he was glad the case of the missing sister was over and done. His leg twitched, as his habitual memory warned him to put it up on a chair. Unfortunately, nothing like that existed in the front office, so if he wanted to take the pressure off his sore foot, he'd have to go back to his own office where he had an ottoman for just such a need.

Grumbling with indecision, Alex checked his pocket watch and found that it was already after five. With a sigh of both resignation and satisfaction, he used the cane to push himself up, then limped to the outer door. Turning the handle on the lock, he heard the bolt snap into place. It wasn't a loud sound, but it carried with it an energy that invigorated Alex. With a spring in his still-limping step, he turned and made his way across the front room to the back hallway and then to his vault.

Since he was still bound by the damnation rune, Alex couldn't modify his vault. Normally, since he was attuned to the vault by virtue of having created it, Alex could shape and mold the walls with his hands, or, more recently, with his mind. With the damnation rune in place, however, the cold, gray stuff that made up the walls were just as unyielding as the stone they resembled.

Still, he had modified some of the vault. The back, left corner had always been a storage area for things Alex didn't want to deal with.

Now all of that had been removed and a large desk occupied the space. It was made of oak and stained a light, golden color with an integrated leather topper and polished brass accents. A sturdy chair sat in front of it and a cork board hung from the wall above it. Beside the desk was a rollaway chalkboard of the kind Alex had seen in universities. The space was designed to be a model of research efficiency.

It was anything but.

The chalkboard was covered in tiny, packed lines of text along with several alchemical formulae. The cork board held so many scraps of paper, it looked like a notepad had exploded, and heaped upon the desk were dozens and dozens of papers and folders.

There was one spot on the desk that was clean, however. Alex had taken great care to make sure nothing encroached on the space. Only one thing stood there, a glass dome mounted to a wooden base and inside, held up by a dowel, was a black lump of rock with green fracture lines running through it.

It was the most hated thing Alex owned.

The veins in the stone seemed to pulse as Alex approached, getting subtly brighter and dimmer, as if the thing were breathing. The glass that encased it warped the image of the rock, a testament to how thick it was. As Alex approached, the glass shimmered with different colors, like a trapped rainbow.

Both Sorsha and Iggy had enchanted the glass to ensure that whatever sickly miasma the stone was giving off could not escape its prison.

Alex ground his teeth at that thought.

It had been almost four months since they'd laid Charles Grier to rest. Four months and Alex was no closer to figuring out what the curse stone was or who thought it was so important that they killed his friend for knowing about it.

Alex swore again, the sound of his profanity echoing off the walls.

A curse stone, that's what Charles had called it. Not a cursed stone, as if the stone itself were cursed, but a curse stone. A stone meant to curse others.

Charles was the kind of man who used language precisely. He was much like Iggy in that respect. If he said that the little bit of pulsating rock could curse people, then that's what it was doing. The damnable, frustrating thing about it was that after four months, Alex was no closer to figuring out what the stone was, or what it did.

With his dying breath, Charles had named the Inquisition as a place to start, but as far as Alex was concerned it was yet another dead end. The only Inquisition Charles could possibly mean was the Spanish Inquisition, a pogrom of torture and murder meant to drive Protestants out of Catholic Spain.

"And to steal as much loot as they could," he added out loud. "Let's not forget that."

Alex had scoured the library for every book they had on the Spanish Inquisition and had learned a great deal about its history, but as far as he could tell, they used neither runes nor alchemy as a matter of course. The only thing he was certain of was that there was no mention in any of his books of magic stones, curse-laden or otherwise.

"Just go down to dinner," Alex urged himself. "Iggy's bound to be cooking; you can talk about the newspaper and worry about this tomorrow."

After a long moment, his efforts to convince himself to just move on began to work, but as he turned away from the new desk, the phone next to his drafting table rang.

Alex considered just letting it ring, but something in the annoying jingle of the bell compelled him to limp across the room and answer it.

"Lockerby," he said, with a bit more vitriol than he meant.

"Oh, I'm glad you're still here," Sherry's voice greeted him, though he wondered why she mentioned his still being in the office.

Someone must be with her, he thought.

"Trouble?" he said, glancing at his gun cabinet.

"I finished the research job at the library," she said as if he hadn't spoken. "I wanted to make sure everything was locked up here and when I got here, I ran into a client who was just leaving."

"Someone I should see tonight?"

"I think so."

"Well, tell him I'll be out in a minute," Alex said, then thanked her and hung up.

With a sigh, he turned back to the little hallway that led to the office door and began limping that way. It wasn't far, but with his limp,

Alex was irritated by the time he reached the door to the office's front room.

Taking a deep breath and letting it out, he took hold of the door handle and pushed it open. In the reception room, Sherry was sitting on the edge of her desk, offering a light to a tall, athletic man with thick brown hair that was going gray at the temples. His hands were calloused, but not so much that Alex would have guessed him to be a laborer. If his hands weren't those of a workman, his clothes definitely weren't. He was dressed in an expensive suit with a gold chain running to his watch pocket and a large gold ring on his middle finger, set with an equally large diamond.

The man leaned in and drew the flame from the metal match of the touch-tip lighter that Sherry held out. A moment later he stood straight, puffing out a cloud of smoke before he turned to the sound of the open door.

"Mr. Lockerby, I presume," he said in an affable baritone.

Alex plastered a smile on his face and limped forward, reaching out to shake the other man's hand.

"Call me Alex," he said, then looked to Sherry.

"This is Holcombe Ward," she said. "We ran into each other in the hall."

"I dare say you're lucky, Mr. Ward," Alex said. "The office is usually empty by five."

"I do appreciate you seeing me," Ward said. "And call me Holcombe."

"Let's go back to my office," Alex said, stepping to the side and indicating the still open door to the back hallway. "It's the last door on the right. I need to confer with Ms. Knox for a moment, but I'll be right with you."

Holcombe nodded and headed into the back hallway.

"Did you find anything? Alex asked once his potential client had found his office.

"Yes," Sherry said, pulling Alex's attention to her. "Between the two of us, we've read every book the library has on the Spanish Inquisition except for two."

"What about those?"

"They've been checked out every time I've been there," Sherry said. "This time I asked the librarian and they said that both books are overdue, so they'd look into it."

"What books?" Alex asked, taking out his notebook.

"Don't bother," Sherry said, handing him a page torn from her notebook. "It's all down there."

"And that's it?" Alex asked, tucking the loose paper into his shirt pocket.

"Unless you want to go see Captain Blood again. I hear the Carson Theater shows it every month or so."

"That takes place during the Monmouth Rebellion in England," Alex said, returning his notebook to his pocket. "Right time period, wrong country."

"Yeah," Sherry said with a contented sigh, "but it has Errol Flynn in it so it would be worth it."

Alex chuckled and clapped her gently on the shoulder.

"I won't tell Danny."

He thanked her and headed back to his office and his potential client. "I'm sorry to keep you waiting," he said when he entered.

Holcombe Ward had taken one of the chairs in front of Alex's desk, the one nearest the door, and was waiting patiently with his legs crossed and his hat perched on his knee.

Alex limped around his desk, leaving his cane in the corner, then sat down.

"What happened?" Holcombe asked as Alex held up his left leg as he swung his seat into position. "If it's not too impertinent to ask."

"I got shot in the foot on a case," Alex replied.

"Isn't that something a simple healing potion could take care of?"

Alex gave the man a sardonic smile.

"Normally, yes," he said, "but I've been busted up, shot, and stabbed so many times that I've developed a mild allergy to healing potions. I have to heal up the usual way."

That was true, strictly speaking, but Iggy had suggested it as a way to avoid too many questions.

"Now, Mr. Ward, what is it I can do for you?"

Holcombe's affable expression soured and he took a deliberate breath, giving himself time to organize his thoughts.

"I want you to investigate the death of a friend of mine," he said at last.

"You suspect foul play?" Alex asked.

"I don't know what I suspect," Holcombe admitted with a sigh.

"What do the police say?"

Holcombe took a drag from his cigarette and blew out a long plume of smoke.

"They say it was an accidental drowning," he said, "but I don't buy it. Ari was a strong swimmer, had been all his life."

"That's your friend's name," Alex asked, picking up his pen to make notes.

"Ari Leavitt," he said with a nod. "I've known him since we were at university together."

"What university?"

"Harvard," Holcombe said.

Alex wrote that down, giving himself time to think. He knew several people who'd been to the elite Massachusetts college, Andrew Barton among them. They tended to think highly of their education and didn't let lesser mortals forget it. He focused his mind on the task at hand, not wanting to make a bad impression.

"Tell me how your friend, Mr. Leavitt, came to drown," he said.

"He was at a soirée up on Long Island," Holcombe began. "The Daltons have it every year for the pros on the circuit."

Alex held up a restraining hand as he finished scribbling on his notepad.

"I'm going to need a bit more information, Holcombe," he said. "Who are the Daltons, and what circuit are these pros a part of?"

"Oh, sorry," Holcombe said, somewhat abashed. "Maybe I'd better begin with the background information. I'm the president of the USLTA, uh, that's the United States Lawn Tennis Association."

"So these are professional tennis players," Alex said catching on quickly.

"Yes," Holcombe went on, "Beals Dalton is one of our biggest supporters, he loves the game, though he has no talent for it himself."

"So the parties are at his home, where is that?"

"The Hamptons."

"Beals comes from money, then?" Alex said. It wasn't much of a deduction, most people in the Hamptons had mansions and Ari had drowned while swimming in February, which meant an indoor pool was involved.

"Oh, yes," Holcombe supplied. "His old man supplied railroad ties for the whole transcontinental railroad, had them coated in some alchemical concoction that made them last twice as long as regular ones. Made a fortune."

Alex wrote that down.

"Now, your friend, Ari, was he a tennis pro as well?"

"No, Ari was one of our top umpires. He was the chair umpire for most of our finals matches."

Alex raised an eyebrow at that, but decided to let details of tennis match mediation go for now and come back to them later.

"And what were the circumstances of Mr. Leavitt's death?"

Holcombe Ward cleared his throat and took another puff from his cigarette.

"The party wound down around midnight," he said. "I had already retired—"

"You were staying at the Daltons' house?" Alex interrupted.

"Yes, Ari, myself, and a few of the more well-known pros." He tapped his cigarette over the ash tray on the desk and continued. "Anyway, from what the police were able to piece together, Ari left the party shortly before midnight to go swimming in the Daltons' indoor pool."

"Did he often go for a swim after a party?" Alex asked.

"Oh, yes," Holcombe confirmed. "He was on the Harvard swim team back in the day. He loved the water."

"Do you know if he'd been drinking excessively at the party?"

Holcombe looked a bit nervous and shifted in his seat.

"Well, I can't swear to it," he admitted at last, "but Ari was a man of moderate habits, and I never saw him drink to excess in all the years I knew him."

"What did the police say about the drowning? Did they find anything suspicious?"

"No. Ari was found floating face down in the pool by one of the pros." Holcombe cleared his throat. "Apparently he and a single young lady were looking for some, uh, privacy."

"I see," Alex said, sparing the distinguished man from having to go on with a more detailed explanation.

"Anyway, the police didn't find any evidence of foul play, though I don't know what they could find on a waterlogged body."

"More than you'd think," Alex said. "What makes you think Mr. Leavitt didn't just have a heart attack?"

"The coroner insisted he didn't," Holcombe said, punching his right fist into the palm of his left hand. "Something's just not right, Mr. Lockerby. Ari was an excellent swimmer, there's just no way he'd drown in a swimming pool. I need your help, Alex. I need someone to find out what really happened to my friend."

Alex let that statement hang in the air for almost a minute. Drowning someone in a swimming pool wasn't really that hard. Making it look like an accident was a bit more involved. If Holcombe was right, his friend was strong and fit. Drowning someone like that would be difficult since he would undoubtedly fight back, leaving traces on his body and on the body of the killer.

"All right, Mr. Ward," he said at last. "I can't promise you I'll give a better answer than the police, but I'll take your case."

2

ABSENCES

"Well, here you are at last," Iggy said when Alex came limping into the brownstone's kitchen. He was sitting at the head of the massive oak table with the equally solid chair pushed back so he could cross his legs while he read the paper.

Alex just shrugged as he hooked his cane over the back of a chair.

"A client came in at the last minute," he said, sliding gingerly into the chair.

"Completely understandable," Iggy said, splitting his attention between Alex and the paper. "Interesting case?"

"The president of the U.S. Lawn Tennis Association thinks that one of his umpires was murdered," Alex said. "So it could be interesting."

"I take it the police disagree," Iggy said.

"The man drowned in a heated swimming pool without a mark on him," Alex said.

Iggy made a non-committal noise in throat.

"Hard to drown a strong swimmer without leaving some kind of evidence."

"What makes you think he was a strong swimmer?" Alex asked.

"Well, first, he was swimming in February," he said. "That's dedication, unless there was a lady involved, and you would have mentioned that detail had it been true."

"And secondly?"

"His good friend thinks it wasn't an accident," Iggy said with a shrug. "Only a strong swimmer would elicit such doubts, especially in the face of the official police findings."

Alex chuckled.

"Well, you've got it exactly," he said. "I told Holcombe, the client, that it's not very likely that the police were wrong, but I'll look into it."

"Good of you to warn him before he spends too much money," Iggy said, returning to his paper.

Alex was about to ask about dinner but Iggy dipped his paper enough to look over the top.

"Did you say your client's name was Holcombe and he was involved with tennis?"

"Yes," Alex confirmed, suspicion in his voice.

"Not Holcombe Ward?"

"Yes," Alex repeated.

"Tall fellow, big chin?"

"That's him," Alex confirmed. "Why?"

Iggy's face, which had been suffused with a beatific smile, suddenly fell and he rolled his eyes.

"I forget just how deprived your childhood actually was," he said with a sigh. "Holcombe Ward is the closest thing you Yanks have to tennis royalty. He won seven U.S. national championships during his career...a magnificent player."

"If you say so," Alex replied, trying to hide a grin. It wasn't often he saw the old man this enthusiastic about anything other than crime.

"I saw him play once, you know," Iggy went on, somewhat indignant over Alex's reaction. "It was back in aught-one at Wimbledon. Holcombe didn't win, but he was a joy to watch."

"You want me to introduce you?" Alex offered.

"Better not. I actually met the man back then. If he's got a good mind, he might remember me."

"Oh, well," Alex said. "I'm starving, are we waiting for Sorsha?"

"Dear me," Iggy said, folding the paper and setting it aside. "I almost forgot. She came by earlier and said she wouldn't be joining us tonight."

Alex raised an eyebrow.

"Anything I should know about?"

"She said that her team has been pursuing new markets in the Midwest and in California," Iggy explained. "Apparently, she needs to sign a half dozen contracts and the marketing people promised her new customers that she'd do it in person."

Alex understood that. He was lucky that he had regular access to sorcerers, but to most people, they were nigh unto mythical figures. Sorsha's presence at a business meeting would go a long way to sealing the deal.

"So, she's headed out of town?"

Iggy nodded.

"Said she'd be gone a week at least," he added.

"Why didn't she just teleport?" Alex asked.

"Don't be peevish," Iggy admonished him. "You know she hates teleporting almost as much as you do. Don't put her through all that just because you'll miss her."

"I wasn't suggesting that," Alex lied. "But if we're not waiting for her, what can I help with? I'd like to eat."

"All right," Iggy said with a sardonic smile behind his bottle-brush mustache. "Get the plates and I'll get dinner out of the oven."

Alex sat back from the table with a satisfied sigh. Iggy had prepared a glazed ham with fresh rolls and baked green beans. It was one of his absolute favorite meals and he'd eaten a bit more than he should have.

"That was excellent," he said as Iggy puffed a post-meal cigar to life. "Thank you."

"Not at all, lad," his mentor intoned, blowing out a fragrant cloud of bluish smoke. "Cigar?"

Alex selected a wrapped cigar from Iggy's pocket humidor.

"Don't mind if I do," he said as he pulled out his jackknife to trim the cigar.

"So," Iggy began while Alex cut the cigar tip, "anything in the paper grab you?"

"You saw the story about the letter bomb?"

"I figured you'd notice that one," Iggy said, shaking his head. "Especially after your experience with the Brothers Boom. Pick something else."

Alex favored his mentor with a sly grin.

"That's not how we play this game," he admonished. "I want to talk about the bombing."

Iggy sighed, then chuckled.

"All right, all right," he said, holding up a placating hand. "According to the Times, some industrialist was killed in his office by an explosive sent to him in the mail."

"Reginald Aspler," Alex supplied. "Owner and operator of the Aspler Shipping Company. According to Who's Who, Aspler owns a fleet of ships on both coasts and several dozen trains to connect the two."

Iggy raised an eyebrow and blew a smoke ring at Alex.

"You did research?" Iggy chuckled. "You really are interested in this case."

"Not really," Alex admitted, "I just had some extra time in the afternoon."

"Well, there really wasn't much about the bomb in the paper," Iggy said. "What do you think?"

"Could be anything," Alex said. "Maybe a jealous husband or a disgruntled competitor? Maybe the Galleanists are active again."

Iggy chuffed at that, shaking his head.

"I think your police rolled up that cult of communist adherents," he said. "I suspect your first guesses are closer to the mark. It shouldn't be too difficult for the police to find the killer, though. It takes specialized knowledge to make a mail bomb, to say nothing of acquiring dynamite."

Alex didn't want to agree, but Iggy was right. Very few people knew how to build a bomb that would survive a trip through the mail and still explode at its destination.

"What about that jewel store robbery in the diamond district?" Iggy said.

"Inside job," Alex said. "The owner said that the thieves only took his best pieces. Normal thieves wouldn't know which were the best, they had to have an inside man."

Iggy nodded sagely.

"What do you think?" Alex pressed.

"Insurance fraud," he said. "The owner did say that only his best pieces were taken, so he should have come to the same conclusion you did."

"But he didn't tell the police he suspected inside help, so he must be the inside man," Alex agreed.

"That's my read on it. What about that case with the missing wife?"

Alex had seen that story; a well-to-do doctor had come home a few days ago to find his wife simply missing. The house was undisturbed and her clothes and things were all accounted for, as far as anyone could tell. This struck Alex as a runaway: the wife had wanted out and she'd gotten out. If she'd been taken, there would be some sign of a struggle and if she'd just gone to visit a friend, she'd have taken a suitcase.

He relayed his conclusions to Iggy and they spent an enjoyable hour discussing that and other news.

"My cigar is out," Iggy said at last, dropping the stub into the ashtray on the table. "I think it's time for me to do a little reading, then retire." He stood up from the table and inclined his head to Alex. "I'll leave the dishes to you."

Alex groaned, but got up and got to work anyway. Between his time with Father Harry and living with Iggy, he'd washed enough dishes to start his own restaurant. Still, washing dishes was the kind of mindless task that gave a man time to think, and Alex enjoyed that.

He'd just drained the sink of soapy water when someone rang the bell.

"I have it," Iggy's voice came from the library.

Alex hung up his towel, picked up his cane, and began limping toward the little hallway that separated the kitchen from the library and the foyer.

"Right this way, Lieutenant," Iggy was saying as he passed through the vestibule.

Alex met him as the older man stepped aside, revealing the stocky form of police Lieutenant James Detweiler. He had his hat in his hand, revealing his bald pate, surrounded by a fringe of black hair. Alex had known the man for years and his relationship with the serious-minded and irascible lieutenant had always been a bit rocky.

"Lieutenant," Alex greeted him, "to what do we owe the pleasure?"

Detweiler took a deep breath and let it out.

"I got a serious question for you, Lockerby," he said. "Maybe we better sit down."

Alex exchanged a glance with Iggy but his mentor could only shrug. The lieutenant looked tired and haggard, like he'd had a long day and it wasn't remotely finished.

"Right this way," Alex said, turning and heading back into the kitchen. "Can I get you something to drink?"

Detweiler sighed as he took a seat at the kitchen table.

"I could use a beer."

Normally neither Alex nor Iggy were big fans of beer, but ever since Alex became a part owner of Homestead Brewery, he felt obliged to keep a few bottles in the icebox. He retrieved one and placed it on the table in front of Detweiler along with a church key.

"So," Alex said, seating himself on the opposite side of the table from the lieutenant, "what's your question?"

"That bank robbery case a few years ago, the Brothers Boom?"

"I remember," Alex said. "Does your question have something to do with that industrialist who was killed, Reginald Aspler?"

"We saw the story in the paper," Iggy inserted, lest Detweiler get the wrong idea.

For his part, the lieutenant took a sip of the beer and sighed.

"This is good stuff," he said, looking at the label, then he looked up at Alex. "I should have known you'd be out ahead on this. I just came from the offices of Aspler Shipping Company. That bomb that killed the boss..."

"Let me guess," Iggy said, "he didn't get any packages delivered with today's mail."

"No," Detweiler said, "he didn't."

"So," Alex summed up, "either someone planted an explosive device in his office last night or the explosive was in one of the letters he received."

"Which would make it a rune bomb or something alchemical," Iggy added.

"And," Alex continued, "if it were alchemical, there'd be residue for the police investigators to find. Since you're here, Lieutenant, I'm guessing they didn't find anything."

Detweiler shook his head.

"I have to ask, Lockerby," he said, setting the beer aside, "did you ever figure out how the Brothers Boom did it? Do you know how to make an explosive rune?"

Alex shook his head.

"No," he lied. "I have no idea how to make a rune explode."

In point of fact, Alex had one of Arlo Harper's explosive runes in his rune book right at that moment. It was just in case of an emergency, of course, but he had it nonetheless. Fortunately, even if Detweiler or another runewright examined his book, they wouldn't know the rune for what it was.

The lieutenant held Alex's gaze for a long moment, then drained the beer bottle and set it aside.

"In that case," he said, "I've come to ask for your help. This time whoever's making exploding runes isn't just stealing money, this time they're killing."

"Any idea who had a beef against Mr. Aspler?" Iggy asked.

Detweiler gave Iggy a patronizing look.

"He was an industrialist, who didn't have a beef with him?"

"I think Dr. Bell meant someone particularly motivated," Alex said.

"Don't make me say it again, Lockerby," Detweiler growled. "The man was a lowlife, I've seen shorter enemies lists from mob bosses."

"So plenty of suspects, but a very specific type of weapon," Alex said. "That ought to narrow the suspect pool down significantly."

"A little too well, as it turns out," Detweiler said. "So far, no one we've looked into has any connection to rune magic at all."

"Lash yourself to the mast, Lieutenant," Iggy said. "It only takes one, and if your suspect pool is as deep as you say, there's plenty more suspects to go through."

"Well, you aren't wrong."

"What do you need from me, Lieutenant?" Alex asked.

"Come with me over to Aspler Shipping with your bag of tricks and see if you can find something, anything, to help break this case."

Alex thought about that for a moment. He was tired and wanted to go to bed, but if there really was someone running around with Arlo Harper's exploding rune, Alex needed to get them off the street before they killed again.

"As it turned out," he said, making his voice upbeat as he stood up, "I have a free evening. Let me get my 'bag of tricks' and we can head over to Aspler Shipping."

"Do you mind if I have another beer while I wait?" Detweiler said. "These are pretty good."

Alex gestured toward the icebox as he headed for the stairs.

"Help yourself," he said.

Almost an hour later, Alex set his crime scene kit down on the top of what used to be the desk of Reggie Aspler's secretary. It was made of a light-colored wood with a clear varnish and even under the layers of sludgy debris and blood, it still managed to look refined.

The rest of the outer office was similarly destroyed. The explosion had been centered on Reggie's desk in the inner office, but whoever had made it had given the bomb much more power than it needed to kill one man. The inner office was almost completely destroyed and the door separating it from the outer office had been blown off its hinges, embedding itself in the wall opposite.

Detweiler had given Alex the rundown on the way over, so he knew that the blood on the desk belonged to Reggie's secretary, who was clinging to life at Bellevue. Alex bent down and picked up a cracked picture frame from the ground. Turning it over, he saw a middle-aged woman with long, dark hair standing next to a blond man in a button-up shirt and a bow tie. A boy that looked about ten stood between them and they were all smiling. Now the dapper man might lose his wife and the boy his mother.

"All because someone wanted to make a point," he said, setting the picture down on the ruined desk.

"The question is, what point?" Detweiler said, coming up beside Alex.

Alex took a deep breath, filling his nostrils with the scent of soot, sweat, and blood.

"Don't know," he admitted, opening his kit bag. "Let's see what we can find."

The inner office had been pretty well destroyed, so he didn't bother giving it the once-over for evidence. Between the explosion, the shop hands who had extinguished the fire, and the subsequent herd of policemen, any small evidence would have been obliterated. That being the case, Alex decided to start with his multi-lamp.

Setting the egg-shaped frame on the desk, he removed the oil burner with the ghostlight formula in it, then the yellowish spectacles that would allow him to see what the lamp revealed.

Slipping the earpieces of the spectacles behind his ears, Alex settled the frame on his nose. He used to have a set in the pince-nez style, but they hurt his nose during long investigations, so he left them in the case with the other spectacles.

With a quick flick of his lighter, Alex lit the burner, then slipped it into the bottom of the lamp, securing it in place. Normally, Alex would have only one side of the lamp's four lenses uncovered, making it easy to focus on a single spot. In the aftermath of an explosion, however, there wasn't really any specific place to focus, at least not at first, so he removed all the covers from the lamp.

Holding the lamp up, Alex scanned the outer office. Through the lenses, he could see traces of magic and runes. There was a privacy rune on the back of the door out into the hall, which was usual for industrialists and other professionals wary of having their business overheard.

Another concentration of magic glowed from inside the remnants of a cabinet that originally had a glass front. As Alex held the lamp close, he could see pages in thick folios emanating a faint light.

"Sealing runes or revealing runes," he said out loud.

"What?" Detweiler asked.

"Contracts," Alex explained. "Lots of contracts use runes to keep them from being altered, or prevent unauthorized people from reading them."

He moved on, satisfied there wasn't anything more to see in the outer office. As he passed through the ruined doorway, the lamp began to pick up a glowing haze in the air. Turning to look at the wall, Alex found them speckled with a glowing green residue. The remnants of Reggie Aspler's desk, however, positively glowed with the leftover magic.

Squatting down, Alex ran his hand across what remained of the desk's top. The formerly smooth surface was rough and pitted, exactly what Alex would have expected in an explosion. The surface was so bright with magical residue, he was surprised he needed the lamp at all.

Taking off the glasses, Alex raised the lens in the multi-lamp and blew out the burner.

"Well?" Detweiler asked, impatience in his voice.

"We don't have to wonder if anyone knows how to make one of Arlo Harper's boom runes," Alex said. "They do."

3

TELL NO TALES

Alex sat on his bed smearing a thick, jelly-like cream into the crevasses of his unhealed foot. Since the bullet went straight through his foot, he had to apply the greasy ointment to the top and bottom of his foot to help it heal.

That was Iggy's story and the old man was sticking to it, but Alex knew better. The ointment was mostly to keep dirt and other foreign material out of his wound. When he'd first been shot, Iggy had packed the wound with a healing paste suspended by a cloth that would deteriorate as the wound closed. Unfortunately, neither he nor Alex had taken into account the damnation rune on his chest. Normally such runes were doled out as punishment to offending runewrights, to block them from accessing their magic. In Alex's case it was a bit different: it still cut him off from using his magic, but it also had the side effect of drawing out the leftover magic energy in his body. Since Alex had effectively poisoned himself with excessive amounts of life energy going in and out of himself, to say nothing of his far-too-casual use of Limelight, the rune was there to purify him. He'd been warned that the process would be slow, maybe even taking more than a year to complete, but at the end, he would be healthy enough to use magic again.

The unfortunate reality of Alex's situation was that the healing putty Iggy had used on the bullet wound had its magic pulled away by the damnation rune. What was left behind was a still-open wound, but one that had healed up inside. Alex had checked with a doctor who told him the only way to get the wound to close would be to surgically cut out the prematurely healed tissue and let the wound heal naturally. As bad as that sounded, however, the real bad news was that without magical healing, the delicate bones in his foot wouldn't be restored, which meant he'd have to undergo another surgery once he could be affected by magic.

For the time being, Alex had to accept that he was a man with a limp and a cane. It wasn't so bad, but his days of running after suspects were temporarily over.

With a growl of frustration, he tugged on his socks, then stood to pull on his trousers and buckle his belt. Next came his suit coat, and then Alex began loading his pockets with the various gear he carried. When he picked up his rune book, with its new shielded cover, a slip of folded paper slipped from under the cover and dropped to the floor.

Alex just looked at it for a second, trying to remember where it came from.

"Sherry," he said as he leaned down to pick it up. Opening the note, he found the names of two books in his secretary's neat script along with a string of numbers that Alex knew would correspond to the Dewey library cataloging system. He'd forgotten about the two missing Inquisition books, but he wasn't going to have time to dig into that today, so he opened his rune book to the back and slipped the paper into the little pocket.

Checking the wind-up alarm clock on his bedside table, Alex noted that it was about half-past seven, meaning he should go straight to his office. Still, the foolishness with his foot had him feeling peevish and he decided to have breakfast first.

Normally, when Alex had breakfast, he went through his vault to his unused apartment in Empire Tower, then down the elevator to the cafe in the sky crawler terminal. Today, however, he wanted something more familiar, more real than the gilded opulence of Andrew Barton's signature station.

"The Lunch Box," he said out loud. It was only a block and a half away, though he'd still need a cab, but these days he could afford one. Picking up the telephone on his bedside table, Alex gave the operator the number of a local company, then headed downstairs to wait.

A quarter of an hour later, the taxi dropped Alex off in front of the little diner that had been his second home for a good part of his residence at the brownstone. Much to his surprise, he realized that it had been months since he'd been back, maybe as much as half a year. Originally, the diner had been a greasy spoon that didn't open until eleven, but ever since Mary started working there, the quality, the cleanliness, and the hours had improved.

Alex limped to the glass door and pulled it open, eliciting a jingling tone from the bell over the door. Everything that greeted him, the sights, smells...it was all as he remembered it.

As it should be.

"Good morning," an unfamiliar voice greeted him. "What can I getcha?"

Alex turned to find himself looking at a short woman with brownish hair, blue eyes, and a wide smile on her painted lips. She wore the apron of the diner over a cream-colored blouse and a pair of grey slacks with, "Milly," displayed on her name tag.

"Uh," Alex managed. "Where's Doris?" Truth be told, Alex wasn't certain that Doris didn't live in a room in the back of the diner as she always seemed to be there whenever he came in.

"Oh," Milly said, her cheeks going suddenly pink. "I'm sorry, I thought everyone knew. Doris passed just after Thanksgiving."

Alex just stood there with his mouth open. He knew Doris lived alone after she kicked out her cheating husband a few years ago, but not much more than that. She mentioned having kids once, two girls and a boy if Alex remembered right, but he'd never been able to learn more. Despite her gregarious nature, Doris had been very close-mouthed about her private life.

"I..." Alex began, then cleared his throat and tried again. "I was out of town for a few months, I hadn't heard. What happened?"

"Heart attack," Milly said, "least that's what I heard."

When no other information was forthcoming, Alex looked back toward the kitchen.

"Is Mary here?" he said. "Maybe she'll know something."

"Mary Powell?" Milly asked. "I guess if you didn't know about Doris, you wouldn't know about Mary; she left after Christmas."

That shocked Alex more than the news of Doris' death. Mary had loved cooking and she'd been the head cook here for years.

"Did she say why?"

"Nothing to it," Milly said with a nonchalant shrug. "She married a swell and they opened a restaurant over on the West Side somewhere."

Alex knew that Mary and Danny hadn't been a couple for a while, but he hadn't heard she had a new beau.

"So what do you want this mornin'," Milly asked, her pen poised to take his order.

Wow, Alex thought, *you fall into one drug induced coma and the whole world changes.*

Out loud he said, "Poached eggs on buttered toast."

Milly gave him a pretty smile, then she turned and headed for the kitchen.

"And coffee," Alex added toward her retreating form. "Lots of coffee," he muttered as Milly disappeared into the back.

Alex propped his cane against the inside of the phone booth and closed the door behind him. Dropping a nickel into the slot, he gave the operator the exchange for his office and waited to be connected.

"Lockerby Investigations," Sherry's voice greeted him in a far-too-cheerful manner.

Alex's eggs had been hard, his toast has been burned, and Mary had taken the secret for their better-than-average coffee with her when she left. To say the least he was a bit out of sorts.

"It's me," he said, biting back a cross remark. "I'll be in shortly, and I want you to pull the files on Ray and Arlo Harper. Just leave them on my desk."

"Sure thing, boss," Sherry said, her enthusiasm undiminished. "Though I think you'd better make plans to stop off at the Central Office. Lieutenant Detweiler called a few minutes ago, and he wants to see you."

Alex had hoped to go over the files on the Brothers Boom before he met with Detweiler, but he'd just have to go from memory.

"Anything else?" he asked.

"Yes," she said. "Holcombe Ward called and said he can meet you at the Suffolk County coroner's office this afternoon."

"Find out where that is and get the train schedule for Grand Central," he said. "Call Holcombe back and tell him that I'll be there and that I'll call him before I leave so he'll know when to meet me."

"Will do," Sherry said.

Alex was about to say goodbye and hang up, but he remembered the slip of paper in the back of his rune book.

"One more thing," he interjected, taking the book from his pocket. "These books the library is missing," he fumbled for the paper, finally managing to press it flat on the little shelf by the phone, "why is there a book about the Knights Templar in there? The Templars were destroyed by King Phillip of France, they don't have anything to do with the Spanish Inquisition."

Alex squinted at the paper now that he had it open. The first book was entitled, "*The Heresy Trials*" and presumably dealt with some of the more sensational trials from the Inquisition. The second book, however, was called "*Stories of the Inquisition*." It had the words 'Knights Templar' written beside the name and didn't sound like a scholarly work at all.

"I asked the librarian about that," Sherry explained. "Apparently I'd only asked about the Inquisition, not specifically the Spanish Inquisition. I didn't know this, but the Templars were destroyed under the authority of an Inquisition, just not the Spanish one."

Alex stifled a sigh and pinched the bridge of his nose. He was about to complain that he didn't need another Inquisition, but then Charles Grier's dying words came back to him. He said he'd learned about curse stones when he'd been investigating "the Inquisition." Alex had assumed he'd meant the Spanish Inquisition, but Charles hadn't said that.

"This might be helpful," he admitted at last, explaining his thoughts to Sherry.

"Does this mean we have to look up this inquisition against the Templars?" she asked, a little despair creeping into her voice.

"Hold off and let me look into it first," he said. "For right now we're at the end of the line."

"I can do that," she said.

Alex looked at his pocket watch, then started tucking the paper back into his rune book.

"I'd better get going," he said, "Detweiler is an impatient sort of fellow. I'll call you back when I'm on my way to Grand Central."

Sherry assured him she'd have the train schedule and the stops for him when he did, and Alex hung up.

Alex leaned on his cane as the elevator in the Central Office of Police ascended up to the fifth floor. When it finally rumbled to a stop and the doors slid open, he limped off and made his way along the hallway to the end where it turned left. As the hallway continued, Alex passed the offices of the lieutenants that ran the various divisions with jurisdiction over Manhattan. When he reached Danny's office, he stuck his head in but found the office empty.

Detweiler's office was three doors further along the corridor, and when Alex stuck his head in his door, the lieutenant was hard at work at his desk. His hair was unkempt and he leaned heavily on his elbow as he paged through an open folder.

"You look like hell," Alex said as he stepped around the door.

Detweiler looked up and stifled a yawn.

"Some of us have to work whatever hours they have to," he muttered.

"Late night?"

"I'll let you know when I get a chance to go home," the lieutenant growled. "I was up most of the night briefing the captain and going through Reggie Aspler's appointment book."

"That wasn't blown up with the rest of his desk?" Alex asked as he eased into the chair in front of Detweiler's desk.

"His secretary kept it," Detweiler replied, leaning down to pick up something on the floor. "Even his personal appointments were in here." He came up with a leather-bound book about a foot square with a spiral binding, and placed it on his desk. "Including some very enlightening entries."

Alex raised an eyebrow at that.

"He kept his less-savory activities on the books? His secretary must be making a mint."

Detweiler opened the book and paged through it.

"There are appointments at hotels in the middle of the day," he said, "lunches at fancy restaurants for two, and trips to Tiffany's with very pricey expenses listed by the appointment."

"So he had a mistress," Alex concluded. "That sounds like motive for his wife."

"More than you know," Detweiler said. "The hotels and the lunches and the little trips come and go. Some months there's a bunch of them, other months are clean."

"Multiple mistresses," Alex amended his statement. "Sounds like lots of motive for the wife."

"We already talked to her," Detweiler said with an exhausted sigh.

"You don't like her for this?"

"It's possible, but Mrs Aspler never left her home upstate, and she's not a runewright."

"Is she a homebody," Alex asked, "or did Reggie make sure she stayed there?"

"She seemed happy as a clam about her living arrangements," Detweiler said. "She also wasn't too upset that her husband was plastered all over the walls of his office, no matter what the initial report said."

"So who else had a motive?" Alex said, steepling his fingers in front of his face. "There's his paramours, of course. Any of them could resent him for any number of reasons. What about his company, any feuds with members of his board?"

Detweiler shook his head.

"We don't know yet," he admitted, pinching the bridge of his nose. "I've got Detectives Nicholson and Harlan talking to everyone we could find, and I'll have their interview notes by tomorrow. Did you learn anything?"

"I haven't had the chance to through my notes on Arlo and Ray Harper yet," he said. "As far as I remember, the boom rune wasn't made with any pricy inks or special paper." Of course he knew that, since he'd made and tested his own version of Arlo's explosive rune, but he wasn't going to tell Detweiler that.

"Is that important?" the lieutenant asked.

"Well, if the rune had required expensive or uncommon inks, we might be able to trace our bomber by learning where they bought them, but with normal ingredients, they could be getting their supplies anywhere."

"That's it?"

Alex shrugged.

"Sorry, Lieutenant."

Detweiler sighed.

"All right," he said. "I'll go through the witness statements as they come in. If I find anyone worth talking to, I'll give you a call."

Alex nodded, then stood and picked up his cane.

"I've got to run up to Long Island," he said, "probably for the rest of the day, but I'll be back tonight."

"I don't expect the first of the interviews until lunchtime tomorrow at the earliest," Detweiler said. "After that, I'll want your undivided attention."

"Well," Alex said, pulling the conversation around to his point, "I've got a long train ride ahead of me, so if you don't need it, I can go over Reggie Aspler's appointment book."

Detweiler looked up at him with a pair of tired, bloodshot eyes.

"Are you suggesting my boys and I missed something?" he growled.

Alex cleared his throat, but before he could respond, the lieutenant picked up the leather-bound book and held it out.

"Because if you are, I can understand why."

Alex accepted the book, clutching it under his arm.

"Don't lose that," Detweiler said.

"Perish the thought."

4

BOXES

It was well after noon when the train pulled in to Hauppauge station. The town was located in the center of Long Island, almost equidistant from the east and west coasts, and even though Ari Leavitt died in Southampton, the coroner was located here.

"I guess that's a good thing," Alex said as he carried his kit bag across the terminal, heading for the street outside, "not having enough murder to keep more than one coroner busy."

"Alex," he heard his name once he passed through the station's front doors.

To his left was Holcombe Ward, leaning on the fender of a shiny new Mercedes-Benz painted two-tone in burgundy and white. He had a newspaper that he was rapidly folding to tuck under the arm of his overcoat.

"Thanks for meeting me," Alex said, even though it hadn't really been his idea. Originally, he'd intended to take the train from Hauppauge to Southampton, but Holcombe had insisted that would take too much time and Alex might arrive too late to talk to the detective handling Ari's case.

"I'm glad you could come," Holcombe said. "It's only been a few days, but I feel like the sand is slipping out from beneath me. If you don't get this case figured out soon, it might just be too late."

"Don't worry, Mr. Ward," Alex said as Holcombe directed him to the backward opening door on the passenger side of the car. "There's still plenty of time to make inquiries."

Holcombe pressed the starter and the car roared to life.

"I hope you're right," he said, then pulled out onto the road.

The trip to the coroner's office took less than five minutes. The office was in a building that looked like it had once been a post office, but had been converted. A bored-looking woman sat behind a high desk that also served as a counter. Like the building and the woman, the desk had seen better days.

"Can I help you," the woman asked in a toneless voice.

She wore a dark dress with short sleeves and a wide collar that at looked clean, though it was at least a decade out of fashion.

"My name's Lockerby," Alex said, handing her his card. "I need to speak to the coroner."

The woman took the card, but made a face when she read it.

"If you want to talk to anyone here, you need to get permission from the police chief," she said, handing the card back. "We don't allow civilians access to police business."

Alex had heard this song-and-dance many times in his career, but had gotten away from it of late. With Callahan running the Manhattan Central Office and Danny and even Detweiler using his services, most other officials played ball.

"Where is the chief's office?" he asked, taking his card back.

The woman started to answer, but Holcombe interrupted her.

"Perhaps I can be of some help," he said. "I already talked to Chief Peterson. I'm Holcombe Ward, I believe he called you about me."

The woman seemed to see Holcombe for the first time and her mask of indifference cracked.

"Oh, of course," she said, sounding genial. "The chief did say you'd be by, but he didn't mention a private detective."

"I'm sorry he wasn't clear," Holcombe said, taking her hand and speaking in a soothing tone. "He does know that my friend, Alex, is here, and he was okay with that."

The woman hesitated, wondering if she should believe Holcombe, but the earnest smile in his handsome face seemed to convince her.

"Let me just call Dr. Flaherty for you," she said, waiting for Holcombe to let go of her hand before she reached for the phone.

A few minutes later, an older man with silver hair and a pair of square spectacles stepped through a door at the back of the room. He was average height with slightly stooped shoulders, a short nose, and the pale complexion of someone who doesn't get out of doors much. All Alex could see of the man's attire was a pair of decently polished, dark shoes, sturdy trousers, and a doctor's white coat. The coat didn't appear new, and bore many marks and stains, but they were all faded, as if the laundry staff did their best to keep Dr. Flaherty looking respectable.

"Which one of you is Holcombe Ward?" he demanded, squinting through his glasses as he approached. "Oh," he continued before anyone could answer, "it's you."

He held out his hand to Ward, who took it in a friendly grip.

"I saw you play back in aught-four, at the Nationals," Flaherty said. "What a tournament that was."

Holcombe chuckled and continued to shake the doctor's hand. "We won that one," he said.

"So, what brings you here?" Flaherty asked, finally releasing Holcombe's hand.

"The death of Ari Leavitt," he answered.

Flaherty looked surprised at that.

"It's a simple drowning," he said, "nothing suspicious about it."

Holcombe nodded but continued.

"I have some questions I'd like answered," he said in an apologetic voice. "That's why I've asked Mr. Lockerby here," he indicated Alex, "to poke around a bit, for the sake of my suspicious mind."

Flaherty eyed Alex up and down and the excitement that had been on his face when he met Holcombe drained away.

"Private dick, eh?" he asked. When Alex nodded, he shook his head and sighed. "I don't usually indulge you fellows," he admitted. "I have enough trouble with the regular detectives who always want favors or expedited reports. Still, as a friend of Holcombe Ward's, I'll see what I can do. Ask your questions."

"Did you know that Avi Leavitt was a strong swimmer" Alex asked, pulling out his notebook.

"That's true," Holcombe added before the doctor could reply. "Ari swam almost every day."

"I don't see how that's relevant," Flaherty replied.

"He was a strong swimmer and managed to drown in a pool," Alex pointed out. "You don't find that the least bit suspicious?"

"I suppose I would have," Flaherty said, "if there had been any signs of violence on the body, but there weren't."

"Would you mind if I took a look?" Alex asked.

Dr. Flaherty glared at Alex from under his white eyebrows, but then seemed to relax.

"I suppose I wouldn't but it's a moot point."

"Why?" Alex and Holcombe asked at the same time.

"I've already sent out Mr. Leavitt's body," he said. "It went to Albany where his parents live."

"What do you mean you shipped out the body?" Alex demanded. "The police are finished with this case already?"

"I imagine not," Flaherty said, taking off his glasses and polishing them with his handkerchief, "but they were satisfied with the rather obvious cause of death and the family was eager to get the body returned for burial."

"I thought it took longer for the authorities to release a body," Holcombe said, looking confused.

"It does," Alex confirmed.

"Not in cases like these," Dr. Flaherty corrected. "Mr. Leavitt was of the Jewish faith, and, in their tradition, a body must be buried as quickly as possible."

"If you shipped the body to his parents yesterday," Alex asked, starting to feel a bit alarmed, "Ari could have been interred today."

"Most likely," Flaherty admitted.

Alex pinched the bridge of his nose.

"Did you do a toxicology report on Mr. Leavitt?" Alex asked.

"There wasn't any need," Flaherty said with a shrug. "His blood alcohol level was quite high. My findings were that he was impaired by drink and drowned. No foul play, I'm afraid."

"Could I see your report?" Alex asked.

"Sorry," Flaherty said. "I already submitted it to the Southampton police. You'll have to take it up with them. Now, if there's nothing else, I have to get back to work."

Alex was forced to admit that there wasn't anything else, since all the evidence and any notes on the evidence were no longer present. He did, however, manage to keep from expressing his opinion of this too-sure-of-himself doctor while the man said goodbye to Holcombe Ward.

"That didn't seem very productive," the tennis pro said once they were back in his car.

"Got it in one," Alex said.

"Was any of it useful?"

"Flaherty said that Ari had a high blood alcohol level," Alex said. "Is there any chance he was too drunk to swim and Flaherty is right about his cause of death?"

"No," Holcombe declared with surety. "Ari could hold his liquor, and this wouldn't be the first time he went swimming after a party."

"Did he do that a lot?"

Holcombe nodded.

"His apartment building in the city has a heated pool. He swam every day."

That didn't mean that Ari couldn't have drowned, of course, but Alex didn't think it was likely that a practiced swimmer would have simply drowned from being drunk. Still, he'd need to see the police report to see just how intoxicated Ari really was.

"Do you know the police chief in Southampton?" he asked as Holcombe turned onto the main road out of town.

"We've met," Holcombe said, a touch of evasion in his voice.

"I take it he's not a tennis fan."

"No," Holcombe admitted. "He and Beals Dalton lock horns all the time."

"Which makes you collateral damage because you're a regular house guest at Mr. Dalton's estate."

"Yep," Holcombe said as he picked up speed when Hauppauge fell away behind them.

Alex took a deep breath, then let it out slowly. He hadn't wanted to take this case in the first place and now it was shaping up to be an uphill slog the whole way. Sliding down in his seat, Alex pushed his hat forward over his eyes.

"When we get to Southampton, find someplace with a telephone," he said, "I need to make a call."

Alex stood in the phone booth in the rear of a little diner on the outskirts of Southampton. Holcombe was sitting at the counter finishing up a sandwich, so he had a few minutes. Shutting the door behind him, Alex took out his rune book. He hesitated when he saw the new metal cover, running his thumb over the smooth surface. According to Iggy, the metal would block the damnation rune from draining his runes, allowing him to carry the book in his inside coat pocket instead of in his kit bag.

He hesitated as he looked at the changed rune book. The covers were stronger than the old paperboard covers, but he just didn't like them. Or, maybe he just disliked what they represented, the fact that his magic was gone.

"Shake it off," he told himself, opening the book.

Flipping past the first few runes, he came to an elaborate safe rune. Technically, it was a vault rune, just scaled down to a smaller door. Alex came up with this so he would be able to get his crime scene kit from his vault without having to actually open his vault. He'd been lucky up to now, but opening his vault in front of strangers was just asking for trouble. The safe was just an enclosed box against his vault wall that the little vault door opened into, making it appear to be a safe.

At the bottom of the modified vault rune page there was a small dot in the left hand corner. Paging forward, Alex reached a copy of the rune with two dots at the bottom. Tearing it out, he touched the corner of the paper to his tongue and stuck it to the side wall of the booth. A moment later, after he'd lit the rune with his cigarette, a smooth, metal door melted out of the wall.

Looking over his shoulder to make sure no one was paying attention to him, Alex took out his key ring and opened the safe door. Inside was a small space with only one thing inside, a candlestick telephone with a twenty foot cord. Behind the box, the telephone was wired into both the brownstone's line and his office line. In the back of the box was a small lever switch that would change the phone between the two lines.

Checking to make sure the switch was in the up position, and thus connected to the brownstone, Alex picked up the receiver and gave the operator the exchange for the Central Office of Police. He could have just used the phone in the booth, but this far away from his office it would incur long distance charges, so this was a way to get around that problem. Also, Alex could access this phone from anywhere, not just from a building with a phone line.

"Central Office of Police," the operator announced when the call connected.

Alex asked for Danny, but he wasn't in, so he hung up and dialed back, this time looking for Callahan.

"I'm sorry," the operator said after the phone rang for almost a full minute. "Your party doesn't answer."

Alex thanked her, then dialed again.

"Lockerby investigations," Sherry greeted him.

"It's me," he said, "I'm up in Southampton."

"What's wrong?" she asked. "Before you ask, I can hear it in your voice."

Alex explained about the coroner and Ari's rapid burial.

"I guess you could dig him up, but do you have any idea what you're looking for?"

"Not really," Alex admitted. "He might have been knocked out and dumped into the pool, he might have slipped on wet tile, hit his head, and rolled into the pool. Hell, he might have had an aneurysm for all I know, but we'll never know thanks to a lazy coroner and Jewish burial traditions."

"You'll figure it out."

"I don't know what could've given you that idea," Alex said with a chuckle.

"I have faith in you," Sherry said.

"Well, faith could use a little push," Alex said. "The police chief up here is a guy named Peterson. I need Danny or Captain Callahan to give him a call and get me access to his police report."

"I take it they're not in right now?"

"I tried them first," Alex said. "I'll try and get it on my own, but the sooner you can get ahold of one of them, the better."

"Will do," Sherry said, then she hung up.

An hour later Alex and Holcombe were back in his Mercedes outside the Southampton police station.

"Well, that was a bust," Holcombe said.

"We'll deal with Chief Peterson later," Alex said, frustrated after their talk with the irascible man. The chief really seemed to dislike Holcombe, Beals Dalton, and even Ari Leavitt, for reasons that made no sense to Alex. He didn't even know Ari.

Surprisingly, the man hadn't given Alex so much as a dirty look, his status as a private detective notwithstanding. A call from Captain Callahan should grease the wheels enough to get Alex a look at the police report. With the body unavailable it might be his only chance to find clues to what actually happened to Ari Leavitt.

"Let's go take a look at the swimming pool Ari drowned in," he said. "Is your friend Beals in town?"

Holcombe nodded, starting the car.

"I talked to him this morning. He said we could come by anytime."

The home of Beals Dalton wasn't just large, it was enormous, at least three stories high with a square tower that went up the left side. It sat on a hill, commanding an impressive view of its wooded grounds and the ocean beyond. The boards had been whitewashed, leaving it to shine in the afternoon sun, with sky blue shutters and shingles, giving it a splash of color.

The drive that led up to the house was at least a quarter of a mile long, giving anyone approaching plenty of time to appreciate the grandeur of the place. Even in February, the exterior of the house and the flower beds were well maintained and free of leaves or debris.

Growing up poor, Alex had often fantasized about owning a place like this, but after living in the brownstone for the better part of a decade, he just considered the big house a place that would take a long time to clean.

Holcombe piloted the car up the winding drive and around the circle drive in front of the house. A paved parking area was located on the far side of the house where it was hidden from view.

"This is it," he said, letting the car glide to a stop in the parking area. "Quite the pile of bricks, isn't it?"

Alex agreed, then followed as Holcombe led the way along a brick path to the front door. Like the house, it was larger than it needed to be, made of perfectly sanded white oak boards held together with steel bands that had been blued. It was wider than normal and taller too, with a rounded top, like something Alex had seen in paintings of European castles. In the center of the door was an enormous knocker made of the same blued steel and Holcombe lifted the clapper, then let it fall.

The sound resounded through the house like thunder and less than a minute later Alex heard the tromp of heavy footsteps from inside. The lock clicked and the door was pulled open by a tall, broad shouldered man in his fifties. He had an angular face with prominent cheekbones, a long, thin nose, and dark, intelligent eyes.

"Mr. Holcombe," the man said in an upper-class British accent. "It's pleasant to see you again."

He stepped back, taking the door with him so Alex and Holcombe could enter.

"Who is your friend?"

"Milton, this is Alex Lockerby, he's a private investigator, one of the best."

Milton inclined his head.

"Mr. Lockerby," he said. "I am Milton Thornhill, Mr. Dalton's butler. Please call me Milton."

Alex had to admit he was impressed. He'd seen professional men, butlers and valets and such, but other than Andrew Barton's valet, Gary Bickman, most of them seemed like overpaid place-holders. Milton Thornhill exuded confidence, like he, rather than Beals Dalton, was master of the house.

"Mr. Dalton called about your visit," Milton said.

"You mean he's not here?" Alex interrupted.

"No, sir," Milton said. "His work is in the city, so he's only here on the weekends. He did instruct me to give you the run of the house and see to any of your needs while you're here. I assume you'd like to see the pool first."

"That would be great," Alex said.

Milton shut the heavy door and made certain it was latched before turning toward an opening in the side of the foyer.

"This way, gentlemen."

5

SWIMMINGLY

Alex limped after Beals Dalton's butler, Milton, through elegant rooms and along tiled corridors until they finally reached a spiral stair going down. At the bottom was the basement level, with a large room for entertaining bordered by a long bar complete with shelves of bottles on the wall and a brass rail in front of it.

"This is where the party was held?" Alex asked as Milton turned left toward the back of the room.

"Yes," he said. "Here and outside. The house has a walk-out basement with a large patio and a small lawn beyond. From there, steps go down to the beach."

"Seems a bit cold to be outside," Alex remarked.

"People want to see the ocean when they drink," Holcombe supplied. "Besides, there are gas heaters on the patio."

Alex flipped open his notebook and jotted down the relevant points.

"The pool is back here," Milton said, indicating a door that led to a narrow hallway.

As soon as Alex entered, he could smell the chemical odor of treated water. At the end of the hall were two doors that led to changing rooms and a third that accessed the pool itself. When Milton opened that door, Alex had to descend down a flight of stairs to the level of the pool deck.

The room was massive and everything from the walls to the floors was covered in mosaic tiles. The tiles depicted a scene as if the pool were out of doors, down on the beach, with sand and scrub grass where the wall met the deck, and blue skies with fluffy clouds as the arched ceiling went up. All around the deck were bright lights mounted with reflectors to shine upward, illuminating the tiled sky and reflecting the light back down to the pool below.

Alex whistled.

"This must have cost a fortune," he said, mostly to himself.

"I don't know the exact figure," Milton said, "but it's a hundred thousand dollars at least."

Alex whistled again, looking the pool over. The shallow end was on his left, closest to the stairs, with the deep end on the right. It was a long pool, suitable for swimming laps and there was even a rope, with cork buoys set along it, lying coiled on the far side.

"How deep is this pool?" Alex asked Milton.

"Ten feet on that end," the butler replied, "but it rises steadily until it's only three feet deep on this end."

Alex wrote that down, then circled the pool looking for anything that might be out of place. There wasn't any water on the deck and nothing suspicious. He was certain the police had made a mess when they came to get Ari's body, so that meant the place had been cleaned. No doubt the household staff had seen to that the moment the authorities left.

Still, since the pool was full, and the party was only four days ago, that meant they hadn't drained the water. It would take quite a while to drain the pool with a submersible pump, to say nothing of refilling it from the city tap. That would take days all by itself.

"How often is this pool serviced?" he asked.

"On the first Wednesday of every month," Milton replied. "We have a man who comes out."

Alex noted that down, then stopped where a metal door had been set into the floor. Reaching down, he pulled it up, pivoting the metal plate on its hinges until it pointed straight up. Underneath was a sump with a basket inside made of metal mesh.

"You said Mr. Leavitt was staying here?" Alex said, directing the question to Holcombe.

"He had a room upstairs," the tennis pro supplied.

Alex turned to the butler.

"Is that normal?"

"Oh, yes sir," he said. "There are a dozen bedrooms upstairs and Mr. Dalton offers them to certain of his special guests so they don't have to drive home or take the late train into the city. Mr. Leavitt always stayed with us."

"What brought that question on?" Holcombe asked.

Alex picked up the mesh basket by its wire handle.

"This is the pool filter," he said holding it up. "It's designed to catch any debris that might end up in the pool before the water gets sent to the pump."

"And?" Holcombe prodded.

"And, I'm sure the police checked it when they did their investigation," Alex turned the wire basket upside down to emphasize his point. "However," he went on, reaching down into the sump where the basket normally rested. "They missed something."

Alex lifted his hand, revealing a sopping wet bit of white fabric.

"Is that a handkerchief?" Holcombe guessed.

Alex set the basket aside and stretched the fabric out so the other could see it.

"It's a woman's brassiere," he said. "Are you certain Ari was alone when he went swimming?"

Holcombe opened and closed his mouth in rapid succession before spluttering a denial.

"Ari is a gentleman," he insisted.

"That's hardly a proscription against having a girl," Alex pointed out, keeping his voice free of judgement.

"Not Ari," Holcombe insisted. "I've known him for years, since we went to university together. If he were seeing someone, I'd know about it."

Alex shifted his gaze to Milton, but the butler only shrugged.

"I've been here for almost 10 years," he said. "You'd be amazed what the maids find when they clean the rooms. I don't know if Mr. Leavitt's room ever required..." he cleared his throat, "special cleaning, however."

"Besides," Holcombe added. "That brassiere was underneath the filter, it could have been there for years."

"No," Alex corrected. "It's been here less than a month. I can understand the police missing it, because it's the exact color of the sump, but there's no way the regular pool man would miss it. Whoever owns this garment, lost it in this pool in the last few weeks."

"That still doesn't mean whoever owns that was here with Ari," Holcombe pointed out.

"No, it doesn't," Alex admitted, setting the brassiere aside and replacing the filter basket, "but it could. Are you sure you want me to continue pursuing this case?"

Holcombe just stared at Alex for a long moment, expertly hiding the war of emotions going on inside his head. Finally, he sighed and nodded.

"I have to know," he said. "If it turns out Ari was doing something he shouldn't have been, I don't have to let anyone else know."

"All right, then," Alex said, using his cane to push up to his feet, then moving to the stairs where he'd left his kit bag. "Let's do some investigating."

"If you don't need me," Milton said, "I shall return to my duties. If you require anything, just call."

"Before you go, there are a couple of things I will need," Alex said.

Milton, who had mounted the stairs, turned back to regard him with a curious face.

"I assume someone from your cleaning staff tidied up here in the pool area," Alex said. "I'd like to talk to them, along with the maid that was responsible for Mr. Leavitt's room. Also, I need to know who found Mr. Leavitt's body."

"I believe that was one of the guests, sir," Milton offered.

"Someone must know which guest, see if you can get me a name."

"Very good, sir," Milton said, then he turned and headed up the stairs.

"So what now?" Holcombe asked.

"Now comes the boring part," Alex said, pulling his multi-lamp from his bag. "I'm going to go over every inch of this place and see if there's anything the police and the cleaning staff missed. You might want to find a place to sit, and maybe have Milton bring you a book."

Rather than looking dejected, Holcombe's face blossomed with interest.

"I'll stay and watch if you don't mind."

Alex chuckled as he clipped the silverlight burner into the lamp.

"Suit yourself," he said, "Just save your questions until the end."

Almost two hours later Alex slumped down into a pool chair next to Holcombe and slipped the shoe off his wounded foot so he could rub it.

"That was actually quite interesting," the tennis pro said. "Can I ask what you found?"

"I did say I'd answer questions after the performance," Alex admitted with a chuckle. He let go of his foot and leaned back, covering his eyes with his forearm "As expected the deck, the furniture, the tables, and everything that might have been a wealth of physical evidence has been thoroughly cleaned by your friend's dutiful staff."

"Are you suggesting one of them had something to do with Ari's death?"

Alex sighed.

"It's possible," Alex admitted, "but unless I find a motive, I doubt it. Plus, a house this big has what, a dozen people on staff? That's too many people to keep secrets. If someone here was involved with Ari, in any regard, the others would know."

"But you haven't talked to them."

"Don't need to," Alex said, still covering his sore eyes. "The police will have seen to that, and, if someone was romantically involved with Ari, they would have arrested that person already."

"So what else did you discover?"

"Well, there's a truly disconcerting amount of bodily fluids on the walls, up above where a maid would normally clean."

"You mean..." Holcombe let his question trail off.

"Yes," Alex said, not elaborating. "This pool is quite the little love nest. There are lots of fingerprints around the door to the equipment room and on the tool handles, but nothing out of the ordinary. Assuming the coroner was correct, Ari wasn't bludgeoned anyway."

"Is that all?" Holcombe demanded. "You were at it for over an hour."

"I did find one thing," Alex said, finally sitting up. "I don't know what to make of it yet, but I'm absolutely sure we need to talk to your friend Dalton's pool man."

"Why?"

"Because the water in this pool isn't water, or rather it's not just water. It's giving off a faint magical aura."

"What does that mean?"

Alex shook his head.

"I don't know," he admitted. "It could be nothing, or..." he sighed.

"Or?" Holcombe prodded.

"Or someone might have put something in the water that killed Ari."

"Wouldn't it have killed the police that went in to get his body?"

"Maybe," Alex said, "but it might have lost its potency by then. One thing is for certain," he said, standing up, "we won't figure it out sitting here."

Holcombe pulled his car up in front of a simple garage standing at the corner of a residential street. A hand painted wooden sign had been nailed above the garage, proclaiming it to be the offices of Addams Pool Service. The carriage door to the garage was closed against the weather, but there was a regular door on the side of the building, and Alex could see light through the frosted window in it.

"This is it," Holcombe announced unnecessarily.

Alex got out and limped to the door with the glass panel. A curtain had been hung behind the door, so he couldn't see in, but a shadow was moving around inside.

"Someone's home," he said, then knocked.

A moment later the door was opened by an older man with gray hair and a gray mustache. He had a roundish, affable face with the thin, muscular build of someone who engaged in manual labor.

"Can I help you?" he asked.

Alex handed him his card and explained why he and Holcombe were there.

"I have a few questions about the work you do for Beals Dalton," Alex said. "May we come in?"

The man stepped back to allow Alex and Holcombe in. His workshop was neat and orderly, with cans of chemicals lining shelves and a work table where he was filling glass jars with some powdered substance. There were hoses and pumps stacked in one corner along with what looked like a small alchemist setup on a rollaway table.

"Look," the man said as he closed the door behind him, "I heard about what happened at Beals' place, but I can assure you it has nothing to do with me."

"Mr...?" Alex prompted.

"Addams," he said, sticking out his hand. "Harry Addams."

"The reason we came by, Mr. Addams, is because there is a residue of magic coming from the water in Mr. Dalton's pool." He turned and looked at the rollaway table with its alchemy equipment. "I was wondering if you used any alchemical products in your work?"

"I do," Addams admitted, "but I don't make them. That equipment is for testing water samples I take from my client's pools."

"So what is it you use?" Alex continued.

Harry Addams turned to a nearby shelf and pulled down a rectangular metal tin with a lid.

"I add this to my chlorine powder and it keeps mildew from growing on the walls in underground pools. It's a real problem in humid regions."

Alex knew that; he only showered once a day, but if he didn't scrub the grout once a month, mildew would grow.

"Are you sure it's harmless?" Alex asked.

"Of course," Addams said, a touch of offense in his voice. "It's been approved by the American Alchemical Conclave and I've been using it for almost four years now." He sounded both confident and dismissive. "I…I hardly ever have to scrub mildew any more."

Alex picked up the tin, noted the name of the alchemist who made the mildew killer, then set it down. He was reasonably sure Addams was telling the truth and, if he was, the magic residue in Beals Dalton's pool water was likely a dead end. Still, he'd taken a sample of it that now resided in his kit. When he got back to the city he'd have Charles…he'd have Linda test it for anything toxic.

With that done, Alex thanked Harry and he and Holcombe headed back to the car.

"What now?" the tennis pro asked.

"I'm hungry," Alex said, "and I need to make another phone call. Let's find a decent diner."

"Lieutenant Pak," Danny's voice greeted him when Alex finally managed to catch him.

"It's me," Alex said.

"About time you called," his friend chided him. "I had a nasty phone call with that police chief up in Southampton. I didn't know you were rustling feathers up north."

"I told you, I'm looking into a suspicious death," he explained.

"That's not what the chief told me," Danny countered. "He said you're making waves over a man who drowned in a swimming pool."

"That's what the coroner said too, but from what he told me, he wasn't very thorough. I need to see the police report."

Danny chuckled at that.

"Well Callahan did you a favor on this one, apparently he pulled some strings and got the Southampton chief to let you see the police file along with the coroner's report. You just have to go by the station and look at them there."

Alex didn't like that; he'd much rather take them home and study them at length.

"Beggars can't be choosers," he said as he checked his watch. "I've got to get going then, it's after four and I bet the chief will kick me out at five."

"Good luck," Danny said, then hung up.

Alex closed the safe door that concealed his phone, and headed back to the booth where he and Holcombe had been having an early dinner.

"Let's go," he said. "I got us access to the police file on Ari's death."

Alex limped down the brownstone stairs at a quarter to seven, pausing every third step to let the throbbing in his foot subside.

"Rough day?" Iggy asked from where he stood at the front window, looking out.

"I was on my feet more than I would have liked," he said, limping to his reading chair and dropping into it. "And I have a case that's probably an accidental death but my client insists it's murder."

"That's not too big of a problem," Iggy said. "Did you examine the body?"

"The body of Ari Leavitt has already been interred."

"When did he die?"

"Late Saturday or early Sunday."

"Leavitt," Iggy said, more to himself than to Alex. "Jewish funeral?"

"Got it in one," Alex sighed, propping up his sore foot on the ottoman.

"Have you seen the police report?"

"Yes, but neither the investigating detective nor the coroner believed there was anything suspicious about Mr. Leavitt's death."

Iggy sighed and stepped back from the window.

"I detest incurious investigators," he said, sitting down in his own chair. "Cigar?" he offered, holding out his portable humidor.

Alex accepted the offer and slipped his hand into his pocket for his jackknife.

"Why does your client think Mr. Leavitt's death was not an accident?" Iggy asked as he trimmed his cigar.

"He was a strong swimmer, who swam every day in his apartment building's indoor pool. He was also on the swim team in college and despite all that, he managed to drown in an indoor pool."

"Was alcohol involved?"

"Ari Leavitt was drunk, but not incredibly so," Alex supplied. "Most people who drown while drunk do it by falling and hitting their heads, or trying to swim in the ocean, not from swimming in pools."

"True," Iggy said, puffing his cigar to life. "Even drunk people will lift their heads out of water. So how did Mr. Leavitt drown?"

"For all I know he had a heart attack," Alex said, trying and failing to keep the irritation out of his voice.

"Not helpful, lad," Iggy said. "Stop worrying about what you don't know and focus on what you do."

Alex puffed on his cigar while he collected his thoughts.

"Ari was in his early fifties, so I can't rule out a medical issue."

"Even young people have medical issues," Iggy said, a touch of indignation in his voice.

"He might have banged his head and passed out after he got in the water."

"Even the most inept investigator would notice a contusion on Mr. Leavitt's head," Iggy fired back. "Next."

"Poison?"

"Usually leaves traces. Foam around the mouth, skin rash, a blue tinge on the lips, nails, or skin."

"All things even my lazy coroner would have noticed," Alex confirmed.

"So, what did you see in the police report?"

Alex closed his eyes and reviewed his time with the police report. For the second time today he was irritated by the lack of information in a file. The coroner's file wasn't much better; all it included was a few pictures of the body and the meaningless measurements about Ari Leavitt's physical dimensions and blood alcohol level.

As he reviewed the pictures in his mind's eye, one thing did jump out at him. He'd seen it when he first reviewed the file, but he had no context for it.

"Is it normal for a dead body to smile?" he asked.

Iggy puffed on his cigar, giving him a moment to think.

"Not usually," he said. "When the body dies, the muscles relax. If someone were to use some device to form a smile on a corpse, it would stay during rigor, but that's only a temporary state. I'm assuming this isn't an academic question?"

"Ari Leavitt had a crooked grin on his face in the coroner's photos."

"Was there anything in his notes about broken bones?"

Alex thought for a moment, then shook his head.

"No," he said, "but I'm starting to think it's important."

"A smile like that could mean that Mr. Leavitt's jaw was fractured on one side."

"What would that mean?"

"Well," Iggy said, blowing a smoke ring across the room. "I doubt Mr. Leavitt went swimming with a broken jaw."

"No," Alex admitted, "he wouldn't. So, assuming his jaw was broken, how did that happen?"

"Since we're firmly in the land of supposition, I'd guess he experienced a particularly strong muscle spasm. Something similar to lockjaw."

"What causes that?" Alex asked.

"Tetanus," Iggy supplied. "That would also explain his drowning since other symptoms are muscle spasms all over the body."

Alex sat up a bit straighter at that thought. Full body cramps could make even a strong swimmer drown. Something about that tickled his memory.

"Unfortunately it takes a couple of weeks for tetanus to turn into lockjaw," Iggy went on, "and there are symptoms long before that."

Alex slumped back down again with a frustrated sigh.

"Do I really have to spell it out for you?" Iggy said, irritation blossoming in his voice.

Alex's wandering mind snapped back into focus. Now that he thought about it, he recognized the symptoms Iggy described, but not associated with tetanus.

"Your monograph on poisons," he said, his memory finally retrieving the information. "Strychnine."

"Indeed," Iggy said, blowing another smoke ring. "A poison that causes severe muscle spasms would kill Mr. Leavitt quite effectively."

"But there's still no way to prove it."

"Without Mr. Leavitt's body, you're correct," his mentor said in his smug, I-figured-it-out voice.

"But the broken jaw should be enough evidence to get the body exhumed," Alex finished the thought. "Assuming I can convince the police that Leavitt's jaw was broken in the first place."

"I'm sure if you had access to a competent doctor," Iggy suggested, "he might be persuaded to issue a report calling the coroner's conclusions into question."

"Maybe one who has worked with the police as a consultant in the past," Alex supplied.

"The ideal candidate," Iggy intoned with a smirk.

6

BETWEEN THE LINES

The automatic elevator dinged and the outer door rumbled open to reveal the fifth floor of the Central Office of Police. Alex unhitched the inner cage door and pushed it open before picking up his kit and stepping into the hall. His foot felt better after a night of rest, but that still left him with a headache he couldn't shake.

Limping along the hall, he skirted the open bullpen where the detectives of the various divisions had their desks. At the end of the hall he turned left and progressed along the back wall where the offices of the lieutenants were located. Technically, he was headed for Detweiler's office, to go over the witness statements in the explosive death of Reggie Aspler, but, before that, he needed to talk to Danny.

"Knock, knock," he said, stepping through Danny's open door. His friend's office appeared much as it had when it had been Captain Callahan's office. There were file cabinets along the far side wall, a desk in the center, faced by two wooden chairs, a moth-eaten couch below a window that looked out into the hallway, and a trophy wall to the left. A large window occupied the space behind the desk, revealing the city and letting in copious amounts of the morning sunlight.

Danny sat behind the desk, leaning back in his chair with his legs crossed. He was reading from a file folder while the lit stub of a cigarette trailed a thin spire of smoke from his ashtray.

"Alex," he said, setting the folder aside. His face split into a wide grin and he stood up to shake his friend's hand. His face seemed almost as young as it had been when he and Alex first met a decade ago, but there were a few lines beginning to creep in at the corner of his dark eyes. He wore the police lieutenant's uniform, a suit made of sturdy fabric in a dark enough color to hide any stains that might be picked up on the job, and his gold badge hung from the outside breast pocket of his coat.

"I wasn't expecting you so soon," he said as Alex clasped his hand.

Alex pulled an envelope from his pocket and dropped it on the desk.

"Iggy wrote it out last night after we talked," he said. "It's not the first time, so he had it done in a few minutes."

Danny just shook his head with a laugh.

"I wish Wagner or any of his orderlies would work that fast," he said, picking up the envelope and examining the letter within.

"That should be enough to get you an exhumation order if you know a friendly judge," Alex said.

"That's Callahan's department," Danny said, tucking the letter back into the envelope. "I've already briefed him, so he's expecting this."

Even though his friend's voice gave no inflection of any kind, Alex flinched a bit at the statement.

"Was he mad?"

Danny shrugged as he tucked the letter into the inside left pocket of his coat.

"At first he was livid," he said. "Jumping other investigator's cases is frowned upon, even little departments like the Southampton P.D."

"I don't imagine Chief Peterson is going to like it much," Alex admitted, though based on how uninterested the man had been at the possibility of a murder in his own back yard, Alex didn't really care what he thought.

"When I told the captain that this was at the behest of Holcombe Ward, he cheered up quite a bit."

"He's a tennis fan?" Alex asked, not believing the words as they were coming out of his mouth.

"Mrs. Callahan," Danny supplied. "I'm pretty sure the price of Callahan's assistance on this is going to be a luncheon with your client, the captain, and his wife."

Alex was never one for the game of tennis; he wasn't even sure he understood the rules, but this was the second time someone offered to help when they found out about his famous client. He resolved to use that to his advantage if he could.

"I'm sure I can arrange that," Alex said with absolute confidence. "Will Callahan get the case transferred to you?"

Danny gave him a weary smile and chuckled.

"Let's see if there's actually a case first," he said. "Though it wouldn't hurt if Mr. Ward could get a list of everyone who was at the party the night Ari Leavitt drowned."

Alex pulled out his notebook and jotted that down, along with a note to ask Holcombe about a meet-and-greet with the Callahans.

"When do you think you'll know about the broken jaw or the strychnine?"

"It'll be a while," he said. "First we've got to convince a judge to order the exhumation, then, once we get the body, Wagner's got to do a proper autopsy."

"Don't dawdle," Alex advised, then explained about Jewish funeral practices.

"I know," Danny said, "and even if I didn't, Dr. Bell mentions it in the letter."

"I'll leave you to it, then," Alex said. "If you need me, I'll be with Detweiler, he's got me consulting on the bombing case."

"I thought you two were on the outs again," Danny said, moving around the desk.

"I can never tell with Detweiler," Alex admitted. "He usually just shows up when he needs my help."

"Good luck," Danny said as they both stepped out into the hall.

Alex wished him luck in return, then turned down the hall toward his destination.

Lieutenant Detweiler's office was similar to Danny's, though the chairs in front of the short man's desk were padded and the couch was a bit more run down. Just like Danny, Detweiler was hard at work over a stack of folders. As Alex rounded the door, he looked up with bloodshot eyes.

"Oh, thank God," he managed. "Please tell me you brought some of that coffee from Empire Station."

Alex hadn't but it would be child's play to have Sherry get some, put it in his vault and then fetch it in 15 minutes.

"Sorry," he said, setting his kit bag down on the lieutenant's desk. "I did bring your copy of Aspler's calendar back though." Alex withdrew the stained book and placed it on the lieutenant's desk.

Detweiler looked at the leather-bound book for a long moment, then sighed.

"No coffee, though?" he said in an exhausted voice.

Alex had spent a long time disliking the balding little man, and, to be fair, Detweiler had the kind of bulldog-ish personality that made him hard to like. In that moment, however, Alex felt for the man.

"Let me use your phone," he said, turning the black object around.

"Help yourself," Detweiler said, then began sorting through the stack of folders on his desk.

Alex gave the police operator the number of his office and, in a few moments, he was connected to Sherry.

"Hey, boss," she said upon hearing his voice.

"Listen," he said, "I need you to do me a favor."

"If it's about two thermoses full of coffee," she interrupted him, "I had a feeling you'd be needing them. I had Mattie fill them up and then I put them in your vault."

Alex suppressed a laugh at that. In Detweiler's condition, it might provoke the little man.

"That's great, doll," he said. "I'll meet you in the lobby in fifteen." In reality, he'd just have to step away for a few minutes to open his vault, but he wasn't going to tell Detweiler that.

"I take it you're in Lieutenant Detweiler's office," Sherry said.

"Right," Alex confirmed. "If anything important comes up, you can reach me here, and if Holcombe Ward calls, tell him I'll call him back as soon as I know something."

"Gotcha," Sherry said. "Anything else?"

Alex said that there wasn't and they both hung up.

"Did you just have your secretary send coffee over?" Detweiler asked, prying one eye open wide to stare at Alex.

When Alex nodded, he went on.

"Bless you. Next time you're up to your neck in something shady, I might just look the other way."

"Why, Lieutenant," Alex mocked, "that's really very decent of you."

"I said 'might'," he growled back.

"While we wait for my secretary, why don't you explain what all this is?" Alex said, indicating the pile of files.

"These are the witness statements from Aspler's office staff," Detweiler said, picking a folder off the top of the pile and passing it to Alex.

"Anything interesting?" he asked as he opened the file.

"Nothing," Detweiler sighed. "I've been through these twice and there isn't anything in there that's remotely interesting." He pushed the stack of blue folders away from him and folded his arms on the desk. "See what you can make of them," he said, putting his head down on his arms, "and wake me when the coffee gets here."

Alex picked up the stack of folders and transferred them to the battered couch. By the time he'd settled down to read, Detweiler was snoring softly.

Alex read through all the folders over the next half hour and he was forced to admit, the inner workings of Aspler Shipping Company were excessively tedious. As far as anyone knew, Reggie Aspler had no enemies, at least not any that were mad enough to kill him, and was a man of regular habits. He had an apartment in the city and a country home upstate, where he spent his weekends.

At the country estate, he had a wife, Janet, and two children. While the children were reportedly distressed by Reggie's death, the investigating detective wasn't so sure about the wife. For her part, however, Janet stayed in the country so much that none of the office staff ever remembered actually meeting her.

On the day of the bombing, none of the office workers noticed anything out of the ordinary. The mail had been delivered in the morning, but Reggie never got to it until after lunch, which was consistent with the time of the explosion.

With a sigh, Alex closed the last folder and stretched. Deciding he needed to exercise his good leg, he got to his feet and, patting his pocket to make sure his rune book was there, he headed toward the janitor's closet at the end of the hall.

The closet was both wide and deep and filled with the various tools of the janitorial trade. Because of its size there was a significant portion of bare wall that Alex had used in the past to open his vault. Chalking a door in that area, he opened his vault and limped inside.

Sherry had left two green thermoses standing on the reading table in his library area and Alex limped over to them, grabbing them both by their handles with his right hand, then heading back to the closet. Usually when Alex opened a vault in this particular closet, it was to make a quick exit from the Central Office, so the door was only open for a few moments. This was longer than he liked the door to be open since he couldn't tell when a janitor might decide he needed something from the closet.

With a sigh of relief, Alex set down the thermos bottles on the floor and pulled his vault door closed, waiting until the smooth steel had melted away, leaving only the plastered wall behind.

Once he'd returned to Detweiler's office, Alex filled up the lieutenant's empty coffee cup with Marnie's magical brew. He had to hunt a bit, but eventually found an empty whisky glass in one of Detweiler's file cabinets.

The coffee was hot enough that he had to drink it from the glass cup in short sips, but that was just fine by Alex. It made the coffee last longer.

"Eh?" Detweiler mumbled, suddenly rousing himself. He sniffed the air and that led him to his cup. "You're a prince," he declared, taking a long sip of the steaming liquid.

"I'll remember that you said that," Alex laughed, taking a quick sip himself.

"So," Detweiler said after he'd drained, refilled, and drained his cup. "Did you read everything?"

Alex nodded.

"What do you think?" Detweiler asked.

"I think your original assessment was right," he admitted. "There isn't much here."

"What about his calendar?"

Alex shook his head as he took out his cigarette case.

"Let's stay with the eyewitness reports for now," he said, offering Detweiler a cigarette before selecting one of his own. "There were a couple of details that stood out to me. First, I'm fairly certain we're dealing with a runewright, a good one."

"Why?" Detweiler asked.

"Because the mail came in early, but the bomb didn't go off until after lunch," Alex explained. "The staff said that Reggie didn't open his mail until after lunch."

"So the bomb didn't just go off," Detweiler said, "it exploded when Aspler opened the letter."

"And since we know it was a magical explosive, that means that there was an activation rune, maybe written across the envelope flap or the top of the folded paper, that only triggered the explosive rune when the letter was opened."

"Is that hard to do?"

Alex nodded.

"Activation runes are fairly rare. Other than myself and Dr. Bell, I only know one other person who can make them."

"Sounds like a suspect," Detweiler said. "We should go talk to him."

"Jimmy Cortez," Alex said, "He'll be easy to find, he's in prison. He was part of that crew that tried to rob the American History Museum back in thirty-four."

"Prisoners can still send mail."

"Yes, but during the attempted robbery, they used dynamite," Alex pointed out. "If he knew how to make a blasting rune, he wouldn't have bothered with the hassle of acquiring dynamite."

"Okay," Detweiler said, somewhat deflated. "We're looking for a runewright and they're talented enough to have a blasting rune and a... what did you call it?"

"Activation rune," Alex supplied.

"Could they have learned the blasting rune from Arlo Harper?"

"It's certainly possible," Alex admitted, "but if they were friends of Arlo and Roy Harper, why didn't they send me a bomb, or you? We were involved in their deaths, a friend might want to get revenge for that?"

"You make a good point, but that begs the question, how does this new bomber know about blasting runes and activation runes? According to you, one is rare and Arlo's blasting rune died with him."

"What one man can discover, another can uncover," Alex repeated one of Iggy's maxims.

"So he's talented and smart," Detweiler said, coming at last to the same conclusion Alex had. "Anything else?"

"Two things actually," Alex said. "First, I found it odd that several of the office staff made a point to say that they'd never met Reggie's wife, Janet."

"I thought that was strange too," Detweiler admitted, "but it's a two-and-a-half hour train ride out to that estate where she lives. Maybe she doesn't like to travel."

"Makes sense," Alex said, "but her husband spends most of his time here in the city."

"So?" Detweiler said. "We already know that he was running around on his wife."

"What if she knew it too?" Alex said.

"How did you get from no one seeing her to her knowing about Reggie's affairs?"

Alex stood and picked up the burned and bloodstained calendar.

"Look at this," he said, paging through it until he found the entry he was looking for. "Six-thirty on Thursday last it says that Reggie had a meeting with someone called WW." Alex pointed to the entry.

"So?"

"So…" Alex said paging backward through the book. "WW appears twice the previous week, three times the week before, and then," he turned more pages, "it skips a month, but reappears…here."

"You're thinking WW is Reggie Aspler's mistress?" Detweiler said.

"I did initially," Alex said, "but then I went back to the beginning of this book." He paged some more, opening to the first week covered. "This calendar started at the first of last year."

"I don't see a WW here," Detweiler said, leaning over the book to get a better look.

"That's because it first appears here," Alex turned to the next week and indicated another evening meeting, but this time instead of initials, there was a name written out.

"Widow's walk?" Detweiler read before giving Alex a confused look.

"I don't think WW is a person," Alex said. "I think it's code for a location."

"You mean Aspler met his mistress somewhere other than his apartment?" Detweiler asked incredulously. "Why would he bother?"

"The only reason that makes sense is that Janet was having his apartment watched," Alex said. "Maybe she paid off the superintendent, maybe a neighbor, but if I'm right, Reggie didn't want to be seen at his apartment with a woman."

"He'd need a love nest," Detweiler agreed. "So how do we find it?"

Alex shook his head.

"All we know is the name Widow's Walk. I'll have to do some digging in the library, try to find out what that means, and maybe we can figure it out from there."

Alex was expecting Detweiler to get angry or at least annoyed, but instead a predatory grin spread across his face and he laughed.

"You mean there's something the great Alex Lockerby doesn't know?" he scoffed.

Alex was puzzled by this reaction, but he kept his cool.

"There's plenty of things I don't know," Alex said. "I'm wrong all the time, I just don't stop digging. That's how I get to right."

"Relax, Lockerby," Detweiler said, chuckling all the while. "I'm just savoring this moment. A widows walk is a footpath along the ridge of a house, usually surrounded by railings. According to folklore, they were built so that wives could stand out there and look to the sea, watching for their husbands to come home. It's sometimes called a captain's walk, because captains home from the sea would pace up there, anxious to be back on board their ships."

Alex processed that information for a moment, then reached for Detweiler's phone.

"Who are you calling?" the lieutenant demanded.

Alex just held up a finger, then had a brief conversation with the man who answered the phone.

"Thanks, Mick," Alex said at last, "I owe you one."

"I reiterate, who was that?"

"Mick Chambers," Alex said, jotting in his notebook. "He's the concierge at the Waldorf. The way I figure it, a swell like Reggie Aspler isn't going to take his mistress to some cheap hotel, he's going somewhere with class."

"No self-respecting mistress would accept less," Detweiler agreed.

"Well, according to my friend Mick, the only high-class hotel in the city that has a widow's walk is the Plaza, over by Central Park."

"I knew I kept you around for a reason," Detweiler said, pouring and downing another cup of Marnie's coffee. "Let's go see if anyone at the Plaza remembers Reggie."

"And maybe who he came in with," Alex said, recapping the thermos and placing it into his kit along with the second one. "We'll bring these along," he said with an extremely self-satisfied grin.

7

THE CAPTAIN'S WALK

The manager of the Plaza Hotel was a small man, shorter even than Lieutenant Detweiler, though he had a full head of bushy brown hair. Despite his diminutive size, Alex could almost feel an aura of pompous self-importance emanating from the man. He was dressed in an immaculate silk tuxedo with a gold watch, several diamond rings, and a fat cigar clenched in his teeth.

"I'm sorry, Detective," he was saying in a nasal voice that grated on Alex's nerves. "The Plaza simply does not discuss our patrons, or anyone who might have been a patron, with outsiders," he took the cigar out of his mouth and flicked the ashes at Detweiler, "especially the police."

"First of all," Detweiler growled, clenching his fists, "it's Lieutenant, and secondly, if I want to know what size jockey shorts you're wearing, you're going to tell me."

"Not without a warrant," the manager pushed back, seeming to be oblivious of Detweiler's building rage.

"Listen, pencil neck," Detweiler snarled, reaching for the man's lapels.

"I think we've wasted enough of this gentleman's time," Alex interrupted, putting a restraining hand on Detweiler's shoulder. "If he won't help the official investigation into Reggie Aspler's murder, I'm sure the press would love to know about that. I do have a friend over at the Times and one at The Midnight Sun."

"Aspler?" the manager gasped, clearly recognizing the name.

"He's the person who was murdered," Detweiler said, giving Alex a dirty look.

Technically he wasn't supposed to name the subject of an investigation, but Alex figured dropping it would be easier than trying to get a warrant. Historically judges were reluctant to grant warrants for Manhattan's swanky hotels, mainly because they catered to the kind of rich political donors all politicians needed to get elected.

The Plaza's manager wavered, considering what Detweiler and Alex had said. He paled, probably realizing that Alex had mentioned talking to the press, something that might cost the officious little man his job. He hesitated for a moment, then clasped his hands together and plastered an ingratiating smile on his formerly smug face.

"If the Plaza can help the police solve the murder of one of our valued patrons, we'd be happy to help."

Detweiler gave Alex another, much less hostile look, then turned back to the manager with a smile.

"According to our information," he said, pulling a folded sheet of paper from his coat pocket, "Reggie Aspler stayed here on theses dates." He passed the paper to the manager. "We'd like that confirmed and we'd like to see the room, or rooms, he stayed in."

The manager glanced over the paper, then turned toward the front desk.

"Let's go to my office and I'll get that information for you."

He led the way across the lobby to a gilded door behind the main desk. The name Adam Finch adorned a brass plaque next to the door and the tuxedoed man went inside without pausing.

The inside of the office was the most opulent space Alex had ever seen, and he'd been in both Sorsha's and Andrew Barton's homes. Crown molding with dentil work, wainscoting with chair rail, and sconce lighting that appeared to be made of gold. The carpeting was a deep shade of burgundy and the furniture was carved and tipped with gold accents. As they crossed the room, the carpet and the wallpaper muted the noise, making the office seem, not just dignified, but sacred.

Alex tried not to judge rich people, as they were the bulk of his clientele in this stage of his career; still, this office was seriously over-the-top. Of course it wasn't really the diminutive Adam Finch's decor, as the office came with the job, but whoever set it up wanted any visitors or petitioners to feel the weight of the occupant's perceived importance.

Finch sat down at his desk and Alex had to stifle a smirk. He literally had to step up into his chair, probably because he had a book on the seat to prop up his diminutive frame. Reaching over, Finch punched a button on an intercom and asked for someone to bring him the reservation book. A moment later an attractive young woman entered carrying an oversized leather book. She put it on the desk, then left without a word.

Finch opened the book to the first page, which had the word 'February' printed in a flowing font across the top.

"This covers the last month," he said. "If your dates are accurate, there should be several reservations for Mr. Aspler here. What was the first one in February?"

Detweiler checked his list.

"February second," he read.

Finch turned to the first page, then ran his finger down a list of names.

"Here it is," he said. "He rented the northwest penthouse for one night. The captain's cabin."

"Captain's cabin?" Alex asked.

"It has a nautical theme," Finch said. "All the penthouses have a theme. The captain's cabin even has a widow's walk, though we keep it locked in the winter."

Alex exchanged a look with Detweiler.

"Show us," he said.

Equal & Opposite

The Captain's Cabin turned out to be a suite on the penthouse level of the Plaza Hotel. It reminded him of the suite Sorsha had used at the Waldorf back when German agents had tried to start a sorcerer's war in New York. There were five rooms in the suite, including the master bedroom, a lounge, a solarium, a guest room, and a small kitchen. It was bigger than most New Yorkers' apartments.

A long row of windows in the lounge included a glass door that led out to the captain's walk. Through the glass, Alex could see a path that led down to the edge of the roof, to a platform with a table and two chairs for dining outdoors in better weather.

Finch had said that the room had a nautical theme, but it wasn't as over-the-top as Alex had expected. The room had paneled walls of dark wood, with artwork of ships and the sea. The long wooden bar in the lounge area had brass accents, polished to a high shine, as did the heavy doors and the furniture. It was subtle, and Alex could see why Reggie Aspler would stay here. The entire room was tasteful and elegant.

"Lovely," Detweiler said, looking around with his hands on his hips. "Now, why are we here? Aspler hasn't been here for almost a week; there isn't going to be any evidence left behind."

Alex gave him a patient smile, then turned to Finch, who was standing impatiently in the entryway.

"This suite comes with butler service, correct?"

"Of course," Finch said. "We have only the finest amenities here."

"How do I summon the butler?"

"There's a button near the phone," Finch said.

The phone in the lounge was on the end of the bar, and, as Alex moved to it, he saw a white button with a brass collar mounted into the top of the bar. Pushing the button, Alex held it for a moment, then let it go. Almost before Alex returned to where Detweiler stood, there was a polite knock at the door.

"Mr. Finch," a cultured voice said from the hall, "did you need something?"

"In here," Finch said, standing back from the door to admit an older man with a gray mustache and a glossy tuxedo. "These gentlemen are with the police," Finch said, "I assume they have a few questions for you. Take care of them and then lock up the room when you're done."

With that, Finch turned without a word and stalked out of the room.

The butler watched him go, then turned to Alex with an inquisitive look.

"My name is Colin Balsam," he introduced himself, "you need only call me Balsam. Now, how may I be of service?"

"Reggie Aspler," Detweiler said. "We know he was a regular in this suite."

Balsam looked suddenly uncomfortable and he hesitated.

"I won't deny that Mr. Aspler was a guest here," he admitted. "I suspect you learned that from Mr. Finch. That said, if you want to know about Mr. Aspler's time here, I'm afraid you'll have to ask him. I'm not at liberty to discuss a hotel guest."

"Hey," Detweiler barked at the man, "I'm getting tired of—"

"If I may," Alex cut him off, earning him a dirty look, "I realize that a big part of your income depends on your serving your guests, and that means keeping their secrets. Unfortunately, Mr. Aspler is dead. He was murdered two days ago. We're trying to figure out who might have killed him."

"We know he brought a woman here who wasn't his wife," Detweiler said. "Having a mistress is one of those things we cops call motive."

"I, uh," Balsam stuttered. "I'm not sure—"

"Don't tell me you don't know her name," Alex said, keeping his voice calm and easy. "A man with the credentials to be the day butler in one of Manhattan's best hotels knows everyone he serves. He knows their likes and dislikes, their habits, and, most importantly, their names."

"So tell us, Mr. Balsam," Detweiler said, his voice quiet. "Who did Mr. Aspler bring when he came here?"

Balsam held up both his hands in a gesture of compliance, then took a minute to collect himself.

"Please, gentlemen," he said, "I'm not trying to say that I don't know names or that I won't tell you, but you seem to be under some misapprehension. Mr. Aspler did, in fact, bring a companion when he booked the Captain's Cabin. It was not, however, just one woman."

Alex looked at Detweiler who rolled his eyes.

"He came with a group?" Alex asked, a bit incredulous.

"Oh, no sir," Balsam said, his voice high and his speech quick. "What I mean to say is that there were several different women over the course of time."

"How many?" Detweiler asked.

"During the two years I have been with the Plaza, Mr. Aspler was accompanied by seven different women when he stayed with us."

"Of course he was," Detweiler said, opening his notepad. "I need you to give me their names and, if you can remember, when they were here with Mr. Aspler."

"Of course, sir," Balsam said.

Alex slid into the passenger seat of Detweiler's car, pulling the door shut behind him.

"What do you think?" the lieutenant said as he pressed the starter. "If there had only been one mistress, I'd be more suspicious, but seven? He couldn't have dated any one of them for more than a couple of weeks."

"I've seen people get attached in less time than that," Alex said, rubbing his forehead.

"Still," Detweiler said, pulling out into traffic, "I don't think this is much of a lead."

"Do we have any others?"

Detweiler sighed before answering.

"The Captain and I are meeting with the lawyer for Aspler Shipping after lunch," he said. "He's going to go over the company holdings and debt. We'll see if anything there jumps out. Maybe Aspler was moving goods for the mob and got greedy, or maybe someone wanted to buy him out and he said no."

From the sound of it, Detweiler didn't think those options were likely, but as Iggy often said, you never knew what people might have buried until you started digging.

"I'll take the mistresses then," Alex said, pulling out his notebook and going over the list of names. Some of them he recognized, mostly Broadway actresses and fashion models. There were a few names he didn't recognize, but Sherry could help with them.

"You just want to talk to the pretty girls," the lieutenant groused.

"It's a tough job," Alex said with feigned magnanimity, "but someone must do it."

"Get it done by tomorrow," Detweiler said. "The Captain wants this business settled and I'm coming up with nothing. That does not look good."

"If I find anything, I'll call you right away," Alex promised.

"You'd better," Detweiler growled.

Alex put his notebook away and lit a cigarette. It shouldn't take too long to track down Reggie's mistresses, but based on the names he recognized, none of them had any runewright knowledge. The list was more than likely a dead end. Still, he needed something to do until Danny got Ari Leavitt's body exhumed. He checked his watch and found it was a quarter to noon. If he wanted to get Sherry working on the unknown mistresses before lunch, he'd need to hurry.

"There's a sky crawler station in the next block," he said to Detweiler. "Drop me there."

"Hey, Boss," Sherry said as Alex pushed open the front door. "How'd it go?"

"The coffee was much appreciated," he said, setting down his kit and extracting the two thermoses. "I think there's even some left if you want it."

Sherry broke out in a dazzling smile, then opened a drawer in her desk and retrieved a ceramic coffee mug.

"I never turn down Marnie's coffee," she said.

"Anything important come up while I was out?"

"Danny called," she said, pouring steaming liquid into her mug. "He said they got the exhumation order and that he'd probably know something late this afternoon."

That made sense, it would take a while for the body to be dug up and transported to the morgue, then Dr. Wagner would have to run the test for strychnine and do the autopsy.

"Dr. Bell called as well," Sherry said, settling down in her chair with her coffee. "He wanted to talk to you, but when I told him you were out, he said it could wait."

It was unusual for Iggy to call Alex's office, unless he was helping Alex with a case.

Maybe he figured something out about Ari Leavitt's death, Alex thought.

He discarded that thought as soon as it came. If Iggy had something that important to tell him, he would have insisted Alex call him as soon as he returned.

"I've got to make some calls," he said, pushing his mentor from his mind. "Then, I'll have to go out for a few hours. Apparently Reggie Aspler was quite the ladies man, so I need to talk to his mistresses and see if any of them hated him enough to kill him."

He pulled his notebook from his pocket and flipped it open.

"While I'm busy, I need you to figure out who these three names are," he said. "Brooke Margrave, Carmine Ott, and Lana Redgrave." He paused while Sherry took down the names. "The rest of the list are actresses and fashion models, so I'm guessing these are more of the same. You should probably start with the casting agents."

"I'll check Who's Who first," Sherry said. "Maybe I'll get lucky and they're debutants."

"Good thinking," Alex acknowledged. "If you find them fast, I'll be in my office."

With that, Alex headed into the back hallway and down to his office. He stopped at the middle room and stuck his head in, but his apprentice, Mike Fitzgerald, must have been out on a case, because the room was empty.

The fact that Alex didn't know where the diligent little man was bothered him and he made a mental note to have Sherry start an active case sheet for Mike that Alex could review every morning. It was a tribute to Mike's skills that Alex didn't need to keep close track of him, but he didn't want Mike getting in over his head either.

Satisfied that he'd learned all he could from the empty room, Alex proceeded to his own office. There was a small stack of blue folders on his desk, cases Sherry wanted him to review when he had time. From the way his day was shaping up, he'd be able to look over them this evening before he went home.

Putting his cane in the corner by the bookshelf, Alex limped to his chair and sat down, propping his sore foot up on the small ottoman he'd acquired just for that purpose. He lit another cigarette and pulled the telephone within easy reach. His black phone book was in the center drawer of his desk and he pulled it out and set it on the table. Next he retrieved a bottle of good bourbon and a glass, filling the latter with the former.

Once he'd had a few enjoyable sips from his cup, he picked up the phone and gave the operator the number of the largest casting agency on Broadway.

"Louie," he said once he'd been connected, "it's Alex. How are things in the world of the theater?"

"What do you need, Lockerby?" a tired voice came back at him.

"That's what I like about you, Louie," Alex said in his most ingratiating voice, "you don't beat around the bush."

"And you don't call unless you want a favor," Louie responded. "I've got actual work to do, Alex."

"I just need to know what shows a couple of your girls are doing right now," Alex said. "Nothing big."

"Uh-huh." Louie responded, sounding thoroughly unconvinced. "And what do I get out of helping you?"

Alex thought quickly.

"Tell you what," Alex said, "have you got a show that's good but isn't doing well?"

"I've always got at least two of those," Louie said. "Why?"

"How about I get Sorsha Kincaid to come out to one of them?"

Louie started to say something, but hesitated.

"She has to look like she's enjoying the show," he said, "smiling, clapping, that sort of thing."

"I can guarantee it," Alex said, "but it would have to be next week," he added hastily, "Sorsha's out of town right now."

"All right," Louie finally capitulated. "Who are you looking for?"

A few minutes later, Alex had the addresses of the theaters where three of Reggie Aspler's mistresses were performing. Now all he needed to do was call around to the various modeling agencies until he found the one remaining girl. Alex wasn't exactly fashion conscious, but he recognized her name, so she must be well known in the industry.

Before he could pick up his phone again, however, it rang.

"Lockerby?" Detweiler's voice came down the wire.

"Lieutenant," he said, trying to sound chipper. "I've found three of Reggie's girls already, and I'll be heading out to interview them in just a few minutes."

"Never mind about that," Detweiler said, his voice heavy and tired.

"Why not?"

"There's been another bombing," the lieutenant said. "I need you to grab your bag of tricks and get over here."

8

THE POTIONEER

Alex took a cab from his office at Empire Tower east to Second Avenue in Turtle Bay. Second Avenue in this part of town was the demarcation line between the end of the Mid-Ring and the start of the outer. As such, there was a Consolidated Edison power plant just a few blocks further east, giving the life sustaining electricity needed by all the industrial businesses.

After the Civil War, Turtle Bay had consisted mostly of brownstones and small houses, but now there were breweries, stock yards, coal warehouses, and rail yards everywhere. Second Avenue ran along the short side of the rectangular New York blocks and attracted smaller storefronts the likes of laundries, dry goods stores, pawn shops, dime stores, and tradesmen of all kinds. Most were the kinds of businesses that catered to the laborers who worked in the adjacent factories and tended to be of the rougher variety.

The Thrifty Potioneer was a shop like that, or, rather, used to be a shop like that. According to its neighbors, the store advertised alchemical potions and materials at bargain costs. In truth, its proprietor and resident alchemist, Matthew McDermet, was known to skimp on ingredients and the volume of his potions. It kept costs down, but at the expense of his doses actually doing their job. Many of The Thrifty

Potioneer's patrons had to return for a second dose of a curative that should have worked the first time, had it been properly prepared.

Now, of course, it was a moot point. When Alex stepped out of his taxi, the entire store was open to the street, its front facade having been blown completely off. Debris littered the sidewalk and out into the street, consisting of colored stains, broken potion bottles, smashed ingredient cans, along with glass and wood from the building itself. Most of the big and dangerous debris had been cleaned from the street by the police, making it safe for cars, but much of the sidewalk was still being blocked off by officers.

"He's waiting for you," a big policeman who Alex didn't recognize said, jerking his thumb over his shoulder at where an exhausted-looking Lieutenant Detweiler stood.

"Thanks," Alex said, stepping around a broken potion bottle, while being careful not to step in any of its spilled liquid. Most potions only worked when ingested, but there were a few that turned acidic when they spoiled and Alex wasn't taking any chances.

"This is a real mess," he said as he joined the lieutenant just outside where the ill-fated store's front door had been.

Detweiler nodded.

"It's a bigger blast," he said, "that's for sure."

"What do we know?"

"Not much," Detweiler said, pulling a flip notebook from his suit coat pocket. "We found a body inside, we can't be certain, but it appears to be one Matthew McDermet, the owner. According to the neighbors, he worked here by himself. There was a delivery boy who worked on weekends, so it might be him if he was here for some reason."

"Did McDermet or the delivery boy have enemies?" Alex asked, surveying the damage.

"No idea. McDermet had a reputation for shoddy work, so there's bound to be someone squawking about it."

Alex looked around at the remains of the shop and the businesses on either side. None of them were what he would call 'classy.' Certainly not the kinds of businesses that attracted clients with the knowledge to make rune bombs.

"How certain are we this was a letter bomb?" Alex asked. "If McDermet was as bad an alchemist as you say, he might have just blown himself up."

"I was hoping you could use your bag of tricks to tell me that," Detweiler admitted.

Alex surveyed the damage, noting all the stains on the walls, ceiling, and out into the street.

"There's too much magic already in the air," he said. "My oculus won't be of much use."

"Great," Detweiler sighed.

"Fear not, Lieutenant," Alex said, affecting a radio announcer voice. "We can still investigate the old-fashioned way."

"Great," Detweiler repeated.

"Give me a few minutes," Alex said, setting his kit bag on the sidewalk next to the lieutenant.

Alex stepped over the ruins of The Thrifty Potioneer's facade, limping his way carefully through the destruction. As he went, he tried to imagine what the shop looked like before the blast. From what he could tell, the bomb went off in the back room, right about where a covered body lay on the floor.

All right, he thought, *let's see what we can see*.

More than an hour later, Alex came limping out of the remains of the cut-rate alchemy shop. His foot was killing him and his stomach was a bit queasy after what he'd found during his investigation.

"You look terrible," Detweiler said as Alex limped up to him. The lieutenant was leaning against the fender of a patrol car with the unlit stump of a cigar clenched between his teeth and a newspaper under his arm.

"I need to sit down and I could use a cup of coffee," he admitted, "so let's get this over with."

He turned and motioned for Detweiler to follow him back into the building and walked up to where the ruin of the main counter still stood.

"The explosion was centered here," Alex said, pointing down at where some of the wooden counter had been blown downward and into the floor. "If you stand here," he said, moving aside so the lieutenant could take his place, "you can see the blast lines where the other furniture gouged the floor."

Detweiler turned in place, noting what Alex had seen, and nodded.

"So do you think it was a rune bomb then?" Detweiler asked. "Maybe McDermet was standing behind the counter opening his mail?"

"I'm certain of it," Alex said, pointing to a spot on the floor where a bit of the back wall still clung to the brick side wall. There were several torn and shriveled letters caught there.

"Why didn't they catch fire?" Detweiler asked.

"Probably were blown away by the force of the blast before any heat was generated," Alex said. "Regular explosives are created by burning gunpowder or TNT, but runic ones use pure magic. They only burn once the explosive pressure reaches a high enough temperature."

Detweiler looked like he wanted to ask more, but the little man thought better of it and shrugged.

"What else?"

"McDermet," Alex began, then paused, "and I'm pretty sure the corpse in the back is McDermet, got blown back by the initial blast." Alex paused and took a deep breath before continuing. "The force blew the head right off the body and destroyed the face enough to make standard identification impossible." Alex jerked a thumb over his shoulder. "It's back there if you want to look."

"I'll take your word for it," Detweiler said, "but if the face is destroyed, how can you be sure it's McDermet's head?"

"Over here," Alex said, motioning for the lieutenant to follow. He stopped and pointed to the remains of a human arm that had been severed at the elbow. "This belongs to the body," he explained. "My best guess is that the force of the explosion blew Mr. McDermet through the door that separated the front of the shop from the back. His arm got caught on something and tore free."

Detweiler made a noise in his throat and turned a little green. Alex didn't blame him one bit.

"Note the back of the hand," Alex said, indicating it with his cane.

"Liver spots and loose skin," Detweiler said after squatting down for a better look.

"Whoever was answering the mail had to be at least fifty and, if your canvass notes are correct, the only other person that ever worked in here was the delivery boy, who we may assume is under twenty."

"We can?" Detweiler asked.

"We can," Alex confirmed, "if he'd been older than twenty, the neighbors would have referred to him as a clerk, not a delivery boy."

Detweiler looked like he might argue with that, but just didn't have the energy.

"Are you sure it's a rune bomb?" he said instead. "Not some potion that got out of hand?"

"A potion exploding would have burned the mail," Alex said. "Plus, there's no basement in this building and the upstairs is McDermet's apartment."

"You mean his alchemy lab isn't here?"

Alex shook his head.

"Based on what I've seen and what you told me, I'm betting that McDermet didn't have a lab anywhere."

Detweiler's head snapped up from his notebook at that.

"You mean he was using unlicensed alchemists to make his stock?"

"That's the way I figure it. It explains the lack of a lab and the inconsistency of his potions. Some were made by competent alchemists, others by barely passable hacks."

Detweiler swore under his breath.

"This is a real mess," he said, "and I don't mean the shop. We'll have to start an investigation into his suppliers and chase down his clients...it'll take weeks."

"And meanwhile," Alex said, cutting to the heart of Detweiler's frustration, "none of that has anything to do with our bomber."

"Do you think there's a connection between McDermet and Aspler?"

Alex shrugged.

"Not unless one of Aspler's mistresses is related to McDermet."

"What about first aid kits?" Detweiler said. "Aspler owns warehouses, ships, trucks, and even a few trains, he'd need first aid kits for all of those. Maybe he was skimping on the healing potions by buying them here."

Alex chewed his lip for a moment. He hadn't thought of that, and it was certainly possible. Laws governing working conditions in the state were becoming prominent, after all. Reducing expenses with cheaper, less reliable regeneration potions sounded like something a cost-cutting company president might do.

"If Aspler bought from McDermet, there'll be records of it," he said. "McDermet's office is upstairs and didn't get hit too bad by the blast. I'm sure your boys can find those records...assuming they exist."

"So that puts us back at square one," Detweiler said, clenching his teeth around the stump of his unlit cigar.

Alex sighed and shrugged. He didn't really have a good answer for that statement.

"I guess I'll continue on with the mistresses," he said, pulling out his pocket watch. It was just after four in the afternoon. "I'll start with them first thing in the morning, and I'll call you if anything turns up."

"That leaves me to head upstate tomorrow and see the widow Aspler," Detweiler said. "I'd like to think Aspler's death is a simple case of jealousy over his infidelity, but unless his widow is a top tier runewright, it doesn't seem likely."

"Look on the bright side, Lieutenant," Alex said in his most cheerful voice. "Maybe she hired the bombing out to someone who *is* a top tier runewright."

"I doubt I'm that lucky."

It took Alex a few minutes to hail a cab, but once it pulled out into traffic headed north to the brownstone, Alex had the cabbie pull over almost immediately.

"Thanks a lot," the cabbie groused as Alex got back out, leading with his cane. "The fare's ten cents."

Alex dug a half dollar out of his pocket and passed it over.

"Keep the change," he said, immediately brightening the cabbie's mood.

The reason he stopped was a little shop nestled between a cobbler and a laundry. The paint was faded and cracking on the sign hanging over the door. Two windows faced the street, with crowded displays behind them, but the glass was so dirty they were more like vague shapes.

As Alex drew closer, the name of the shop could be seen, just as he remembered, *Bell's Book and Candle*.

As Alex pushed the door open, a bell hung above rang, and the aroma of exotic incense, mixed with old books, greeted him.

"Be with you in a minute," a muffled voice came from somewhere off to Alex's left. The shop seemed unchanged from the last time Alex had seen it, with shelves along the walls loaded down with books, candles, and knick-knacks of all description. In the center of the floor were tables that held merchandise too large for the shelves, including what Alex hoped were models of shrunken heads.

"Mr. Lockerby," a delighted voice drew Alex's attention to the back of the store.

A short man with slicked back hair and spectacles emerged from a beaded curtain that separated the back of the store from the front. He wore pinstriped trousers with a white shirt and a red vest with satin lapels. Alex didn't realize it had been so long, but it looked like the man had lost at least fifty pounds.

"Theo," Alex greeted him. "You look great."

"It's been a while," Theodore Bell said, sticking out his hand for Alex to shake. "What brings you around?"

Alex hesitated, then plowed forward.

"I need to know if there was anything magical or paranormal about the Inquisition?"

"The Spanish Inquisition or one of the others?" Bell asked.

"I should have come to you first," Alex grumbled. "The one against the Knights Templar."

"Ah," Theo said. "France, thirteen o'seven. What did you want to know about it?"

"Did you ever hear of something called a curse stone?" Alex asked, getting right to the point.

Theo thought about that for a moment before answering.

"I don't know about curse stones," he said, "but there was this one book..." His words trailed off and he turned to his bookshelves. "I remember reading something, just a story, really. It didn't claim to be historical, but it had the kind of details that made you think it was real."

"What book was it?" Alex asked as the shorter man searched among the many shelves lining the walls of the shop.

"I don't remember, exactly," Theo said, pulling books out from their fellows enough to see the title, and then shoving them back in line. "I do remember it had a green cover, though."

After another minute of searching, Alex grew restless.

"Do you remember anything about this story?" he asked.

"Well," Theo said, not giving up his search just yet, "it starts with the founding of the Templar order. According to what is known, the Templars were founded in the early eleven hundreds by a group of knights. They were part of the force that held Jerusalem after the First Crusade."

Alex searched his memory for any details about the crusades, but he just hadn't learned any of it. Those things were too distant for either Father Harry or Iggy to teach him.

"They were based in the ruins of the Temple," Theo was saying when Alex's attention snapped back. "That's where they got the name 'Templar', or Knights of the Temple."

"Okay," Alex said, trying to move the story along. Theo was a well-spring of obscure and occult knowledge, but his train of thought had to be directed or he'd take hours to explain a simple point.

"Well, according to the story in the green book, the knights found...something, something about a Vision Stone."

"What's a vision stone?" Alex asked.

"Well, according to the story, it's a rock that's been imbued with magical power," Theo explained. "This one was supposedly how the biblical figure, Joseph of Egypt interpreted dreams."

Alex whistled. The story of Joseph had been part of his training at the hands of Father Harry. If Joseph really did have some kind of magic stone that gave him visions or let him see the future, that would be incredibly powerful.

"What happened to this stone?" he asked.

"I have no idea," Theo admitted. "What I do know is that, historically, the period from the time of Joesph to the Exodus of the children of Israel is considered one of the high points of Egyptian civilization."

"Because of this magic stone?"

Theo shrugged.

"It's possible."

"But what does this have to do with the Templars?" Alex pressed.

Theo could only shrug.

"There is one other bit of historical information that you might find interesting, though. When they returned home from the Crusades, the Knights Templar grew and eventually became one of the wealthiest and most powerful organizations in all of Europe."

"The implication being that they found the stone," Alex said.

"It would certainly fit the story," Theo said. "Though it wouldn't explain how the Templars were taken by surprise on Friday the thirteenth of October, thirteen o'seven."

Alex rubbed his chin as he thought. A magic stone that granted prosperity would certainly be something worth killing for.

Was that what Phillip the fourth of France was really after? he wondered. *And what, if anything, do curse stones have to do with this?*

It was true the story Theo remembered didn't have curse stones in it, but the fact that it had a magical stone in it at all made the story worth pursuing.

"You sure you can't remember the title of that book?" he asked.

Theo thought for a moment, then sighed and shook his head.

"Sorry," he said.

"Well, if you remember," Alex said, taking out his flip notebook, "give me a call."

He began to write the high points of the story Theo had told him, but then he remembered something.

"Would you know the title if you saw it?"

"Probably," Theo said with an air of confidence.

Alex returned his notebook to his pocket and took out his red rune book. Opening it to the back, he pulled out the folded slip of paper Sherry had given him.

"How about, *The Heresy Trials* by Phillip Tanner?" he asked.

"No," Theo said, "that's not it."

"What about, *Stories of Inquisition* by Conner Gertz?"

Theo hesitated for a long moment.

"That could be it," he said. "I can ask around to other bookshops and see if anyone has a copy, if you like."

"Do it," Alex said. "And if you come across any other references to magical stones, cursed or otherwise, let me know."

9

DINNER AND A SHOW

Alex thought about going back to his office and contacting at least one of Reggie Aspler's mistresses, but he was tired and his foot was killing him. On top of that, Iggy had called his office about something that he ultimately decided wasn't important enough to leave a message about.

Alex found that intriguing.

So he called a cab from the public booth in a hardware store and made his way back to the brownstone. When he paid off the cabbie, Alex noted a car parked down the street a few houses further on where there wasn't usually a car. When he'd first woken from his enforced coma, there had been a car on the opposite side of the street with two men who were watching the brownstone. Alex learned that they worked for a Jersey FBI director named Washburn. When Alex first met the man, he ranted about Alex helping Lucky Tony Casetti, the mob boss, go straight. Busting Casetti would have made Washburn's career, but putting surveillance on Alex seemed a bit much for even that. Alex had the uncomfortable feeling that a bigger game was being played, one he couldn't see.

As Alex limped up the steps in front of the brownstone, he glanced over his shoulder at the parked car. Unlike the glossy black Ford the

FBI men had been using, this one was an old model, painted brown and with many dents and other damage. It seemed to be empty and none of the windows were fogged up, so he kept going up to the door.

I'll have to ask the neighbors if it belongs to any of them, he thought as he used the gold key on his ring to open the front door.

"I'm home," he announced as he passed through the vestibule and into the small foyer that also served as the landing for the staircase going up.

"In the kitchen," Iggy called.

He really didn't need to announce himself. Since Iggy did all the cooking for the brownstone, there was nowhere else he was likely to be a mere half-hour before dinner.

Alex limped into the kitchen and dropped heavily into one of the chairs around the table, sticking his leg out straight to take any weight off his sore foot.

"That kind of day, eh lad?" Iggy said. He was puttering by the stove where several steaming pots rested.

"You have no idea," Alex said, resting his head against the high back of the chair.

"I saw in the paper that there was an explosion down in Turtle Bay," his mentor went on as he shook out some salt into one of the steaming pots. "The police are saying it was an improperly maintained gas line."

"Nope," Alex said, closing his eyes. "It was another rune bomb, bigger than the last one. It blew the entire front off the shop."

Iggy whistled.

"That means our bomber is well versed in their rune lore," he concluded. "If they were just an amateur who ran across the boom rune, or even someone just skilled enough to work it out for themselves, they wouldn't be able to control the scale of the blast."

"Not precisely, anyway," Alex agreed.

"I'm assuming by your dour countenance, that there isn't any obvious connection between your first victim and this latest one?"

Alex sighed, then told Iggy the whole story of Reggie Aspler and his philandering ways, then moved on to Matthew McDermet and his cut-rate alchemy shop.

"I'm going to interview the mistresses tomorrow," Alex concluded, "but as of right now, I don't see any connection between the two victims."

"Quite the contrary," Iggy said, forcing Alex to open his eyes and pay attention.

"What?"

"To my mind, both men are scoundrels, the kind of people who draw out the anger of others just by existing."

Alex thought about that for a minute. He'd come to much the same conclusion himself, but failed to see how such a revelation was relevant.

"I wouldn't be surprised," Iggy went on, "to learn that the shipping magnate's wife knew all about his mistresses."

"I suppose," Alex said. "People bought from McDermet's shop despite his reputation for shoddy alchemy. I guess the world is full of liars and cheats."

"Not of this caliber," Iggy said. "The glorious bastards of the world are a fairly small fraternity."

"Do they have club meetings?" Alex asked.

"No," Iggy admitted, "but I dare say they are connected, either through an acquaintance, a business deal, possibly even one of their victims."

Alex found that difficult to believe; Aspler and McDermet traveled in very different circles. The likelihood that they even knew of one another was minute.

"I'll worry about that tomorrow," he said finally.

"Well," Iggy said, setting out several covered dishes on the table. "If you're tired of the mad bomber, how about your tennis judge?"

"Danny got the exhumation order," Alex reported, "so Dr. Wagner will run the test for strychnine as soon as he gets the body. Danny said there's going to be a full autopsy as well. Even if he got the body today, it'll be tomorrow at the earliest before I hear anything."

"Pity," Iggy said, dishing out a thick meat stew into a bowl for Alex, then topping it with a scoop of finely whipped potato. "I was looking forward to that one."

Alex was too tired to be disappointed by the lack of news, and the aroma of the bowl placed under his nose was diverting his attention.

Once the meal had been served, Alex said grace and the two men began to eat. Alex recognized Iggy's long-cooked pot roast as the meat in the stew and took his time savoring every tender bite. Once he'd made his way through half of the bowl, Alex began to relax and enjoy the warming effects of the meal.

"Hey," he said, as his brain began firing on all cylinders again. "Sherry said you called but didn't leave a message. What was that about?"

Iggy blotted his mouth with his napkin before replying.

"Just a strange incident earlier today," he said. "A caller came looking for you around noon."

That took Alex aback. While it was true he was a public figure these days, appearing in the newspaper at least twice a year, the only mention of where to find him was at his office. To his knowledge, his residence at the brownstone was only known to a select few.

"Why didn't you just send him over to the office?"

"I tried to," Iggy said, "but all he would say was that he'd call again."

"Did he say what he wanted?"

"No," Iggy reported, "but he did seem a bit skittish."

That wasn't uncommon in people who sought out private detectives, but if the man wanted Alex's help, then his office was the logical place to seek it.

"What did he look like?"

Iggy sat back in his chair and thought for a moment before replying.

"He was a little below average height," he said, "probably five foot four. His complexion was pale with light blond hair, of Nordic heritage, I'd say. His hands were rough and his shoulders were broad, indicating a trade with lots of manual labor."

"What about his clothes?"

"Durable and worn, though kept in good condition," Iggy finished.

"I wonder what such a man wants with me," Alex said, feeling the weariness of the day starting to creep back in. "He did say he'd come back. I guess I'll find out then."

Iggy looked like he wanted to comment further, but at that moment the phone rang. Alex looked over at the phone where it was mounted on the wall. Above the device were two lights, one red and one yellow, next to a short lever. Since Alex's vault now connected the brownstone to his office, he'd wired this phone into his office line, just like the candlestick phone in his vault and the one in his room.

"It's for you," Iggy said, noting the yellow light was illuminated.

With a sigh, Alex stood up on his sore foot and limped to the phone. Taking hold of the lever, he turned it toward the yellow light, then picked up the earpiece.

"Lockerby," he said.

"It's Danny," his friend's voice greeted him.

"Did you get Ari Leavitt's body exhumed?"

"Yes. Wagner has it now and he said he'll have a full report in the morning. You want to meet me over at the coroner's office at nine?"

Alex thought about that, but couldn't find a good reason not to go. He wasn't thrilled about autopsies, but he owed it to his client to see the matter through.

"All right," he said. "I'll see you then."

He asked if there was any other business and, when Danny said no, they hung up.

"An autopsy report at nine and Mr. Aspler's mistresses after that," Iggy said, lighting a cigar as Alex returned to the table. "You've got a busy day tomorrow."

The morning came faster than Alex expected and before he knew it, he was late to meet Danny. He thought briefly about stopping somewhere for something to eat, but Dr. Wagner might not be done with the autopsy and the last thing he needed for that was a full stomach. He did, however, require coffee, so he went through his vault to his Empire Tower apartment and took the elevator down to the terminal level with a thermos in his kit bag.

One cup of Marnie's coffee and a cab ride later, Alex limped through the door of the Police Annex Building, where the morgue was located.

"How can I help you?" a severe-looking woman with her blonde hair in a tight bun asked him.

It took Alex a moment to process what he was seeing. For the last five years at least, no one had occupied the front desk but Sergeant Charlie Cooper. The man had been a patrol officer for decades and the job of desk sergeant had been a way of keeping him on the force after his twenty years of service.

"Where's Charlie?" Alex asked.

"Retired," the woman said with a disinterested tone.

"Why?"

"Don't know," she admitted. "Now, what's your business?"

"I'm here for autopsy results," Alex said, biting back a terse remark. He'd ask Danny about Charlie later, so there was no reason to prolong his conversation with the obnoxious blonde.

"Is the coroner expecting you?" she asked in a voice that clearly indicated that if the answer was 'no,' Alex would be denied entry.

Reaching in his pocket, Alex handed over one of his cards.

"I'm Alex Lockerby," he introduced himself. "I'm a consultant for the department and Lieutenant Pak is expecting me."

The woman looked as if she might argue, but after a long moment, she handed back the card.

"You know where the morgue is?" she asked, no doubt as a last test of Alex's validity.

"Downstairs," he said, accepting the card back, "and you have to use the elevator because the lobby stairs are locked."

When the elevator doors opened, Alex stepped off, into the dimly lit, tiled hallway of the morgue. Turning left, he headed down the hall, past the offices, to the end where the operating theaters were located. Before he was even halfway there, Alex could hear raised voices. The doors to the operating theaters were closed, so he couldn't make out what was being said, but the discussion was heated.

When he reached the outer doors to the theater, Alex saw Danny and Dr. Wagner inside next to a table with a covered body on it. A man and two women stood up against the inner doors, obviously trying to stay as far away from the body as possible. The man was shouting something while Danny was trying to keep him calm. Wagner was on the phone, no doubt summoning officers to the surgery.

"Something I can help with?" Alex asked, raising his voice a bit while he pulled open the inner door. As he did, he understood why the women had handkerchiefs over their faces; the odor of decomposition and medical disinfectant was strong inside.

The man turned and Alex knew immediately who he was. His resemblance to Ari Leavitt was plain to see.

"Who are you?" he demanded.

"This is Mr. Lockerby," Danny said, his tone exasperated. "He's—"

"You," the man rounded on Alex. He was dressed in an expensive suit, so Alex wasn't worried he was going to get physical, but he was clearly upset.

"Take it easy, Mr. Leavitt," Alex said, putting up his hands in a placating gesture.

"Easy?" Leavitt demanded. "These idiots dug up my brother's body, apparently on your say-so! Don't tell me to take it easy!"

"This is Aaron Levitt," Danny said, "Ari Leavitt's brother."

"I understand you're upset," Alex said, jumping in as Aaron took a breath to shout some more, "but there's a real chance your brother was murdered. I'd think you'd want to know if that's true."

"Ridiculous," Aaron scoffed. "Ari drowned, the police said so."

"That's true," Danny said, "but that might not be the whole story."

"There were no marks on the body," Aaron said, "Ari drowned and we had to bury him. Now you're putting his poor family through this?" He waved at the two women whom he had yet to introduce.

"Your brother was a strong swimmer," Alex explained, "how do you explain that he drowned in a heated pool without large amounts of alcohol in his system?"

"Are you saying that couldn't happen?" Aaron demanded.

"Not at all," Alex continued, "but there is physical evidence that Ari was poisoned. Don't you want to know if your brother Ari was murdered, Mr. Leavitt?"

Aaron stepped closer to Alex, almost chest to chest, and looked up into his face.

"Are you saying I don't care about my brother?" he demanded in a soft voice.

"That's enough," Danny said, grabbing Aaron's arm and shouldering his way between him and Alex. "No one is saying you didn't love your brother."

Danny shot Alex a dirty look, then refocused on Ari's brother.

"Right now," he went on, "we only have circumstantial evidence, but that's why Ari's body is here."

"You don't have to wonder any longer," Dr. Wagner said, hanging up the phone on which he'd been talking quietly. "That was the police laboratory. They tested the sample of Ari Leavitt's blood and tissue I sent over and they found traces of strychnine. It's a certainty, Mr. Leavitt was given enough poison to lock up his muscles while he was swimming. Without someone there to help him, there was no chance he'd be able to get out of the water."

Aaron and the two women with him just stared at Wagner for a long, silent moment.

"I'm afraid your brother was murdered, Mr. Leavitt," Wagner finished.

Aaron staggered back as if he'd been struck, bumping into the women with him.

"I think you should go home, Mr. Leavitt," Danny said, stepping up to the group. "We'll make sure your brother is reinterred as soon as possible and we'll find Ari's killer."

One of the women leaned in and whispered something to Aaron, who nodded after a short pause.

"All right," he said. "I'm sorry if I caused you trouble. Please let me know when you'll return Ari to his grave."

Danny handed Aaron one of his cards while putting a comforting hand on the man's shoulder.

"I will," he said. "I promise we won't re-bury him without you and your family."

Aaron thanked him, then turned and ushered the two women out. Once they were fully gone, Alex turned to Danny.

"Who were the women with him," he asked.

"His sisters," Danny explained. "They're all that's left of Ari's family; his mother and father passed a few years ago."

"Do you like him for the crime? Was there any inheritance?"

"No," Danny said, flipping open his notebook. "I checked into Ari's family while we were waiting for the exhumation. Ari was estranged from his parents. Apparently they didn't like him being a tennis player and referee."

"Was there money involved?"

"Not on Ari's side," Danny said, "Aaron inherited their father's business in the diamond trade."

Alex whistled but didn't have any more questions. Unless there was something they didn't know, it looked like Aaron had no financial motive against Ari.

"Ari didn't marry Aaron's girl, did he?" Alex asked, grasping at straws.

"Ari was a bachelor," Danny said.

"Right," Alex said, managing not to blush at forgetting such an important detail.

"If you two are quite finished," Wagner said, irritation in his voice. "I'd like to give you my findings so I can get on with my day."

"Sorry, Doctor," Danny said, opening his notebook. "Go ahead."

Alex bit his tongue. He and Wagner hadn't liked each other ever since Alex threatened to expose his affair back when they first met, but their hostility had been dormant for a year or so. There was no need to pick at the scab of their feud.

"The level of strychnine in Mr. Leavitt's system was enough to cause muscle cramps within an hour after consumption."

"So he was dosed at the party," Alex said.

"Something he ate or drank?" Danny asked.

"Drank, most likely," Wagner said. "Strychnine is bitter, so you'd have to put it in something strong, like alcohol."

Alex looked at Danny with a raised eyebrow.

"If it was in a bottle, more people would have been poisoned," he said.

"So whoever made him his drink added the poison at the time," Danny guessed. "That means we won't have any physical evidence. There's no doubt everything from the party has been cleaned up by now."

"Maybe," Alex said, rubbing his chin, "but we do know one thing for certain."

Danny gave him a quizzical look.

"Whoever made Ari Leavitt that deadly drink was at the party, and they knew Ari well enough to know how to kill him in a way that looked accidental."

10

FAMILY MAN

Once Alex was out of the morgue and breathing the air on the street, he started to feel better. By the time he got out of a cab in front of Empire Tower, even his appetite had returned, so he stopped on the terminal level to get some poached eggs on buttered toast from the café. It felt like he'd been rushing everywhere for the last several days, so he just sat at the counter, eating his breakfast, like he hadn't a care in the world.

It felt decadent.

Despite his reveling in not doing anything work related, the tasks didn't go away, so with great reluctance, Alex put forty-five cents on the counter, plus a dime for the waitress, and headed for the elevator.

"Morning, boss," Sherry said when he entered the office a few minutes later. "I've found out who belongs to those names you gave me."

Alex raised an eyebrow at that, but he wasn't too surprised. Sherry was very good at research.

"That was quick," he said as Sherry picked up one of the many notepads on her desk.

"Carmine Ott," she read, "she's a singer from Cuba, well, her family is from Cuba. She's a regular on NBC's radio programs, Chase &

Sanborn, Jack Benny, that sort of thing, mostly fill-in and background work."

"What about the other two?"

"Lana Redgrave and Brooke Margrave are actresses," she said. "They've been in working in Hollywood for the last three weeks."

"So, they're out as suspects," Alex said. He gave Sherry a smile as he jotted that down in his notebook.

"How did you find Carmine so quickly?"

"I went down into the terminal and asked people getting on and off the sky crawlers if they'd ever heard the name," Sherry said with a smirk. "I figured with all the other girls being models and Broadway starlets, Carmine had to be in the same category, and that meant someone would know her."

"How long were you down there?" Alex asked, genuinely impressed.

"Ten minutes," she said, trying to hide a smile as she lit a cigarette.

"Good work," he said, "I'll call NBC and get a time to interview her along with the others."

The thought of that made Alex tired again. There was a time when the prospect of spending the morning questioning attractive young women would have energized him. Of course he didn't have money back then and, unless he was very much mistaken, that was what this list of women found attractive.

Alex headed for his office, then gratefully sank into his chair, putting up his sore foot.

An hour later he had interviews set up with each of Reggie Aspler's mistresses. None of the agents or producers he'd talked to wanted to allow Alex to talk to their pet starlets, but when Alex pointed out that they could let him interview the girls, or Lt. Detweiler could show up with a warrant and an army of officers and talk to everyone, they quickly relented.

With the next few hours of his day organized, Alex picked up his cane, dropped off his kit bag in the vault, then headed back out to the elevators.

"Reggie was fun," the dusky singer, Carmine Ott, purred as she sat across from Alex in the little dressing room at the NBC Radio studios. "I knew he was married, but I have a career, Mr. Lockerby, and I'm not looking to settle down."

"Did Reggie try to hide the fact that he was married?" Alex asked.

He could see what Reggie Aspler saw in Carmine; she was beautiful in an exotic, yet classic way. Her skin was the dark tan typical of a Latin, with a mass of dark, curly hair on her head, and dark eyes that gleamed mischievously through half-closed lids. The bright red lipstick she wore was the perfect contrast for her skin and added a wanton sensuality to her.

"He did at first," Carmine said, taking a cigarette from a pack on the dressing table, "but after a few dates, he gave up the pretense. We both knew what we wanted from a relationship." She placed the cigarette in her mouth, but didn't bother looking at the table for a match. "Do you have a light, Mr. Lockerby?" she asked, dropping into her husky purr again.

As Alex retrieved his gold lighter, he reminded himself it came from his beautiful, powerful, and given to jealousy fiancée. Flicking it to light, he held it out so that Carmine could lean in and draw the flame to her cigarette.

"I can see why Mr. Aspler would ask you out," he said, flipping his lighter closed, "but I'm a bit confused why you'd say 'yes'?"

Carmine smirked at Alex while she took a long puff from her cigarette.

"Surely you know that such relationships are...mutually beneficial," she said.

Alex knew it, but he never thought Carmine would come right out and admit it. She was brash, bold, and absolutely gorgeous. For a moment, Alex envied Reggie. Then he remembered the absolute goddess he was going to marry.

"Reggie was a man of influence," Carmine went on. "He spoke to some of his friends about me and now, I'm going to be the voice of the Queen of Sheba on *Captain Midnight*. If that goes well, I'll get other voice acting roles."

"But you're a singer?" Alex said.

"Sure, but the people who produce the radio dramas are the same ones that produce the variety shows," she said, her smirk back. "If they like you, you can punch your own ticket."

"To where?" Alex pressed.

"My own show," Carmine said with no trace of modesty. "Hollywood? The sky's the limit, baby." She took a long puff on her cigarette. "Anything else? I've got a rehearsal in ten minutes."

"No," Alex said, flipping his notebook closed. "Thank you for your time."

He stood and made his way back into the hall, closing the dressing room door behind him. Normally after an interview, he'd take a few minutes and go through his notes and add anything he might have missed, but Carmine had been the last of his interviews and it was just like all the others. The only real differences were the people Reggie promised to talk to. The Broadway actresses got introduced to producers and Hollywood people. The fashion model had already been picked up by a Paris designer and would be leaving the country at the end of the month. Reggie had been their shortcut to success, and he'd delivered. Alex couldn't imagine any of the mistresses speaking badly of Reggie, much less killing him.

It was looking like Reggie's extra-marital partners were a dead end.

That still leaves his wife, Alex reminded himself, *or maybe some embarrassed member of his extended family. Hopefully Detweiler is having better luck.*

Alex trudged off the elevator on the twelfth floor of Empire Tower and turned left toward his office. He hadn't done a ton of walking but his foot hurt anyway, no doubt in sympathy for his headache.

Not wanting to present an exhausted countenance in case he had any potential clients that might be in his outer office, Alex took a cleansing breath and straightened up into a posture Father Harry would approve of.

"Welcome back, boss," Sherry said as he came in.

"Anything urgent?" he asked, stepping inside and closing the door behind him. Since the outer office was otherwise empty, he limped over to Sherry's desk and sat heavily on the corner, folding his left leg under him.

"Just a call from Holcombe Ward," she said, handing him a torn note page with the tennis pro's number on it. "He'd like an update."

Alex briefly wished once again that he hadn't taken the case of Ari Leavitt's death, but at least he had some news to pass on.

"All right," he said, pausing to light a cigarette, then offering one to Sherry. "I'll give him a call, then I'll go through the folders on my desk. If you need me, that's where I'll be."

Sherry wished him good luck, then he headed along the back hallway to his office. He'd been there just this morning, but it felt like a year ago. Flopping down in his chair, Alex leaned back, enjoying his cigarette for as long as it took to smoke it. Finally, he crushed it out and sat up, reaching for the phone. Giving the number Holcombe had given Sherry to the operator, he waited for the call to connect.

"Hello," a distinctly female voice greeted him.

"I'm looking for Holcombe Ward," Alex said, not sure he'd gotten the right number.

"He's in a meeting," the woman said. "Is there a message I can give him?"

"Let him know that Alex Lockerby called, that I'm in my office, and that he can call me back at his earliest convenience."

"Oh, just a minute, Mr. Lockerby," she said, her voice suddenly energetic. "He said to get him if you called."

There was a clack as the unseen woman set the phone receiver down on a hard surface, then half a minute later, Holcombe himself came on the line.

"Alex?" he asked. "Have you found anything?"

"I have," Alex said, keeping his tone professional. "The police exhumed Ari's body last night and conducted an autopsy."

"Why didn't you call?" Holcombe demanded, cutting in.

"I didn't call," Alex explained, "because the police didn't know anything until just this morning. The coroner got Ari's blood results from their lab and they found traces of strychnine. Right now, Lieutenant Pak of the Manhattan Police is at your friend Beals Dalton's house looking for the source."

"Pak?" Holcombe said, an edge in his voice. "Not that Nip the cops have working for them?"

Alex bristled. Nip was a common slur for someone Japanese, deriving from the native pronunciation for Japan — Nippon. It was something Alex had heard many times around his friend, but that didn't make him tolerate it.

"Mr. Ward," he said, keeping his voice even. "I can assure you that if you want justice for your friend, Danny Pak is the man you want on the case. That's my good friend, Danny Pak, to you."

Holcombe grumbled an apology, then asked Alex if there was anything else.

"Ari's family wasn't too happy about his body being exhumed," Alex said. He went on to relate the entire incident, including Danny's research into the family.

"I can't say for sure," Alex hedged, "but I don't think they had any obvious motive to kill Ari."

"Ari and his brother Aaron were never close," Holcombe said, "but there wasn't any bad blood between them. His ex-wife, however, she's wanted Ari dead for twenty years."

"Ari was divorced?"

"Yes, he was married a long time ago to a real looker," Holcombe said. "She divorced him when Ari gave up his stake in the family business."

Alex wrote, 'gold digger,' in his notebook.

"Do you remember her name?" he asked.

"Elie Berrin," Holcombe replied without hesitation.

"Does she live in the city?"

Holcombe made a noncommittal noise.

"She married someone in the publishing industry," he said. "I see her at society affairs every now and again, so I suspect she's still in town. I don't remember her new married name, though."

That didn't bother Alex; he still knew people in the publishing industry after the affair with Margaret LaSalle. It shouldn't be too hard to track Elie down. It didn't seem likely that Elie would poison Ari twenty years after their divorce, but stranger things had happened.

"All right," Alex said, flipping his notebook closed. "I'll follow up on Elie and I'll find out if the police found anything with their search. I'll call you tomorrow morning and give you an update."

Holcombe didn't sound excited about that, but there wasn't really anything else to be done, so he thanked Alex and hung up.

Alex sighed and returned the handset to the phone's cradle. It was too early to have a theory in Ari Leavitt's death, especially with such a small amount of evidence. Sitting there in his office chair and reviewing the case in his mind, Alex simply didn't have a clue where the case would lead.

A thought struck him and he reached for the intercom.

"Sherry," he asked once he depressed the talk key. "I need a copy of Ari Leavitt's divorce decree. Also, if there was a lawsuit from a woman named Elie Berrin, I want the filing."

"I'll call over to the hall of records," she said. "If they can find it fast, I'll go over today."

"Thanks," Alex said. Before he could sit back in his chair, however, Sherry's voice came back at him.

"There's a Mr. Eccles here for you," she said. "He says it's urgent."

Alex sighed, then nodded, even though Sherry couldn't see him.

"Send him back," he said.

Alex pushed his telephone to the side and sat up straight, moving a blank notepad in front of him. He was tempted to pour himself a bourbon, but reckoned he didn't have time. The idea, however, made him thirsty.

The door to his office opened and a weary-looking man came in. His clothes were worn, but well-kept and he had the kind of tired eyes that Alex saw in the bread lines and soup kitchens. His face was haggard and wrinkled, giving him the look of someone in his late fifties, though Alex suspected he was younger than that.

"You'll forgive me if I don't stand up," Alex said, indicating his cane in the corner.

"That's all right," the man said, reaching out to shake Alex's hand. "I'm Nils Eccles, Mr. Lockerby, and I need your help."

Something about his name triggered a memory. Iggy had told him that a Nordic-looking man had come to the brownstone looking for him. Eccles was a Norwegian name.

"Have a seat, Mr. Eccles. How can I help you?"

Eccles sat down and fidgeted with his hands for a moment before looking up.

"I'm trying to talk to my sister," he began, then hesitated.

"Is she missing?" Alex asked.

"No," Eccles said, hesitating again. "We're just estranged. I haven't seen her in person for almost twenty years."

"Why reconnect now?" Alex asked, wondering what Eccles wanted him to do about his relationships.

"It's our father," Eccles said. "He passed last week and I want her to have the chance to pay her respects."

Why do I get the feeling the sister isn't going to have any respects to pay, Alex thought.

"Well, I appreciate your intentions, Mr. Eccles," Alex said out loud, "but I still don't see how you'd require my services."

"Aren't you dating her?" Eccles asked, looking up at Alex for the first time.

"Excuse me?" was all Alex could say.

"Sorsha Kincaid," Eccles said after a moment of silence, "she's my sister, Kjirsten Eccles."

Alex knew he had a look on his face like he'd just been brained with a two-by-four, but he just couldn't wrap his mind around what he heard. He knew that Sorsha was older than him, well into her forties at least, but she'd never mentioned having any family. That probably meant that she was estranged from all of them.

"Kjirsten?" was all he could manage.

Alex picked up the phone for the seventh time, then immediately replaced it in the cradle. Opening his right middle drawer, Alex pulled out a bottle of good bourbon and a tumbler. Pouring himself a full glass, he sat back and sipped it while he stared at the phone. Normally he went over his notes a few times before he had a difficult call to make, but there was no need in this case.

He tipped up the glass, downing the bourbon without savoring it, and grabbed the phone.

"Chrysler-six, fifty-one hundred," he told the operator. A moment later there was a click and Inge Halverson's voice answered.

"Kincaid Refrigeration," she said.

"Inge, it's Alex," he said. "I need to talk to Sorsha as soon as possible."

"Didn't she tell you she'd be out of town?" Inge asked, the slight trace of her Swedish accent peeking through.

"She did," Alex admitted, "but this is a bit of an emergency. Does she check in with you?"

"No," Inge said, "but she does with Miss Burnside."

Carolyn Burnside was Sorsha's personal secretary, a red-headed Southern belle with the organizational skills of a German mechanic.

"Tell Carolyn to call me," Alex said. "I've got some news Sorsha really needs to hear."

Inge promised to relay the message and Alex hung up.

"Kjirsten," he said again, pouring himself another drink. That was going to take some getting used to.

11

FAMILY MATTERS

"You're early," Iggy said as Alex came limping down the stairs at the brownstone. He was standing in front of the bookshelf to the right of the hearth with his hands behind his back.

"Looking for something to read?" Alex asked, heading for his reading chair.

"I thought I had a volume on the psychology of bombers," Iggy said, scanning the shelves.

"By a psychiatrist named Hambley?" Alex asked. "It's in the library in my vault. I borrowed it during the Brothers Boom incident."

"Borrowing involves returning," Iggy chided.

"Tomorrow," Alex said, raising his hand in the gesture of a pledge, "I promise."

"Fair enough," Iggy said, turning toward the kitchen. "I'm running a bit behind my time today," he continued.

"What does that mean?"

"It means it's leftover night."

Alex's mind drifted back to the leftover nights he had at the Brotherhood of Hope Mission. They consisted of day-old soup and stale bread. Iggy's leftovers were considerably more appetizing.

"In that case," he said, levering himself back to his feet, "I'll help."

Ten minutes later, Alex and Iggy were tucking in to a wildly eclectic meal of cold potatoes and roast beef, with some day-old rolls that had been reheated in the oven. The entire affair had been garnished with some fresh cucumber, carrots, and celery.

"Sorry for the poor fare, lad," Iggy said as he loaded some of the cold beef onto a roll to make a sandwich.

"Any meal I don't have to make is okay with me," Alex replied.

"So how is it going with the mad bomber?"

"Mad bomber?" Alex asked. Iggy wasn't usually given to hyperbole.

"That's what the papers are calling him. Haven't you been keeping up with your reading?"

"Didn't have time," Alex admitted. "Well, that's not technically true, but I had a lot on my mind."

"For instance?"

Alex sighed as he dipped a bit of roast beef in a blob of mustard. He'd been struggling to organize his thoughts after his meeting with Nils Eccles, without much success. Going over it with Iggy would help, so he took a deep breath and launched into the story.

"Kjirsten?" Iggy said when Alex finished.

"That's what I thought."

"That's an interesting story," Iggy went on.

"I tried to get ahold of Sorsha, but all I could do was leave a message for her secretary to call me."

Iggy made a contemplative noise and rubbed his chin.

"You don't think I should tell her?" Alex guessed, a bit shocked.

"No," Iggy said at last. "I wouldn't, at least not till you've had a chance to investigate this Eccles fellow. Plenty of people want access to someone powerful, like a sorceress, and they'd make up any story if they thought it would get them that access."

Alex hadn't thought of that. Nils had seemed quite confident in his story; he even assumed that Alex knew Sorsha's real name. If he had, and Nils had made one up, that would have exposed him right there.

"True," Iggy said when Alex voiced these concerns, "but even if he is Sorsha's brother, or some other shirt-tail relative, it doesn't mean his intentions are honorable."

It was a good point. Before Alex got Sorsha involved, he needed to do some due diligence on Mr. Nils Eccles.

"I'll find out where he lives," Alex said. "See if he has any warrants or a criminal file."

"Did he leave you his address?" Iggy asked.

"No, but if his father just died, the obituary will be in the papers sometime in the last week. If I find a deceased Eccles with a surviving son named Nils, I can get his info from the funeral home."

"Jolly good," Iggy said, genuinely pleased with Alex's mastery of finding people. "Now," he said between bites of his sandwich, "tell me about your dead tennis player."

"Ari Leavitt hasn't been a player for several decades," Alex said, trying not to talk with his mouth full. "The police dug him up and you were right, he was definitely poisoned with strychnine."

"That means he was poisoned at that party," Iggy said. "Probably in a drink, Strychnine has a strong, bitter flavor."

"Wagner said the same," Alex confirmed. "So cocktails made with bitters."

"Or bitter alcohol," Iggy pointed out.

"I'll call Danny and update him.."

"Is young Daniel still on the case? I thought the crime was committed up in the Hamptons?"

"Callahan pulled a few strings," Alex said, "jerked them, actually."

Iggy chuckled at that.

"I take it Daniel is up there now looking for the source of the strychnine?" Iggy said.

Alex set his fork down and put his napkin next to his plate.

"I need to make a phone call," he said.

Pulling out his notebook, Alex looked up the phone number for Beals Dalton's estate, then gave it to the operator through the kitchen phone.

"Dalton Estate," a male voice answered.

Alex recognized Milton Thornhill, Beals' butler.

"Milton, this is Alex Lockerby."

"I remember you, sir; how can I help?"

"Are the police still there?"

Milton sighed audibly.

"Unfortunately, sir."

"I need to speak with Lieutenant Pak, please."

It took a few minutes, but finally Danny picked up the phone.

"Alex?" he said. "Did you find something?"

"Sort of," Alex replied. "Iggy confirmed what Wagner said about strychnine being bitter, so if he got it in a drink, it would have to contain bitters or bitter alcohol."

"Makes sense," he said. "We still have to test everything, but that'll help us prioritize."

"How much alcohol does Beals have?"

"All we're doing is taking samples and labeling the bottles and I'm going to be here most of the night."

Alex wished him luck, then hung up and went back to his dinner.

"I don't envy Daniel his job," Iggy chuckled as Alex rejoined the table.

"That's why I'm not a cop," Alex said.

"Yes," Iggy said, his voice full of sarcasm, "that's the reason."

Alex winked back and they continued eating.

"Now that you're done with that," Iggy said, "tell me about the mad bomber."

"Two victims so far, but you know that. Still no connection between the two, none that the police can find at any rate."

Alex went on through everything they knew about the case, which didn't take that long. Still, Iggy listened quietly, interrupting only to ask the occasional question.

"It's not very encouraging, is it?" he said when Alex finished. "Still, there must be some connection; the alternative is too horrific to consider."

"Alternative?" Alex asked.

"That these bombings are completely random," Iggy said. "That would make the bomber some kind of maniac."

"And very difficult to stop," Alex added. "Still, I think you're right, there has to be some connection, something that makes the bombings make sense."

A long moment of silence stretched between them.

"I'm sorry to say it," Iggy said, "but you may have to wait for a new victim to find your connection."

Alex had come to the same conclusion, but didn't want to say it out loud. There just wasn't enough data between the two victims. When it was just Reggie Aspler, the mistresses seemed like the right angle, but Matthew McDermet was a bachelor and, as far as anyone knew, didn't have a girlfriend or even any female relatives. What he needed was more data, and Iggy was right, the only reliable way to get more was for there to be another victim.

That thought made Alex clench his fists.

"Easy, lad," Iggy said in a quiet voice. "There's nothing you or I can do. Evil will be evil and the best we can do is stop it as soon as we can."

Again his mentor was right, but again, Alex didn't like it.

After Alex helped Iggy clean up and then did the dishes, he joined his mentor in the library to read in front of the fire. Alex was working his way through Iggy's copies of Margaret LaSalle's mysteries. After helping to catch her murderer, Alex felt like he needed to know her work better. He'd just gotten to a detail-heavy interview with the man Alex considered the prime suspect, when the phone in the kitchen began to ring.

Iggy had dozed and the sound roused him slightly.

"I'll get it," Alex said, before his mentor could get up. His foot was feeling all right and he left his cane leaning against his chair and just limped to the phone.

"Hello," he said, picking up the earpiece and pressing it to the side of his head.

"Alex?" a familiar voice with a southern twang asked.

"Carolyn," Alex said, recognizing the voice of Sorsha's secretary. "How is it on the road?"

"Busy," she said in a slightly irritated voice.

"Then I'll get right to the point: how much do you know about Sorsha's family?"

It was clear Carolyn wasn't prepared for such a question and she hesitated.

"Only that Sorsha is estranged from them," she said.

"Estranged how?" Alex pressed.

"I don't know the whole story," Carolyn said, "but I know it comes from before she was a sorceress."

That made sense; few people wanted to fall out with a powerful and soon-to-be-rich emerging sorceress.

"I'm assuming you're not asking a rhetorical question," she continued.

"No," Alex admitted. "Something's come up, but I don't want to bother Sorsha with it until I get more information."

"What is it?" Carolyn demanded.

Alex hesitated, wondering just what he could tell the clever and extremely loyal Carolyn Burnside.

"A man came by my office today," he said. "He claimed to be Sorsha's brother. I'm going to check him out tomorrow and if he passes muster, I'll give you all the details."

"I don't think Ms. Kincaid will be happy to hear that news," she said.

"I don't know how she'll take it, but if this guy is an imposter, then it's something Sorsha never has to know about, right?"

There was a pause where Alex could hear Carolyn breathing.

"I guess that's acceptable," she said at last, "but I'm going to call you tomorrow night for an update."

"That'll be fine," Alex said, then hung up the phone.

Alex got to bed fairly early, but he must not have slept well, because when his alarm went off, he felt like he'd just laid down. He muddled his way through a shower and managed to cut himself shaving before heading through the vault to his Empire Tower apartment.

Repeating his actions of previous mornings, Alex rode the elevator down to the security station in Empire Terminal, then had breakfast in the terminal café along with a cup of Marnie's coffee. It was the fourth time he'd been to her little coffee counter when Marnie hadn't been there, and he was starting to miss her.

I'll have to come down for the lunch rush, he told himself. *Marnie's always working then.*

Half an hour after Alex ordered his breakfast, he was walking through the front door to his office. As usual, Sherry had beat him into work and was sitting comfortably behind her desk, smoking a cigarette.

"I'm going to assume you didn't find Ari Leavitt's divorce papers yesterday," he said.

"No," she shook her head, "but my source over at the records office promised she'd look for it again today."

"While you're at it, have your source look for anything they can find on a Nils Eccles."

"The man from yesterday?"

"He claims he's Sorsha's brother, but I'm not so sure," Alex explained. "I want to know if there's any record of him owning land or a business."

"What about police records?"

"I'll handle that," Alex said, knowing he needed to call Danny anyway. He could request an arrest record search.

"Library?" Sherry asked.

"I'll take care of that one too," Alex said. He didn't want too many people knowing about the possible death of Sorsha's father. In fact the fewer people who knew that Sorsha might have a family, the better.

"Is Mike in?" he asked, heading for the back hallway door.

"Not yet," Sherry said. "He was out late following a suspected jewel thief."

Alex was impressed by that news. Mike had taken up the slack when Alex had been in a magical coma, and the little man's skills as an investigator had really improved.

"Well, tell him to come see me when he gets in, I need a few runes for my book."

Sherry promised to relay the message and Alex limped back to his office.

He thought about calling Danny first to get the police looking for

Nils Eccles, but he remembered that his friend had probably been up all night looking for strychnine, so he called Detweiler first.

"How did it go with Reggie's wife?" Alex asked once the line connected.

Detweiler sighed.

"She's not all broken up that her two-timing husband is dead," the lieutenant said, "but she could barely keep eye contact with me. The woman's a mouse. If she's the killer, then I'm the Duke of Ellington."

"Kids?" Alex asked. "Maybe someone defending their mother's honor."

"Two," Detweiler said, "a boy age six and a girl age 9."

"Unless one of them is a prodigy, they're too young to blow up their father with runes," Alex admitted.

"Based on your questions, I'm assuming you came up with nothing on the mistresses."

Alex relayed his experience with Reggie's cavalcade of companions and how he helped all their careers.

"So no motive there," Detweiler concluded.

"And no real connection between our victims," Alex said. "Did your detectives find anything useful in McDermet's place?"

"We got a list of his unregistered alchemists, but as soon as we picked up the first two, word got around. The rest scattered like cockroaches when you turn the light on."

Alex swore.

"We did learn one thing," Detweiler said. "That partner that left McDermet all those years ago was forced out."

"Do you have a name?"

"Nope," Detweiler said. "We're looking for the original business license, but the hall of records isn't exactly a model of efficiency."

"Well, let me know when you get a name," Alex said.

He was about to hang up when the lieutenant spoke again.

"Do you think there's going to be more of these letter bombs?" he asked.

"Yes," Alex admitted. "All we can do is hope they give us the clues we need to catch this sick bastard."

"From your lips to God's ears," Detweiler said, then he hung up.

Alex needed a drink after that conversation, but he passed over the bourbon in favor of an expensive Scotch whiskey. Pouring two fingers' worth, he nursed it for a full fifteen minutes while he thought.

The only thing he could really do now was go to the library and check for notices of Sorsha's father's death. After that, he could call Danny and get him looking for Nils in the police files. He probably should call Theo Bell too, just to see how he was coming on finding a copy of the elusive Inquisition book.

It wasn't a scintillating itinerary, but it would carry him through to at least lunch. By then Holcombe Ward would probably have called, looking for an update.

Alex suddenly sat up straight in his chair and reached for his phone.

"Ward," Holcombe's voice greeted him.

"It's Alex, and before you ask, there's nothing new, but I did have a question."

"Shoot."

"Did Ari have a drink?"

"A drink?"

"Yeah, something he really liked or something he'd order all the time."

"Sure," Holcombe said. "Whenever Ari was in a good mood, he'd order a Manhattan."

Alex scribbled that down.

"You're sure?"

"Of course," Holcombe said, "I introduced him to that drink, he loved it."

Alex thanked him and was about to hang up, but Holcombe kept speaking.

"Do you think that's how he was poisoned? In his drink?"

"Strychnine is bitter," Alex said, "you'd have to put it in something bitter to hide the taste, so a cocktail is a good choice."

"Manhattans are made with vermouth," Holcombe said. "That's bitter."

Alex jotted that down too.

"Thanks, Holcombe," he said. "I'll get this information to the police right away."

With that, Alex hung up. It was still too early to call Danny, and the police would have already sampled any bottles of vermouth at the Dalton estate, but knowing what to test would speed up the confirmation of the poison.

"Not a bad morning," Alex said as he stood up and grabbed his cane. With any luck, he'd find out at the library that Nils was a fraud and not have to bother Sorsha with his story at all.

"A very good morning," he repeated, then headed out toward his front office and the elevators beyond.

12

BLIND ALLEYS

It had been a month or more since Alex had been in the New York Public Library, but the building and its contents never changed. He inhaled the smell of old books and wood polish, then moved across the main floor to the stairs leading down to the newspaper archive.

With his foot, it took a bit longer than usual to reach the lower level, but Alex got the papers he wanted quickly enough, so he was soon sitting at a sturdy table with a light over it. He was looking for evidence of the death of someone named Eccles, so all he had to do was check the obituaries in the Times and the Post going back two weeks.

It didn't take long for Alex to locate the entry he was looking for. According to the Times, a Roland Eccles died of a stroke on the previous Friday. His wife, Loraine, had passed more than a decade ago and he was succeeded by three children, Nils, Kjirsten, and Mia. The funeral was going to be the day after tomorrow at Hudson County Burial Grounds in New Jersey.

Alex copied the relevant data into his notebook, then checked the Post, but found no corresponding entry. Alex wasn't too surprised;

from the look of Nils, his family wasn't exactly well off, so putting an announcement in both papers would have been considered a luxury.

Folding the papers back together, Alex rose and limped over to the circulation desk to return them. He couldn't fault Nils Eccles' story, but he wasn't sure he wanted to involve Sorsha yet.

"Doesn't matter what you want," he mumbled as he limped his way back up the stairs, "the funeral is in two days, you have to tell her."

Normally, Alex was happy to have a decision made, but this time it didn't sit right. Sorsha had obviously cut off contact with her family for a reason, and he didn't want to reopen that wound. On the other hand, this would be the only chance for Sorsha to attend her father's funeral.

As Alex reached the main floor of the library, he pushed Nils and the Eccles family from his mind. Carolyn would call him tonight and he could have her pass the message to Sorsha. After that, the whole matter would be out of his hands. Sorsha hadn't ever mentioned her family and Alex wasn't one to pry; after all, a woman was entitled to her secrets.

Moving toward the doors, Alex diverted to the line of phone booths on the wall by the entrance. Closing the door, he dropped a nickel into the phone and gave the operator the number for the Central Office of Police.

"Lieutenant Pak," Danny said once he picked up the phone.

"It's me," Alex said. "How's the Ari Leavitt case going?"

"We're still looking for the source of the poison," he said. "My boys are rounding up everyone on Beals Dalton's guest list. If we get lucky, maybe someone saw something."

"I can't help with that," Alex said, "but I talked with Holcombe Ward this morning and I might be able to narrow down your search for the poison."

"How?"

"According to Holcombe, Ari was a fan of the Manhattan," Alex explained. "Apparently it was all he drank at parties. Now, strychnine is bitter, and Manhattans are made with whiskey and vermouth."

"And vermouth is bitter," Danny finished.

Alex could hear the scrape of a pencil on paper, then Danny called out to someone in his office area. He had a brief conversation that Alex couldn't really hear, then he came back.

"Thanks," he said. "If you're right, the lab will be able to track down the poison today."

"There is one other thing," Alex said. "Ari has an ex-wife."

Danny paused on the line.

"Was it a contentious divorce?"

"Don't know," Alex admitted. "Sherry is pulling a copy of the decree and I'll let you know what I find. I do know the divorce was years ago."

Danny paused again.

"I'd like the ex better if the divorce was recent," he said. "Get me the info and I'll look into her."

"You've got enough on your plate," Alex countered. "Let me take a look at the divorce and maybe talk to the ex. If there's anything there, I'll let you know."

"Well, there's something else on my plate that I'd like your help with."

"Go on."

"I was just handed the warrant to get into Ari's apartment, I'd like your help to go through it."

Alex hesitated. Usually the police only called him in when there was something magical to investigate.

"What do you need me for?" he asked.

"Turns out Ari is a neighbor of yours," Danny said. "He lives in the Cormac Building."

Alex knew that name, it was a thirty-story building full of luxury apartments that was literally across the street from Empire Tower. He could see the building from his apartment.

"I can probably do that," he said. "I'm at the library now, but I can be over there in fifteen minutes or so."

"All right," Danny said. "Wait for me in the lobby."

Alex promised he would, then hung up.

He was about to leave the booth when he remembered that he was headed back to the office to see what Sherry dug up.

Dropping another nickel in the phone, he called his office.

"Hey, boss," Sherry said before Alex could even speak. "Did you find what you were looking for?"

"I did," he replied. "By the way, if anyone from Sorsha's office calls, I want to know about it the second I call or come in."

"Will do."

"Have you heard back from your friend at the records office?" Alex pressed on.

"I went over an hour ago and looked at Ari's divorce decree," she replied. "You want the short version?"

Alex flipped open his notebook and set it on the little shelf below the phone.

"Go ahead."

"Ari's wife was a woman named Elie Berrin. They were married for four years and had a daughter, Barbara. According to the documents, the divorce was Elie's idea. She expected Ari to join his family business and when he became a professional tennis player, she wanted out."

That tracked with what Holcombe Ward had told Alex, Elie wanted a comfortable, privileged life and Ari denied her that.

"Any idea what happened to Elie?"

"I had my friend look for her name and found a marriage certificate," Sherry said. "She got married to a banker named Harold Rollings, three years after her divorce. I then found a record of Harold adopting Barbara."

That took Alex by surprise.

"Ari would have had to sign away his parental rights for that to happen," he said.

"I don't know what to tell you," Sherry said. "He signed."

"Do you have an address for the Rollings?"

Sherry rattled off a Core address that was surprisingly close to Ari's apartment building.

"Thanks," he said, flipping his notebook closed. "I'm going to meet Danny and look over Ari's apartment. After that I'll grab your boyfriend and we'll go see Elie."

"Say 'hi' for me," Sherry said, and Alex hung up.

Alex whistled when the manager of the Cormac Building pushed open the door of Ari Leavitt's apartment. It wasn't up to the standards of Andrew Barton's decorator, but it was pretty darn close. The space was large, which was to be expected in a Core building. It had a large parlor with tasteful leather furniture all round. The walls were hung with newspaper clippings, awards, and pictures of Ari with people in tennis attire and luminaires dressed to the nines. A bookshelf was tastefully decorated with knick-knacks and tchotchkes mixed in with blocks of leatherback books.

"I didn't know tennis paid so well," Danny said, taking in the room.

An open hall led to the rear of the apartment and Alex could see lots of natural light coming from somewhere.

"Consider who goes to tennis matches," Alex replied. "The King of England attends at Wimbledon."

"Where?" Danny asked.

"It's a high-end tennis club in England. They have a big tournament every summer. Holcombe Ward played there when he was still a player."

"I assumed that Beals Dalton was the benefactor," Danny said, moving into the room. "It was his mansion in the Hamptons that hosted all the parties."

"He is," Alex said, examining the bookshelf. "Ari lived here, but he couldn't afford a house in the Hamptons."

"So Ari was rich, but Beals is super rich."

"Exactly," Alex said. "Have you talked with him yet?"

"We spoke on the phone," Danny said. "He's in Florida right now."

Alex considered that as he walked along the wall of photographs.

"Don't you find that suspicious?"

"No," Danny said. "Beals was staying at the Waldorf here in Manhattan for the last two weeks so he could attend meetings, and he flew out for Florida yesterday."

That grabbed Alex's attention.

"He wasn't even home for the party at his house?"

"Apparently that's not uncommon," Danny said, nodding toward the hallway. "Let's get to work."

Alex opened his rune book and tore out a safe rune.

"I'll get my kit," he said, drawing a rectangle on the back of Ari's front door. A moment later, he had his beat-up doctor's bag and followed Danny into the rear of the apartment. He thought it would go back to a bedroom and maybe an office, but it was actually bigger than that. There was a guest bedroom, a second bathroom, an office, a kitchen, and a formal dining room.

"I'll start in the office," Danny said. "You take the bedrooms and the bathroom."

Alex nodded and headed for the master bedroom first. It was immaculate, with no sign that anyone lived there at all.

"He's either obsessively neat or there's a maid service in the building," Alex muttered, setting his bag on the bed. "It doesn't matter if the maid's been in, Ari," he said to the empty room, "you can't hide your secrets from me."

Almost two hours later, Alex had to admit defeat. Apparently Ari could, and did, keep his secrets hidden.

"Anything?" Danny asked as Alex leaned against the office door frame.

Alex shook his head.

"I've been through everything," Alex said, "including Ari's underwear drawer. There's no sign of anything suspicious, no magical residue, no suspicious or illegal substances — nothing."

"Any sign he had a girlfriend?"

Again Alex shook his head.

"No suspicious bodily fluids in either of the bedrooms and only one toothbrush in the master bathroom. If Ari kept female company, it wasn't here. You find anything in his papers?"

Danny sat at Ari's desk with several stacks of papers in front of him. When Alex asked about his progress, he sat back in the chair and sighed.

"Most of these are requests for Ari to talk about his time as a tennis pro," he said. "There are several offers for him to work as an umpire at tennis matches, but he rejected all of those. Apparently he only books his services through the USLTA."

"Bank book? Lease? Legal filings?" Alex suggested.

Danny held up a slim book with a black cover.

"Ari has sixty thousand dollars in his account and, as far as I can tell, no debt."

Alex nodded.

"I should have gone into tennis."

"Not unless you're good with money," Danny said, indicating a stack of paper. "Ari took his tennis winnings and plowed them into the stock market."

"Shouldn't he be broke, then?" Alex asked.

"Nope," Danny said, picking up the stack of paper and holding it up. "Ari's investments were in companies that didn't crash. Oh, he had a few turkeys," he admitted, "but on balance, Ari made thousands."

"That explains how Ari lives here," Alex said, "but not why he's an umpire for tennis matches?"

"Based on the letters he gets from schools and tennis appreciation associations, Ari loved the game."

Alex could understand that. He had more money than he knew what to do with, but he wasn't going to be giving up his detective business any time soon.

"What would you do if you made that kind of money?" he asked his friend.

"Nothing," Danny said, giving Alex a sly look, "for the rest of my life."

"Funny," Alex chided. "So, are we thinking Ari's murder was about his money?"

"Maybe his ex-wife found out?" Danny suggested. "I didn't find a will in here, so his daughter would likely inherit."

Alex shook his head.

"Ari signed away his parental rights," he said. "She might be able to sue Ari's estate, but legally, she's not his daughter."

"What if this isn't about Ari's family?" Danny said. "He was poisoned at that tennis party where a bunch of players attended. What if this is about his umpire job?"

Alex thought about that. Family and money were two of the most common motives for murder, but revenge was high on that list as well. He'd been to a few sporting events during previous cases and crowds got rowdy if they thought there was a bad ruling from an official.

"Did you find any threatening letters?"

"No," Danny admitted.

Alex hesitated, then made a decision.

"Holcombe didn't mention Ari having a beef with anyone, but I'll call him and make sure. You finished here?"

Danny sighed and nodded.

"I've got some of the boys on the way here to collect this stuff, but you can go if you want. Call me after you talk to Holcombe."

"I was hoping I could borrow you," Alex said. "Ari's ex lives half a block from here and I thought it might be useful to talk to her."

Danny chuckled.

"So, you figured she'd be more likely to talk if I'm the one asking?"

"And people say you aren't that smart."

"Cute," Danny said.

"Ari Leavitt is a bastard," the gaunt woman said, a sneer on her face. "When he married me, he was going to join his family's business. With his mind, he'd be running it by now, but no, he had to play tennis."

Elie Rollings had a long, angular face with brutal cheekbones and a severe nose. There was a shadow of beauty in her face, but from where Alex sat, it was almost entirely gone. Whatever Elie had lost, she had gained quite a bit along the way. Her apartment wasn't as nice as his or Ari's, but it was definitely upper class, and her clothes were the latest fashion.

"What's he done this time?" Elie continued. "Has he taken up another juvenile hobby?"

"He's dead," Danny said, his voice unemotional.

Elie's look of superior derision slipped as she realized how her words would have been perceived by the strangers in her apartment.

"We were wondering what you could tell us about your ex-husband," Alex said.

"Well, obviously, I'm not involved in his life," Elie said. "I didn't even know he'd passed."

"What about your daughter," Danny asked, checking his notebook, "Barbara?"

"Barb hasn't ever spoken to Ari," she said. "Harold, that's my husband, adopted her when she was three."

"Does she know that Ari is her father?" Alex asked.

"Harold is her father," Elie spat.

"Her natural father then," Alex amended.

"Barb doesn't know anything about Ari," she insisted.

"You sure about that?" Danny asked. "Does she like tennis?"

Elie went purple and spluttered for a full ten seconds before she got herself under control.

"I would like you to leave," she insisted. "If you have any further questions about my unfortunate mistake, you can talk to my husband. He'll be home after five."

Alex exchanged a knowing look with Danny, then the latter closed his notebook and rose.

"Thank you for your time, Mrs. Rollings," he said as Alex rose too.

Elie harrumphed, then stood and led them to the front door. Alex and Danny left without a word and Elie slammed the door as soon as they were out in the hall.

"That was a bit much," Alex said when they reached the elevator at the end of the hall.

"It was pretty clear Mrs. Rollings didn't know Ari was dead," he said. "I just wanted to give her an opportunity to gloat about Barbara inheriting."

Alex snorted at that. It was a good trick. If Elie had designs on Ari's money, she would have talked up Barbara's relationship with her biological father.

"You realize this leaves us back at square one."

"Not at all," Danny said, elbowing Alex. "You still need to talk to your client. Be sure to tell him it was my idea."

"I will," Alex laughed. "He'll love that."

13

MOTIVATION

Alex decided to call Holcombe Ward from the lobby of Elie Rollings' building rather than going back to his office. It was possible the tennis pro would give him useful information and, in that case, Alex wouldn't have to go out again since he was already out.

Calling Holcombe's office number, he once again reached the perky secretary. This time, however, Alex was told that Holcombe was in a meeting and couldn't be disturbed. With a sigh of resignation, Alex asked for the address of the US Lawn Tennis Association and was given a Mid-ring address fairly close to the Core.

The office itself was on the top floor of a five-story office structure and reminded Alex of Sorsha's office. Everything was done up in light colored woods with accents of green and gold. For an organization that mostly scheduled tennis matches, it seemed awfully tony, but Alex supposed Holcombe and the other administrators needed a place to welcome VIPs and such.

"Can I help you?" a woman asked as Alex entered their front lobby. She was young, probably in her early twenties, with strawberry blonde hair that hung down to her shoulders and brown eyes. Even sitting down, Alex could tell she was slim and fit, the kind of secretary an athletic organization would favor. The fact that she was uncommonly pretty probably helped as well.

As Alex crossed from the door to her desk, the blonde smiled and batted her eyelashes at him.

"I'm here to see Holcombe Ward," he said, handing over one of his business cards. "My name's Alex Lockerby."

"Oh," the girl said with a genuine smile. "Nice to put a face to the name." She handed the card back to Alex and glanced at the clock on her desk. "He's in a meeting right now, but they should be wrapping up any minute if you'd like to wait."

She indicated a waiting area off to Alex's left with several green and white striped couches and a coffee table piled with what he assumed to be sports magazines. Thanking the pretty girl, Alex excused himself and sat down to wait. Several of the magazines on the table were dedicated to tennis and Alex wondered if any of them would be running an obituary or story about Ari in their next issue.

While he waited, Alex flipped open his notebook and paged through it to remind himself of the details of Ari Leavitt's death. He knew that Ari's death was, in fact, a murder, and even what method was used to kill him. What he didn't have yet was a motive. After having met Ari's family and his ex-wife, Alex was fairly certain none of them had killed him, though there could still be a motive there. Fortunately the police would be pursuing that angle, looking into everyone's financials and business dealings for anything fishy.

That left Alex with Ari's professional life.

Someone had hated Ari enough to kill him. Usually that kind of thing built up over months and even years. In that case, Alex was certain the killer had expressed his dislike in public at least once.

"Someone knows," he said as he rescanned his notes to make sure he didn't miss anything.

"Beg your pardon?" Holcombe's voice cut through his thoughts.

Alex looked up to find the athletic man striding across the carpet toward him.

"Just going over a few things," Alex said, standing and extending his hand.

"Does your visit mean you've found something?" Holcombe asked.

"No," Alex admitted, "in fact we're losing suspects fast."

"How?"

Alex explained about Ari's family and his ex as Holcombe led him back to a sumptuous corner office with a nice view of the city.

"Why are you talking to Ari's family?" Holcombe demanded, leaning on his large desk. "He was poisoned at Beals' party, none of his family were there, clearly he was poisoned by someone else."

"Take it easy," Alex said, nodding toward a liquor cabinet that stood in the corner. "Have a drink."

That seemed to make Holcombe even angrier.

"What am I paying you for, Lockerby?" he demanded.

Alex just kept his face neutral. Dealing with angry clients who didn't understand how investigations worked was just part of the job.

"You pay me," Alex said, moving to the liquor cabinet and opening it, "because I know that finding motive is a much better way to figure out who a murderer is than chasing shadows."

Alex poured what looked like cognac into a tumbler and handed it to his employer. Holcombe hesitated for a moment, then took the glass.

"I assume you can explain what you just said," he growled before sipping from the glass.

"When someone gets murdered," Alex began, pouring himself a glass as well, "there's always a reason. Find out *why* someone was killed and it usually points directly at *who* killed them."

"I guess that makes sense," Holcombe said, nursing his drink.

"There are three main reasons people kill each other," Alex said, shutting the liquor cabinet and turning to face Holcombe. "The first is the big one…money. Either the victim had money, or they were stopping someone else from getting money, and the killer needed them out of the way."

"Ari was rich," Holcombe said. "He was very good at investing, and he didn't have any family beyond his ex and his daughter, who, as far as Ari knew, didn't even know he existed."

"And Ari's family is in the diamond business," Alex added. "They seem to be doing well."

"What's reason number two?"

"Revenge," Alex said. "The victim did something to the killer in the past. Maybe it was justified, maybe it wasn't, but in the killer's mind, the scales of justice are out of balance."

Holcombe shook his head.

"Ari didn't have any enemies," he said. "Even his ex-wife didn't hate him that much."

He had a point, Elie clearly despised Ari, but she seemed more interested in seeing him suffer with their absence than enacting any actual revenge. Of course, she may have found out how much better he was doing than she was, but Alex was pretty sure of his deduction. She hadn't known Ari was dead when he talked to her.

"So what's the third reason?" Holcombe pressed.

"The third main reason is jealousy," Alex said. "The victim has something the killer wants very badly."

"Isn't that the same as money?" Holcombe asked.

"No," Alex said. "With money, that's what the killer wants, so it's an easy motive to track. A jealous person could want their victim's job, or their apartment, or their lover, or their car, or just to punish them for being them."

"Sounds like that would make the motive difficult to find," Holcombe observed.

Again, Alex disagreed.

"The thing about jealousy is that it can't keep its mouth shut," Alex said. "Jealous people love to complain, to talk about what the object of their jealousy did wrong, or how they don't deserve their success."

Holcombe sighed and pursed his lips for a moment.

"I can't think of anyone like that," he said. "Ari was a good guy, I mean he had his faults, but he never held a grudge, and he was always fair."

"How about at his job?" Alex asked. He wasn't much of a sports fan, but he'd read an article years ago about a fight that broke out in Yankee Stadium over a bad call made by an umpire. As he remembered the story, the fight spilled out into the streets before it was contained. "People seem to get very passionate about their sports, could someone be holding a grudge over a bad call?"

Holcombe actually laughed at that.

"Sure," he said. "I'm sure lots of people do, although I suspect it's not a grudge directed at Ari, but rather at the rules of tennis in general."

Alex didn't understand that, and he said so.

"People bet on tennis," Holcombe said, "just like horse racing or baseball. If their chosen player loses because of a questionable call, they usually get mad. We sometimes even get letters from them, but that's as far as it goes. Only the people who work the games and the spectators in the stands know who umpires a specific match."

"That's still a lot of people who do know," Alex pointed out. "Besides, if I lost a lot of money and blamed it on the umpire, I bet I could find out his name with just an afternoon's work and a five-spot for a bribe."

"But you're a detective," Holcombe protested.

"Never assume a bad guy is stupid or unskilled," Alex said. "Whoever killed your friend was smart enough to give him a poison that would make his muscles cramp up while he was taking a swim. If you hadn't insisted there was foul play, no one would have caught on."

Holcombe cleared his throat, looking a bit chagrined.

"I see your point," he said.

"So," Alex said, pulling the conversation back on point, "are there any calls Ari got wrong, or maybe some that might be questionable?"

Holcombe sipped from his glass again.

"Too many to count," he admitted after a long moment. "Tennis, like all sports, has rules that the officials have to interpret. Whether a ball is in or out, whether a serve was proper, those kinds of things. We have several officials watching the game at all times, of course, but the man who ultimately makes the decision is the chair umpire."

"And that was Ari's job?"

"Yes." Holcombe nodded.

"So a bad call from one of the other officials might still be blamed on him if he backed that call."

"Yes."

"Again," Alex said, "are there any of those calls that blew up, maybe in the papers or you got letters?"

"Only two I can think of off the top of my head," Holcombe said.

"There was a match about six months ago where Ari called a fault on an ace serve, he said the girl's foot touched the line."

"What's an ace?"

"The person being served didn't return the ball when they should have," Holcombe explained. "Lizzy would have won the match if Ari hadn't called the foot fault."

"Was her foot out?"

Holcombe shrugged.

"I wasn't there, but if Ari said she touched the line, then she touched the line."

"I'm going to assume that she went on to lose the match," Alex said, scribbling in his notebook.

"And the championship," Holcombe admitted. "Lizzy Tizzy lived up to her name on that one, she was furious."

"Lizzy Tizzy?"

"Sorry," Holcombe said. "Her real name is Elizabeth Tisdale, she's an up and comer, very talented. The press dubbed her Lizzy Tizzy because she has a bit of a short fuse."

Alex was always amazed at the names the press gave to sports figures, it was like some kind of game to see who could come up with the most ridiculous sounding moniker.

"Abbot and Costello were right," he mumbled. "How mad was Lizzy Tizzy?" he directed the question to Holcombe.

"Like a wet hen," the tennis pro chuckled. "I'm surprised the police didn't have to drag her away. Eventually her mother calmed her down."

"Her mother?" Alex asked.

"Elizabeth is only just eighteen," Holcombe said. "The rules require that she have an adult chaperone on tour, and that's always been her mother."

Alex noted that down. He wanted to make Elizabeth Tisdale his prime suspect for Ari's death, but with a name like Lizzy Tizzy, he assumed she wasn't the brightest star in the heavens.

She could be hiding a clever mind, he reminded himself, but out loud he said, "Did she make threats toward Ari or anyone else?"

Holcombe cleared his throat again, looking a bit chagrined.

"She did," he said, "but it was the kind of thing you'd expect in the heat of the moment."

"Was Miss Tisdale at the party at Beals Dalton's house?"

"Of course. Everyone who's anyone in the tennis world was there."

"Did anything happen between Ari and Elizabeth at the party?"

Holcombe shook his head and shrugged.

"If anything did, I didn't hear about it. You could ask around."

Alex made a note to do just that. The police had already taken statements from the party guests, but they didn't know what to look for. Alex would have to repeat the interviews, a prospect he was not excited about.

"You said there were two matches where Ari made a controversial call," Alex prodded after a moment.

"The other was a similar event; Ari called a ball out and it ended the match."

"That doesn't sound like a big deal," Alex observed. "You said things like that happen all the time?"

"Not during nationals," Holcombe said.

"So Ari's call cost the player the championship?" Alex asked. When Holcombe nodded, he went on, "And the loser got angry?"

"Not as much as I expected," Holcombe admitted, finishing his cognac. "The player's name is Freddy Hackett, he's one of our rising stars. I wouldn't be surprised if he won nationals this year."

"And you think he would have won last year but for Ari's call?" Alex prodded.

"Probably," Holcombe said with a dismissive shrug. "I would have been furious, but Freddy brushed it off pretty quickly."

"Maybe he only pretended to let it go," Alex said, making more notes in his book. "Maybe Freddy nursed a grudge. I assume he was at the party as well."

Holcombe nodded.

"Everyone who's anyone on the tour was there," he reiterated.

"Anyone else you can think of who had a problem with Ari?" Alex asked.

"Not off the top of my head," Holcombe said. "Let me think about it and call you tomorrow. I can also make a few calls and see if any of the other officials know something."

"What about the other officials?" Alex asked. "Did any of them have motive to get Ari out of the big chair?"

"I doubt it. Ari and the other officials were friends. If there was ever any trouble, Ari would take the heat. I don't think any of them would lift a finger against him."

Alex wasn't sure he bought that.

"Just the same," he said, "put together a list of the officials Ari worked with so I can talk to them."

"They aren't going to like being suspected of murder," Holcombe pointed out.

"I'm not going to ask them about the murder," Alex said, closing his book. "I'm going to ask them about Ari's relationship with Freddy and Elisabeth and if any of their answers strike me funny, I'll ask them some more pointed questions."

Holcombe shook his head.

"There seems to be a lot of deception in the private investigation business," he said.

"We wouldn't need those techniques if people were honest," Alex admitted, "but then if people were honest, we wouldn't need private detectives."

Alex called his office from the lobby of the building that housed the USLTA. After his conversation with Holcombe, he had plenty of research that needed doing so there was no reason to physically return to Empire Tower.

"Sherry?" he asked when she picked up. "Did I see you reading a tennis magazine this morning?"

"No," Sherry said in a coy voice, "but you might have seen one on my desk."

"By any chance were there any articles in it about a woman named Lizzy Tizzy, or a man called Freddy Hackett?"

"Just a minute," she said and Alex could hear her turning pages. "I found Freddy," she said. "Ooo, handsome."

"Anything salacious in the article?"

"Just about him being the new heartthrob in the tennis world after Marvin Thaw retired last year."

"What about Lizzy?" Alex said. "She may be listed as Elizabeth Tisdale."

There was more page turning, then Sherry had to report failure.

Maybe Lizzy isn't the new girl any more, Alex thought. *If Ari's call had cost her a championship, maybe she lost her confidence. That kind of thing ended careers, and Lizzy might blame Ari for that.*

"I'm going over to the Midnight Sun and see if their sports gossip expert knows any dirt on those two, so if you need me, I'll be there."

"You want me to find out who their agents are, boss?" Sherry said.

"Do that," he said, "and find out if Lizzy and Freddy are still in town."

"Will do."

Alex thanked her and was about to hang up when Sherry spoke again.

"Oh," she exclaimed, "Dr. Bell called for you. He said it wasn't urgent, but you should probably call him anyway."

Alex promised that he would and hung up.

Digging another nickel out of his pocket, he gave the operator the number of the brownstone and waited for her to connect the call.

"How's your investigation into the bomber going?" Iggy asked once the call went through.

"No idea," Alex admitted. "Detweiler and his boys are digging into our two victims to see if there's any connection between them, but if they found something, they haven't told me."

"Well, what are you working on, then?"

"Ari Leavitt's death. I think I might have some viable suspects."

Iggy growled in his throat, a sign he was not pleased that Alex was working what he considered to be a less interesting case.

"I was thinking that there might be an avenue you haven't explored with regards to your bomber," he said.

Alex wasn't too proud to accept a good suggestion, so he urged his mentor on.

"The Office of Magical Oversight," Iggy said. "It's their job to keep track of magical practitioners in the city, so if there's a runewright with the kind of talent necessary to recreate Arlo Harper's boom rune, then they might know about them. At the very least, they might be able to point you in the right direction."

Alex wasn't so sure of that. He'd had to register as a runewright back when his father first started training him, and then again when he turned sixteen, and once more when he opened his detective agency, but all of that was years ago. He doubted the Office of Magical Oversight even knew his name. Still, it was a potential lead, which was more than he had a minute ago.

"All right," he said, making a decision. "I've got to interview some suspects right now, but I'll stop by Magical Oversight on my way home."

"Good lad," Iggy said, then hung up.

14

INSIGHT AND OVERSIGHT

The offices of The Midnight Sun were attached to the industrial building that housed their printing presses in the East Side Mid-ring. Alex had been there many times over the years since he first met Billy Tasker, so he knew his way around. When he limped in through the front door, he passed the reception desk and headed straight for the back hallway that lead to Billy's office.

As he passed the desk, Laura, the secretary, gave him a cold look. When Alex first visited the tabloid offices, she'd flirted outrageously with him. At the time Alex had been preoccupied with other things and hadn't responded, an oversight that Laura took personally and was still a sore spot with her.

Paying the irritable secretary no mind, Alex proceeded down to the end of the hall to Billy's corner office. Thanks in no small part to Alex, Billy had moved up rapidly at The Midnight Sun and was now one of their senior editors.

The door was closed when Alex reached it, so he took off his hat and knocked.

"Come," Billy's voice greeted him.

Opening the door, Alex stepped inside. The last time he'd been in Billy's office, the place had been an exercise in chaos. This time was no exception. Papers, files, notebooks, and stacks of newspapers littered the desk, along with at least two ashtrays, both of which were full. Alex couldn't discern any pattern among the maelstrom of paper, so he shifted his gaze up to the man behind the mess.

Billy was in his early thirties with a serious baby face that made him look much younger. He had brown hair and eyes with a narrow nose and a dimple in his left cheek. It was the dimple that first suggested to Alex that he might be related to Duane King, the Ghost Killer. Alex had learned that Duane had died in prison, but he'd been dying when Alex first met him, so that came as no surprise.

"Alex," Billy said, setting aside his cigarette and standing. "To what do I owe the pleasure? Something good, I hope."

"Maybe," Alex said, shaking the newsman's hand. He'd learned to undersell anything he took to Billy, since tabloid writers weren't exactly hesitant to run a story before all the facts were in. Billy was fairly trustworthy when it came to not filling in gaps in a story with wild speculation, but Alex still liked to err on the side of caution. "Do you cover any sports, or just sports gossip?" he asked.

"We cover anything interesting," Billy replied, motioning for Alex to sit before dropping back into his own chair. "Usually that's stories about individual athletes, but every once in a while we cover a game if there's enough drama, like Babe Ruth's first games for the Yankees. What are you looking for?"

"Tennis," Alex said. "Is there anyone consistently making headlines?"

Billy thought about that for a moment.

"There's aways someone who gets pictured sneaking out of a hotel room with a few ladies," he said with a shrug. "Then there's that official who drowned at a party upstate. That looked good for a few hours, but the police ruled it an accident and closed the case so, there's nothing there."

"Don't be so sure," Alex said, raising an eyebrow.

Billy sat up, leaning forward over his desk.

"What can you tell me?"

"I was hired to look into it," Alex said.

"And you found something," Billy guessed, a conspiratorial grin slowly creeping across his face.

"It wasn't an accident," Alex said.

"And..." Billy prompted, picking up one of his notepads and a pencil.

"And that's all I can tell you right now, but I do need some help." Alex left the thought hanging.

"So you'll bring the story to me first?"

"It probably won't be a very deep story," Alex said, "but yes, I'll make sure you get it before anything is released by the police."

Billy's grin slipped a bit when Alex mentioned the pedestrian nature of the story, but he was a man who was used to making lemonade from lemons, so he just shrugged.

"Okay," he said. "What do you need to know?"

"Does your sports writer know anything about a tennis pro named Freddy Hackett or Elizabeth Tisdale? She goes by—"

"Lizzy Tizzy," Billy said with a nod. "We get a lot of pictures of her from independent photographers. She's pretty and those tennis skirts are short. The photographers we use like taking her picture," he added.

"Do you print all those pictures?"

"Sometimes," Billy admitted. "She's been around in the tennis circuit for a few years, but she turned eighteen last year and she's been enjoying the privileges of being an adult."

"Lots of men?" Alex asked.

"Not as many as I'd like," Billy admitted. "Mostly she gets pictured being carried to cars from nightclubs because she's blind drunk."

"Is that affecting her performance?"

"Not even a little," Billy said. "She's favored to win the nationals coming up next month."

Alex made a quick note of that. With all his investigations into Ari Leavitt's death, he hadn't looked up the man's work schedule. He'd assumed that Ari would be working the big tournaments, but he didn't know for sure.

A competent investigator would look into that, he thought as he scribbled notes.

"Do you know if she had a beef with any of the officials?"

"Like the man who drowned?" Billy guessed.

"Anyone," Alex said.

"I wouldn't know about that," Billy said. "Do you want to know about Freddy Hackett as well?"

Alex nodded.

"All right," Billy said. "I'll have my boys look into it. Give me a day or two."

Alex thanked him and stood up.

"Call me the second you know something," Alex said, heading for the door.

"I will," Billy promised. "Close the door on your way out."

Alex gave him a quizzical look.

"Ever since you told me about the leak here at the Sun, I've had to be more careful."

"I'm surprised you haven't managed to ferret the leaker out," Alex said. Billy was a great investigative reporter in his own right.

Billy shrugged.

"You never know when I might need something leaked to the police," he said. "Accidentally, of course."

"Of course," Alex agreed.

He hadn't thought about that angle, but the cops would be much more likely to believe a trusted inside source rather than if Billy went to them directly.

Alex bade his friend farewell, then shut the door and limped back to the lobby where he endured the secretary's angry gaze until he reached the street.

The Office of Magical Oversight was located in a government building on the south end of Manhattan in the Mid-Ring. Some government buildings were more like temples, complete with Doric columns and marble façades, but those buildings were for important offices. Magical Oversight, on the other hand, was a plain, beige, five-story building on a side street two blocks from the important government buildings.

The lobby reminded Alex of the Police Annex building, with a black and white tiled floor and secondhand furniture in a basic waiting area. The only real differences were the lack of a police guard, and the absence of a freight elevator.

Checking the registry, Alex found that the Office of Magical Oversight was on the third floor, and a short elevator ride later, he was standing outside a plain door. *New York Office of Magical Oversight*, was engraved on a plaque attached to the door at eye level.

Without hesitation, Alex turned the knob and stepped inside. The office beyond was much bigger than he expected. It was a large open space with rows of filing cabinets against the back wall. To the left, Alex could see two offices with frosted glass windows and closed doors. In the middle of the space were three desks, arranged in a bit of a semi-circle, with clerks going through stacks of papers.

The desk on the left had a young, earnest-looking man who was typing something from a sheet of notes he kept squinting at. Alex deduced he was new to the job, because his typing skills were still a bit rough. The middle desk was occupied by a man in his forties with a pencil mustache and thick hair. His shirt was perfectly ironed and his cufflinks gleamed; clearly he was a detail man, right down to his appearance.

At the last desk sat a woman. She was pretty, looking to be in her middle thirties with short brown hair and a competent appearance. She wore a floral blouse with a vest over it and slacks, a style that reminded Alex of Sorsha. Like the young man, she was typing, but unlike him, her fingers flew over the keys as she read from a handwritten paper on her desk.

"Can I help you?" the precisely dressed man in the middle asked, looking up from his work. A brass plate with the name Jeremy Clark stood on the desk.

"I'm a consultant with the Manhattan Police," Alex said, stepping up to the desk and handing the man one of his cards. "I have a few questions if you can spare a moment."

"Alex Lockerby," Clark read, "Private Investigator?" He looked up with questioning eyes. "Since when do the police work with P.I.s?"

"It's legit," Alex said. "Call over to the Central Office if you don't believe me. Captain Callahan will be happy to confirm my bona fides."

"No need," he said handing the card back. "How can I help you, Mr. Lockerby?"

Something in the background noise changed and it took Alex a moment to realize that the regular rhythm of the woman's typing had skipped a beat.

"I'm a runewright," Alex began, "and I was wondering how closely you monitor runewrights and alchemists in the city?"

"Monitor?" Clark asked.

"Do you have notes or files on prominent runewrights or alchemists?"

"What?" Clark asked. "Are you trying to get into Who's Who?"

"No," Alex said, keeping a tight rein on his temper. "A runewright who seems to have a lot of skill is a suspect in a murder. I was wondering how much information you had about who might have his kind of skill?"

Clark thought about that for a long moment and Alex could tell he was trying to find the most diplomatic way to get rid of him.

"Mr. Clark," the woman said from her desk. "I can help Mr. Lockerby with his questions."

Clark looked annoyed for a moment, clearly irritated by the woman's interruption, but his desire to get rid of Alex won out.

"Miss Carson will assist you with your questions," he said, nodding in the woman's direction.

Alex was tempted to keep badgering the man just for spite, but decided he'd rather have his questions answered, so he turned to the woman at the right-hand desk. Unlike Jeremy Clark, there was no brass nameplate on Miss Carson's desk, so Alex stepped up and held out his hand.

"Nice to meet you," he said. "I'm Alex—"

"Lockerby," the woman finished, blushing a bit. "I heard. My name's Kim Carson. Are...are you the runewright detective?"

Alex raised an eyebrow at that. Every once in a while someone recognized him from one of the stories in the newspaper, but that didn't happen very often.

"I am," he said, putting on an affable smile.

"I've followed your career," she said, blushing furiously. "It's quite impressive."

Alex had to hesitate for a moment, not sure what to do with that information.

"You've...followed me?"

"Of course," she said. "You're one of the most impressive and important runewrights in the city."

Alex had met people who followed Sorsha's exploits and looked at her with something akin to hero worship, but he'd never experienced it himself.

He had a fan.

"Do you know about other runewrights?" he asked.

"Some," Kim said, looking nervous. "I'm a runewright too, we all are here, so whenever one of us gets in the paper, I pay attention."

"I'm looking for someone powerful enough and smart enough to make an explosive rune," he said. He really shouldn't have mentioned that, but he couldn't figure out how to get the information he wanted without being specific.

"Like the ones the Brothers Boom used?" she asked, wide-eyed.

That took Alex aback. The papers didn't print anything about the Brothers Boom using runes; in fact, they heavily implied that Roy and Arlo had used dynamite.

"What makes you think the Brothers Boom used runes in their robberies?" he asked.

She gave him a coy look, then looked over at Mr. Clark to see if he was listening.

"Well, they used a vault room to rob the banks," she said, keeping her voice low. "Vaults are pretty high level stuff, so I figured that they probably used some kind of explosive rune too. Especially since dynamite isn't that easy to come by."

"You do remember that they robbed a hardware store?" Alex said.

"Yes," she admitted, blushing slightly, "but if they'd gotten away with dynamite, it would have been all over the papers. Besides, if they didn't use a rune, I suspect you wouldn't be here asking about one."

Alex hid a smile. This girl was smart, for a bureaucrat.

"Well, I can't speak to Arlo Harper," Alex said, attempting to get the conversation back on track, "I just want to know if anyone you keep track of is smart enough to figure out how to make a runic construct that explodes?"

She put a finger to her lip and thought for moment.

"There are only two runewrights that I know about who might be able to do something like that," she said at last. "The first is you, Alex."

Based on her earlier comments about him, he should have guessed that response.

"The other would be Dr. Ignatius Bell," she finished. "I know he taught you a great deal, but he also used some very impressive magic a year or so ago, when that sky crawler derailed."

That caught Alex by surprise. Most people never bothered to wonder where Alex learned his more impressive tricks. He wondered if his mentor was more visible than he'd thought. It could be bad if anyone recognized him, after all.

Deciding to ignore the praise being heaped upon him and his mentor, Alex went on.

"No one else?" he asked.

"Not that I know of," Kim said, shaking her head. "Unless Arlo Harper's lore book got out. I mean no one seems to know what happened to it, and according to the police, his vault was left open. That's how they recovered all the money he stole."

Alex wasn't worried about Arlo Harper's lore book, especially since it was on a shelf in his vault library at that very moment, but of course he couldn't tell Kim that. Instead, he reached into his shirt pocket for one of his business cards and placed it on the woman's desk.

"Well, if you notice anyone from our community suddenly making waves, I'd appreciate it if you gave me a call."

Kim picked up the card, blushing again, then nodded.

"I will," she promised. "It was nice to finally meet you, Alex. After reading so much about you, I mean."

"It was nice to meet you too, Kim," Alex returned, then he excused himself and headed for the elevator.

He hadn't expected much help from the Office of Magical Oversight, so he wasn't too disappointed. To his knowledge, he'd never had any professional interactions with them beyond registering as a runewright when he turned sixteen and updating those records when he became a private investigator. It seemed logical that other magical practitioners had the same experience.

The elevator came to a stop at the lobby, and Alex headed for the phone booth by the door. After dropping a nickel in the slot, he gave the operator the exchange for his office.

"How's it going?" he asked when Sherry answered.

"It's good here," she said. "Nothing Mike can't handle. There was a call for you, though, from Theo Bell."

Alex felt a chill pass through his body at the mention of Bell's name, followed by a flash of anger. He'd gotten so tied up with his current cases, that he'd forgotten about Theo, and why he'd gone to the little man's shop.

"What did he say?"

"He said he wants you to stop by," Sherry relayed. "Apparently, he has something for you."

"All right. If you need to reach me, I'll be at Bell's Book & Candle."

Sherry assured him that she'd hold down the fort, and Alex hung up.

The distance between the government buildings and Theodore Bell's hole-in-the-wall shop wasn't as great as one would expect, so it was only about ten minutes later that Alex got out of a cab in front of the place. It looked as it always had, maybe a little dirtier from the front, but something about it caught Alex's attention. It might have been his own desire to find out why someone had killed Charles Grier, but he felt an electricity in the air.

Shaking off the feeling, Alex limped across the sidewalk to the door and pushed it open. The broken bell above the door gave out an anemic, off-key chime as he entered. As before, the shop was filled with the aroma of incense, candles, and old books. There weren't any patrons inside that he could see, so Alex moved to the counter and struck the little bell atop it.

"Just a minute," Theo's voice came from the thick curtain that separated the front of the shop from the back room.

True to his word, about a minute later, Theo Bell came bustling out of the back. He looked a bit flustered as he smoothed down his hair then adjusted his vest.

"Thank you for waiting," he said. "How can I — Alex."

This last came out as a gasp and he seemed to deflate a bit in relief.

"I was worried you wouldn't get my message."

"Why's that?" Alex asked, genuinely curious. Sherry was an excellent secretary who, as far as he knew, had never lost a message.

"Your secretary doesn't seem to like me very much," Theo said. "She was very short with me on the phone."

Alex made a mental note to ask Sherry about this then pushed it aside to deal with later.

"So, why did you call? Did you find a copy of that missing book?"

"No," Theo said, with energy in his voice, "and that disturbs me greatly. My business is locating rare and valuable knowledge, I know everyone in the trade, and none of them had a copy of *Stories of Inquisition*, by Conner Gertz."

"Are you sure that's the book with the green cover?" Alex asked, remembering Theo's original description.

"I wasn't at first," he admitted, "but I am now."

"What made up your mind?"

Theo looked around as if he were worried about being overheard in his empty shop, then took a half step closer to Alex.

"Because," he said in a low voice. "I checked with my library contacts, and they checked with their contacts, and so on until..." He paused and mopped his face with his handkerchief. "Alex," he went on, "there isn't a copy of that book for sale or rent anywhere in America, not in a library, not in a bookstore, nowhere. It's like someone has deliberately taken them, specifically so that they can't be read."

Alex wasn't sure he believed Theo, but if the little man was right, he was dealing with an incredibly well-organized group, not some seedy back-alley alchemist. The thought sent chills up his spine. He was still curious, though. What could be so important in a book about the Inquisition against the Templar order?

Reaching out, Alex took hold of Theo by the shoulders.

"Tell me everything," he said.

15

CLARITY OF VISION

"Let me lock up the store," Theo said, despite the fact that it was early afternoon.

Alex watched him turn the sign over to Closed, then turn the lock until it snapped into place.

"Come into the back," he said, returning to the counter where Alex waited.

Alex followed him without comment, through the curtain behind the counter and into the back. The rear of Theo's store looked a lot like a warehouse with crates and boxes stacked along the walls. The freestanding shelves in the middle were loaded down with all manner of books and unidentifiable oddities and there was packing straw everywhere. To the right was a small table that was conspicuously bare.

"Sit," Theo said, indicating one of the wooden chairs.

While Alex pulled up a chair, Theo opened a filing cabinet and withdrew a bottle of bourbon and a pair of glasses.

"What haven't you told me?" Alex asked as Theo poured some of the amber liquid into the cups.

"Just because something isn't in a library or a bookstore, doesn't mean it's gone," he said, pouring bourbon into the second glass.

Alex raised an eyebrow.

"You found a copy," he guessed.

"I have a few friends who aren't in the business, but still have deep knowledge of the occult," Theo said, sitting down and pushing one of the glasses to Alex. "I called around and finally remembered a woman I know in New Orleans, Abigale Flick."

"Flick?" Alex asked, having never heard that surname before.

"I think she made it up herself," Theo said, unruffled by the interruption. "The important thing is that she has an absolutely iron-clad memory. Anything she reads, she remembers — forever."

Alex sipped on the bourbon and was surprised by the quality.

"So she doesn't have a copy of the book, but she remembers it?" he said.

"That was my hope," Theo said, leaning forward across the table. "When I called her, however, she actually had a copy of *Stories of Inquisition*."

"Is she sending it to you?" Alex asked. "I'm sure I can convince Sorsha to take me down there, if I need to pick it up."

Theo shook his head.

"Abigale is very protective of her library," he said, holding up a hand as Alex took a breath to argue. "She'd never give up her copy, but I don't think we need it. After I talked to her about the curse stone and Charles Grier's death, she read me a passage out of the book and I think it's exactly what you're looking for."

Alex wasn't convinced, but he was willing to let Theo make his case, so he sat back in his chair and sipped his bourbon.

"There's a story in the book that talks about the original organization of the Knights Templar," Theo began. "As we discussed, the Templars were created when the individual knights who were helping to hold the city of Jerusalem decided to form an alliance. All that history remembers about the event is that the knights had quartered themselves in the ruins of the Temple in Jerusalem."

Alex remembered the story. He didn't know much about the Templars personally, but he'd been brought up reading the Bible, so he knew about both Solomon's Temple and the Temple that Herod built after it had been destroyed. According to the biblical account,

Solomon's Temple was supposed to have been covered in gold and jewels and other things of value.

"Were they treasure hunting?" he asked.

"That's what I always thought," Theo admitted, "but not according to Gertz. The knights were men of faith, determined to hold the Temple as the last bastion of Christianity, should the Arab hordes retake the holy city."

"Okay, so why do we care about how they formed their brotherhood?"

"Because Gertz says something in his book that I've never heard before," Theo said, his eyes alight with excitement. "According to him, the knights were excavating a partially collapsed basement room when they discovered a bronze tablet hidden behind a façade that broke away from the wall as they worked."

Alex nodded along. Bronze was a strong enough metal to survive for a thousand years, so that part of the story made sense.

"What was written on this metal tablet?" he asked.

"It contained a story, part from the Bible, but with other details added in," Theo began. "You remember that I told you about a legend that said that Joseph of Egypt used a magical stone to interpret dreams?"

Alex nodded. That was certainly new information for him. The Bible contained no references to any device or focus required for Joseph to understand the dreams of others.

"According to Gertz, Joseph had a piece of clear crystal, about the size of a pool ball, that he would stare into and, apparently, receive information through. The account on the tablet ascribes the power of the stone to magic, rather than divinity."

"Meaning you don't have to worship Christ to make it work," Alex guessed.

"That's the conclusion the Templars came to," Theo agreed. "They guessed that anyone who held the stone, if they had some affinity for magic, could use the stone. They were terrified at that prospect."

"Why?" Alex interjected. "I can't remember the last time I had a dream, there can't be much call for dream interpretation."

"That's just it," Theo said, then drained his glass. "The stone was capable of far more than simply revealing the meanings behind dreams. According to the bronze tablet, if the person using the stone was powerful enough, the stone would show them anything, anywhere on earth. They might even be able to see the future, or revisit the past."

"That sounds a bit far-fetched," Alex said.

"Not really," Theo said. "Some of the dreams that Joseph interpreted dealt with the future."

Alex raised an eyebrow at that. A magical device that could reveal the future would be powerful indeed. Of course, he'd had dealings with Augury, his secretary being one, and he knew how fickle and unreliable such power could be with regards to the future. Still, even if the vision stone only parsed out a few details every once in a while, a smart man could make that work for him.

"So what happened to the stone after Joseph died?" Alex asked. "If what you told me last time was right, the Templars ended up with it somehow."

"Remember," Theo said, an intense expression on his face, "Joseph of Egypt married one of the daughters of the Pharaoh, meaning his children were tied into the royal line."

Alex hadn't thought about it that way, but he supposed that was correct.

"So," Theo went on, "when Joseph died, the stone would have gone to one of his relatives."

"Like his in-law," Alex guessed, "the Pharaoh?"

Theo snapped his fingers.

"Exactly," he said. "Now imagine what you could do as the ruler of an empire if you had a stone that let you see the future?"

Alex was imagining; such a device could make its owner rich beyond their wildest dreams, could attract the women they desired, could even reveal traitors or other enemies. Alex didn't know exactly when Sherry had brought down Egypt's magical empire, but from what she told him, it was well before the time of Joseph. The opportunity for a later Pharaoh to regain the ability to know the future would have been irresistible.

"The exact historical timelines aren't known," Theo continued, "but the period leading up to, and directly succeeding the biblical

Exodus was the pinnacle of Egypt's power and wealth," Theo pointed out. "Historians call it the Eighteenth Dynasty."

It took Alex a moment to unravel the threads of the story to figure out where it was going.

"So Conner Gertz is saying that the Pharaohs of this Eighteenth Dynasty were so rich and powerful because they had Joseph's bit of crystal?"

"That's exactly what he's saying," Theo confirmed.

"So what happened to it?" Alex asked, starting to catch a bit of Theo's enthusiasm.

"It was passed down in the male line of the Pharaohs of the Eighteenth Dynasty," Theo said. "All the way down to the last male member of the line, a young man named Tutankehaten, who later changed his name to Tutankhamun."

"King Tut?" Alex asked, somewhat shocked by the revelation. Tutankhamun's story had been in all the newspapers after the discovery of his tomb in nineteen twenty-two.

"The Templars believed that the vision stone was not passed on when Tut died, but was buried with him in his tomb."

Alex looked up in alarm at that.

"So this powerful magical stone is just sitting behind glass in a museum somewhere?"

Theo gave him a conspiratorial smile.

"Not according to Gertz," he said. "In the book, he says that the real reason the Templar order was formed was to send an expedition to Egypt, locate Tut's tomb, and retrieve the stone."

"That's crazy," Alex protested. "No one knew where Tut was buried, that's why it took archeologists so long to find his tomb."

"Not exactly," Theo corrected him. "I remember reading in the paper that when the seal on Tut's tomb was exposed, there was evidence that it had been broken in to at least twice."

"So you think the Templars found it?" Alex asked. "The stone, I mean."

Theo paused and poured another bourbon for himself and Alex.

"You do know why King Phillip the fourth of France wanted the Templars eliminated, don't you?"

"I assume he wanted their money," Alex replied. "They were reputed to be very rich…"

Alex stopped as the realization hit him.

"They were rich because they found the vision stone," he said.

"And they used it," Theo added. "One other funny thing, when the Inquisition finally broke into those Templar castles and strongholds, they only found a tiny fraction of the wealth the knights were supposedly hoarding. It was almost like they'd been warned in advance and moved their cash."

Alex sat back in his chair, dumbfounded. The tale of Joseph of Egypt and his chunk of magic crystal seemed ridiculous when Theo first presented it, but the more he thought about it, the more it seemed that the influence of the stone was plain to see.

"So where did the Templars take the stone?" he asked, letting a bit of frustration creep into his voice. "And where is it now?"

"Gertz didn't know," Theo admitted. "Or, if he did, he didn't put it in his book."

Alex sat and thought about that for several minutes while Theo drank his bourbon and refilled his glass for a third time.

"So I need to have a talk with Conner Gertz," Alex said.

"Unfortunately, Mr. Gertz is dead," Theo said. "Almost ten years now."

Alex sighed. Everything about these curse stones was two steps forward and one step back.

"Is there anything you can tell me about this Vision Stone," Alex asked Theo, "or where it might be?"

"I can tell you this," Theo said. "There have been rumors of the Templars' escape from King Phillip dating all the way back to the event itself. Some say they put their treasure into ships and carried it off to England or Africa. Some even say they made it all the way to the new world."

"But what became of them?" Alex asked. "Are there any Templars today?"

Theo shrugged.

"If there are any still around, they're keeping quiet," he said.

"Though there are rumors and legends that the Templars are the ones who started the modern version of the Freemasons."

Alex knew of the Masons, of course; many of America's founding fathers had been Masons, including Benjamin Franklin, who had also possessed, and made notes in, the Archimedean Monograph.

It was quite the coincidence.

Alex felt his stomach sour at that thought. The Freemasons existed all over the U.S. and Europe.

The stone could be anywhere, he thought. *Worse, it could be sitting in a box of forgotten things in someone's basement.*

"Is there anything else?" Alex asked, dreading what the answer might be.

"Only one thing," Theo said. "The Inquisition against the Knights Templar accused them of heresy. Apparently they found strange jewels in what was left of the knights' treasure, only they weren't jewels, they were curse stones, just like the one that got Charles Grier killed."

"Why would the Templars make something like that?"

"Gertz doesn't say, but for my money...they were trying to make more vision stones."

Alex took a deep breath and let it out slowly. He hadn't considered the idea that the curse stones were failed experiments put to an alternative use.

"Listen Alex," he said, his voice dropping low again. "Whoever is grabbing up all the books is willing to kill to keep the knowledge of the vision stone secret. If what you told me about this new curse stone is true, they're also trying to make new ones."

"And if they do that," Alex concluded, "they'll be able to see the future, or anything in the present that they want. Can you imagine that kind of power in the hands of Stalin, or Hitler?"

Theo shivered.

"Heaven forbid," he said.

Alex held up his bourbon, staring at the amber liquid for a long moment.

"So what now?" Theo asked at last.

"I can't stop whoever is doing this if I don't know how you go about trying to make a vision stone."

"Only the Templars can tell you that," Theo pointed out, "or the Freemasons, if you believe that legend."

"You're wrong," Alex corrected his friend. "Someone else knows, someone who's making curse stones. Someone who killed Charles Grier when he got too close."

"I suppose that's true," Theo admitted, "but it still leaves you with no course of action."

"Not entirely," Alex countered, a smile drifting across his face. "I can always ask a Freemason if they know anything about it."

"How are you going to find one?" Theo asked. "Just walk up to their lodge building and ask the first one you see?"

"No," Alex said. "I was thinking about asking the one I live with."

Twenty minutes later, Alex limped into his office, on the way to his vault. He needed to go see Lizzy Tizzy and Freddy Hackett, but he was determined to pursue the curse stones now that he had an actual lead. If Theo's friend was reading the right book, and if the author, Conner Gertz, wasn't just some nut, then the origin of the curse stones was more complex than he could have imagined. Alex wasn't convinced yet that the information in the Gertz book was anything other than an entertaining fairy tale, but at least he had a lead to follow.

"I'm going home for an hour or so," he said as he crossed the waiting room. "Hold my calls."

"About that," Sherry said in her bad news voice. "I just got off the phone with Lieutenant Detweiler. He wants you at a home on the West Side." She tore a page off one of her notepads and held it up. "There's been another bombing."

Alex looked at an address that turned out to be pretty close to the Inner-Ring and the park.

"Did he say anything else?"

"Just that the victim was a professor at Columbia," Sherry said.

"All right," Alex said after a moment's struggle with himself; he still wanted to talk to Iggy about the Masonic traditions, but his paying cases had to take precedent.

"I also found the agents for those tennis pros," Sherry went on. "Both Miss Tisdale and Mr. Hackett are in town and will be until the nationals next week."

"All right," Alex said, jotting the information in his notebook. "If Detweiler calls back, tell him I'm on my way."

"Will do, boss," Sherry replied, flashing him a smile. "You want me to give Dr. Bell a message for you?"

"How did you know I wanted to talk to Iggy?" Alex asked, assuming her gift had informed her.

"I don't have to be a detective to know that when you go home in the middle of the day, you want to consult with the good doctor," she said with a smirk.

Alex was impressed and he said so.

"I guess you're rubbing off on me," she said as he turned to leave.

"You want me to start giving you cases?" Alex asked, only half joking.

"No," she declared. "I like my job...people don't shoot at me."

Alex chuckled as he headed back into the hallway in the direction of the elevator.

In recent years, most of the West Side neighborhoods, the ones with neat little houses, had been turned into business blocks and apartments. When Alex's cab turned into a tree lined lane of small homes, he was a bit surprised. There appeared to be at least two blocks' worth of the legacy houses still existing in the middle of a city that was steadily growing up toward the sky.

As Alex leaned toward the window, it became obvious where he was bound. About half a block up, several police cars were parked along either side of the road in front of a house with a gaping hole in the side.

Once he paid the cabbie, Alex limped up to the cop at the front door, a stone-faced man he hadn't seen before, and handed the officer his card.

"Inside," the man growled after scrutinizing the card.

"Thanks," Alex said, not feeling gracious, but determined to be civil. After all, as Iggy often pointed out, you never knew when you might have to work with someone, so it was best to stay professional.

The inside of the house looked like the race track after the crowds had gone. Papers, scraps of cloth, and bits of lumber were everywhere, even a few embedded into the walls. The aroma of fire clung to everything, though it was obvious that whatever had burned had been put out. To make the chaos worse, at least ten policemen were moving around, contaminating the scene.

Deciding to salvage what he could, Alex took a close look at the front room. Even with the destruction he could see what the room had once been. Along the wall that separated the room from the back of the house stood the remnants of a well-worn couch. The wall on the right hand side was mostly gone, revealing a room beyond that Alex assumed was an office, and the left wall revealed faded patterns in the wallpaper, showing where pictures had hung. A few of the more hardy ones were still in place and, in one of them, Alex could see photos of a pudgy, bespectacled man in a dark suit standing in front of what looked like a government building. A comfortable looking easy chair stood next to the door, completing the little room, and Alex could imagine that, before it was destroyed, it had been quite cozy and inviting.

"Alex," Detweiler's voice broke into his thoughts.

"I came as soon as I got your message," he said, looking up to find the police lieutenant coming out from the rear of the house.

"I'm glad you brought your bag," he said. "This is a complete mess."

"What do you know?"

Detweiler pulled out his notebook and flipped it open.

"The victim's name is Brian Rodgers," he read. "According to the neighbors, he was a quiet man with regular habits, though that's all they knew. They said he was a college professor, and with Columbia just up the street, I sent some uniforms over there to find out more."

"Call them back," Alex said, stepping over to the left-hand wall and picking up a framed document that had been knocked off the wall. He shook the debris off the glass, then handed it to Detweiler. "According to this, Professor Rodgers teaches magical theory and application at New York University."

"That's not very close," the lieutenant observed.

Alex shrugged at that.

"There's a sky crawler station a block from here," he said. "The line goes right past NYU, so it's probably a fairly short trip. That's why he used his house to meet with students."

"What makes you think that?"

Alex pointed at the easy chair.

"Notice the pattern in the seat cushion," he said. "Someone sat here regularly. Then look at the couch, it's not old, but the fronts of the cushions are worn. The professor would sit in the chair and his students would sit there."

"You can't be sure of that," Detweiler said, dismissal in his voice.

"Well, it's either that or he had neighbors over to visit regularly and from what your men found out, they don't know him well enough for that."

"Okay," Detweiler said. "I'll have one of my boys call NYU and find out if Rodgers was one of their professors; in the meantime, do your thing. I want to know if this was another letter from our bomber, or a student who didn't pass his class."

16

RETURN TO SENDER

Alex found himself dozing on what remained of Professor Rodgers' consultation couch as Detweiler argued with a veritable army of reporters who had gathered around the exploded house in what could only be called an encampment. Up to now the police had been able to control access to the scenes of the bombings, but the word was out now and the press were as thick as flies on a two day old carcass.

When the press had arrived, Alex kept a low profile. Plenty of reporters knew that Alex worked with the police from time to time, but if anyone saw him, tales of a rune bomber might creep into the evening editions of the more inventive tabloids. He had been publicly associated with the Brothers Boom case after all. So, after clearing the debris off the blue couch, Alex slumped back with his feet out and his hat down over his eyes.

"You awake?" Detweiler's voice pulled his wandering mind back to reality.

"Yes," he said, sitting up. "How goes it with the hoard?"

"I gave them an official statement, so hopefully they'll begin to disperse," he said. "Still, you'll probably be here at least another hour."

Alex grunted at that. He could leave any time he wanted using his

Equal & Opposite

vault, of course, but no one else on site knew that was a possibility. The last thing Alex needed was his vault transportation ability getting out.

"I wish the bomb hadn't knocked out the professor's phone," Alex said, staring and stretching. "I need to call in to my office."

"Run me through your findings," the lieutenant grumbled, "then I'll see if I can find an officer to sneak you out the back."

Alex sighed and dropped his hat on the couch before rubbing his eyes.

"This bomb was exactly like the last two," he said, reaching for his notebook. "The professor was sitting at his desk when it went off, and I know that because his shoes are still under the desk, with bits of his feet still in them."

"Yuck," Detweiler added.

"I can't be certain," Alex said, checking his notes, "but I think this bomb was more powerful than the last two."

Detweiler looked back into the space where the office had been, noting that most of the walls had holes in them.

"Is that important?"

"Could mean our bomber really hated Professor Rodgers," Alex said with a shrug.

"What we need is some kind of connection between our victims," Detweiler groused. "You didn't happen to find anything like that, did you?"

"Possibly," Alex said. "Professor Rodgers taught magical application, and McDermet sold cheap magical supplies, there's a chance they knew each other."

Detweiler shook his head almost immediately.

"There's no chance that New York University was buying their magical supplies from the likes of McDermet," he said.

"No," Alex agreed, "but I went through the professor's papers, the ones I could find anyway, and teaching wasn't his only job."

The balding police lieutenant raised an eyebrow at that.

"Go on."

"According to his employment papers from the University, he was the dean of something called the School of Runic Constructs."

"Never heard of that," Danny admitted.

"Me neither, but I found a letter saying that Professor Rodgers was dismissed from the program when it dissolved eleven years ago."

"He was fired?"

Alex shook his head and rose, motioning for Detweiler to follow. Leading the way into the broken room, Alex picked up a typewritten letter on NYU letterhead from a stack he'd left on one of the still-standing shelves.

"This is the letter," he said, handing it to Detweiler. "The short version is that the university president thanks him for heading up the School of Runic Constructs and says that the school is being eliminated. He goes on to offer Rodgers his old job as professor."

"So he wasn't fired, he was demoted," Detweiler said, skimming the letter.

"That's the way it looks," Alex said. "Of course we're reading between the lines here, but the letter seems straightforward enough."

"I could see that making the professor angry," Detweiler said, putting the letter back on Alex's stack, "but I don't see how that would make him a target."

"Who had the job of professor before Rogers was demoted?" Alex suggested.

"Point," Detweiler admitted, taking out his notepad and scribbling in it. "What do you think NYU was trying to do with their rune college?"

Alex could only shrug. He'd never been to any form of higher education, so his knowledge of how they worked was significantly limited.

"If I had to guess, it looks like they were trying to make NYU a repository for rune lore, maybe standardize the practice?"

"Sounds reasonable, I wonder what happened to it?"

"My guess, they couldn't get enough participation," Alex said. "I'm sure they could buy all the lore they wanted from poor, destitute runewrights, but the ones with valuable skills, the kind of skills that make money? They'd never give up their secrets so a university could teach them to a bunch of kids. They'd be cutting their own throats."

Detweiler sighed and nodded.

"This is interesting, but it isn't getting us anywhere," he declared.

"Sorry," Alex said, "it's the best I've got. I just don't see how a company president, a cut rate potioneer, and a university professor are connected."

Detweiler looked like he was about to agree, but suddenly cocked his head as his bushy eyebrows dropped down over his eyes.

"Wait a minute," he said, grabbing Alex by the forearm. "This kind of collaboration isn't unusual, you do this all the time."

Alex just stared at the little man.

"Think about it," Detweiler said, "you work with Andrew Barton, then there's your friend the gangster."

"Ex-gangster," Alex pointed out.

"Whatever," Detweiler growled, clearly not convinced. "The point is this; let's say you're a businessman who has an idea for some new product or service."

"One that requires magic?" Alex suggested, catching the lieutenant's train of thought.

"Exactly. You find someone to partner with, someone who can do the heavy lifting, magically speaking."

"Someone like a college professor who specializes in runic constructs," Alex said.

"Then, once it was all worked out, all you'd need is someone to provide the supplies you'd need to mass produce your idea," Detweiler finished.

"Someone like Matthew McDermet," Alex said, nodding. "It's just a guess, but it fits."

"And," Detweiler said, "if that's right, our bomber could be someone who got cut out of the deal."

"Or maybe Reggie Aspler stole the idea and the original creator wants revenge," Alex suggested.

"Either way, we need some proof," Detweiler said, a shrewd look spreading across his face. "I don't remember seeing anything about a magical product in any of the documents recovered from the victims."

"Something like this wouldn't be laying around in their papers," Alex said. "If you're right, whatever this is, it's strictly hush-hush. The best place to start looking, though, would be in Reggie's office at Aspler Shipping."

"Why there?"

"Because," Alex said, "between the industrialist, the professor, and the shopkeep, Reggie is the only one in a position to pay the bills. Whatever they're doing, it had to cost money, and in a big company like Aspler Shipping, money leaves a trail."

"Right," Detweiler said, catching on. "I'll have our accountant go over Reggie's books. If it's in there, he'll find it."

Alex smiled. For the first time in days, he felt like they were making progress on this case.

"If we're done here," he said, "I really need to get back to my office."

It took almost twenty minutes for a summoned taxi to reach Alex where he waited, two streets away from Professor Rodgers' home. It would be at least half an hour more, with the traffic, before he'd get back to his office, so Alex had the taxi drop him at the first diner they came across and wait while he called in.

"Boss?" Sherry gasped as soon as the line connected.

"Uh, yeah," Alex stammered, caught a bit off guard by the intensity of her greeting. "What's wrong?"

"I think," she began, but hesitated. "No, something's wrong."

Everyone experienced moments of unease, of course, but when Sherry had one, Alex paid attention.

"What's the problem?"

"I was sorting through today's mail, a few bills and a note from one of your former clients."

"And?" Alex demanded when she didn't continue.

"Well, there's a letter addressed to you, but…it's not right."

Alex felt a prickling jolt of electricity run up his back.

"Is it handwritten or typed?"

"Typed," Sherry said, "and there's no return address."

"What about a stamp?"

"No."

"Where is the letter now?" he said, trying to keep his voice calm.

"I'm holding it in my hand."

"Sherry," Alex said, slowly and deliberately. "I want you to put the letter on your desk, gently."

"Okay," she said after a moment. "It's down."

"Is Mike in the office right now?"

"Yes," Sherry said, "he's in the map room."

"Good," Alex said. "Get that key I gave you, the one that opens my vault door. Once you have that, get up from your desk, get Micheal, get inside my vault and close the door. Don't run. When you get inside, use the phone by my drafting table and call Iggy, tell him to bring you inside the brownstone. Do you understand?"

"Get Mike, go to your vault, call Iggy," she repeated.

"Right," Alex said. "Now hang up the phone, gently, and get going."

There was a click as Sherry hung up and Alex realized he'd started holding his breath. Leaving the phone booth behind, he jogged out to the still waiting taxi, ignoring his sore foot.

"You can go," he said, thrusting three dollars into the cabbie's hand. "Keep the change." Without waiting for a response, Alex turned and hustled around the side of the diner and into the alley behind it. Pulling out his chalk, he hastily drew a door on the back of the building, then retrieved his rune book.

Opening the book, Alex was briefly taken aback. He still wasn't used to seeing Iggy's writing on his rune pages. Flipping through until he found a vault rune, Alex carefully tore it out, then touched the paper to his tongue and stuck it to the back wall of the diner, inside his chalked door.

A flick of the gold lighter Sorsha had given him and the paper vanished, leaving a glowing silver rune emblazoned on the wall. A few moments later, a solid steel door with a brass plate in its center melted out of the rough brick surface.

Alex fumbled a bit with the large skeleton key that would open it, but his trembling hands eventually got it into the lock. With a quick turn, the door slid away from the wall, opening soundlessly into the space beyond.

To Alex's relief, his vault was still as he left it. The only things out of place were Sherry and Mike standing in the middle of his great room.

"Alex," Sherry gasped, wringing her hands together.

Alex limped inside, pushing the vault door closed behind him. Before he could say anything, however, Iggy's voice boomed through the space.

"What's so important that I had to come right away?"

The man himself immediately followed, striding out of the brownstone hallway in his smoking jacket and slippers.

"I got a hand delivered letter at the office," Alex said, crossing to the center of the room where Sherry and Mike waited.

Iggy was brought up short, then stroked his mustache.

"Take them to Sorsha's castle," he said, taking charge.

"Won't they be safer at the brownstone?" Alex asked.

"The brownstone is the safest place to open the letter," Iggy said, heading for Alex's office. "I'll get the letter, but they need to be gone when I get back."

"Right." Alex took hold of Sherry's arm and headed for the door to Sorsha's foyer. He hadn't considered that the protections woven into the brownstone might keep a rune bomb from activating when it was opened, but they had been designed against rogue magic.

"Is the letter a bomb?" Mike asked as Alex fished in his pocket for his key ring.

"Yes," Sherry said, her voice dry and hoarse.

"Don't worry about that," Alex said, pulling the door open. Beyond was the front foyer of Sorsha's flying castle and her very surprised ladies' maid Hannah. "Sorry," Alex said, leading Sherry into the space so Mike could follow behind. "I need to stash these two for an hour or so. Sorsha won't mind."

"O-of course," Hannah said.

She looked like she intended to say something more, but Alex was already heading back through the door, closing it behind him. Iggy had just emerged from the office hall as Alex closed the cover door behind him. His mentor was moving slowly and deliberately, carrying the letter between two fingers while walking steadily.

"I don't think it will activate until the envelope is opened," Alex said, limping up behind him and heading for the brownstone.

"No sense taking chances," his mentor said. "Frankly you shouldn't be here. If this thing goes off, it's the end of both of us."

"I need to know who's doing this," Alex said, getting the door for Iggy. "You're not keeping me out."

"So be it," Iggy said in a nonplussed voice that belied the seriousness of the situation.

Alex contemplated closing the steel door behind his cover door, thus shutting his vault off from the brownstone, but he thought better of it. So far the rune bombs hadn't been powerful enough to destroy more than a single room, and he might need something from his vault in a hurry.

"Kitchen table, I think," Iggy said, heading down the stairs. "Bring your kit."

Alex turned back to the door he'd just closed and fished out his key to open it. After examining the crime scene at Professor Rodgers' home, he'd returned his kit to the fake safe in his vault, so now he hurried across the floor, cursing his sore foot, to get it.

Once Alex returned to the brownstone, he descended to the first floor and headed for the kitchen. Iggy had laid the explosive envelope on the surface of the heavy table and pulled several chairs out of the way so he could lean over it. A silver cigarette lighter stood open and burning a few feet down the table, and Alex recognized it.

"You think your obfuscation rune will stop the boom rune from activating?" Alex surmised, setting his kit bag gently on the table.

"It should," Iggy said. "There has to be an activation rune on either the envelope or the folded paper, maybe both," he said, more to himself than to Alex. "With the obfuscation rune in effect, the activation rune shouldn't be able to set off the boom rune."

"What if it doesn't work?" Alex asked, not sure he really wanted an answer.

"It's not one of my runes," Iggy said.

"Why is that relevant?"

"Only runes based around my basic structure should be able to activate inside the brownstone," Iggy said, motioning for Alex to open his bag.

"Is that why you made me redo all the runes from my father's book?" Alex asked, pulling out his multi-lamp and clipping the ghost-light burner into place.

For his part, Iggy simply waggled his eyebrows at Alex in return.

Alex mumbled a curse under his breath. Half his father's runes simply stopped working when he'd moved into the brownstone, and it took him weeks to redesign them based on what Iggy had taught him.

"Wait a minute," Alex said. "I've used outside runes in here before — what about those Happy Jack books?"

"My protections are stronger now than they used to be," was all his mentor would say.

Alex remembered that Iggy had redone all the protections in the brownstone while he was out of town with Andrew Barton in Washington D.C. He'd asked about that at the time, but Iggy had been similarly vague. There was probably something there he should investigate, but Alex had enough on his plate as it was, so shrugged it off.

"Spectacles," Iggy said, holding out his hand.

Alex pulled his glasses case from the bag and handed it over.

"The yellow ones," he said.

Iggy opened the case and withdrew two pairs of pince-nez style spectacles. Alex lit the burner in his lamp and turned the open lens toward the envelope.

"Now," Iggy said, clipping the spectacles to the bridge of his nose, "let's see what we have here."

Alex followed his mentor, clipping on the spectacles. The envelope glowed with green images, bulging out from the paper as if it were stuffed with twisted wire. From what Alex could see, the magic on the paper inside the envelope was folded up on top of itself, matching the paper itself.

"That's a lot of magic power," Iggy remarked. "Whoever sent this meant to reduce you to a fine mist."

"That's definitely more than needed for the job," Alex confirmed, "sloppy too."

Iggy nodded.

"That's not too surprising," he said. "Most runewrights don't bother to conceal the power of their runes."

"Most don't have much power to conceal," Alex observed. "Whoever did this is not your typical runewright."

Iggy grunted something in response, leaning close to the envelope to examine the runes with a magnifying glass.

"It appears to be stable," he said, straightening up. He passed the magnifier to Alex. "Take a look."

Alex took the glass and leaned in. Since the rune was folded in on itself, he couldn't see the construct clearly. The lines of magical force might be all over the place, but the line work of the construct itself looked clean and confident.

"What now?" he asked at last.

"Now we open it," Iggy said. "With any luck, the sender will have a distinctive style we can trace."

"Should we put up a barrier rune?" Alex asked.

"No point," Iggy said, retrieving a letter opener from the drawer in the China cabinet. "If this decides to explode, a barrier rune would only slow it down for a second." He gave Alex a reassuring look. "As long as the doors are all shut, the protection on the house should keep it from exploding.

As if on cue, the sound of a door opening descended from above.

"Alex?" Sorsha's voice followed it.

Alex wanted to be happy to see the sorceress, but his eyes were drawn to the envelope as the green glow around it suddenly flared into a blinding brightness.

17

COMBUSTION

"**A**lexander!" Sorsha shouted from upstairs, her angry voice echoing off the walls. "What is going on?"

The light from the activation rune in the letter bomb had shifted from green to purple and it glowed like a spotlight, rooting Alex to the ground. He wanted to ignore his injured foot and run, to tell Sorsha to close the cover door to his vault, but blazing purple light pulsing from the table had him rooted to the floor.

"Alex!" Sorsha yelled again, her voice going up half an octave.

"The nullification rune is preventing it from activating the explosive," Iggy said, breaking the spell and letting Alex breathe again. "Now, please tell your girlfriend to shut the bloody door."

Alex turned and ran along the short hall that connected the kitchen from the library.

"Sorsha," he said, trying to make his voice commanding but not strong enough that Sorsha would start an argument. "Shut the cover door to the vault."

"What?" she demanded as Alex reached the foyer.

"The door," he said pointing emphatically up as Sorsha descended to the second floor landing. "Close it, now!"

Sorsha opened her mouth as her darkened eyebrows dropped down over her eyes, but when she saw Alex's face, she turned and waved her hand. From above, Alex heard the cover door to his vault slam shut and he turned back to the kitchen. The purple glow still pulsed along the hallway wall without abating.

"What—," Sorsha began, but Alex darted back into the hall.

Iggy was leaning over the glowing rune, staring at it through the pince-nez spectacles.

"Why is it still glowing?" he demanded as he reached the kitchen.

"Shhh," Iggy shushed him. "It's already expended its energy," he said, using a pencil to point to the rune. "When the door opened upstairs, it weakened the sealing runes and the activation rune did what it was supposed to do."

Alex glanced at the still burning cigarette lighter.

"But the nullification rune is holding?"

"For now," Iggy said, his voice calm despite the warning in his answer.

"What's all this?" Sorsha demanded, sweeping into the kitchen in a cloud of frost vapor.

"Someone sent Alex a bomb," Iggy said without looking up. "We're trying to prevent it from exploding, now quiet, please."

"Let me—," Sorsha said, reaching out her hand.

"No," Iggy said, grabbing her wrist. "The magic is active. Any interference could set it off."

Sorsha gave him a patronizing look.

"Don't you remember the last time you handed me an explosive?"

Alex did remember, the snow globe Paschal Randolph had turned into a magical bomb. Sorsha had managed to contain the explosion, barely. Even then the explosion blew a hole in the side of the hotel where Randolph had been staying.

"We need to examine the rune," Alex said as Iggy carefully slid the letter free of the envelope. "The person who wrote it has already killed three people."

Sorsha looked from Alex to the bright purple light emanating from the folded paper on the table.

"What can I do then?" she asked.

"Put a shield around yourself and Alex," Iggy said, opening his rune book. "If this doesn't work, Alex, there's a copy of my vault rune in that hidden safe in your vault, along with my will leaving you everything."

"Don't talk like that," Alex said, taking an involuntary step forward. As he shifted his weight, he bumped into an invisible barrier and suddenly the sound of Iggy moving about the kitchen stopped. Sorsha had already put up her shield.

Oblivious to Alex, Iggy tore a page from his rune book and quickly stuck it to the envelope. Tearing a second rune out of his book, Iggy moved to the wall, and quickly drew a door.

Alex wanted to ask what he was doing, since there was already an open door into his vault on the wall next to the telephone, but Sorsha's shield prevented it. Iggy took out his keyring and selected an old-fashioned key, inserting it in the brass plate in the center of the newly appeared steel door.

"What's he doing?" Sorsha asked, her voice cool and even.

"I honestly don't know," Alex replied.

As he said that, Iggy pulled open the vault door and bright sunlight filled the room. At the same time, the flame coming from the silver lighter wavered and dimmed.

"That's not Iggy's vault," Alex said, more to himself than to Sorsha. It didn't make any sense, doors opened into vaults, but they didn't open from one place directly to another.

As Alex puzzled, Iggy opened the silverware drawer below the glass doors of the china cabinet and pulled out a long wooden spoon. Opening his rune book again, he paged through until he found what he wanted, then tore out a paper and wrapped it around the handle of the spoon.

The flame above the silver lighter was weak, but it was more than enough to ignite the flash paper as Iggy held the spoon's handle over it. The rune flashed briefly gold as the paper vanished and Iggy hurled the spoon through the open door. An instant later the activation rune pulsed and purple light streaked across the kitchen and out through the open vault door. Before Alex could take a breath of relief, Iggy slammed the heavy door closed and it melted back into the wallpaper.

"Can I lower the shield now?" Sorsha asked. Her voice was calm, but Alex noted a bead of sweat on her forehead. He didn't know if it was from the exertion of maintaining the shield or worry for Iggy, but he suspected it was the latter.

"Yes," he said in response. "Iggy dissipated the power of the activation rune, so the boom rune is inert. Unless you light it on fire," he added.

Sorsha gave him an unamused look as the barrier between them and Iggy vanished.

"My apologies for not welcoming you properly," Iggy said to Sorsha as she and Alex approached the table. "I was a bit preoccupied."

As he spoke, Iggy leaned over the table and carefully pulled the folded letter open. With no more fear of the activation rune, the heavy paper was just as harmless as any other rune, but he handled it delicately just the same.

"Is that actually a bomb?" Sorsha asked, starting to lean forward, but catching herself at the last minute.

"Very much so," Iggy said, examining the rune on the folded piece of paper.

Alex leaned in as well, taking in the form of the construct and the runes used in its creation.

"It's not based on Arlo's design," he concluded, after studying it for a few moments.

"Nor yours," Iggy agreed. "This is something different."

"How did our guy do it?" Alex wondered. The construct had a similar shape to the one he'd made from Arlo's template, but there were several symbols that didn't seem to fit.

"It's raw, like Arlo's was," Iggy said, examining it closely, "but there's an elegance to the conversion of magic that's beyond Mr. Harper's skills."

"The line work's good too," Alex observed, tracing the outer circle of the construct with his finger. Normally, coming into physical contact with a rune like that would make his finger tingle from the magic, but with the damnation rune in place, there was nothing beyond the feel of the paper.

A flash of bitter anger erupted in his mind and Alex felt his jaw tighten. He did his level best to keep an expression of his feelings off his face, but he must have failed, because Iggy's eyebrows rose almost imperceptibly.

"You know," his mentor said, standing up straight again. "It's going to take me hours to decode this, why don't you take Sorsha somewhere for a nice dinner?"

Alex felt his face flush and he was about to protest, but Sorsha laid a firm hand on his arm.

"I think that's an excellent suggestion," she said, pulling Alex around to face her. "I did come all this way, the least you can do is take me out."

Caught, and with no good excuses for staying with Iggy, Alex could only nod his agreement.

"Good," she said. "You go put on your tuxedo while I go return Sherry and Michael to your office."

Since Sorsha had a reserved table at the Rainbow Room whenever she wanted it, Alex told the cabbie to take them there. In the back of his mind, he thought that this would get them in and out the quickest as well. It wasn't that he didn't want to spend time with Sorsha, but he really wanted to get back to the boom rune. When he had his magic, Iggy would never have sidelined him. Even without it, Alex still knew how runes were constructed, so he wasn't dead weight.

"It's not like I'm useless," he grumbled under his breath.

"What are you stewing about?" Sorsha demanded, arms folded in the seat next to him. "I get the feeling you're not taking me seriously."

There was only the barest hint of an edge in her voice, but in Alex's experience, that was enough.

"I'm sorry," he said, taking her hand. "It's just that Iggy sent me away when there's work to be done."

"Because your magic is sealed away," Sorsha stated, leaning in so the cabbie wouldn't overhear.

Alex ground his teeth. It didn't sound any better when she said it.

"Or, perhaps the doctor simply wished to work on the rune in peace," Sorsha went on. "Without me there to ask a million questions."

Alex didn't believe that, but he couldn't deny that Iggy liked to work in silence, and Sorsha didn't. It was a good enough excuse.

For the moment, he thought.

"Good," Sorsha said, correctly reading the expression on his face. "Now we can enjoy our evening."

"Here you go, folks," the cabbie said as the car began to decelerate. "Rockefeller Center."

Alex paid the man, being sure to tip him well, then exited the car and extended his hand to help Sorsha out. They'd barely crossed the sidewalk to the ground floor entrance, when a half-dozen news photographers rushed at them with their cameras flashing.

"Ignore them," Sorsha said, fixing a cold, imperious look on her face.

Alex knew that look, Sorsha had carefully cultivated it to reinforce her Ice Queen persona. It gave anyone seeing her the idea that she was aloof and powerful, someone not to be trifled with.

For his own part, Alex simply let his features go slack, showing no emotion at all. It wouldn't make for a good picture in tomorrow's paper, but he could hardly grin like an idiot next to his sorceress girlfriend.

"Don't worry," Sorsha said, guessing at his thoughts. "They can take some pictures of us enjoying ourselves once we're inside."

"How are we going to eat with the photographers around?" he asked.

When Alex had first started going out in public with Sorsha, she'd impressed on him the rule that he must never be photographed while eating.

"They'll get a picture of you with your mouth open about to shovel something inside," she warned him. *"You'll be on the front page looking the fool."*

"The Rainbow Room keeps a tight leash on them," Sorsha said as they boarded the elevator. "They won't let photographers over until we're finished. I am surprised you thought of that, though," she went on. "You usually don't eat much when we go out."

"I'm usually too busy staring at you."

Sorsha smirked and almost laughed.

"Flatterer," she accused.

Alex held back a smile. He'd been waiting for an occasion to use that line.

As he expected, the moment the elevator arrived, the Maître d' was waiting to whisk them off to Sorsha's favorite table in the back corner. Alex always wondered how whoever was on staff at the Rainbow Room managed to anticipate Sorsha's arrival so expertly. Someone from the ground floor must phone ahead if they see a celebrity going up.

"Now," Sorsha said, once the waiter had taken their orders. "How is it you came to know about my father's death?"

In the shuffle of the last two days, Alex had quite forgotten his conversation with Nils Eccles and the report of Roland Eccles death.

"Is your name really Kjirsten?" he asked.

Sorsha actually gasped at that and pale light flashed in her eyes. She took a deep breath, then let it out slowly before speaking.

"You will never utter that name in my presence again," she said.

Alex expected to hear a threat in that sentence, but instead it sounded a bit like a plea.

"Why?" he said without thinking. "Uh, I mean, it sounds like a perfectly good name."

"I have my reasons," was all she would say.

"All right," Alex agreed. "As to how I know about your father, your brother, Nils, came to my office. He was trying to find you."

Sorsha gave Alex a patronizing look.

"No he wasn't," she said with utter confidence. "My brother is a con man, trained by one of the best in the business."

"Your father?" Alex guessed.

"Exactly. If he came to you, instead of going to my very public office, it's because he wanted to get you on his side of whatever scam he's running."

"I did look in the papers," Alex said, feeling the need to defend himself. "Your father, Roland Eccles, died on Monday and his funeral is Saturday."

"I'm not blaming you," Sorsha said, reaching out to put her hand on his. "It's just been a long time since I thought about my family."

"If your brother is actually running some kind of scam, I expect he'll be back at some point to find out if you're going to attend your father's funeral."

Sorsha scoffed but an angry shadow crossed her face.

"If I want to spit on the old man's grave, I've got another hundred years or so to get around to it." The words were fiery, but Sorsha said them with no emotion in her voice.

"What happened between you?" Alex wondered.

"It's not very good table conversation," Sorsha said. "I'll tell you the story someday, but not tonight. Tonight I want to enjoy the music and the food and maybe dance a little."

"I'm sorry," Alex said, squeezing her hand. "If I'd known how much this would upset you, I'd have thrown Nils out on his ear."

"Nils isn't so bad," Sorsha said, a soft smile playing across her lips. "He was the only one who was kind to me, especially after the death of our mother."

Alex suddenly felt like a heel. He'd researched Roland's death, but hadn't gone any further. He knew from the obituary that Sorsha had a sister named Mia, but no other family members had been mentioned.

"Were you close to your mother?" he asked, genuinely curious.

Sorsha nodded.

"We had many things in common," she said. "Not least of which was a hatred of my father. It was just after she died that I came into my power."

Alex wondered if that particular traumatic event was what prompted Sorsha's elevation, but he decided he'd pushed his luck far enough and kept that thought to himself.

Before they had time to change to a less invasive subject, their food arrived and after that, Sorsha insisted on dancing for an hour. Alex had been so irritated with Iggy that he'd forgotten his cane at home and had to simply suffer through the dances. By the time Sorsha led them back to their table, he was limping heavily.

"Your foot seems to be getting better," Sorsha observed as he slid down into his chair. "You held up quite well."

As sore as it was, Alex had to admit, he didn't really miss his cane until toward the end of their dancing.

Sorsha reached out her empty hand, then closed it, pulling a long wooden cane out of thin air. It was a dark color, though whether it was mahogany or just stained that way, Alex couldn't tell.

"Here," she said, passing it over. "You can use this when we leave."

Alex accepted the offering and leaned it up against the table.

"How much longer do you want to stay?" he asked. "I think I'm through dancing for the night."

"I want some champagne and I want to just listen to the music," she said, stretching luxuriously. "You can bring your chair over to this side of the table and we can watch the band together."

"That's going to make for interesting pictures tomorrow," Alex warned.

"I don't care," Sorsha said, irritation in her voice. "I'm tired of having to sneak around like we aren't an item."

"It was your idea," Alex reminded her.

"Well, I've changed my mind," she insisted. "I'm a woman, we're allowed to do that."

"Does this mean I can take you back to your office when we're done here," he said with a smirk, "and then accompany you to your castle?"

"Of course not," Sorsha said, leaning against him once his chair was in position. "Quite apart from the scandalous headlines that would generate, you'd be completely useless to me."

Alex gave her a raised eyebrow and a challenging look.

"You know very well that you won't be any good to anyone until you've gone back to the brownstone and consulted with Dr. Bell over that rune."

Alex chuckled and put his arm around Sorsha's shoulders.

"You know me well," he said.

18

DECONSTRUCTION

Alex winced as he lifted himself out of the taxi in front of the brownstone. He'd been actively ignoring his injured foot all afternoon and into the evening. It hadn't really bothered him most of that time, but now it felt like he had a thumbtack sticking up through the bottom of his shoe.

"You overdid it," he told himself as he took the stairs one at a time, always leading with his uninjured right foot. At least he was home where he could take some aspirin and put his foot up. "Assuming Iggy's finished with the boom rune," he added.

"You look like you had a good time," Iggy observed as Alex came limping through the vestibule.

His mentor was wearing his purple smoking jacket with a cup of tea in one hand and a newspaper under the opposite arm.

"Since you're heading for your reading chair, I assume you're done with the rune?" Alex said.

"Indeed," he replied, "I left my notes on the table in the kitchen, but based on how badly you're limping, I'd say you need to sit down more than I do. So you sit and I'll retrieve the notes."

Alex wanted to disagree, but his foot wouldn't let him.

As he eased into his reading chair, Iggy set down his tea and paper, then headed back to the kitchen. While he waited, Alex used the borrowed cane to pull the ottoman close enough to rest his sore foot. He absently wished he'd poured himself a whisky before he sat, but he'd already had a few drinks when he was out with Sorsha, so that probably wasn't the best of ideas. He'd need his wits sharp to go over the boom rune with Iggy.

"Have a look at this," his mentor said as he returned from the kitchen. He handed Alex a flip notebook as he passed by on the way to his chair.

Alex flipped open the black cover of the book and scanned the first page. Iggy had made a drawing of the construct with capital letters in place of the individual runes that made it up.

"Seven runes?" Alex said out loud.

"Whoever your bomber is, I'd say he's a devotee of the rune prime theory," Iggy said, sipping his tea.

There were many theories about how runic constructs should be composed for maximum effectiveness. As far as the reality of it, there just wasn't enough evidence to say that any particular structure worked better than any other. The rune prime theory stated that the total number of runes in any given construct should be a prime number. This didn't apply to the smaller groups of runes, called nodes, within the construct, because most of the time when you added two primes, you got a non-prime number, which would mess up the whole thing. Alex always thought that to be a flaw in the theory, but advocates for the prime theory simply ignored it.

As far as Alex could tell, there was no measurable advantage to the rune prime theory. His father's runes had been a jumbled mess and they worked just fine for what they were. Iggy had changed all that when he took Alex in. For Iggy, there was only one proper way to write runes, the rule of three.

As the name implied, the rule of three was an aesthetic that balanced nodes and constructs in multiples of three. Alex had never heard that it made runic constructs more powerful, or easier to write, but it did make constructs more balanced and, in Iggy's opinion at least, more artistic. For all his blustering about being a proper runewright, he put a lot of effort into having his work look nice.

In the early days, Alex argued with him about that affectation, but the older he got, the more he realized that when people saw a good looking, precisely written rune, the more faith they had in it. That didn't make the rune more powerful, of course, but it helped people want to do business with him.

Alex studied Iggy's deconstruction of the boom rune. The first page of the notebook held only the connection lines, the runes themselves were represented by numbers. Turning to the next page, Alex found the names of the runes along with the numbers representing them.

"He's used a flame rune as the base?" Alex said as he finished absorbing Iggy's drawings.

"Fascinating, isn't it?" Iggy said, blowing out a cloud of cigar smoke.

"How is he powering the explosion?" Alex asked, more to himself than to his mentor.

Flame runes were common enough, the rune would ignite when triggered and burn with a hot flame for around a minute. It wasn't really used much due to the fact that the flame wasn't hot enough to weld with, so all it was really good for was starting a normal fire. With the advent of boiler stones, they weren't even used to light boilers anymore. The government issued them in every soldier's field kit in case they had to start a fire in a downpour, but other than that, few people used them. You could simply get a book of matches for a penny, after all.

Alex flipped back to the front page of the notebook and traced the lines of incidence with his finger. In a runic construct, the lines and symbols connecting the runes themselves controlled the flow of magic through the construct. The lines of incidence controlled when the individual runes activated and what other runes they connected to. It was these lines that controlled how the magic manifested and what form it took.

"This doesn't make any sense," Alex declared, "he's got three different tap runes connected to each other and all feeding into a damper that's connected back into the loop."

Iggy blew out another cloud of cigar smoke and nodded.

"I figure he'd be able to loop the magical energy around three times before the damper rune failed," he said.

Alex nodded, finally seeing how the unknown runewright had done it.

"The power builds geometrically each time the magic goes around the loop," he said. "By the time the damper fails, it's enough to overcharge the flame rune and cause an explosion."

"Just so."

Alex wasn't convinced.

"Are you sure this would even work?" he asked, looking up at Iggy.

A look of smug satisfaction crossed his mentor's face and the old man nodded.

"I made one of this exact construct with a weaker damper rune," he explained. "It would serve as an excellent firecracker. I have no doubt that the full version would produce a satisfactorily destructive explosion."

Alex thought about that for a moment. It wasn't the way he did it, nor the way Arlo Harper had done it, but all that really mattered was that it worked.

"These looping pathways," he said, touching the drawing Iggy had made. "They'd have to be exact to get the same explosion each time, right?"

Iggy thought about that, then nodded his ascent.

"That explains why the explosions have been different sizes," he said. "The first one, at Reggie Aspler's office, was smaller than the second one. That one blew the front right off Matthew McDermet's potion shop."

"What about the last one?" Iggy asked.

"It made a wreck of Professor Rodger's office," Alex said, "but that was a small room in a small house."

"You assumed the size was some sort of commentary on the bomber's state of mind?"

"Or his relationship with the victims," Alex added. "Now it looks like it might just have been variations in the way he wrote the rune."

"Well, we can make several deductions based on what we know,"

Iggy said. "First, whoever your bomber is, they're an exceptionally talented runewright."

Alex nodded in agreement.

"Someone like that is going to be relatively easy to find," he said. "They will have made their mark on their profession."

"Something they thought up is bound to be in common use," Iggy agreed, "you just need to find it."

Alex thought about that. Apart from Iggy's finding rune, he'd encountered the works of many talented runewrights in his career. The murdered runewright Fredrick Chance had created the construct that made Waverly Radios reception so clear. Then there was Marnie Talbot, who managed to brew exceptional coffee thanks to some fairly basic, but well used, runic lore. Even Bradly Elder, the runewright who had preceded Alex in Andrew Barton's employ, had designed a construct that would allow him to absorb enough magic to become a literal god.

As Alex ran through the mental list, one thing became abundantly clear.

"This might be harder than we think," he sighed, resting his elbow on the chair and his cheek in his palm.

"How so?" Iggy asked, genuinely curious.

Alex reiterated the list he'd just recalled.

"You mean that all of those people were virtual nobodies, despite their skill," Iggy concluded.

"Yep. Our bomber could be laboring away at some highly specialized job, doing amazing work, but getting no outside recognition."

"In that case," Iggy said after a moment's thought, "You'll have to figure out what the victims have in common."

"Assuming they have anything in common," Alex said.

"Tosh," Iggy scoffed. "Of course they have things in common. All of the victims were in positions of authority, all of them were older, and all of them were men."

"Jealous lover?" Alex quipped with a smirk.

"Hardly," Iggy replied. "What girl goes from a captain of industry, to a cheapskate potion dealer, to a college professor just a few years from retirement?"

The old man had a point. That didn't sound like the success track an ambitious young woman would take.

"So, whoever it is," Alex surmised, "it's likely they have, or had, some professional connection to the victims. Maybe he took Professor Rodgers' class in college, then worked for McDermet and Aspler."

"What about working together?" Iggy suggested. "Aspler is the kind of man who could afford to fund magical research projects."

"Detweiler and I thought of that," Alex said. "He's got one of the boys from accounting going over Reggie's books."

"Well, let's hope that yields some fruit," Iggy said. "In the meantime, keep looking for exceptional runewrights. Whoever did this is good, and someone must know him."

Alex thought about his visit to the Office of Magical Oversight. The girl there had known him, but his name was in the papers a few times a year. Whoever the bomber was, they had a much lower profile. That meant the newspapers weren't likely to be much help either.

"I'll go down to Runewright Row tomorrow," he said. "There's always lots of gossip there."

"An excellent plan," Iggy said, tapping out the stub of his cigar. "How did it go with Sorsha this evening? She seemed especially agitated with you earlier."

Alex chuckled at that. Sorsha had been way past agitated.

"It wasn't me," he defended himself.

"The news about her father's death," Iggy said, nodding sagely.

"Surprisingly not," Alex countered. "She was very explicit that she didn't care at all that her old man took a dirt nap. I think she was more angry that I'd been drawn into her family affairs."

"All you did was meet her brother and look up the obituary," Iggy said.

"That was enough."

"Did she say why that was so upsetting?"

Alex sighed and shrugged.

"Just that her father, Roland Eccles, was a con man," Alex said, "and that her brother Nils was an apple that fell pretty close to the tree."

"Well, the funeral is tomorrow," Iggy observed. "After that I don't think you'll have occasion to see Mr. Eccles further."

Alex wondered about that, but decided not to waste his thoughts on the subject.

"If there's nothing else," Iggy said, standing and stretching. "I believe I shall go to bed."

"What if someone slips another letter bomb under our door during the night?" Alex asked, only half in jest.

"In that case," Iggy said, "the vestibule is more than capable of containing the blast."

Alex chuckled at that. Like many homes in frigid New York, the brownstone had a vestibule to keep cold winter air from getting into the house proper when someone opened the front door. It was a decorative space, meant to be welcoming, with a map of Manhattan laid out on the tiled floor and glass panels that looked in on the foyer. The inside door had a wooden frame but with glass panels instead of wood. To the untrained eye, it didn't appear capable of stopping a determined child. That was utterly incorrect, of course, since the glass was stronger than steel, thanks to the runes that were present, but beyond normal vision.

Vision, Alex thought.

"One more thing," he said as Iggy headed for the stairs. "I learned something interesting about the curse stones today."

This brought Iggy up short and he turned with a look of profound interest on his face.

"The book I was looking for, the one about the Inquisition in France," he began. "Theo Bell found someone with a copy."

Iggy inclined his head, then moved back to his chair.

"Perhaps you'd better tell me all about it, then."

Alex went on to relate what they'd learned from the passages Theo's friend had read him about the vision stone, its supposed power, and its rumored fate. When he finished, Iggy paused for a moment, then rose and moved to the liquor cabinet.

"Care for a belt?" he asked, pouring himself two fingers of twelve-year-old Scotch.

"Do I need one?"

Iggy didn't answer, just set out another glass and poured two fingers' worth.

"Here," he said, moving back to his chair. He set the glass down on the reading table between their chairs and pushed it toward Alex. "I assume," Iggy went on, "that you're telling me this in the hope of enticing me to regale you with tales of my days in the Masonic order."

Alex took a sip of the Scotch and shrugged.

"The thought crossed my mind."

"Well, prepare to be disappointed," Iggy said. "Most of the things we talked about in the lodge dealt with charity work."

"So no trips to some forgotten ruin to see a magic crystal?" Alex asked, managing to sound only a little disappointed.

"If there'd been some of that, I would have attended the meetings more often," Iggy admitted.

"So why the somber tone and the Scotch?" Alex asked. "Not that I mind."

"The one thing I did find interesting in the Masonic tradition is all the symbolism," Iggy said. "Much of their lore is preserved in stories, rituals, and symbols."

"I take it you're not telling me this for rhetorical reasons," Alex prompted when his mentor stopped.

"Don't rush an old man, boy," he said with mock irritation.

Finally, after what seemed like a full minute, Iggy got up and walked to the bookshelves on the left side of the fireplace. Selecting a thin, leather-bound volume, he paged through it for a moment, then turned back to Alex.

"Take a look at this," he said, handing over the book.

On the left-hand page were two circles, one with an eagle behind a shield painted with the American flag and the other with an Egyptian pyramid surrounded by Latin text.

"What's..." he paused, leaning down to read the tiny text under the illustration, "the Great Seal of the United States?"

"Technically it's the coat of arms of this country," Iggy explained. "Like in former days, the seal is a stamp that can be put on official documents to authenticate them."

"Why are there two of them?"

"The one with the pyramid is the obverse side of the seal."

"How does a stamp have a back side?" Alex asked.

"The design is more like a coin than a stamp, even though the actual use is a stamp with the front side on it."

"That makes no sense," Alex said.

"We're getting off track," Iggy said, reaching over the top of the book to tap the picture of the pyramid. "What do you notice about this?" he said.

"There's an eyeball on top of it," Alex said, knowing he'd seen that before.

"It's on the back of the one-dollar bill," Iggy supplied, correctly guessing Alex's question.

"What does it mean?"

"Can you translate the Latin above it?" Iggy said, ignoring Alex.

Iggy had forced Alex to learn Latin during their early days, but he hadn't used it in quite some time.

"Annuit coeptis," he read. "Something about good fortune?"

"Loosely translated, it means 'fortune favors us,'" Iggy explained. "It refers to the eye at the top of the pyramid."

"So it's a Masonic symbol?" Alex guessed.

"It is," Iggy said. "It's known as the eye of providence, and the superscription indicates that favors America."

"So, what you're saying is that this eye of providence could be a representation of the vision stone," Alex said. "Does that mean that the founding fathers had it?"

Iggy waggled his eyebrows at Alex, then shrugged.

"I can't say one way or the other," he admitted, "but I have always wondered how a bunch of farmers and tradesmen could beat the best trained, best equipped army on the planet during the war of independence."

It took Alex a full ten seconds to wrap his mind around that concept before he could speak again.

"Does this mean the government has it now?"

"Based on the market crash of twenty-nine, I'd say not," Iggy said, "but I suspect some of America's founding fathers did. It's no coincidence that they put the eye of providence atop that pyramid."

"It could easily be a coincidence," Alex said. "Lots of the founders were Freemasons, including Ben Franklin. They would have known about the eye since you said it's a Masonic symbol."

"Possibly," Iggy admitted, "but let me give you one more piece of information you might find interesting. The eye of providence has another name, a less formal name, in masonic tradition."

"Yes?" Alex prodded when Iggy didn't continue.

"It's also known as the 'all seeing eye'."

19

TIZZY

Alex had been up for hours after his discussion with Iggy. He sat in his reading chair, going over what he'd learned until the wee hours. When his alarm clock rang at six-thirty the following morning, he simply turned it off, rolled over, and went back to sleep. By the time a knock came on his door, the clock read nine-twenty.

"Iggy?" he asked, not being able to imagine who else might be at his bedroom door.

"Are you dead in there?" his mentor's voice demanded.

Alex's tired mind took a moment to process the words before he was able to mumble a response.

"Give me a minute and I'll let you know."

There was a click and Iggy opened the door. He carried a tray in one hand with a coffee cup and a covered dish on it.

"At least your sense of humor seems to have survived," he said, setting the tray down on the bedside table. "I was starting to worry."

"Why didn't Sherry call?" Alex mumbled, swinging his legs out of bed so he could stand.

"She did," Iggy said. "After it rang a half-dozen times, I picked it up downstairs."

That got Alex's attention. The candlestick phone on his bedside table was loud when it rang and only two feet from his head. He must really have been exhausted to have slept through it.

"Thanks," Alex said, finding it difficult to keep his balance as he stood up. "I…I'll shower then head over there, unless there's something urgent."

"Other than your absence, nothing is out of the ordinary," Iggy said. "I've brought you some breakfast, so eat that while it's hot, then shower and get on with your day."

Alex dropped back down onto the bed, then pulled the tray closer and uncovered two soft-boiled eggs, with sausages and toast.

"Rough night?" Iggy asked, sitting in the reading chair while Alex ate.

"Couldn't sleep," he managed.

"Yes," Iggy said, "I should imagine not. I, myself, had difficulty getting to sleep, but a nightcap with a bit of valerian in it helped immensely."

Alex took a swig of the coffee in the ceramic cup and wished he'd thought of that.

"Did you figure out what to do next?" Iggy asked when Alex didn't respond.

That was a good question. Yesterday he was at loggerheads with his cases but now he had some decent leads.

"I wanted to go over to Aspler Shipping and review their new projects file," he said between bites of egg.

"I thought Lieutenant Detweiler had people doing exactly that," Iggy said.

"He does," Alex confirmed. "That's why I'll probably spend the day talking to a couple of celebrity tennis players instead. I'd like to look into the vision stone more, but short of breaking into the local Masonic Temple, I don't know what to do."

"I had a thought about that," Iggy said, taking out his cigarette case. "After our discussion last night, I'm fully convinced that Benjamin Franklin must have known about the vision stone. It seems clear to me that the leaders of the revolution had access to it and, if the Masons had it, Franklin would have known."

It made sense. Franklin was one of the most prominent figures of the Revolutionary War, and one of the most senior statesmen. If anyone had access to the stone, it would have been him.

"How does that help us?" Alex said, feeling fully awake at last.

"We know that Franklin had the Archimedean Monograph," Iggy said, as if that explained it all.

"We've been through the monograph backwards and forwards," Alex pointed out. "There's no reference in there to the vision stone."

Iggy lit his cigarette with a match, then blew out a puff of smoke.

"Have you ever heard of the concept of synchrony?"

Alex hadn't and he said so.

"It's the name for things that seem to be linked together, but are, in fact random," Iggy explained. "For example, have you ever been looking for someone with a distinct feature, like a Van Dyke beard or red hair? What happens?"

Alex nodded, starting to catch on.

"One time I was looking for a left-handed man with a limp," he said. "I found twenty of them before I ran into the right one. It's like suddenly they were everywhere."

Iggy nodded.

"You have your brain to answer for that," he said. "Those twenty people were always there, but you weren't looking for them, so your brain filtered out those particularities."

Alex thought about that for a minute.

"You're saying that maybe Ben Franklin, or some of the other authors of the monograph did write about the vision stone—"

"Likely in very indirect ways," Iggy added.

"But, because we weren't looking for magical, future-seeing stones, we didn't recognize it."

"Precisely," Iggy said as Alex polished off the last of the sausages. "So, while you shower and pursue Mr. Leavitt's killer, I'll go back through the monograph and see if there's anything helpful there."

Alex wasn't sure he liked that idea. Iggy had a history of hiding things he judged that Alex wasn't ready for. Still, it wasn't a bad idea, and he could always go through the monograph himself later.

"Sounds good," Alex said, returning the now empty plate to the tray. "Now, I need to get to work."

Half an hour later, Alex limped through the cover door that separated his vault from his office. Sitting behind his large desk, he keyed the intercom twice in quick succession to let Sherry know he was in.

"Everything okay, boss?" her voice came back at him from the little speaker on the intercom.

"Yes," he replied. "I just had a late night. Is there anything pressing?"

"No," she said. "So far no one's called for you. I put the numbers for those tennis agents on your desk if you still want to talk to their clients."

"Thanks, doll," he said, then released the talk button.

He had a momentary thought of calling Danny to see if the lab boys had found the poisoned bottle of vermouth yet, but if they had, Danny would have already called him. Alex even considered calling Lieutenant Detweiler, but there really wasn't anything more they could do, and the irascible man would just yell at Alex for bothering him.

With a sigh, Alex picked up the phone and dialed the agent for Lizzy Tizzy.

Elizabeth Tisdale was originally from Boston and maintained a home there. When she came to New York, she stayed in the Grand Imperial Hotel, a small but well-appointed lodging near the theater district. It was just before noon when Alex rode the elevator up to the hotel's top floor.

Miss Tisdale's room was a suite in the farthest corner from the elevator and, when Alex knocked, the door was opened by a handsome woman in her late thirties, with shoulder length brown hair and a serious face.

"Mrs. Tisdale?" Alex asked, remembering that Lizzy Tizzy traveled with her mother.

"Are you the detective?" the woman demanded.

Alex handed over one of his cards, which the woman studied intently for almost a full minute before she stepped back from the door.

"Come in, then," she said.

Alex stepped inside and was surprised by the room. He'd been in suites before, but this one was tiny. Just a front room, a parlor, and a door that Alex presumed led to the bedroom. It was only slightly larger than the room he'd stayed in while he was in Washington D.C. with Andrew Barton.

"Who was that?" a young sounding voice called from the bedroom.

"The private detective is here," the older woman said, her tone conveying that she'd just discovered dog excrement on her shoe.

A moment later a young, fit woman came bounding out of the bedroom. Her hair was the same brown as her mother's, but darker as it was still wet. Based on the steam coming from the now open bedroom door, Alex guessed that she'd just finished showering.

"Did I interrupt your practice?" he asked.

The girl looked startled for a second, then smiled and shook her head.

"I see why the police sent you," she said, her tone light and full of amusement.

She's supposed to have quite the temper, Alex reminded himself. That might not come up in an informal interview, but it was useful information nonetheless.

"I'm Alex Lockerby," he said, extending his hand to her.

She shook it and Alex was surprised at how firm her grip was.

"Lizzy," she introduced herself. "That's Mary, my mom."

Alex stuck out his hand to Mary, but she just rolled her eyes and headed across the parlor to a liquor cabinet.

"Mom's a little protective," Lizzy said, leaning in and keeping her voice low.

Alex could understand that; Lizzy was more than passingly attractive and she seemed to have the headstrong personality of someone who knows exactly what they want.

"So what is it the police want to know?" Lizzy said, moving to a comfortable looking couch in the parlor. She motioned for Alex to take the seat next to the couch and he sat.

"You know about the death of Ari Leavitt?" Alex asked. "The chair umpire for USLTA events."

"I heard he drowned," Lizzy said.

"Technically he did," Alex said, choosing his words carefully.

"What do you mean 'technically'?" Mary asked, from the far side of the room. She had appeared to not be listening as she made herself a cocktail.

"I mean," Alex replied, "that while Mr. Leavitt did drown, that was the result of someone poisoning him earlier in the evening."

"Poison?" Lizzy said, suddenly sitting up. "Why?"

"That's something I was hoping you could tell me," Alex said, keeping his voice calm and nonchalant. "Was there anyone who disliked Mr. Leavitt, or had a grudge against him?"

Lizzy scoffed and Mary gave her a hard look.

"Who didn't," the younger woman said with a flip of her wet hair. "The old geezer was blind as a bat, and there isn't a player on the circuit who hasn't had a bad call from him."

"Anyone hate him enough to want him dead?"

Lizzy outright laughed at that.

"Maybe in the heat of the moment," she said. "A lot gets said on the court."

"What about you?"

"Don't answer that," Mary snapped, her face going flushed. "He's trying to trick you."

Despite Mary's reaction, Lizzy didn't seem fazed at all.

"Did I want that old goat dead?" Lizzy asked. "No."

Alex was pretty good at reading people and Lizzy's response seemed legitimate.

"I heard he made a call that cost you a championship," Alex pressed.

"So have other umpires," Lizzy said with a shrug. "It's just part of the game."

"Did you attend the party at Beals Dalton's house?"

For some reason, this question made Lizzy grin. It wasn't the kind of grin one got from happiness, but rather one of mischief.

"Of course," she said, "but I'm sure you already knew that. Everyone who was anyone was there."

Alex caught the briefest movement in the background and shifted his gaze to Mary for a moment. The muscles in the older woman's face had tightened and her cheeks were flushed again.

"Did you see Ari at the party?"

Lizzy shook her head.

"I didn't notice him, but of course I was busy."

Mary's jaw clenched and Alex could see her knuckles whiten around the glass in her hand.

"Doing what?" he asked.

"I found this absolutely marvelous new player, from Romania," Lizzy said. "We spent most of the evening in each other's company."

"You speak Romanian?" Alex asked.

"No," Lizzy said with a languid smile. "But we weren't really talking."

Behind her, Mary was squeezing her glass so hard, Alex was afraid it would break. With each declaration from Lizzy, her mother had only gotten angrier.

She's trying to get a rise out of Mary, he thought.

Clearly the older woman was on the verge of a full-blown rage, but when her eyes met Alex's, she seemed to regain control of her temper.

"When did your mother insist that you leave the party?" Alex asked.

"What makes you think Mother was there?" she asked.

"The way you told the story," Alex replied, allowing himself a predatory grin of his own.

"It was around ten," she said.

That was too early to have poisoned Ari herself, but she could still have poisoned the bottle of vermouth. That would have been risky, though, since anyone could have used the tainted bottle. It was more likely that the killer had brought the bottle with them, then used it to make Ari's Manhattan for him after the party was over. Still, a bold poisoner might have spiked the bottle and not cared who drank from it.

So far Lizzy Tizzy is pretty bold, Alex thought.

"I think that's everything," Alex said, standing. "If the police have any more questions, I'm sure they'll contact you directly."

"Leaving so soon?" Lizzy said, not bothering to get up from the couch.

"I'm afraid so," Alex said.

He turned and headed for the door, but stopped before reaching it to turn back.

"Did you drink at the party, Miss Tisdale?" he asked.

"Of course," Lizzy said, "but only to excess."

That wasn't surprising; based on what Alex could tell about Mary, she had a tight leash on Lizzy before she turned eighteen. Now Lizzy seemed determined to flaunt her freedom in her mother's face.

"And do you mix your own drinks?" Alex continued.

Lizzy shook her head.

"No," she said with a dreamy sigh. "I haven't had enough practice."

Alex could believe that.

He thanked her again, including Mary this time, then let himself back out into the hall.

The lobby of the hotel had a row of telephone booths, so Alex stopped to call his office. It was a short call since Sherry had nothing new for him and within five minutes, Alex was on his way across town to the home of Freddy Hackett. Unlike Lizzy Tisdale, Freddy's family lived upstate, so when he started making money on the tennis circuit, he bought an apartment on the east side of Manhattan.

Half an hour after hailing a cab, Alex stepped onto the sidewalk in front of Freddy's building. It was at least fifteen stories with the modern look of a recently built structure. The same brown bricks that gave brownstones their name were used as decorative façades around windows and structural features. Looking north, Alex could see the Chrysler building stretching into the sky, and he remembered that he hadn't called Sorsha yet. She would be interested in his discussion with Iggy and keeping her waiting wouldn't make her happy.

Deciding to make her a priority, Alex entered the apartment building and moved to the pay phone in the lobby. After a few pleasantries exchanged with Inge Halverson, Sorsha's receptionist, the sorceress herself came on the line.

"How did you know I was deciding whether or not to be cross with you?" she asked in an amused voice.

"I'm blessed with good timing," he replied, letting a smile play across his face.

"So," Sorsha said after a short pause, "tell me what you and Dr. Bell found out about your homicidal missive."

Alex took a deep breath and walked Sorsha through their discussion.

"So you really don't know anything about the person who's trying to blow you up?" Sorsha concluded once Alex had relayed the entire story.

"Sorry," he said.

"So, you stayed up late talking with Dr. Bell," Sorsha assumed. "Since it clearly wasn't about exploding runes, what did the two of you find so fascinating?"

Alex hesitated. Sorsha knew about the cursed stones, of course, she'd been present when Alex found the original. This new information, about the vision stone, the Templar, and the Masons, was something he wanted to keep to himself. After another moment of hesitation, Alex took a deep breath and brought Sorsha up to speed on his discoveries.

"I don't like it," she said once he'd finished.

"Well, until I can talk to a Mason and find out what they know, I'm afraid that's all there is," Alex said.

"Tell me where you are," Sorsha said.

"Why?" Alex asked, genuinely curious.

He could hear Sorsha sigh on the other end of the line and he had a sudden mental picture of her pinching the bridge of her nose.

"Someone has been watching you on and off for months," she began. "You find this curse stone and someone kills poor Charles before he can tell you anything about it. Now you've learned about some mythical crystal ball and someone sends you a runic bomb through the mail. Am I the only one who sees a pattern here?"

Alex was certain that her question was rhetorical, so he didn't answer it.

"The watchers were thanks to that Jersey FBI man," Alex fished in his memory for a name, "Washburn."

"You think that," Sorsha countered, "but you don't know for sure."

"Then there's the bomb," Alex went on, ignoring her protest, "I'm working a case where someone is sending boom runes through the mail and I'm sent one. You don't have to be Sherlock Holmes to figure out where that came from."

There was a silence on the line and Alex could almost feel Sorsha stewing.

"Where...are...you?" she demanded again.

"I'm at an apartment building a few blocks south of your office," he said. "I'm about to interview a tennis pro named Freddy Hackett."

"Of the Long Island Hacketts?" Sorsha asked.

"You know them?"

"I seem to remember going to a party at their house back during Prohibition," she said. "I suppose it will be all right for you to talk to him without me."

"Got a meeting to go to?" Alex guessed.

"Yes," she growled. "It's only an hour, so when you're done with the tennis player, I want you to meet me here."

Alex wanted to argue, but with Sorsha there was no point. Once she'd made up her mind, that was it, and it wasn't wise to annoy a sorceress, even one that was in love with you.

"All right," he acquiesced. "I'll swing by as soon as I'm done."

20

KING OF THE CLAY

The apartment of Freddy Hackett was on the top floor of the building and the elevator was surprisingly slow. Alex figured the ride from Empire Station to his apartment on the Barton Electric residence level took less than half the time to go more than twice the distance.

When the elevator finally did arrive on the fifteenth floor of the building, Alex followed the hall around to the left and down to the end until he found Freddy's door. After a quick knock, a young man that looked to be in his early twenties opened the door. He had classically handsome features with a square jaw, complete with cleft chin, strong cheekbones, a narrow nose, and deep blue eyes.

"You the private dick?" he asked in a bored voice.

"Alex Lockerby," he said, sticking out his hand.

"Whatever," Freddy said, opening the door and turning back to the room. "The police already wasted an hour of my time, and now they say I have to talk to you, so let's get to it."

Alex shrugged and closed the door after stepping inside. Freddy was dressed in tennis shorts and a collared knit shirt with a towel around his neck. He had the long, lean muscled body of an endurance athlete, covered with a sheen of sweat like he'd just stepped off a court.

"Since the police already talked to you, I assume you know why I'm here," Alex began.

"That guy that drowned at the party in the Hamptons," Freddy said, rubbing his hair with the towel.

"Ari Leavitt," Alex supplied.

"Sure," Freddy said with a shrug. "I'll save you some time, I never saw him or the pool."

Alex gave the young man a hard look, then cleared his throat.

"But you were at the party, right?"

"Of course," Freddy said, sitting down in a chair made of woven wood strips. "All the important people in the tennis world were there."

"Did you know Ari Leavitt?"

"No."

"The man who cost you the win at nationals last year?" Alex pressed. "You don't remember him?"

"Ok, I remember him," Freddy said, an edge of irritation in his voice, "but I don't know him. He's just some official from the USLTA, why would I care about him?"

"Last year's loss springs to mind," Alex said, trying not to sound overly sarcastic.

"Lockerby, was it?" Freddy said. "Do you have any idea how many times I've lost games, lost championships, or lost opportunities?"

Alex didn't and he said so.

"I'm not some kid who had it easy," he growled, "I had to work for every inch of ground I got. Hell, I was kicked off my high school team. The coach said I'd never amount to even a mediocre player."

"Clearly he was wrong," Alex said, not sure where young Freddy was going with his tirade.

At that, Freddy calmed down immediately, and a wide smile spread across his face.

"No," he said, "he was right about me. Back then, I didn't have the skills to make it."

"So, what did you do?"

"I hit the clay," he said. "Our neighbor had a tennis court and my mother convinced him to let me use it. I was out there for hours after school, running laps around the court or hitting balls from the machine. The only problem was the court didn't have lights, so I had to come in when it got dark."

Alex didn't want to be impressed, but that kind of dedication took effort, mental as well as physical.

"So you got on the team the next year," Alex guessed.

Freddy chuckled to himself.

"No," he said. "I was so bad the previous year, the coach didn't even let me try out."

Now Alex was confused.

"Mom and I were going to go over his head to the principal, but one of the other kids on the team got hit by a car when he was running in the dark. He was okay, but it broke his leg. After that, coach gave me another chance. By the end of that year, I was the third best player on the team."

The kid had work ethic, no doubt about that, but he rattled off the high school kid's injuries as if they were nothing. Alex made a note of that in his book.

"How does that translate to you not taking last year's loss personally?" he asked.

Freddy shrugged again, looking bored.

"Losses happen," he said. "The only thing you can do is work harder and come back better. Speaking of that, I need to get back to work, I've got a court on the roof and it's time to hit some balls."

"One more thing," Alex said as Freddy stood up. "Did you drink a lot at the party?"

Freddy laughed at that, but his cheeks got a bit pink.

"I was smashed before nine," he admitted. "A couple of the other guys had to carry me up to my room."

"You stayed at the Dalton home?"

Freddy nodded.

"Beals always invites the top players to stay at his house," he said. "Wouldn't want any of us getting picked up by the local cops for driving drunk."

Alex could only imagine the headlines.

"If that's all, Lockerby, I really need to get back to work."

Alex flipped his notebook closed and stood.

"Thanks for talking to me," he said, then headed for the door. "I'll see myself out."

Alex's interview with Freddy didn't last as long as he thought it would, so Alex arrived in Sorsha's office on the sixty-fifth floor of the Chrysler Building ahead of schedule. Since he had access directly to Sorsha's office through his vault, it had been a while since he'd been to her lobby. The only thing that seemed to have changed was that the front office secretary, Inge, was wearing clothes that bordered on baggy. That was out of place for her. Alex couldn't remember a time when the slim blonde wasn't clad in a form-fitting dress.

Tightening his focus, Alex noticed that her fingers appeared to be a bit swollen. Normally that might be a symptom of weight gain, but there was no alteration in Inge's face. Glancing at the base of the desk, he could see that the secretary had taken her shoes off, and that they were flats rather than her usual pumps.

"Hello, Inge," he said when he reached her desk. "Sorsha said to meet her here."

"She's still in a meeting," Inge said with a radiant smile. "Are you going to wait or do you want me to give her a message?"

"I'll wait," Alex said. He started to turn toward the part of the reception area where they had couches and chairs, but stopped halfway. "On second thought, I think I'll go down to the lobby and make a few phone calls. I'll be back in fifteen minutes or so."

"Don't be ridiculous," Inge said. "You can use the telephone in the conference room."

"Isn't that where Sorsha is having a meeting?"

"No, she's in her office."

"Okay," Alex said, glad to not have to spend the nickel on the call. He turned toward the back of the offices.

"Wait," Inge said, pushing herself up from the desk. "It's locked."

She bent stiffly, and pulled a ring of keys out of her desk. When she straightened up, Alex knew why she had changed her wardrobe. It wasn't much, but she was showing signs of motherhood.

"How are things with you and David?" he asked as she led him through the office. He knew she'd been married about a year ago because he'd attended the wedding with Sorsha.

Instead of answering, Inge blushed a bit and unconsciously touched her abdomen.

"He's been promoted at work," she said. "Now he's the sales rep for the northern midwest."

David Halverson worked for U.S. Steel. He'd met Inge when he arranged to sell Sorsha the steel bars she used in making her cold disks.

"So, Sorsha's going to have to get a new secretary?" Alex asked.

Inge blushed furiously at that.

"There's still a few months before that becomes necessary," she said. "Here we are."

She stopped in front of a door that consisted of a thin wooden frame around an enormous panel of frosted glass. Deftly inserting the key, she turned it and pushed the door open, stepping back for Alex.

"Take all the time you need," she said. "When Miss Kincaid gets out of her meeting, I'll tell her you're here."

Alex thanked her and shut the door as she withdrew.

He hadn't been in Sorsha's conference room for years, but it looked pretty much the way he remembered it. A large, oval table dominated the center of the space, with padded, high-backed chairs all around it. In the center of the table stood a sculpture made out of glass that resembled a spire of ice or crystal. Other than that, the polished table was unadorned. A large window dominated one wall, giving a spectacular view of the west side of Manhattan, and several chairs had been set up, facing out, no doubt for more intimate discussions. A liquor cabinet stood against the back wall and a small desk was nearby, opposite the windows. Alex knew from experience that the desk was there so a secretary could take minutes and other notes during meetings.

It also had a telephone on a shelf under the desk.

Moving over to the secretary desk, Alex took out his notebook and sat down. Beneath the desk were two shelves, one above the other. On the top shelf was a new, rotary-style phone with a unified handset, and below it was a compact stenotype machine. Apparently Inge had picked up some new skills when it came to taking notes.

Moving the phone from its shelf up to the desk, Alex picked up the handset and dialed the operator, giving her the exchange for the Midnight Sun.

"Tasker," Billy's voice greeted him.

"It's me, Alex," he said. "Did you find out anything about those two tennis pros?"

"Not really," Billy said. "I've mostly been focused on a string of bombings throughout the city. You wouldn't know anything about that, would you, old friend?"

Alex could tell just from the tone in Billy's voice that he'd been found out.

"That's supposed to be a secret," he growled.

"The bombings?" Billy scoffed. "It's all over the morning papers."

"My involvement," Alex said. "That bit's not in the papers, I checked. How did you find out?"

"One of my boys saw you leaving the home of Professor Brian Rogers yesterday. I'm wounded you didn't tell me about all this."

"You know the drill," Alex said. "When I'm on the Central Office's dime, I can't say anything."

"That's never stopped you before," Billy shot back.

"Sure it has," Alex retorted. "I don't bring hot stories to you until I get the okay from the police or my clients. I'm just good at convincing them that controlling the press is better than letting the story get out naturally."

"Is that what I am?" Billy said, "your way of spinning a story?"

"Of course you are, and you know it," Alex said. "Now can we get back to business?"

"Fine," Billy said, all traces of anger instantly gone from his voice.

Alex hadn't been worried his friend was seriously upset; news was all about telling a story, and the better the story, the more papers they sold. All Alex did was provide a good story so they didn't have to make up their own. Billy appreciated that and Alex knew it.

"So, when were you going to tell me about the bombings?" Billy asked.

"As soon as I know who's doing them," Alex said. "The other papers can print whatever sensational nonsense they want, but you'll get the details before them."

There was a pause and finally Billy acquiesced.

"What do you know about Lizzy Tizzy and Freddy Hackett?" Alex pressed.

"Not much," Billy said. "Hackett would make a good Cinderella story if his parents didn't live in a mansion upstate."

"How so?"

"I guess he wasn't a very good player when he started out, so he had to work hard to get where he's at," Billy said. "But nobody wants to read about a poor rich kid who had to practice to become the world's best tennis player."

Alex had to admit, coming from a rich family kind of took the Horatio Alger feel out of the story.

"What about Lizzy?"

"She's a different story," Billy said.

Alex could hear paper shuffling through the phone, then Billy went on.

"She comes from money too, but it seems like she's a real natural talent. Her mother had her entering tournaments when she was just fourteen."

"So nothing interesting," Alex sighed. Without a viable suspect in the murder of Ari Leavitt, he was back to square one.

Maybe Danny's having better luck, he thought.

"No," Billy said, pulling Alex wandering attention back to the conversation. "She's plenty interesting. My sports guy has done a bit of research on her, even been to see her play. He says that even though she's eighteen now, her mother is still running her tennis career."

"So?" Alex said. He already knew that, of course, from his interview with Lizzy herself.

"Apparently, Lizzy doesn't like it," Billy said, "not one bit."

"Why doesn't she fire her mother?" Alex asked. It was a harsh move, but Lizzy was a legal adult.

"There's some kind of contract that Lizzy signed when she was just starting out. It made her mother her agent and manager in perpetuity."

Alex made a note of that in his book.

"That might explain her attitude," he admitted.

"It explains more than that," Billy went on, "because last month she accused her mother of stealing money from her."

"If her mother is her manager, she would have had access to Lizzy's accounts while she was a minor."

"Exactly," Billy said. "My man did some digging and found out that the police investigated, but didn't find anything."

"Lizzy just made it up?"

"That's the interesting part. I know a guy at the bank Lizzy uses and he said there was money moved out of her account, but it wasn't moved into the mother's account. Someone took it out in cash."

Alex thought about that for a minute, remembering how Lizzy kept trying to get her mother's goat when he interviewed her.

"Sounds like Lizzy took the money," he said. "She's feathering a nest somewhere so she can get away from her mother."

"You think?" Billy replied. "That would be one hell of a story."

"I wouldn't run with that unless you had some proof," Alex said. "Lizzy seems like the kind of girl who would sue for libel."

"You bet," Billy said. "If you happen to find something in your investigation, be sure to let me know."

"You'll be the first," Alex promised. "If you hear anything more about Tisdale or Hackett, call my office and leave it with Sherry."

Billy agreed, then hung up.

"Well, that sounded like an interesting conversation," Sorsha's voice came from behind him.

He turned and found her leaning against the heavy conference table with her arms crossed. Today, she wore a dress with cap sleeves, a plunging neckline and a form-fitting waist that spread out into a loose skirt. It was almost as startling as Inge's attire had been. When at work, Sorsha usually wore a shirt and pants.

"You look nice," he said, rising.

"Did you expect something else?"

Alex crossed the intervening space and gave her a chaste kiss on the lips.

"No," he admitted, "but between you and Inge it's like the dress code changed around here. You don't happen to have the same issue as her, do you?"

Sorsha looked shocked for half a second, then snorted with laughter and covered her mouth.

"And if I did?" she challenged him once she'd regained her composure.

"Then I'd say we needed to move up our wedding."

Sorsha slipped her arm around his back and put her head on his shoulder.

"Good answer," she said. "And no, I am not, currently, with child."

Alex had been making light of the whole subject but he had to stop himself from trembling as a wave of relief washed over him.

"Now," Sorsha said, stepping away from him. "What are we investigating?"

Alex had forgotten the reason he'd come to Sorsha's office, and he had to force himself not to react. The prospect of spending the day with Sorsha wasn't exactly repulsive, but he disliked the thought of a babysitter.

Sorsha seemed to read those thoughts, and a predatory grin ghosted her lips.

"I was thinking about visiting a family upstate, and maybe a high school tennis coach."

Sorsha's smile slipped.

"Does that mean you want me to teleport us?"

Alex didn't like that idea any more than Sorsha did, but having her around meant he had access to her abilities.

"It would make the trip a lot faster," he said.

Before Sorsha could object, there was a polite knock on the door and Inge came in.

"I'm sorry to interrupt," she said, holding a folded note out to Alex, "but your secretary called. The police want you at this address."

Alex opened the paper and read the note as Inge withdrew.

"What is it?" Sorsha asked.

"Looks like we'll be spending the day in the city," he said. "You know that bomber I've been trying to track down? Well, they've struck again."

"Where?"
"The Office of Magical Oversight."
"Was anyone hurt?"
Alex handed the note to her.
"One person was injured," he said. "Two were killed."

21

RED TAPE

Alex offered Sorsha his hand as she got out of the cab in front of the government building that housed the Office of Magical Oversight. Even if Alex hadn't been there before, he couldn't have missed the blown-out window on the third floor. A white curtain hung out through the empty window and waved in the wind like a flag.

Sorsha followed his gaze upward and shivered. Despite the February weather, Alex knew she wasn't cold.

"You don't have to come up with me," he said as she took his arm.

"I appreciate your chivalry," she said, "but I'm a big girl."

Alex didn't press her; she had worked for the FBI, after all. He was sure she'd seen many unpleasant things during that time.

A uniformed policeman met them at the elevators and, after verifying Alex's identity, sent them up to the third floor.

When the elevator doors opened, Alex found the hall filled with debris. A janitor who probably worked in the building was sweeping up the bits of wood, glass, and paper. Several uniformed officers stood at the far end of the hall talking with a detective in a suit.

The place where the door for the Office of Magical Oversight once stood was a gaping hole and the smell of smoke permeated everything.

Being careful not to step on anything sharp, Alex headed for the scene, letting Sorsha trail behind him as he picked out a path.

"Lieutenant," the detective called toward the destroyed office, "your scribbler's here."

A moment later, the man himself appeared.

"Lockerby," Detweiler said in a relieved tone, "Am I glad to see you. The mayor has been all over my—"

He drew up short when Sorsha stepped out from behind Alex.

"Uh, M-Miss Kincaid," he stammered. "To, uh, to what do I owe the pleasure of your company?"

"Sorsha," Alex said, trying and failing to hide a smile of amusement, "this is Lieutenant James Detweiler of the Central Office of Police. Lieutenant, Sorsha Kincaid."

"Nice to meet you, Miss Kincaid," Detweiler said, the shock of seeing a sorceress at his crime scene having worn off.

"A pleasure," Sorsha responded. "Don't worry, Lieutenant," she continued, "I'm just here to keep an eye on Alex. He's been getting into more trouble than usual of late."

Detweiler raised an eyebrow at that, then looked to Alex.

"Our bomber sent one of his exploding letters to my office yesterday," he admitted.

"What," Detweiler said in a voice that clearly indicated that he'd have shouted it if Sorsha had not been present, "and you didn't call me?"

Alex shrugged.

"Doctor Bell and I managed to open it up without the rune exploding, but examining it didn't yield anything important. If we find a sample of this guy's runes, we can try to match it to the boom rune, but that's it."

Detweiler looked like he wanted to read Alex the riot act, but Sorsha's presence made him think twice.

"I want that letter for the evidence file," he growled.

"That's not a good idea," Alex said. "The boom rune is inherently unstable. Right now we've got the rune stored in a dampening field to make sure it's not a threat."

"The rune that was delivered with your mail?" Detweiler said, clearly not buying Alex's story.

"At that point, it was contained by an activation rune," Alex explained. "We had to remove that to open the envelope. In its current state, anything could set it off."

"Define anything," Detweiler said.

"Dropping it on the floor," Alex said with a shrug, "bumping the shelf it's on."

"Smoking in the same room with it," Sorsha added. "The rune needs to be contained by an expert."

"And that's you?" Detweiler asked Alex.

"Dr. Bell is handling that," Sorsha said. "In my professional opinion, there isn't anyone better in the state, maybe not even on the eastern seaboard."

Detweiler considered that for a long moment. He clearly didn't like having evidence out there in the wild, but he didn't want to argue with a sorceress.

"Fine," he said at last, "but you need to get Captain Callahan to sign off on this."

"I'll have Dr. Bell give him a call once we're done here," Alex said. "Now, tell me what happened."

Detweiler pulled out his flip notebook and went back a few pages.

"The target was the head honcho here, one Hector Iverson. He was in his office when the letter exploded."

Alex looked at the shattered opening where the outer door to the office used to be. Clearly this was the most powerful boom rune yet.

"I take it he's one of the victims?"

Detweiler made a face.

"The blast blew the top half of his body off," he said. "The other victim was one of the workers, Benjamin Moss. His desk was closest to the center of the explosion. There were two other people here, Kimberly Carson and Jeremy Clark. Kimberly was unconscious when the first people got here, so we sent her over to Bellevue."

"How badly was she hurt?" Alex asked, remembering the helpful young woman.

"I don't know," Detweiler admitted, "They'd already taken her out when I got here. I was planning on going to interview her once we're done here. You can tag along if you want."

Alex was glad that Kimberly had survived the blast, the world didn't have enough helpful people in it, after all. He reminded himself that the fact she was hero worshiping him while he was here had nothing whatsoever to do with it.

"What about Jeremy Clark?" Alex asked, picturing the man who sat at the center desk.

"He's fine," Detweiler said. "He was in the bathroom down the hall when the bomb went off."

"That's convenient," Sorsha observed.

Alex agreed with her; his being completely out of the blast zone might be a simple coincidence, but he hated coincidences.

"Is Mr. Clark still here?" he asked.

Detweiler nodded.

"We've got him stashed in the office down the hall." He jerked his thumb over his shoulder toward the doors at the far end.

"Do you believe his story about being in the bathroom?" Alex said.

"He seems pretty shaken," Detweiler said with a shrug.

"All right," Alex said, mentally pushing the extraneous information to the side. "Keep him on ice until I've had a chance to examine the scene."

"Are you sure?" Detweiler said, sarcasm dripping from his voice. "I would never have thought of that."

Alex managed not to smirk.

"Get to work," Detweiler growled. "I want to be home in time for dinner, Cynthia's making a roast chicken."

"Yes, boss," Alex said, stepping around the lieutenant and heading for the crime scene.

Stepping through the remains of the office door, a scene of chaos greeted Alex. When he'd been to the Office of Magical Oversight before, it had been a neat, open space with the three desks for the workers in the center and orderly rows of file cabinets along the right side and back walls. Now the desks were moved, their files, typewriters, and phones scattered around the room. The left hand wall, where there had been two glassed-in offices, now had no enclosures, and file cabinets close to them had been overturned, spilling their contents across the floor.

Despite having never met the man, Alex could tell where Hector Iverson's office had been. It was the one with the blown-out window. The remains of his desk stood in the middle of the ruined room with most of its top missing. Whatever had been in the unfortunate man's office had been scattered all over the room, with little possibility of separating it from the rest of the debris.

"Watch your step," Alex said, as bits of the former glass wall crunched under his foot.

In response, Sorsha put her hand on Alex's arm.

"Hold still," she said, then reached out and pulled a pair of heavy leather boots out of thin air. Dropping them on the floor, she stepped out of her stylish flats and into the boots.

"There," she said, picking up her shoes and vanishing them.

Her access to her magical storage was always impressive, but Sorsha knew how Alex reacted and leaned into it, showing off as much as she could. Alex rolled his eyes as she released his arm, then moved to a mostly undamaged spot of wall to open his fake safe and retrieve his kit.

"That takes a while, doesn't it?" Sorsha said as Alex shut the door, leaving it to melt back into the wall.

"Well, I suppose I could let you keep it for me," Alex chuckled. He'd said it as a joke, but if Sorsha was going to insist on tagging along with him, it might not be a bad idea to make up a third version of his crime scene kit and let her keep it in her magical storage.

"So you do want me along with you," she said with a smirk. "How sweet."

"You say that now, but just wait until I'm sorting through all this junk looking for clues. You're going to be so bored you'll wish for another explosion."

With that, Alex moved to the desk that belonged to Kimberly Carson and set his bag down. It was less damaged than the other two, but there were scorch marks on the top. He wondered just how badly Miss Carson had been hurt.

Opening his bag, he took out his multi lamp and the ghostlight burner. Normally, with a magical explosion this big, he would be able to feel the magical residue in the air. Locked away from such abilities by the damnation rune, he had to rely on more conventional methods.

"Can I have a pair of those?" Sorsha asked as Alex slipped on the yellow spectacles. He'd used the pince-nez pair with Iggy, but those had been the ones his mentor had handed him, and he still disliked using them.

He removed the spectacles, handing them to Sorsha, then pulled out his backup pince-nez pair from the glasses case.

"What am I looking for?" she asked as Alex inserted the burner in his lamp.

"Nothing yet," he said, taking out his gold lighter and igniting the wick. Closing the lantern, Alex stepped back from the beam of sickly green light.

Sorsha gasped.

"What's all this?" she wondered.

"Do you feel the magic in this room?"

"Of course," Sorsha said, "but a magical bomb went off here, that's bound to leave traces behind."

Alex held up the lantern, revealing a greenish mist in the air.

"That's what this is," he said.

Sorsha stretched out her hand, pushing it through one of the thicker parts of the magic.

"It's thicker here," she said, her voice filled with delight. "I can feel it."

"I've still got a few tricks up my sleeve," Alex said. "Let's see what else we can find."

Two hours later, what Alex found was precious little. All the ghostlight told him was that an intense amount of magic had been used in the office, something he knew already. Silverlight yielded fingerprints on the desks and filing cabinets, all the places one would expect to find them, and a copious amount of blood spattered on the remaining structures of Hector Iverson's office.

He did have some luck with amberlight, which showed him what pieces of the debris field had started off in Hector's office. By the time he'd gathered enough to get a picture of what the Magical Oversight director had been working on, it turned out to be utterly mundane.

"Is this really what you do all day?" Sorsha groaned, putting her hands behind her to stretch her back.

"Of course not," Alex said, "sometimes I read old newspapers at the library."

"How do you stand the tedium?" she said with no trace of humor.

Alex shrugged and gave her a smile.

"I like puzzles."

"Well please tell me you've figured out something about this one," Detweiler interrupted. "I just got off the phone with Callahan and everyone from the mayor to the chief is raising hell. He did talk to the Doc, and he's okay with you holding on to the bomb letter, but only until the case is over. Now, what have you got?"

"I wish I had better news," Alex sighed, "but other than confirming that this was another rune bomb, I've got nothing. Do you know if Mr. Iverson was connected in any way to any of our other victims?"

"You mean other than the fact he worked in an office that licenses alchemists and runewrights?" Detweiler shot back. "No. Detective Arnold is talking to his wife, and we haven't been able to reach his boss at the city licensing office yet. I'll know more in the morning."

"There has to be something that connects the victims," Alex said, more to himself than anyone else.

"Why?" Sorsha asked.

"Because if there isn't," Alex explained, "then these bombings are random, the work of a genuine madman."

"No," Detweiler said, shaking his head. "Whoever's behind this, they have a plan, otherwise why send a bomb to your office?"

Alex just shook his head.

"I don't know," he admitted. "Maybe I know the bomber, maybe I'm part of his plan somehow."

"Nonsense," Sorsha said. "You don't know any of the other victims."

"As far as we know, neither did they," Detweiler pointed out.

"I still say there's some rational thought behind all this," Sorsha declared. "You didn't get sent a bomb until you came here, a place the bomber had on his list."

"When were you here?" Detweiler growled at Alex.

"Two days ago," he said. "I wanted to find out if they kept records on powerful or highly skilled runewrights."

"And?" the lieutenant asked.

"They don't."

Detweiler looked around at the ruins of the room.

"I suppose that means that the bomb was meant for Iverson, not to destroy some specific records."

"That's our guess," Sorsha said. "Now, if you're finished with Alex, I'd like to get off my feet."

"I thought you wanted to talk to Jeremy Clark."

Alex had forgotten about the disinterested man he'd met before.

"You still have him?" he asked.

"He's across the hall in the dog licensing office," Detweiler said. "He's already given a statement to my boys, so as soon as you're done with him, he can go."

"Heading home?" Alex asked.

Detweiler shook his head.

"Every time you interview someone when I'm not around, I end up out of the loop," he said, then indicated the door across the hall. "So this time, I'm going to listen in."

"I'll do my best to hurry," Alex promised.

With that, Alex held out his arm to Sorsha.

"Shall we?"

Out in the hallway, the janitor Alex had seen earlier had finished his job and the plaster, wallpaper, and bits of door and lath were all gone.

"Good," Sorsha said, pulling her flats into existence. "Let me change out of these boots."

"Why?" Alex mocked. "I was thinking of taking you out for dinner; they'd look great at the corner lunch counter or a greasy spoon."

Sorsha gave him a patronizing look as she dropped her shoes on the floor in front of her.

"You are not funny," she said, slipping out of the boots and into the shoes.

The Dog Licensing Office turned out to be much smaller than its neighbor across the hall, though with a fair number of filing cabinets along its walls as well. A chest-high counter stretched most of the way across the room, separating the file area from the front. A few couches and chairs lined the front walls so patrons could wait, and Jeremy Clark sat on one of them, looking a bit grey and unsettled. A uniformed policeman sat in a chair by the door looking bored.

"You," Jeremy said when he recognized Alex.

"I told you I worked with the police," Alex replied.

"You can go," Detweiler told the waiting policeman.

The officer got up and left without a word and Alex waited until the door was shut before turning back to Mr. Clark.

"I already told the police everything," he said in a weary voice. "I just want to go home."

"I'll try not to detain you any longer than necessary," Alex said. "Tell me about Hector."

Clark drew a trembling breath.

"He was my boss. I worked for him for ten years."

"Was he a good boss?" Sorsha asked.

Clark's eyes seemed to go out of focus for a moment, then he looked at Sorsha. To Alex it seemed like he hadn't noticed she was there.

"Yes," Clark replied. "He was a good man, he didn't deserve this."

"I don't remember seeing him when I was in your office the other day," Alex said.

"He was out. Hector was due to retire at the end of the month, so he's been meeting with some of the higher ups. You know, making sure it's a smooth transition."

That bit of information piqued Alex's interest.

"Do you know who will be replacing him?"

Clark brightened up at that question and some of his color came back.

"Actually, I am. I got the word last week."

"Why you and not Benjamin Moss or Miss Carson?" Alex pressed.

"Well, Moss is new to the office," Clark said. "He hasn't even been here a year."

"And Miss Carson?"

"She's only been here five years," he said. "I have seniority."

Sorsha took a breath to ask a question, but Alex put his hand on her arm.

"I only have one more thing," Alex said, setting his kit down and opening it. "In cases like these, I need to make sure you weren't exposed to any dangerous magic."

"As I told the police," Clark said, "I was in the gents when the bomb went off."

"It's just routine," Alex said, clipping the ghostlight burner into his lamp. He quickly lit it, then set it on the office counter while he dug out the yellow spectacles. As soon as Alex had them on, he swept the light from the lantern over Clark, then back again.

"Well, that's it," he said, returning the lamp to the counter. "As long as you're feeling all right, you're free to go."

Clark thanked them, then stood and left.

"Why did you stop me from asking him a question?" Sorsha asked. "And what was all that about being exposed to dangerous magic?"

"I didn't want you to spook him until I could look at him under ghostlight," Alex said, putting his equipment away.

"But why did you want to see him under ghostlight?"

"Because, if Mr. Clark was really in the toilet when the bomb went off, he shouldn't have any magical residue on him. The bathrooms are at the far end of the hall."

"And did he?" Sorsha asked when Alex didn't elaborate.

"No," he said in an irritated voice. "That would have been too easy."

"It doesn't mean he's not the bomber," Sorsha observed, "but if he's telling the truth about his promotion, then why would he risk a police investigation days before he's due to take over?"

"Assuming he's telling the truth about the promotion," Detweiler said. "I'll have one of my boys find out in the morning."

22

VISITING HOURS

By the time Alex, Sorsha, and Lieutenant Detweiler reached Bellevue, it was after five. Surprisingly, it wasn't the lieutenant who was upset by the hour, but rather the ward nurse on the floor where Kimberly Carson was being treated, who insisted that visiting hours were over and they would have to leave. Eventually Detweiler had to threaten to have the nurse arrested before she revealed what room Miss Carson was in.

When Alex entered, Kimberly was sitting up in bed with her bandaged left arm in a sling. There were a few scrapes on her forehead and on her cheek, but other than that, she was none the worse for wear.

"Alex," she said with surprised smile. "What are you doing here?"

"Kimberly, this is Lieutenant Detweiler," Alex said, as the others came in. "I know you've had a rough afternoon, but he'd like to ask you a couple of questions."

"Miss Carson," Detweiler said, nodding in her direction. "How are you feeling?"

Kimberly's smile vanished and she shrugged.

"As well as I could be, I suppose," she said. "My arm took the most of the damage."

"Where were you when the bomb went off?" Alex asked.

She took a deep breath and let it out slowly.

"I was at my desk," she said.

Alex thought back to the layout of the office before the explosion. The three desks had been in the center of the room, with Jeremy Clark's desk facing the door. Benjamin Moss, the other victim, had his desk to the left of Clark's with his back to the office that was the origin of the blast. Kimberly's desk was on the other side, furthest from the bomb. It made sense that she wasn't hurt as badly as Benjamin.

"Did you see anything strange during the hours leading up to the explosion?" Detweiler asked, notebook in hand.

"No," Kimberly said, shaking her head.

"Anyone come into the office?" the lieutenant continued.

"No, it was a quiet morning."

Kimberly reached across her body with her right hand and grabbed her opposite shoulder. Alex could see her trembling slightly.

"They told me Ben didn't make it," she said, her voice dropping to a whisper.

"That's true," Alex said. "I'm sorry."

Kimberly shivered and Alex could see the knuckles of her hand going white as she gripped her shoulder.

"He was just a kid," she said.

"Where do you pick up your office mail?" Detweiler asked after a moment of silence.

"Down at the front desk," Kimberly replied. "I get it out of our box and bring it up every morning."

"Did you notice any letters without a stamp on them?" Detweiler said.

"No," she admitted. "There's always a few letters, mostly registration forms. I quit reading them years ago. They just go into a box on Mr. Clark's desk. We get to them when we have time."

"Does Mr. Clark sort through them?" Alex asked.

"Sometimes," Kimberly said, "but not always. It depends on how busy we are."

"So how did the letter get onto Mr. Iverson's desk?" Sorsha asked.

Because of her celebrity status, she'd agreed to hang back for fear of distracting Kimberly, but now she was engaged.

"He picks up his own mail," Kimberly said, shrinking back in her bed when she recognized the sorceress.

"Does he get it from the mail room or from the basket on Mr. Clark's desk?" Sorsha pressed.

"From the mail room," Kimberly confirmed. "They put his mail in his own box."

"Why not just have you pick them up and put them on his desk?" Alex asked. "You've got time to sort through the mail on the elevator ride."

"I don't know," Kimberly said. "That's just the way it's always been done. We used to joke that he was getting classified information from the state office, but what would they want with us?"

Alex still had no idea why the Office of Magical Oversight would be run that way, but it seemed like Kimberly didn't know either, so he let it drop.

"Did you notice anything right before the bomb went off?" he asked.

"No," she said, starting to sound tired. "Mr. Iverson came in, went to his office, and a few minutes later...boom."

"Are they keeping you overnight?" Detweiler asked.

"Yes. Just for observation."

That meant that the doctors were worried that she might have some internal injuries that hadn't manifested yet. From Alex's experience, he knew a nurse would be in to check on her every couple of hours throughout the night.

He thanked her and wished her well, but before he could turn away, Detweiler spoke up.

"Don't you want to test her like you did Jeremy Clark?"

When Alex looked confused, he continued.

"To make sure she hasn't been exposed to something magical."

Alex hadn't thought of that, especially since he'd made up that excuse so he could shine some ghostlight on Clark.

"Of course," he said, as he realized what Detweiler meant.

Putting down his kit, he took out his multi-lamp and the yellow, pince-nez spectacles.

"I'm just going to make sure your body didn't absorb any strange magic in the explosion," he explained to Kimberly as he lit the lamp.

Unlike Clark, she seemed interested and eager to watch Alex work.

With the lamp lit and the spectacles in place, Alex shone the ghost-light over Kimberly. As he expected, her arm still glowed faintly from its exposure, while the rest of her had lost any trace of the residue entirely. That wasn't surprising as residual magic was eventually absorbed back into the universe.

"All right," he said. "It looks like you're going to be fine."

Alex returned his gear to his bag and picked it up.

"One more thing," he said. "Was Mr. Iverson retiring?"

Kimberly nodded.

"At the end of the month," she said. "We just got word that Mr. Clark would be replacing him."

"Thank you, Miss Carson," Alex said, giving her a smile. "I'm glad you're okay."

"Would you sign my autograph book?" Kimberly asked, looking at Sorsha. "It's just that I've met lots of runewrights and alchemists, but I've never met a sorceress before."

If this request was strange to Sorsha, she didn't show it.

"Of course," Sorsha said, stepping up beside the bed.

Kimberly picked up her handbag from the bedside table and, after digging around in it one handed, produced a small, leather-bound book. She tried to open it with one hand, but the pages kept turning, so Sorsha reached out and took it.

"Just find an empty page," Kimberly said, blushing.

Sorsha did as she was told, then pulled a pen out of thin air and wrote her name in big letters across the page.

"Thank you, so much," Kimberly said, accepting the book back from Sorsha.

Awkwardly, she held the open book with the fingers of her immobilized hand, and pulled a pencil from her handbag with the other.

"I have to write down the date," she said, making slow strokes in the book with the pencil.

"Get better," Sorsha said, then Alex and Detweiler repeated those wishes and they headed back out into the hall.

"Well, that was a bust," the lieutenant said. "Not that I expected her to know much. One minute she's working at her desk, the next, she's flat on her back with bits of office raining down around her."

"She was rattled," Alex said. "When I dropped in to the office earlier, she was the one who answered my questions."

"How did she seem then?" Detweiler asked.

"Competent," Alex said. "She knew her job well, but that's all I can tell you."

"Well, I don't expect I'd be all together if I'd narrowly escaped being blown up," Detweiler said.

"And don't forget she lost a coworker," Sorsha pointed out. "Someone she probably considered a friend."

"What am I going to tell Callahan tomorrow?" Detweiler sighed.

"Tell him we're looking for a connection between the victims," Alex said.

"How?" Sorsha asked. "I thought you already looked."

"There's a new piece to this puzzle," Alex explained. "The bomber sent one of his boom runes to my office. Clearly he wants me off the case."

"And you went to the Office of Magical Oversight the day before the bomb showed up," Detweiler added.

"I'm going to assume you don't think the bombing of that office was a coincidence," Sorsha said.

Alex could only shrug at that.

"I don't know if the bomber hit the Office of Magical Oversight as part of some larger plan or if he did it because I went there," he said. "But if I were a betting man, I'd wager on the latter."

"So was he trying to interfere with your investigation?" Sorsha asked.

"Interfere how?" Detweiler said.

"There must be something in that office that the bomber doesn't want me to know about," Alex declared. "As soon as the government buildings open tomorrow, I'm going to have to do some research."

"Do that and keep me in the loop," Detweiler said as they reached the street. "Now, I'm late for dinner as it is, so I'll talk to you tomorrow."

With that, the lieutenant walked away, headed for where his car was parked along the curb.

"I hope you're not expecting me to teleport you home," Sorsha said, giving him a wry smile.

"No," he replied automatically as his thoughts wandered.

"You've figured something out," Sorsha accused him. "Haven't you?"

"What?" Alex said as his attention snapped back to the present. "No, nothing like that. There are just some things that bother me."

"Well, tell me," Sorsha said, an excited gleam in her eyes.

"Not right now," he said. "I need to look into a couple of things first."

Sorsha's eyebrows dropped down into a scowl, but before she could protest, Alex cut her off.

"I promise that if I do figure anything out, you'll be the first to know."

Sorsha didn't look pleased at that, but she didn't press the issue.

"So how are we getting home?" she asked.

"Have you ever ridden on a sky crawler?"

"That is not how one keeps a low profile," she observed.

"I guess that means we need a cab," Alex said with a chuckle.

"Better," Sorsha said. "I've already signed one autograph today and I want to get to the brownstone before Dr. Bell's dinner has gotten cold."

During the cab ride, Sorsha snuggled up against him with her head on his shoulder and dozed. She'd had a long day of meetings before deciding to chaperone him, so he let her rest.

It was amazing to him how easily she'd become part of his life. It happened gradually at first, but now it seemed like their relationship was changing week to week. He didn't mind, he'd thought Sorsha was gorgeous from the moment they met, but she'd taken her time coming around to him. Now she was eating dinner with Iggy several nights a week and trying to become a partner in his agency.

How did that happen? he wondered.

The only rational explanation was that it had all been Sorsha's idea. If he'd tried to drag her into his cases by taking her to crime scenes for hours, she'd have balked.

I guess she really loves me, he thought.

Somehow her actually telling him that they would get married when the time was right, hadn't done it, but her watching him meticulously sift through bomb debris for hours — that was love.

Putting his arm around Sorsha, he pulled her closer. She didn't need his body heat to stave off the February chill, but let out a soft sound of approval just the same. When the cab finally pulled up in front of the brownstone, Alex was loathe to release her.

"We're here," he said after a pause.

Sorsha roused herself quickly and he helped her out of the car and up the stoop of the building.

Iggy was waiting in his greenhouse, reading a dime novel among his fragrant orchids while something with a more substantial aroma sat simmering on the stove.

"I heard about the bombing at one of the city offices," he said, when Alex stuck his head into the greenhouse door, "I wasn't expecting you back so soon."

"Sorsha's with me," Alex said. "I know this isn't her usual night."

"Tosh," Iggy said, setting his book aside and picking up a lit cigar from the ashtray. "Since I didn't know when you'd be back, I made a stew. It's the perfect meal for the February chill, so I always make extra."

"Of course you do," Alex chuckled. He turned back to the kitchen to find his rich and powerful sorceress fiancée setting the table.

"What?" she asked when she caught him watching her.

"Nothing," he replied, "nothing at all."

"Well, if there's not a good reason for you to be standing there," Iggy interjected from behind him, "move out of the doorway."

Alex stepped aside, and moved to help Sorsha with the silverware, while Iggy shut the greenhouse door. In a few minutes, Iggy had the meal all laid out and Alex held out Sorsha's chair for her. He was about to sit himself when there was a knock at the front door.

"I'll get it," he said, heading for the vestibule.

When he opened the door, his wandering thoughts were jolted back to reality by the sight of Nils Eccles, Sorsha's big brother. He was dressed in a clean, pressed suit, with his hat in his hand and a cardboard box at his feet.

"I know my sister's here," he began without any preamble, "I just need to talk to her for a moment."

Alex held his gaze for a long moment, but Nils didn't turn away.

"I didn't see your car on the street when I got home," he said, "how do you know your sister is here? Did you pay off one of the neighbors?"

To his credit, Nils didn't flinch.

"I just need a moment," he pressed, "I don't even have to come in."

"Sorsha doesn't want to see you," Alex said.

"I know she didn't come to Pop's funeral, and I guess I understand that, but there's a provision in the will that concerns her. I just need to tell her about it."

Alex shook his head.

"When I told her about the funeral, her exact words were that she had plenty of time to spit on her father's grave if ever she wanted to."

Nils did look a bit shocked at that, but only for a moment.

"Please, Mr. Lockerby," he said, "let me see Kjirsten, just for a minute."

Alex laughed at that.

"I wouldn't call her that," he advised. "When I asked about her name, she nearly slapped me. And she loves me."

Nils didn't have a ready response for that, so Alex pressed his advantage.

"Why don't you tell me what this is all about?" he said. "If I think you've got a worthy cause, I'll talk to Sorsha. You leave me a phone number where I can reach you, and if Sorsha wants to, she'll call you in the morning."

Nils looked angry for a fraction of a second, but quickly mastered his emotions. After a long moment, he sighed and reached down into the cardboard box. When he came up, he held a music box that was made to look like a carousel. It wasn't big or elaborate, just four horses made out of thin wood cut-outs mounted around a central pole. The colors of the horses, the poles, and the awning were faded, but Alex could see that they had been expertly applied, making the cheap music box look more opulent than it actually was.

Alex knew it fairly well, since Sorsha had an exact copy of it sitting on one of the decorative shelves in her office. Hers had blue horses while the one Nils held had red ones, but that was the only real difference.

"Your father left Sorsha a music box?" he said.

Nils shrugged and for the first time looked a bit sheepish.

"Not really," he admitted. "This one belongs to Sorsha. Our father got it for her when she was seven. He also got one for our sister, Mia. It looks just like this one, but it has blue horses. Sorsha took that one with her when she...when she left."

"And Mia wants it back?" Alex asked, remembering that Mia was a year older than he was.

"It was my father," Nils said. "He wasn't very coherent during his last days, but he insisted that I get Mia's music box back, made me promise."

"So you're just honoring one of your father's last wishes?"

Nils nodded.

"Why was it so important to him?" Alex asked.

Nils just shrugged and shook his head.

"I don't know," he admitted. "It's stupid, but he made me promise."

All right," Alex said. "I'll talk to Sorsha for you."

Nils brightened up at that.

"Don't get your hopes up too high," Alex cautioned. "There was an accident with Sorsha's castle five years ago."

"What kind of accident?"

"It fell into the Atlantic and sank, along with most of her personal possessions. The castle up in the sky now is a new one."

"So it's gone?" Nils said, sounding way more distressed than Alex would have thought.

"Probably," he lied. "Like I said, I'll ask Sorsha about it and either she or I will call you tomorrow."

Nils clearly didn't like that answer, but he seemed to understand it was the only one he was going to get. With a sigh, he returned the music box to the cardboard box and gave Alex a phone number to reach him.

Alex waited until Nils was down the stairs and onto the sidewalk before he closed the door and returned to the kitchen.

"Who was it?" Sorsha and Iggy asked in unison.

"Persistent salesman," Alex lied. "Let's eat, I'm starving."

23

BREAD CRUMBS

The next day was Saturday, which frustrated Alex to no end. He caught up on some reading, and went through his case files, but with nothing open and most people unwilling to talk business, he felt like whatever momentum he'd gained with his cases was beginning to stall. Iggy and Sorsha happily played pinochle for hours, but Alex wasn't one for games.

When you're married, you're going to have to learn, the more sardonic part of his brain reminded him. *Then you'll have Danny and Sherry over to play bridge.*

Alex shuddered at the thought and retreated to the library to try reading one of Iggy's pulp novels. It actually wasn't too bad, but if the book represented what the public thought of Private Investigators, then Alex wasn't getting into enough fist fights or sleeping with enough beautiful, dangerous women to qualify.

Sure you would, his sardonic mind chimed in. *You get shot way more times than those fictitious P.I.s, and none of them are sleeping with a woman half as dangerous or beautiful as yours.*

That thought made him feel better and, hours later, he returned the book to the steamer trunk where Iggy kept his illicit collection.

Since it was late, and Sorsha had already gone home, he closed the trunk, and headed off to bed.

He rose early Monday morning, hoping to sneak out to his office before Sorsha insisted on tagging along. While he enjoyed her presence, he still chaffed a bit at having a leash, to say nothing of the damnation rune curating his magic. Of course, he'd brought the rune on himself by using Limelight, a substance he knew to be both dangerous and addictive, not that the reality made him feel any better.

He laughed at that thought as he shaved yesterday's stubble off his jaw. The reason Sorsha was wanting to be his permanent sidekick was exactly the same as the rune. He'd pursued her, despite knowing that she was both dangerous and alluring.

"What's so funny?" Sorsha's voice came from the half open door.

"Nothing," he said, winking at her reflection in the mirror.

"What are your plans this morning?" she asked, getting right to the point.

"I've got to make a bunch of calls," he said, "then I was hoping to talk to a few people, assuming I can find them. It's going to be pretty boring, so I'd understand if you didn't want to tag along."

Sorsha smirked at him and her eyes sparkled with mischief.

"I accompany you for less than a full day and you want to get rid of me already?"

"Of course not," he lied, feeling a bit of shame over the thought. "I'm just saying that if you're dead set on coming to the office with me, you should probably bring a book."

Her smirk widened and her nose wrinkled adorably.

"Uh-huh," she said in a tone that practically shouted her disbelief of his statement. "Fortunately for you, I have three meetings today and I'm behind on my enchanting work. I need to do six pallets of steel bar stock before noon, or my shipping coordinator is going be very angry."

"If he's giving you a hard time, I could rough him up a bit for you," Alex said, without allowing himself even the trace of a smile.

"First," Sorsha said, ticking off her index finger, "you will do no such uncivilized thing. Second," she ticked off her middle finger, "I hardly need you to play the white knight for me."

"That's no fun," he protested, tapping his safety razor on the side of the sink to clear it.

As he rinsed it off and closed the tap, Sorsha slipped her arm around his waist and pressed her hip against him.

"I said I don't need it," she purred, "I didn't say I didn't like it."

She looked up expectantly, so Alex leaned down and kissed her.

And you were trying to get rid of her, his brain accused him.

Twenty minutes later Alex was dressed and had raided the icebox for some of the leftovers from last night's dinner. Satisfied he was ready for the day, he limped up the stairs back to the third floor, then used the gold key to open the cover door to his vault. Since he had to ask Iggy and Mike to make all the runes he used, Alex hadn't moved the door back into his room from the hallway where Iggy had put it during his convalescence. Alex would need several complicated runes to detach the cover door, and several more to put it in a new location. Still, having it in the hall bothered him, so he would have to at least start accumulating the runes he would need.

Pushing that thought from his mind, Alex moved to his drafting table in the middle of his vault's main room. It hadn't seen much use of late and Alex missed sitting at it to work. This time, he knelt down carefully and opened the bottom-most drawer on the rollaway cabinet next to the desk. Since it was down near the floor, and hard to access, Alex used the drawer to keep things he didn't need on a regular basis. In this case he was looking for a business card from an old case.

It took him a minute to locate the card, then Alex stood and limped across to the far side of the room, through the vault door, and down the short hallway that led to his office. If history was anything to go by, Sherry would be in the outer office, getting ready for the day, so when Alex reached his massive desk, he tapped the intercom key twice to let her know he was in. She answered with a tap of her own, giving a brief burst of static, to confirm the message was received, but nothing more was forthcoming.

Alex took out a notepad and made a list of the things he needed to do…and it wasn't short.

"Might as well start with the hardest thing," he told himself, then picked up the telephone receiver and gave the operator the number from the business card.

"James," Alex said when the call connected, "Alex Lockerby."

"Alex," James said, sounding delighted. "It's been some time."

Alex admitted that it had been, then rushed on.

"I'm calling about that favor you owe me," he said. "Would now be a good time to collect?"

"Of course," James said. "When can you come down?"

Alex consulted his datebook, then set an appointment and hung up.

"One down," he told himself.

His next call was one he didn't want to make at all, but he picked up the phone anyway.

"Nils Eccles," the voice on the other end of the line said.

"Nils, this is Alex Lockerby. I have good news for you. After a lot of convincing, I got Sorsha to agree to see you on Wednesday."

"Does she have the music box?" her brother asked. "From what you said, I was worried it had been destroyed."

"She does," Alex reported. "I didn't even have to ask her about it. I knew I'd seen it before and I had, Sorsha's using it as a centerpiece for her conference room table."

"That's good to hear," Nils said. "Please tell Kjir— uh, Sorsha that I can't wait to see her."

"I'll let her know," Alex replied, then hung up.

"Two down," he sighed.

The next call was to Lieutenant Detweiler.

"Please tell me you have something?" he growled.

"No," Alex admitted, "but I think we can rule out our bomber just hitting random targets."

"How do you figure that?"

"All the targets are tied to magic," Alex said, "specifically runewrights. Reggie Aspler uses runewrights in his shipping business, McDermet sold runewright supplies, Professor Rodgers was the dean of a college for runewrights, and Hector Iverson was in charge of runewright registration."

"That would be one hell of a coincidence if it's random," Detweiler admitted. "How does that help us? We already know the bomber is a runewright."

"It helps us because now we know for certain that there's some connection between the victims."

"None of my boys have found anything to suggest any of these people knew each other. I supposed McDermet and Rodgers would have had dealings with the Office of Magical Oversight, but you said it yourself, it's mostly just filling out forms."

"Forms..." Alex said.

"Come again?" Detweiler asked.

"What if McDermet and Rodgers met each other at the Office of Magical Oversight?" Alex mused. "What if they talked to Hector Iverson?"

"It's possible, but what could they have said to each other that would make someone want them dead?"

"I don't know," Alex admitted, "but see if your boys can find either of their registration cards and compare the date stamps on them. If McDermet and Rodgers were in at the same time, the dates will match."

Detweiler sighed.

"All right," he said. "It's as good a lead as anything else."

"Is there anything else?"

"I got the report back from the police accountant," Detweiler said. "There were no secret magical projects at Aspler Shipping, and Matthew McDermet was a crook who sold cheapskate potions, but he was no criminal mastermind."

"What about partners, employees?" Alex asked. "Maybe he wasn't the mastermind."

"He's had a couple dozen employees over the years," Detweiler said, as the sound of shuffling papers came over the wire. "Most of them were teenagers. He did have that partner in the beginning, but he left the business within the first year."

"Left or was forced out?" Alex said.

"It doesn't say in my report," Detweiler said. "Just the name, Sam Olsen."

"Do you have a line on this guy?"

"No," Detweiler admitted, "but I'm guessing you think I ought to."

"I think we should ask him a few questions about his work with McDermet," Alex said. "Even if he has nothing to do with the bombings, he might have an idea who would hate McDermet enough to blow him up."

"I'll have my boys look through the Magical Oversight files to see if they can find Olsen in there. It would help your theory if he was actually a runewright."

"Good call," Alex said. "I'm going to dig into Reggie Aspler some more, he's the only victim with a tenuous connection to magic."

Detweiler wished him well and hung up.

Alex spent a few minutes making notes before he reached for the phone again. This time he gave the operator the exchange for the offices of the Midnight Sun.

"I need to speak to Billy," he told the receptionist when she answered. "This is Alex Lockerby."

A moment later his young friend picked up.

"Tell me you've got the dirt on the bomber," Billy said by way of introduction.

"No such luck," Alex was forced to admit.

"Is the case moving? Are you getting close?"

"Just following leads at the moment," Alex said. "Trust me, once there's something real, I'll call you."

"Well, if you aren't calling to make my week, what is it you need?"

"I assume you've been digging into the lives of the bombing victims," Alex said, "I need to know if you learned anything interesting about Reggie Aspler."

Billy let out a long breath before responding.

"Other then his well-documented infidelity?" he asked. "Nothing."

"So his wife doesn't care," Alex said. That tracked with what Detweiler already told him.

"She lives on Long Island in a mansion," Billy said. "From what I hear, her attitude was that she didn't care what her husband got up to as long as it didn't affect her lifestyle."

"What about bastards or kids from other relationships?"

"Janet Aspler is Reggie's first and only wife," Billy said. "He was engaged twice before, but neither crossed the finish line."

"Any idea why?" Alex asked, fishing for anything at this point.

The sound of turning pages filled the earpiece, then Billy came back on.

"According to our reporter, both of the engagements were called off by the brides to be," he said. "The first runaway bride was Lenore Anthony."

"The actress?" Alex asked. He'd seen one of her pictures last year while on a date with Sorsha.

"The very same," Billy said. "Apparently Reggie wanted a meek housewife and Lenore had bigger dreams than that. She ran off to Hollywood and got discovered six months later."

"So, not our bomber," Alex reasoned. "Whoever is doing this has an axe to grind."

Billy chuckled.

"The only thing Lenore Anthony grinds these days is the gears in her car."

"Moving on," Alex attempted to pull the conversation back to the subject at hand, "what about the other bride with cold feet?"

"Anita Powell," Billy read. "Daughter of Kernan and Hester Powell."

"Never heard of them," Alex admitted.

"Old money," Billy supplied. "They live upstate in a house that's more of a castle, complete with a lake."

"I take it they keep to themselves," Alex said.

"No," Billy said, "but you'd need to jump a few social class levels before they took notice of you."

"So what happened to Anita?" Alex asked. "Did Reggie not treat her like daddy's little princess?"

"No idea," his friend said. "When Anita broke off the engagement, she disappeared."

"What do you mean by 'disappeared'?"

"Just what you'd expect," Billy said. "She vanished. Kernan hired a dozen private detectives, even put out a bounty for information about her, but nothing came of it."

"You think Reggie killed her?" Alex wondered.

"No way to tell," Billy said. "I doubt it, though. Reggie Aspler wasn't the kind of man to get his hands dirty."

"Maybe he didn't," Alex said. "It's not that hard to find a hitter if you have the money."

"How long did Reggie take to get married to Janet?" Alex asked. "After Anita disappeared."

"Three years," Billy said.

"There goes the theory that Janet got rid of an obstacle. If she'd been behind Anita's disappearance, she would have moved in quickly."

"Why?" Billy asked. "Wouldn't waiting be better?"

"Too much risk," Alex said. "The longer she waited, the more there was a chance Reggie would find someone else."

"Well, that's a dead end then," Billy said.

"Is there anything else interesting about Reggie?" Alex pushed. "Something in his business life, maybe?"

"Nope," Billy said, "the man was about as interesting as dry toast."

Alex stifled a curse, then thanked his friend.

"Sorry I couldn't be more helpful," Billy said before hanging up.

Alex took a moment and wrote down the names Lenore Anthony and Anita Powell. He doubted anyone would let him get near enough to Lenore to ask her a question, and he'd bet there was a high likelihood that Anita was dead.

Not easy getting answers out of the dead, he thought.

He could still take the train up to Long Island and talk to Janet. With Reggie dead, she'd have no fear of telling the absolute truth about him. Alex added that to his growing list of things to do, but it would have to wait untill tomorrow at the earliest. With any luck, he was about to fill up his afternoon.

Reaching for the phone again, Alex called Holcombe Ward. After talking his way past the secretary, Alex finally got the man himself on the line.

"How is the case progressing?" Holcombe asked.

"I talked to Elizabeth and Freddy," Alex reported.

"Do you think either of them were involved with Ari's murder?"

Alex took a moment to choose his words carefully.

"I think Lizzy could have planned it," he said. "She seems to be quite the schemer. That said, she doesn't seem to have a motive. She didn't even know who Ari was when I mentioned him."

"So you think Freddy has a motive?" Holcombe said.

"Maybe," Alex said. "I'm looking into that now, which is why I called. I need your help."

"Well, I've got a fund raiser to go to this afternoon, but I could meet you tomorrow if that's not too far off."

"Not that kind of help," Alex chuckled. Lately everyone wanted to go with him while he worked. "I need to know where Freddy grew up, and specifically, where he went to high school."

"Madison Preparatory Academy," Holcombe rattled it off. "It's in Albany. His parents have an estate in Syracuse."

"That's not even close to Albany," Alex said.

"No," Holcombe agreed, "but Madison has the best high school tennis program in the state."

"Is it a boarding school?" Alex asked.

"No, but lots of kids stay in the city. Usually their parents rent out an apartment for them."

"High school kids?" Alex said, not sure he believed what he just heard.

"It's customary for a parent or governess to stay with them," Holcombe explained. "I believe it's actually a school rule."

It took Alex a minute to work that out in his head, and it still didn't make a lot of sense.

"But Freddy washed out," Alex said. "He said he didn't make the team when he tried out. Why would his parents send him all the way to Albany unless he was a shoe-in?"

"Rich people don't think like you or me," Holcombe said. "To them, renting an apartment for six months just to let Freddy prove himself was an acceptable expense."

Alex wasn't exactly poor anymore, but throwing that kind of money away just to indulge what might turn out to be an adolescent whim seemed insane.

"Why do you want to know?" Holcombe pressed when Alex went silent.

"Freddy said that he made the tennis team by working hard and getting lucky. Apparently, one of the other players on the team was hit by a car when he was running along the highway."

"Stupid," Holcombe said. "There's a reason schools have an athletic field with a track."

"Well, I was wondering if the boy who got hit had any bad blood with Freddy."

"You're not suggesting that it was Freddy who hit that boy?" Holcombe said, astonishment in his voice. "Just so he could get on the tennis team?"

"People have done worse for far less," Alex said. "Right now all I have are questions," he cautioned. "I'll call over to Madison Prep and see if I can get some answers."

"Well, good luck," Holcombe said with a strange resignation in his voice.

Alex had heard that tone before; it was the moment when someone realized that the criminal they hired Alex to catch might actually be someone they know and even like.

"I'll let you know what I find out," he said, then thanked Holcombe and hung up.

24

SCHOOL DAYS

It took Alex almost half an hour to track down the exchange for Madison Preparatory Academy. Once he had the office secretary on the phone, he spent a further fifteen minutes trying to convince her to let him speak to the principal.

"What can I do for you, Mr. Lockerby?" the man said once Alex finally got to speak to him.

"Principal Martell," Alex began. "I work for the U.S. Lawn Tennis Association and we're putting together an article on Freddy Hackett for our magazine. I believe he was a student at Madison."

"Indeed he was," Martell said, his voice brightening up considerably.

"We'd like to do a side story about Freddy's time at Madison," Alex went on, "especially his relationship with his tennis coach and the team."

"We'd be happy to help out any way we can, Mr. Lockerby," Principal Madison said with a smile Alex could hear.

"I'd like to speak to the coach; is he available?"

There was a pause and Alex wondered if Martell had seen through his cover story.

"Is something wrong?" Alex pressed.

"The coach who worked with Mr. Hackett retired last year," Martell said.

"That's all right," Alex said, "if you can give me his name and number, I'll just call him directly."

Another pause came down the line and Alex could tell Martell was weighing the risks of letting Alex talk to someone he no longer had any control over. If the coach had been forced out, or quit over grievances, Martell wouldn't want Alex anywhere near the man.

"I think we can do that," Martell said at last. "You're looking for Brian Pearson, he was our coach for almost thirty years. I don't have his number, but I'll hand you off to Mrs. Tatum and she can get that for you."

"That would be great," Alex said. "We at the USLTA appreciate your help."

It took Alex a few minutes to disentangle himself from the overly helpful Principal Martell. He couldn't blame the man; the prospect of some good, free press for his school was an irresistible carrot dangling in front of him. As Alex hung up, he almost felt bad for having given him a cover story.

What else could you do, he reminded himself. If he'd mentioned that he was investigating a murder, the principal would have clammed up faster than a witness to a mob hit.

Pushing any self-recrimination from his mind, Alex put in a call to former tennis coach, Brian Pearson. The coach turned out to be a jovial man who seemed lonely in his retirement, at least based on how eagerly he agreed to talk about his former student.

"Freddy, now there was a talent," Pearson gushed. "I could tell from the first moment I saw him."

"But I thought Freddy didn't make the team in his freshman year," Alex said, knowing full well that was the case.

"Oh, that's true," Pearson said, without missing a beat or losing any enthusiasm. "He was good, but he was lazy. It wasn't until he started really working on his skills that he started reaching his potential. It's like I always told the boys, talent is great, but it's the people who put in the work who become winners."

Alex had been patronizing the old man, but he couldn't fault his teaching philosophy.

Especially since Iggy had said pretty much the same thing to him.

"So he worked out and practiced and made the team the following year?" Alex asked.

"No," Pearson said, his voice turning serious. "One of the boys on the team, Martin Pride, was running along the highway and was hit by a car. He survived, but it took him over a year to completely heal."

"That's awful," Alex said, affecting his best shocked voice. "Did the police catch the driver?"

"No," Pearson said, eager to dismiss the topic. "It was just some drunk."

"So with Martin in the hospital, you gave Freddy another shot?"

"Not right away," Pearson said, a bit defensive. "That wouldn't have been right, but Marty gave his blessing after a few weeks in the hospital."

"Did Martin know Freddy, were they friends?"

"I don't know, but I never saw them together," Coach Pearson admitted. "Marty recovered from his injuries, but he wasn't able to play tennis anymore. Still walks with a limp."

"Tell me," Alex asked, getting back to Freddy, "how did Freddy go from a kid who wasn't skilled enough to make the team to one of your best players?"

"I already told you, he did the work."

"But what did he do?"

Pearson chuckled at that.

"He ran," he said, "and when he wasn't running, he was on the court hitting balls from the machine. In his senior year, he'd set up two machines to force him to run back and forth between them."

Alex didn't want to be impressed, but he couldn't help it. Freddy was clearly driven, and Alex knew from experience that driven people were often willing to do whatever it took to reach their goals.

Like mowing down some poor rival while he's running along the highway, he thought.

Alex talked with Coach Pearson for a few more minutes, but nothing of interest came up. The one thing that was clear was that Pearson was proud as a new papa of Freddy's success.

"Time to talk to Martin Pride," he said to himself.

Turning to the other side of his desk, he pressed down the 'talk' key on the intercom.

"Sherry, can you come back here for a minute?"

"Sure, boss," she said. A moment later she stepped through the open door and moved to the nearest chair. "What do you need?"

He tore the top page off his desk notepad and passed it across to her.

"I need you to call over to Madison Preparatory Academy and get the contact information for the parents of a former student, Martin Pride. Tell them you're from the government and you're doing a background check on him."

"You want me to call the parents after that?" Sherry asked.

"Yes, I need to talk to Martin, so find out where he is and get a number for him."

"I'll get on it," she said, standing up. "Are you going to be here, or are you going out?"

"That depends on Sorsha," he said. "If she's available, we're going to Albany for a few hours. I'll check in when we get back to the city."

Sherry gave him a smile and a wink, then stood up.

"I'll hold down the fort," she said, then headed back to her desk.

Once he heard the hall door close at the far end, Alex reached for his desk phone again.

"Hello Inge," Alex said when Sorsha's office secretary answered the phone. "It's Alex. Is Sorsha out of her meetings yet?"

"She is," Inge said in her slightly accented voice. "She isn't here, though, she's at her workshop."

Alex remembered Sorsha said she had to enchant some bars. He also knew from experience that there wasn't a phone in there. The good news was that Sorsha's workshop was in her flying castle and Alex had a direct connection.

He spent a few minutes adding his notes to the Leavitt file, then stood and headed for his vault. Just because he had a door directly into

Sorsha's house didn't mean he could just walk in whenever he wanted, so he stopped at his drafting table. Picking up the candlestick phone, he dialed Sorsha's private number.

"Hello Hannah," he said when Sorsha's lady's maid picked up the phone. Since she lost her butler Malcolm Hitchens, Hannah had had taken over running Sorsha's household. To be fair, with only a chef and a weekly cleaning crew to manage, it wasn't an insurmountable job, but Hannah handled it with the flair of a sergeant major commanding troops.

"Mr. Lockerby," Hannah replied. "How can I be of service?"

"I know Sorsha's working, but I need to talk to her. Would be okay if I went down to the workshop?"

"She said if you called, I should tell you to come by," Hannah said. "I believe the foyer door is unlocked."

Alex thanked her, then hung up.

Crossing his vault to the back wall, Alex used his gold key to open the cover door, then stepped through, into the foyer of Sorsha's flying castle.

A sound drew his attention upward to the balcony above where Hannah waved down at him. She was a woman in her early thirties with shoulder length brown hair, spectacles, and a round, pleasant face.

Alex waved back before shutting the cover door and limping across the vast foyer to a door on the far side. Despite the fact that Sorsha's flying castle inhabited a giant chunk of rock that looked like an inverted teardrop, most of the home was above the foyer. The space below the foyer was reserved for Sorsha's business. The biggest area was her workshop, a massive space with cranes mounted to the ceiling and a loading dock where workmen brought up the steel rods Sorsha enchanted to make her cold disks.

Sorsha had a storage room off the workshop, but it was mostly there to keep whatever furniture or other things she wasn't using out of the way. To everyone else, that appeared to be the extent of Sorsha's basement.

Alex knew better.

At the bottom of the stairs leading down to the workshop was a solid stone wall with a secret behind it. With her power, Sorsha could simply remove the stone, revealing a passage behind it. That led to her spell chamber, the core of her castle where she laid out the spells that kept it airborne and regulated everything from the temperature to the water pressure.

It was in a room very much like the one where Alex first spent a massive amount of his own life energy.

As he reached the bottom of the stairs, Alex ignored the stone cover over the secret passage and turned to the warehouse.

"Come in," Sorsha called as Alex reached for the doorknob.

Alex turned the knob and entered.

"How did you know?" he asked.

Sorsha was standing in front of a long table full of ten foot lengths of steel bars. Each bar was an inch and a half around, ten feet long, and had to weigh close to one hundred pounds. Despite that, Sorsha was balancing one of the bars on the tip of her index finger. With a contemptuous flip, she set the bar spinning.

"Just a minute," she said, her eyes flashing a deep teal blue. She spoke something in a language Alex didn't know, her voice dropping low and echoing off the stone walls of the room. As she spoke, the bar began to glow, turning white. Alex could hear it crackling as frost spread across its surface.

As Sorsha's voice faded away, the frost on the bar evaporated, leaving it a deep blue color. Alex was at least fifty feet away but he could feel a wave of cold wash over him. Before the temperature could drop too dramatically, Sorsha made a come hither gesture with her finger and the bar floated up, over her head, and down into a wooden box behind her.

"There's a switch behind the upstairs door jamb," Sorsha said, smiling at him. "When someone opens the door, that light comes on." She pointed at a bulb sticking out of the wall by the door.

"You should tell people that you sensed them with magic," Alex said with a chuckle. "The lightbulb takes away from your sorceress mystique."

"Considering the only people who would be coming down here are you or Hannah, who am I trying to impress?" she said, sauntering around the table to him. "Now, to what do I owe the pleasure?"

Alex gave her a wink.

"How would you like to visit the police department in Albany?"

"I hope you understand how much I love you," Sorsha gasped, leaning over with her hands on her knees. Alex hadn't been teleported for most of a year now and he was in no condition to answer her. He just stood still, breathing through his nose until the queasiness passed.

"I'll take you out tonight," he promised. "Someplace new."

"You'd better," Sorsha said after taking a deep breath. "Now where is Albany's Central Office?"

The building that served as Albany's version of the Central Office of Police was called Police Headquarters, and only five stories high. In the past, Alex had encountered good and bad cops and detectives in other police organizations, but the Albany desk sergeant was on the ball. The moment Alex held the lobby door open for Sorsha, the man's eyes got wide and he picked up his desk telephone.

"I think you have a fan," Alex said as he stepped inside behind her.

"That could work for us," she said over her shoulder.

"Miss Kincaid," the desk sergeant said when they reached the desk, "how may I be of assistance?"

"This is my friend, Alex Lockerby," she said, putting her hand on Alex's arm, "he needs to talk to someone about an old case of yours."

Uncertainty washed over the man's face as his gaze transferred to Alex.

"Reporter?" he asked.

"P.I.," Alex fired back, knowing the man would have to hide his disdain and managing not to smirk.

"Uh," the Sergeant hesitated, "let me get someone down here for you. If I can just have you wait over there."

Alex offered Sorsha his arm, then withdrew to a bench in the waiting area.

"I notice he's not calling anyone," Sorsha said, not bothering to hide her own smirk.

He didn't have to, of course, his call when Sorsha walked in had undoubtedly gone straight to the chief or the commissioner or whatever they called the head honcho in Albany. They didn't have to wait long, as a man in a blue uniform coat with a gold braid loop on his right arm emerged from the main door in the back of the lobby. He looked to be in his late forties with graying hair in a short, military cut and the kind of haggard features Alex had come to expect on men with great responsibility. The uniform was immaculate, without a loose thread or a speck of dirt, and it was tailored to his athletic physique.

"Miss Kincaid," he said as he reached them, keeping his voice low. "I'm Police Commissioner Roland. I wasn't informed you were going to be visiting us, is something wrong?"

"Not at all, Commissioner," Sorsha said, touching the man on the arm with her most disarming smile. "I'm actually just tagging along with my friend, Mr. Lockerby."

Roland's eyebrow raised at that.

"The famous private detective?" he said, turning to Alex.

Alex was absolutely that, but he never thought that anyone might have heard of him until someone brought it up. The fact that the police commissioner had heard of him could be good or bad, so Alex decided not to antagonize the man.

"I get lucky once in a while," he said. "I'm sorry you got dragged down here, but I just needed to ask one of your detectives about an old case. Nothing controversial."

Commissioner Roland hesitated for a minute, then seemed to decide that keeping Sorsha happy was the priority.

"Do you know what detective handled the case?" he asked.

"I don't," Alex admitted, "but it involves a Madison Prep student who was the victim of a hit and run. Martin Pride?"

Commissioner Roland sighed and nodded.

"I remember," he said, clearly unhappy that he did.

"Was it an important case?" Sorsha asked.

"Whenever Madison is involved, it's important," Roland said. "I don't know what you'd want with the Pride case, though. It was about ten years ago, but as I remember, he was running along the main road when he was hit by a car. Drunk driver most likely."

"Was the driver ever found?" Alex asked.

"Not that I recall," Commissioner Roland said. "It was just a tragic accident."

"All the same, could I talk to the detective who handled the investigation, just for a few minutes?" Alex asked, as politely as possible.

"I'll have to look up who handled it," Roland admitted. "Have a seat and I'll send him down to talk to you." He smiled at Sorsha, then turned and withdrew.

"That went well," she observed. "You said he might be trouble."

"I suspect he would have been if you hadn't been here," Alex said.

Sorsha gave him a smug look, then leaned against him.

"You should bring me along more often," she said, "and not just to teleport you around."

"I promise," Alex said, settling into the bench. Knowing how police bureaucracy operated, it would take Commissioner Roland at least fifteen minutes to track down the detective on the case, if he was even in the building and not out on a new case. "How about we stay in Albany for dinner and go home after that?"

Sorsha sighed and closed her eyes.

"I don't want to teleport home after a few drinks," she said.

Alex gave her a little shove with his shoulder.

"We'll go home through my vault," he said. "How tired are you?"

Sorsha blushed, then laughed.

"Sorry," she said. "I wasn't thinking." She sat up and looked back at him. "That seems to happen a lot around you," she accused. "Maybe it isn't a good idea for me to be with you so much."

Alex was about to apologize for being so manly and distracting, but a man in a gray suit emerged from the back of the office and strode confidently toward him.

"That was fast," he said to himself.

The detective was a tall, thin man with a long, gaunt face and a large nose like a weathervane. He had dark circles under his eyes and his coat was a bit frayed at the cuffs, which didn't fill Alex with confidence regarding his attention to detail.

"I'm Detective Chance," he said, holding his hand out. "I'm very busy at the moment, but the Commissioner said I need to brief you on an old case. The hit and run of Martin Pride?"

"That's the one," Alex said. "You handled it?"

The detective nodded.

"It was a pretty straightforward case," he said, "what is it you want to know?"

"Were there any suspects in the case?"

"Sure," Detective Chance admitted. "There were a couple of guys who had been arrested before for driving drunk, but none of them panned out."

"What about people who disliked Martin," Alex pressed. "Was there anyone with a motive?"

"To try to kill a fourteen-year-old high school kid?" Chance scoffed. "No, nothing like that."

"How did you know that the drunk drivers weren't involved?" Sorsha asked.

"Easy," Chance said, "whoever hit Martin clipped him pretty good. It would have damaged the front of their car. All the usual drunks had old damage on their cars, nothing new."

"Could the driver have been someone from Madison Prep?" Alex asked.

Again, Detective Chance shook his head.

"Students aren't allowed to have cars," he said.

Alex had a sneaking suspicion that a bunch of rich kids would be able to find a way to have a car without the school finding out, but clearly Detective Chance wasn't going to be any help with that. He thanked the man, who seemed grateful to get back to his cases, then took Sorsha by the arm and walked out.

"What now?" she asked once they were on the sidewalk.

"Now we go the Department of Motor Vehicles and find out if Freddy Hackett owned a car back when he went to school here."

25

LUCKY BREAKS

"Well, that was a waste of an afternoon," Sorsha said, leaning down to rub her right foot. She sat next to Alex on a bench in the lobby of the state capital building.

Alex wanted to argue, just to be contrarian, but Sorsha was right. They'd spent hours in the Motor Vehicle Registration office and the only people in Freddy's family who owned a car were his father, Arnie, and his mother, Bess. According to the state of New York, Freddy Hackett had never owned a car.

It was possible, of course, that Freddy had simply not registered his car, but that might have put his position at school in jeopardy, so Alex doubted he'd risk it. He might have used someone else's car to run down Martin, but that would lead to difficult questions from the car's actual owner when Freddy brought it back damaged.

"He could have bought a car under a fake name," he muttered to himself.

"There are much cheaper ways to eliminate a rival," Sorsha said, switching to her other foot.

Alex didn't want to admit it, but she had a point.

"All right," he sighed, standing up. "I need to call Sherry. There's a bit of blank wall around the corner where I can open my vault."

Sorsha looked like she wanted to argue, but nodded and slipped her shoe back on.

"I'm going to need to change before we go out anyway," she said. "After all the walking around and sitting in government waiting rooms, I'm positively filthy."

"We could always go to a greasy spoon and take in a burlesque show," Alex said with an absolutely straight face.

"You are nowhere near as charming as you think you are," Sorsha said, waiting for him to offer her his arm.

"Come on," he said. "You can change while I make calls."

"Why not just go talk to Sherry?" Sorsha asked as they walked away from the more populated areas of the building.

"Someone might be in the office waiting for me," he said. "It would be difficult to explain how I was really in Albany if I walk into the office."

Sorsha sighed and rolled her eyes.

"I've never worried about things like that," she admitted.

"You can teleport," Alex fired back.

He pulled the chalk out of his jacket pocket once they'd rounded the corner and entered a poorly lit back hallway.

"Isn't this still a bit public?" Sorsha asked, looking up and down the empty hall. "There are three office doors down at the other end."

"I'll close the gate," Alex said, leaning down to begin drawing a door. "Besides, I cooked up something with Iggy that I've been dying to try."

Sorsha folded her arms and simply waited for him to explain.

"You're no fun," he said, giving her a wink as he finished up. Then he made her wait another few moments while he found the right rune in his book and tore it out. "See here," he said, pointing to a series of nodes above and to the right of the main rune, "this is a major obfuscation rune."

"So it hides the open door?" Sorsha said.

"Not exactly," Alex said, "the door is still visible, but the magic encourages people to ignore it."

"Like the Archimedean, uh, like the Textbook on the shelf in your front room."

Sorsha had a note of disapproval in her voice, as this was an old argument between her and Iggy. Despite the fact that Sorsha had never noticed the Monograph until Alex had shown it to her, she remained convinced that it was not hidden nearly well enough.

"Exactly like that," Alex said with a smirk that Sorsha couldn't see since he was facing the wall.

"Not nearly charming enough," Sorsha muttered, apparently able to hear Alex's smirk in the tone of his voice.

Alex decided that discretion was the better part of valor and lit the rune paper, stepping back to allow the steel door to emerge from the plastered wall. Normally, he would have felt the pressure from the obfuscation rune clouding his vision, but with his connection to magic blocked, he could see the door without even concentrating. With a flash of irritation, he slotted his key into the lock in the door's center, and pushed it inward.

He stepped back to allow Sorsha to enter, then followed her in. On the inside wall, opposite the open door, was a steel cage door that Alex had gotten out of a police station that was being rebuilt. Once it was closed over the opening in the wall, it locked in place and would prevent anyone from entering, at least without making a hell of a racket.

Once the lock was set, he walked Sorsha to the door leading to her castle, then moved back to his drafting table. Sitting in his work chair, he scooped up the candlestick telephone and gave the operator the exchange for his office.

"Hello, Boss," Sherry said, her voice bright and full of energy. "How are things in Albany?"

"Cold," Alex said, not for the last time wishing he could write up a batch of his climate runes for just such occasions. With any luck, Mike would be able to write them soon, but with Alex's luck it would be spring then. "Anything I need to know about?"

"Detweiler called twice," she said with no urgency in her voice. "He wants to know if you've learned anything new."

"When he calls back, tell him I'm in Albany and I'll call him tomorrow when I get back."

Sherry chuckled.

"Sure thing," she said. "You might want to call your pal Billy over at the Midnight Sun, he called but didn't leave a message. He sounded funny."

"Intriguing," Alex said, scribbling a note on the pad he kept on his drafting table.

"Do you have anything for me?" she asked in a voice that indicated she clearly expected the answer to be 'yes.'

"Yes," he said with a smile, "I need you to find out why Lenore Anthony and Anita Powell refused to marry Reggie Aspler."

"Lenore Anthony the actress?" Sherry asked.

"The very one," Alex replied. "This would have been before she hit the big time and moved to Hollywood."

"But she was probably still an actress then," Sherry finished the thought. "That means she had an agent, a local one."

"Find him," Alex said.

"I can do that," Sherry said. "What about the other name, Anita Powell?"

"Daughter of some old money swell from upstate," Alex explained. "She didn't want to be Mrs. Aspler so badly that she disappeared before the wedding. See what you can learn about her."

"Will do," she said. "Have fun with Sorsha while you're there, and take her someplace nice."

"That's the plan," he said, then hung up.

Glancing toward the door to Sorsha's Castle, Alex released the hook on the telephone and waited for the operator.

"Get me Manhattan three, twenty-two ten," he said.

"Tasker," the next voice on the line said.

"It's me, what's the word?"

"Are you still interested in Freddy Hackett as a suspect for that upstate hit-and-run?"

"Well, I was," Alex admitted. "That accident got him on his high school tennis team."

"But?" Billy asked.

"But, I've looked at the motor vehicle records, Freddy Hackett never owned a car, still doesn't."

The line went quiet for almost a minute.

"Billy?" Alex pressed.

"Well, I don't like that news," Billy said.

"Why not?"

"Because it's a much better story if he did it," Billy said, a strange note in his voice.

"Why?"

"Because," Billy explained, "that kid, Martin Pride, he wasn't the only person who was forcefully moved out of the great Freddy Hackett's way."

That got Alex's attention.

"Someone else got hurt?" he asked.

"No," Billy said, "this time someone got dead."

"Spit it out, Billy."

"When Freddy graduated from high school, he applied to go to Cornell University. It was his father's alma mater and they have an excellent tennis program."

"Reasonable," Alex said, wondering where Billy was going with the story.

"Turns out not as reasonable as you'd think, because despite Freddy being a burgeoning talent at the time, he was rejected by the Dean of Admissions."

"Why would they turn down a rising star for their tennis team?" Alex wondered.

"That's what I wanted to know, so I made some calls and guess what?" Billy said with rising enthusiasm.

"I'll bite," Alex said. "What?"

"The reason Freddy was denied is because the coach of the tennis team used to be a professional player until he quit after a series of humiliating losses."

"And?"

"Alex," Billy said as if his point was self-evident. "Freddy's father, Arnie Hackett, was a tennis pro too."

"Got it," Alex said as everything snapped into place. "The coach lost to Freddy's dad and used his position to keep Freddy out of Cornell."

"Exactly," Billy said.

"And after that, this coach came down with a bad case of death?" Alex asked.

"You said it. He was eating at a diner just off campus, had a bad reaction to something he ate, and dropped dead."

Alex whistled.

"Did the police investigate?"

"I got ahold of the report," Billy said. "According to the investigation, the coach, one Claude Page, died from a shellfish allergy."

"He had to know he was allergic," Alex said. "Seafood in New York is like a religion."

"He did know," Billy went on. "He always ordered meals that had no seafood in them."

"So what happened?"

"The police ruled it an accident," Billy explained. "Their theory was that someone in the kitchen got careless."

"But you think he was murdered," Alex guessed.

"It would make a much better story if he was," Billy pointed out. "Freddy already removed one obstacle to his dream, why not two?"

"Was Freddy anywhere near this diner when the coach was poisoned?"

"Not that I can tell," Billy said, "but that doesn't mean he wasn't."

"How did removing Coach Page help him?"

"Page was replaced with his then-assistant coach, Victor Simms. Simms was the kind of coach who wanted to win tournaments, and he was only too happy to get Freddy into Cornell."

"Then Freddy became a big star, went pro, and the rest is history," Alex concluded. "It makes sense, or at least it would if we could tie Freddy to any of it."

Billy chuckled at that.

"I'm just a simple muckraker," he said, "making baseless insinuations is my job. Proving things is your line of work."

"Well don't rake any muck until I've had a crack at proving this,"

Alex said. "If Freddy is guilty, and he gets even a hint that we know about this, he'll be on the next boat to Argentina."

"The story's not ready yet anyway," Billy admitted. "I've got a couple of my boys digging into Freddy's past looking for more bodies, but Alex, I can't hold this back forever."

"If you have to run with this, keep my name out if it," Alex said.

"As always," Billy said.

"And call Sherry if that digging unearths any more corpses," Alex added.

"Will do."

Alex hung up the phone and set it aside. Turning to his drafting table, he scribbled notes quickly on the pad, then tore off the top sheet and tucked it in his pocket.

"Finished?"

Alex jumped as Sorsha's voice startled him.

"Yes," he said, spinning his chair around toward her. She had changed out of her slacks and button up shirt and now wore a strapless dress of such a dark blue that it appeared black. A half-length jacket of lighter material with silver piping covered her shoulders down to mid-torso and she had on silver gloves.

"Should I put on my tuxedo?" Alex asked, giving her a look up and down.

Sorsha twirled for him, sending the hem of her dress swirling around her calves.

"I think not," she said at last. "I'm not wearing any jewelry, so just put on your black suit jacket."

Alex limped to his bedroom door, then crossed to his wardrobe and switched jackets. As he turned back, he heard his bedroom door open.

"Oh, I thought I heard you up here," Iggy said from the doorway. "Are you and Sorsha going to be home for dinner?"

"Not tonight," Alex said, slipping on his black suit coat. "We're up in Albany and she wants to do the town."

Iggy chuckled and shook his head.

"Ah, to be young," he said. "I shall soldier on alone, then."

Alex laughed at his mentor's feigned distress, but a thought brought him back to reality.

"Quick question," he said. "Is it possible to die from a seafood allergy?"

Iggy looked startled for a moment by the question, then his brows knit together and he nodded.

"Oh, yes," he said. "The medical term is anaphylaxis and it can be quite deadly."

"Quickly?"

"Indeed, sometimes in a matter of minutes it can cause the throat to close, and the victim literally suffocates."

"How easy would it be to poison someone deliberately?"

Iggy considered that for a moment.

"Simplicity itself really. Just a bit of crab or lobster meat mixed into a dish would do it, if the allergy was severe enough. Shellfish is usually the most toxic in these situations."

"Alex?" Sorsha's voice came from the still open vault cover door. A moment later she appeared and took in the room with a glance. "I wondered what was keeping you," she said, giving Iggy a warm smile.

"Apologies, my dear," Iggy said. "I'm afraid I detained your escort for the evening."

"And what is so interesting?" she asked, turning to Alex.

"Auntie-flaxis," Alex said.

"Anaphylaxis," Iggy corrected. "Most likely death by shellfish in this case," he explained when Sorsha didn't respond.

Sorsha gave Alex a suspicious look and a sly grin.

"That must have been an interesting phone call you had earlier," she said.

Alex crossed the room and offered her his arm.

"I'll tell you all about it over dinner," he promised her.

"Dinner and murder?" she said, putting her hand over her heart and batting her eyelashes. "You do know how to show a girl a good time."

"Well, I'm going back downstairs," Iggy said, turning toward the door. "If I'm exposed to any more of this saccharine display, I shall contract diabetes."

The click of a lock being picked echoed in the empty space of the hallway. Nils Eccles held his breath, wary that the sound would carry to a listening ear. He'd spent five torturous hours hiding in the supply closet at the end of the hallway, waiting until the office workers were gone.

A quick trip into the office of the building maintenance department head revealed that he had a twenty-five-minute window between the time the last office on this floor closed and when the cleaning crew arrived.

"More than enough," he whispered to himself, trying to keep his hands from shaking.

Nils blessed his good luck. There was no way his sister would believe anything he could tell her, but her prejudice had worked in his favor. Since she refused to talk to him, that task fell to her pretty-boy boyfriend. He was supposed to be some hotshot detective, but Nils played him easily enough. Like most people, Lockerby was eager enough to help out a person with a good story. Nils was surprised at how young he was, at least a decade younger than Kjirsten, maybe more.

People are so predictable, he thought as the lock on his sister's office clicked open.

Slipping inside, Nils eased the frosted glass door closed, relocking it for good measure. It wouldn't do to have one of the cleaning staff check the door and find it open.

Looking at his watch, Nils was right on time. He had fifteen minutes to find the conference room, make the swap, and get out.

Plenty of time, he thought.

Moving quietly, he padded silently around the receptionist's desk toward the double doors that separated the front office from the rest. He didn't expect them to be locked but he pushed on them gently just to make sure. When they swung freely, he slipped inside, easing them closed behind him.

The hallway beyond the doors was curved, something Nils didn't expect. Building curved walls was much more expensive than simple straight ones.

"Typical Kjirsten," he muttered, pulling a small flashlight from his pocket. "She always had delusions of grandeur."

Shining the light on the first door on the left, the beam revealed his sister's new name, Sorsha Kincaid.

"Speaking of delusions," Nills chuckled, "where did she get that name?"

As much as he wondered about Kjirsten's new life, and what might lie beyond the monikered door, Nils was on a tight schedule. Panning the light further down the hall, he found three more doors, all with names on them. When he reached the end, there was a heavy looking door with the word 'Garage' painted on it.

"Why do you need a garage on the 65th floor," he wondered. For a moment, he was tempted to investigate, but only for a moment.

Shining the light on the opposite wall, he arrived almost immediately at a polished wooden door marked 'Conference Room'.

"Perfect," Nils said, checking his watch. He still had eight minutes, plenty of time.

Turning the handle met no resistance, so he eased the door open silently and stepped through. Unlike the hall, the conference room was filled with a dim light from the windows that ran along the far wall. The lights of the city were on far below and they provided just enough light for Nils to see his goal.

Right in front of him, in the exact center of an enormous table, was the music box. It looked exactly like the one in the sling pack which Nils had thrown across his back.

Moving to the table, he set the bag down and picked up the box. Turning it over in his hands, Nils found the screws that held on the bottom. They were clean, like the rest of the music box, and he could only hope they had remained undisturbed.

Working quickly, Nils withdrew a screwdriver from his pocket and began removing the four screws. Once they were gone, he took hold of the bottom and turned it counterclockwise. At first, it resisted him, then at last, it popped free, turning almost half way around before it released, coming completely free from the body of the music box.

Tilting the box into the light, Nils looked into the exposed cavity. As expected, the clockwork mechanism that played the music took up most of the space, but there was a folded piece of paper tucked into an empty spot, held in place by the device's winding arm.

"Hello, beautiful," Nils said as a wide smile spread across his face. "I've waited a long time for you."

"I've been waiting for you too," a new voice said, "but I don't think you should call me 'beautiful.'"

Nils almost dropped the box in his effort to point the light at the wall opposite the windows. There was a wooden desk attached to the wall so draped in shadow that it was little more than a dark shape. As Nils' light panned over it, he could see that the desk was not empty. Sitting behind it, his suit jacket buttoned up to prevent any light from reflecting off his shirt, sat Kjirsten's boyfriend, the detective.

As if to emphasize his presence, he flicked a lighter to life and sucked the flame into a cigarette in his mouth. Once the tip glowed with its own fire, he snapped the lighter shut and blew out a cloud of smoke.

"Hello Nils," he said. "We need to talk."

26

BEFORE THE FALL

Alex placed his lighter on the secretary desk, next to his 1911, which sat just a bit to the left. Nils stood about six feet away, by the conference table, looking for all the world like a child caught stealing sweets. To his credit, his face clouded over almost instantly, losing all expression, but Alex had already seen his moment of guilt.

"Fancy meeting you here?" Alex said, switching on the light over the desk then picking up his 1911. He held the weapon loosely, pointing it down at the floor.

"Looks like you expected me," Nils said, clearly back in control of his emotions.

Alex had, of course, especially after feeding Sorsha's brother such a tantalizing window of opportunity. Even then, Alex barely had time to get here after being out with Sorsha all evening.

"You're not armed," he asked, casually, "are you, Nils?"

Nils looked down into the open bottom of the music box and extracted the folded paper before setting the box on the table. That done, he held his coat open and turned slowly around.

"What gave me away?" he asked once he returned to facing Alex.

"Your desperation when I told you about Sorsha's original castle,"

Alex said. "You were pretty upset about the potential loss of a music box. If it had been made by Tiffany and had jewels in it, I might understand, but you're talking about something anyone could buy in a five and dime."

"Sentimental value," Nils suggested.

Alex considered that for a minute, then shrugged.

"That might have worked," he admitted, "if your sister hadn't warned me about you ahead of time."

"Dear Kjirsten," Nils said, shaking his head. "Where is she, by the way?" He looked around, trying to penetrate the darkness in the corners of the room.

"She doesn't know you're here," Alex said.

Nils looked surprised at that.

"You didn't tell her," he realized. "Why not?"

"Things the way they are, you're going to be my brother-in-law before too long," Alex said. "I imagine things will go smoother if you're in your sister's life, and that can't happen if you're a wanted fugitive."

"You're assuming she would even care," Nils scoffed.

"Mr. Eccles, I'm an orphan, I understand the importance of family. I'm not about to let Sorsha throw that away unless there aren't any other options."

Nils laughed at that.

"I wish you luck with that," he said.

"Do you?" Alex asked. "Or is that just a con?"

Nils looked down at the music box, then back up at Alex. After a minute, he held up the folded paper.

"You know what's on this?" he asked, holding it up.

Alex nodded.

Nils chuckled, shaking his head sadly.

"This is it," he said. "The big score, the one last job."

"I've heard that from lots of men," Alex said, shaking his head. "It's never that."

Nils closed his fist over the paper.

"Damn it, this is all I have, it's mine."

"No, it isn't," Alex said.

"You don't even know what it is," Nils said.

"Of course I do," Alex countered. "Open it up."

Nils unfolded the paper, then turned it toward the light so he could read it.

"William Halsey of the Green Wood?" he read.

"It means that the money your father stole in the Pittsburg Depository heist of nineteen twenty-seven is buried in Brooklyn," Alex said.

"What makes you think..." Nils started, then stopped.

"That your father was the one who robbed the army's payroll? That was a guess, but I made a call out to the Green Wood Cemetery in Brooklyn. One of the groundskeepers there was nice enough to tell me the date when William Halsey was buried."

"And?" Nils pressed when Alex hesitated.

"Two days after someone broke into the Pittsburg Federal Depository and made off with a cool million dollars of military payroll, William Halsey was buried."

"Coincidence," Nils said.

"It would be if William Halsey's name wasn't on that piece of paper," Alex said. "Your dad had something buried in a cemetery, jewels wouldn't need a hiding place the size of a casket, no, you only need something that big for a lot of cash. Once I knew that, finding the actual crime was easy."

"How did you figure out that the money was buried in a cemetery?"

"I've seen that trick before," Alex said.

A calculating look crossed Nils face.

"Should I assume that since you're here alone, and you haven't told my sister about this, that you're open to an arrangement?"

"I am," Alex said, cautiously. "I doubt it'll be the arrangement you wanted, but I'm not going to give you much choice."

Nils shook his head.

"You sure about that? I mean we're talking about a million dollars. I'd be more than happy to split it sixty-forty, your way."

"I make a fair amount of money, Nils," Alex said, "and your sister is rich."

Nils laughed at that.

"There's no such thing as enough money," he said with a smile.

"Well, you'd better hope there is," Alex said, pulling one of his business cards from his shirt pocket. "My offer is this," he said, setting the card on the desk face down, revealing a phone exchange written on the back. "You're going to call this number and ask for William Donovan, you don't speak to anyone but him."

Nils' eyes darted to the card, then back up to Alex.

"And what do I say to this Mr. Donovan?" he asked.

"You're going to tell him that you are in a position to return one million dollars of stolen government money, and that you'll do just that if he guarantees you a ten percent bounty."

Nils chuckled at that, but it was a sad sound.

"Even if they believed me, which I doubt they will, you can't trust some government agent to honor any deal they make. This Donovan character will probably dump my body in Halsey's grave the moment he sees the money and keep it for himself."

"I know Donovan," Alex said. "He's hired me before because I have some skills that he needs, not to mention access to your sister."

Nils made a face.

"Don't say 'access to my sister'," he said with a shudder.

It took all Alex's willpower not to grin like an idiot, but he mastered himself.

"The point is that Donovan wants to stay on my good side, and he needs access inside the government more than he needs a million dollars."

"Nine-hundred thousand," Nils corrected.

"That too," Alex continued. "Mention my name, and Donovan will deal square."

"And I walk away with a hundred grand," Nils said.

"No," Alex said, causing Nils' eyes to snap to him. "You walk away with one-hundred grand free, clear, and legal."

"Legal," Nils repeated, as if it was a foreign word. "Father would be so disappointed."

"But Sorsha won't," Alex pointed out. "You write her a letter, explaining everything, and I'll see that she reads it."

"Everything?" Nils said with a raised eyebrow.

"You'll leave out this part, of course," Alex said with a conspiratorial grin, then his expression hardened. "And if you ever tell Sorsha about my role in any of this...there won't be enough left of you to bury in that music box. Capiche?"

Nils looked into Alex's eyes, searching for deception or bravado. Finding none, he cleared his throat and loosened his tie.

"You have my word," he said, his voice suddenly hoarse.

Alex held his gaze for a long moment, then smiled and sat back in his chair.

"Good," he said, his voice easy and friendly. "Once you're done, come by the brownstone before you spend any of that money. I'll let you talk to my mentor, Dr. Bell. He can give you good advice about how not to lose it all in the first year."

Nils stood there, like he didn't know what to do with that information.

"Why do you care?" he said at last.

"Because," Alex said, standing and tucking his 1911 into his shoulder holster, "you're going to be my brother-in-law and I can't have you embarrassing my wife."

"So it's a done deal with you and Kjir—uh, I mean Sorsha?"

"It's unofficial at the moment," Alex said, walking over to stand in front of Nils. "One more thing." He reached out and took the music box. "If you did your homework, you know I got my start as a detective with a gold-standard finding rune, the best in the city. It's gotten a lot better since those days; all I need to find someone is something that is, or was, important to them. If you try to double cross me, Nils, if you try to just grab the money and run..." Alex held up the music box. "Understand I can use this to find you. Combined with your sister's power, I'm pretty sure I can find you anywhere on earth. If you make me come find you, Nils...I'll bring the music box."

"Right," Nils said, a tiny note of disappointment in his voice.

Alex was up early the next morning, but his foot regretted the previous day. Quite apart from all the walking and standing while visiting Madison Prep and various government buildings, he'd taken Sorsha out and she'd wanted to dance.

"That'll teach you," he admonished himself as he picked up his cane and limped toward his vault. By the time he reached his office a few minutes and two vault doors later, he threw his cane into the far corner by his desk.

"I'm sick of you," he grumbled. "Might as well start walking by myself."

He sat down behind his desk, resolved to ignore his throbbing foot. Pulling out his flip notebook, he started reviewing everything he'd learned yesterday. Once he was done with that, he'd have to update the individual case files, then he'd need to call Detweiler. He'd used a bunch of runes yesterday, so he'd have to talk to Mike about restocking his red book. Mike was getting good with his rune skills, but there were still runes that were beyond his ability, so Alex would probably have to talk to Iggy about a few of the more exotic ones. And then...

"Enough!" he shouted, slamming his fist down on the leather top of his desk.

Alex sat there with his stinging hand still in the center of the table. Between his foot and the damnation rune, his detective work had been largely reduced to research and phone calls. He'd made it work, but enough was enough.

"Boss?" Sherry's voice broke through his thoughts.

"What!" he shouted before realizing what he'd heard.

Looking up, he saw his startled secretary standing in his doorway with a worried look on her face.

"Boss?" she said again.

"Sorry," he said, the flash of sudden rage draining out of him like water from a broken bucket.

"You okay?" Sherry pressed.

"No," he admitted, "but there's nothing I can do about that right now."

"That new tattoo on your chest got you down?" she asked.

That startled Alex. Sherry knew about the damnation rune, of course, but she'd never mentioned it before.

"A little," he lied. "I'm sorry I startled you."

She gave him a warm smile, then pulled a notepad out from behind her back.

"I'm still looking into the two women you gave me yesterday, but I found Martin Pride."

Alex had forgotten that he asked Sherry to get current contact information for Martin.

"He went to Yale and graduated with a degree in law," she went on. "He's currently working for Richardson, Sanderson, and Michaels, they're a high-end law firm here in the Core."

"You have an address?" Alex asked.

Sherry tore the top page off her note pad and dropped it on his desk.

"Anything else?" she asked.

Alex shook his head.

"No," he said. "I've got to do some work here, then I'll go interview Martin Pride."

"I'll hold down the fort," she said, then winked at him and left.

Alex listened to her footsteps as she retreated down the hall to the front office.

"Tattoo," he muttered, recalling her reference to the damnation rune. He hadn't really thought about how Iggy and Moriarty had managed to put the rune on him, but it did remind him of the escape rune he once had tattooed on his arm. Even that wouldn't work for him now. He'd had to touch the tattoo machine the entire time the artist put it on him in order to fill the ink with magic. The damnation rune would, of course, prevent that.

He unbuttoned the front of his shirt and pulled it open. The damnation rune was there, right over his heart and wrapping around his left side. It clearly wasn't a tattoo. The lines shifted and pulsed with light, like they were more magical energy than physical construct.

"Tattoo," he said again, his voice a whisper.

"Sherry," he said before even pushing the talk key on the intercom. "Sherry," he said again, remembering the key this time.

"Yes, boss," her voice came back.

"Is Mike in?"

"Yes, he's writing runes in his office."

Alex thought for a second, the pain in his foot long forgotten.

"Tell him I want to see him right away."

Equal & Opposite

The offices of Richardson, Sanderson, and Michaels were the kind of overdone opulence Alex had come to expect from businesses that operated in the Core. The waiting area was done up in oak and hickory, stained a warm color and polished to an immaculate shine. The chairs and couches were leather and inviting, with a bookshelf full of literary classics if clients wanted to read while they waited.

A cabinet radio that looked for all the world like a coffin from a movie, squatted in one corner with the strains of some symphony emanating from it. On the opposite side from the radio was a water cooler and a table that held a tray of what smelled like fresh-baked cookies.

"How can I help you?" the secretary at the front desk asked before Alex was even halfway across the room. She was a prim and proper woman in her forties with brown hair going slightly gray that she kept up in a tight bun. Her face was still attractive in a serious way, and Alex got the impression she wasn't someone with an excess of patience.

"I'm Alex Lockerby," he said, handing her one of his cards. "I'm doing some work for Callahan Brothers Property, following up on an old claim that involves one of your associates. A Mr. Martin Pride? Would it be possible to speak with him for a few minutes?"

The secretary scrutinized his card for a long moment, then she looked up at Alex.

"Who are you working for at Callahan Brothers?"

"Arthur Wilks," Alex lied. He was relatively certain Arthur would back him up if the secretary actually called the insurance company, but he hoped having the ready name would prevent that necessity.

To Alex's surprise, the woman sighed and shook her head.

"That man is annoyingly thorough," she said, obviously recognizing the name. "I'll call Mr. Pride, he'll be out when he can."

"I'll wait then," Alex said, relieved he didn't have to make up more details.

Moving to the comfortable looking waiting area, Alex settled in. He had experience with lawyers and the high end ones tended to be rather callous with other people's time. As it turned out, however, Alex didn't have to wait very long. Before he even had a chance to finish the front page of the newspaper he'd picked up in Empire Station, a young man with a slight limp hurried up to him.

"Mr. Lockerby?" he asked.

"Call me Alex," he said, rising and sticking out his hand for the young man to shake..

"I'm Martin Pride," he said. "Janice told me you wanted to ask about an insurance claim?"

"Not exactly," Alex said. "Callahan Brothers Property wants to use me as a regular investigator so they're having me go over some old cases as a sort of audition. One of the ones they gave me is a claim when you were hit by a drunk driver when you were in high school."

Martin's face soured for a moment.

"Yeah, that's about all I remember," he said. "I was running along the road one minute and the next I woke up in a hospital bed."

"Did the police ever catch the driver?" Alex asked, pulling out his flip notebook.

"Nope," Martin said. "But that's all in the past. Except for a bit of a limp, I never think about it."

"I saw something in the file about you being an athlete," Alex said.

Martin barked out a laugh at that.

"Yeah, I was a tennis player on the high school team. Needless to say, my accident was the end of that, but I was never much of a student back then. While I was recovering, I had nothing to do but read and study, so I got my grades up and made it into law school."

"Sounds like you made lemonade," Alex said.

Martin nodded, then pulled up his shirt cuff to check his wristwatch.

"I don't know what else I could tell you," he said, "but I need to get back to work. The partners here expect me to be productive."

"Were there any repercussions at your high school?" Alex pressed.

"Not that I remember," Martin said. "My girlfriend finally had enough of me being in the hospital and moved on to greener pastures, but I got a better one when I got back to school. I married her last year."

"Congratulations," Alex said, giving Martin an ingratiating smile. "Thanks for your time."

Martin shook his hand again and headed off toward the back office. Alex watched him go, irritated that he hadn't learned anything new. As far as he could tell, Martin's accident was just that, and even though it was a boon to Freddy, there was no proof the tennis pro had a hand in it.

Alex resolved to head back to his office where, hopefully, Sherry would have something for him. Sooner or later Detweiler would catch up with him and he wanted to be able to tell him something new.

At least there haven't been more bombings, he thought as he rode the elevator down to the street level. That thought took him aback. If there weren't any new bombings in the next week, it could mean the bomber's work was done. He wasn't sure how to use that information, but it was something to think about.

Later, he admonished himself. *Right now you've got to find a connection between the bomber's victims and tell Holcombe Ward that Ari Leavitt's killer might have gotten away with it.*

"Great," he said to the empty elevator.

27

ON TRACK

To Alex's surprise, his foot didn't seem to be getting worse as the day wore on, but he did stop at the little general merchandise shop in Empire Station to buy a bottle of aspirin before heading back up to his office.

"That was fast," Sherry said when he opened the door.

"Martin's a dead end," Alex said, shutting the door behind him. "Which means that Freddy Hackett is a dead end."

"Really?" Sherry asked. "From what you told me, he's the perfect suspect."

"What I believe and what I can prove are two different things," he said. "I've spent too much time on this already. If I don't get back on the bomber case, Detweiler's going to have my hide."

"He did call while you were out," Sherry reported.

Alex sighed and pinched the bridge of his nose.

"All right," he said. "I'll go call him, then I'll call Holcombe Ward. Let me know if anyone else calls for me."

"There is one other thing," she said as Alex headed for the back office door.

When he turned back, she held out a stack of rune papers.

"Mike's out, meeting with a client, but he said to give you these."

Alex took the papers and thumbed through them. The linking runes were still a little sloppy, but Mike couldn't even write one a month ago.

"These are good," Alex said, folding the papers in half and tucking them into his shirt pocket. "I'll tell Mike when I see him next, but when he comes back, tell him that I said he did great."

"Will do, boss," Sherry said as Alex headed into the back hallway.

There were four doors in the little hall. The first three were on the right hand wall and came with the office. The fourth was at the end of the hall, facing the front office door, but that one was installed by Alex and led to his vault. He passed by the map room and Mike's workroom, turning into his office and heading straight to the bookshelves behind his desk. Most of the shelves had books that Alex referred to every now and again. The third shelf on the right, however, was bare of literature. That was the one Alex used as a liquor cabinet and he took down a bottle of gin, setting it on his desk. Gin was the preferred drink to use with medicine and if he was going to call Detweiler with nothing useful to tell him, he wanted to take the aspirin first.

Ten minutes later, Alex sat behind his massive desk, toying with a half empty tumbler of gin. He knew as soon as he finished it, he'd have to call the lieutenant, so he wasn't really in a hurry.

"Enough procrastination," he said, then drained the glass, setting it aside.

Picking up the phone, he gave the operator the exchange for the Central Office, then gave the police operator the lieutenant's name.

"Detweiler," he said when he answered.

"I heard you were looking for me," Alex said.

"Lockerby," the lieutenant growled. "It's about time, I've got something I need you to look into."

That was surprising. Alex had expected him to demand new information.

"I've got my notepad," he said, pulling his desk pad in front of him. "What have you got?"

"My boys figured out who was supplying Matthew McDermet with his low-quality potions, a lowlife named Benny Thorpe."

"He's an alchemist?" Alex asked.

"After a fashion," Detweiler said. "He's a third-rate talent, but he's very good at making a few basic potions. Clearly he put that to use supplying McDermet."

"What do you need me to do?"

"We still can't find Sam Olsen, McDermet's partner. Based on his notes, he's been doing business with Benny the entire time he's been in business, so it's likely he knows or knew who Sam Olsen is."

"Don't take this the wrong way," Alex said, jotting down the details, "but why do you want me on this? In the time it took you to get in touch with me, your boys could have already sweated that information out of our cut-rate alchemist."

"Benny can smell cops," Detweiler said. "If he even sees one, he'll be in the wind."

"Do you know where he brews his potions?" Alex asked. "I can track him easily with something from his lab."

"That's the problem," Detweiler continued, "we don't know where Benny lives and we don't know where he works."

"Then how am I supposed to find him?"

"We do know that he likes to bet, and we know where. It's a little off-track lounge in the Bowery. The front is an ice-cream shop called the Scoop Shoppe."

"So raid it when Benny's there," Alex suggested.

"That'll take days to set up, scribbler," Detweiler growled. "I don't know about you, but I'd like to catch our mad bomber before he strikes again."

Alex had to admit, the lieutenant had a point.

"All right," he conceded. "How do I get in and when can I catch Benny there?"

"I don't know when Benny will be there, but he's a habitual gambler so you shouldn't have to wait long. As for getting in, ask the soda jerk for a scoop of Rocky Road without nuts."

"Clever," Alex chuckled. "I'll get a racing form from the newsstand downstairs and hit up the Scoop Shoppe at post time."

"You haven't asked how you'll recognize Benny," Detweiler pointed out.

"That part's easy," Alex said. "Alchemists use a special base in their work, and it never fully washes out of their hands, meaning they always have a slight chemical smell. If Benny is the kind of lowlife you've described, he'll reek of the stuff."

"Good luck," Detweiler said. "This is just about the only lead we've got, so don't blow it."

"You really think an old partner of Matthew McDermet will know why someone blew him up?"

"My source didn't know who the partner was, but they did know that McDermet forced him out. Maybe Sam's our bomber."

"What's his beef with Reggie, the professor, and the Office of Magical Oversight?" Alex asked.

"One thing at a time, scribbler," Detweiler said. "For now, find out if Benny knew Sam, and where we might be able to put our hands on him."

"I'll call you as soon as I know anything," Alex promised and hung up.

He wasn't convinced that Sam Olsen was much of a lead, but he'd worked with less. Standing, Alex returned his gin bottle to the shelf, then headed back down the hall.

"I'm going downstairs for a few minutes," he told Sherry as he emerged into the front office. "I've got a lead to follow at a betting parlor so I need to pick up a racing form and some coffee."

"Oh," Sherry said, brightening immediately, "take this and get it filled."

She reached under her desk and came up with one of the office's two thermoses. Alex accepted it and headed out into the hall for the elevator.

Alex sat at his desk reviewing the little paper that detailed races all over the eastern seaboard. From Saratoga to Pimlico and all the way south to Churchill Downs, if horses were running, they were listed. Alex wanted to skip the descriptions, but if Benny Thorpe really was an aficionado, he'd need at least a passing familiarity with the ponies. Lucky for him, the first race today was at two o'clock out of the Aqueduct in Queens. That was close enough that Benny might decide to catch the train and see it himself, but with McDermet's potion shop closed down, he was likely to be tight on cash. That meant he'd probably skip the train ride and head for his favorite betting parlor. Of course, a lack of funds might keep him away from the track too, but there wasn't anything Alex could do about that.

"Boss?" Sherry's voice interrupted him from the intercom.

"Yeah," Alex said, forgetting to push the talk key. "Yeah," he repeated after rectifying his error.

"I just got off the phone with Jared Watson," Sherry said.

"My contact at the Times?" Alex said, anxiety suddenly in his voice. "You know his help isn't exactly free."

"Yeah," Sherry said, in a voice that indicated that she absolutely knew that, "he said to tell you that you owe him a favor."

"Great," Alex sighed. "The last time I owed him a favor he had me chase down a family heirloom his grandmother accidentally sold at a flea market."

"Let me guess, some horrible tchotchke?"

"A ceramic turtle that looked like it was made by a potter with only three fingers on both hands," Alex muttered. "Jared keeps it on his desk and uses it as an ashtray."

"Well, whatever he wants this time, I'm sure you'll be more than capable," Sherry said, not bothering to stifle a giggle. "Anyway, I remembered that Jared's family was old money, so I asked him what he knew about Anita Powell."

"And?" Alex pressed.

"He knew her, not well, mind you, but as a casual acquaintance."

"Does he know why she ran away from Reggie and disappeared?"

"Not exactly, but he did say that her father, Kernan Powell, was a real traditionalist."

"Don't tell me," Alex interrupted, "he wanted a son."

"Anita was an only child," Sherry confirmed, "and her father wanted to use her to cement the family's future."

"So he married her off to Reggie Aspler," Alex said, "or tried to. And Anita rebelled, though running away sounds like an extreme reaction."

"According to what Jared remembers, Anita was quite the modern woman."

"The kind of girl who wouldn't want to have her life laid out for her," Alex said.

"It explains why she disappeared," Sherry said.

"Did Jared know what happened to her? Where she went?"

"If he did, he wasn't talking," Sherry said.

"All right," Alex said with a sigh. "It's a great story, but it doesn't help us. Thanks for running it down."

"Sure thing, boss. Anything else?"

"No, that'll do. Good work."

Alex released the talk key and went back to his racing form. It had been a long time since he'd been to an off-track betting parlor and he'd never been one for the ponies. That kind of thing required money, something Alex had only recently become acquainted with.

Before he could settle in, however, the phone on his desk rang.

"Lockerby," he said once he picked up the handset.

"Please tell me you found something on Freddy Hackett."

"Nice to hear from you, Billy," Alex said. "Unfortunately, I have bad news. I dug around the accident with Martin Pride, the kid from Madison Prep, and as far as I can tell, it was an accident."

"I don't want to hear this," Billy said. "I can't run a story about the crown prince of tennis without at least some evidence."

"I don't know what to tell you, there's no evidence that Freddy ever even drove a car, much less owned one. And, before you ask, none of his friends at Madison had cars either, they weren't allowed and I checked just to be sure."

"Well, that's interesting," Billy said, a trace of smugness in his voice.

"Why do you say that?" Alex asked, sure he wasn't going to like the answer.

"I'm holding a copy of a police report, dated September twenty-third of nineteen thirty-three, that says that one Freddy Hackett crashed his mother's car while driving drunk."

"So?" Alex said. "Freddy was born in nineteen fifteen, that would make him eighteen years old in thirty-three. He was fourteen when Martin Pride was hit."

"But he did know how to drive a car," Billy countered. "He could have easily stolen one to hit Martin."

"All that report proves is that he knew how to drive a car when he was a senior in high school. It doesn't prove he knew that when he was a freshman."

"You are no help this morning," Billy grumbled.

"Tell you what," Alex said. "Whoever hit Martin would have had their car repaired shortly after that. Call around and see if you can find a garage that did front end repairs around the time Martin was hit."

"Wouldn't the police have already done that?"

"Yes," Alex admitted, "but maybe you can find something they didn't."

"Thanks," Billy said, sarcasm dripping from his voice.

Alex wished him well with his research and hung up. He still had two hours before post time, so he picked up his paper and headed down to the cafe in Empire Terminal for a bit of lunch and research away from his phone.

Alex expected the Scoop Shop to be a little hole in the wall attached to an abandoned building. He wasn't prepared for a clean, newly painted, well-lit business sandwiched between a five and dime and a green grocer. A bell above the door jangled pleasantly as he entered and a young man in a clean white apron and a paper hat looked up from behind the counter. A man and woman that appeared to be on a date sat at a little table in the corner, sharing something in a tall glass with two straws. At the bar were two working women, obviously on their lunch break, and other than that, the shop was empty.

"What can I get you, mister?" the young man asked, a cheery smile on his face.

Alex stepped up to the bar, but didn't sit on one of the available stools.

"I'm kind of picky when it comes to ice cream," he said, keeping his voice low, but not low enough to arouse suspicion. "I like Rocky Road, but I want it without nuts."

The young man's smile got a bit wider and he pushed a button on the cash register, causing the drawer to pop out.

"You'll need to check in the back," he said, his voice also low. Reaching into the drawer, he pulled out a large red coin and pressed it into Alex's hand. "For the door," he said, then glanced around to the far side of the room where a hallway went into the back.

"Thanks," Alex said, closing his fist around the coin.

He turned and headed in the indicated direction. Rounding the end of the counter, he passed a phone booth, a small customer bathroom, and a door to the back of the shop. Alex thought that one might have been what he was looking for, but beyond it, sitting against the back of the hallway, was a plain wooden door with no handle. Instead, it had a small coin slot, like the ones used on a cigarette machine, mounted on the jamb.

Raising the red coin, Alex fitted it into the slot and dropped it inside. There was a clacking noise as the coin fell through the mechanism, then the door popped open about an inch. Without hesitating, Alex pushed the door and stepped inside.

Beyond the door was a small landing with stairs that led down, below the ice cream parlor. Behind the door was a man in a tuxedo who motioned Alex in the direction of the stairs. He had the look of a bouncer, but was less bulky than the ones Alex was used to at nightclubs.

Probably armed, Alex thought.

"Welcome, sir," he said, pushing the door closed until it clicked.

Alex nodded at him, then headed down. At the bottom of the stairs was a much fancier, polished mahogany door with brass hardware and a stained-glass panel with the name 'Scoops' laid out in yellow.

Taking hold of the handle, Alex pulled the door open. A wall of sound and smoke assaulted him as he moved inside and stepped down onto the concrete floor. The room was exactly what Alex expected, with small tables scattered around the main area and a long caged counter running along the far wall. A large chalk board was mounted on the right hand wall, complete with slides to make it easy to pull down so the odds makers could update the races and horses as new information came in.

Not wanting to be the first person in the room, Alex had waited until three races had already been run before arriving. Even as early as it was, there were fourteen customers in the room, eleven men and three women. Two men in tuxedos stood at either end of the room, one of them obviously a bouncer, the other most likely the floor manager. Below the chalkboard was a man in shirtsleeves, with a stick of chalk behind his ear, who was sitting on a stool, waiting for updates from a runner. Two waitresses in matching corset tops with stockings under their short dresses were moving between the tables taking drink orders and selling cigarettes. They each had dazzling smiles and an easy, friendly manner, which Alex guessed made selling booze and cigarettes easier.

There were four betting windows, each manned by an attractive girl in a corset-topped dress with bright red lipstick. Behind them, a man in a green eyeshade sat at a desk, reading the long strip of paper emanating from a ticker tape machine. In front of the man was a microphone and his voice droned through the speakers as he read off the details of the current race.

"Afternoon," a voice dragged Alex's attention back to his immediate environs.

Alex turned to find the floor manager standing at his elbow.

"Harrison French," he said, extending his hand.

"Alex Lockerby," Alex said, shaking the man's hand.

"I don't remember your face," Harrison said, "is this your first time visiting us?"

"Guilty," Alex said. "I've been looking for a place to make a few bets."

"Well, you've come to the right place," Harrison said, putting his hand on Alex's shoulder. "We have a little tradition here," he said, steering Alex toward the nearest betting window. "We like to trust everybody, but cops make it hard to stay in business."

"You want me to make a bet to prove I'm not a cop?" Alex asked. He wasn't sure that would actually work, since cops on a sting operation would be able to bet without getting into trouble.

"We find that helps," Harrison said. "The next race is the 3:00 out of Belmont, do you like any of the horses there?"

"Gentleman's Canter," Alex said, thankful he'd done his homework. He pulled out his billfold and dropped a fiver on the counter. "Five to win."

The girl took his money and wrote the details on a betting slip before passing it back through the cage window.

"Good choice," Harrison said. "Gentleman's Canter is having a good season. If he keeps it up, he might make it to the Derby."

"Do you mind if I make a few more bets?" Alex asked.

"Not at all," Harrison said, slapping Alex on the shoulder. "If you need anything, give me a shout."

With that, the front manager left, moving through the tables and speaking to people as he went.

"Friendly guy," Alex said to the girl as he pulled some more cash out of his wallet.

For her part, the girl smiled, but her cold eyes followed Harrison French as he moved through the crowd. She clearly didn't like him.

"Tell me something," Alex said as he laid out two fives, a ten, and a twenty. "I'm looking for a friend, Benny Thorpe."

The girl's eyes snapped to Alex at the mention of the name; clearly she didn't like Benny any more than Harrison.

"Well, not a friend really," Alex went on, "more of a friend of a friend. He's supposed to be a regular here, but he hasn't been seen in his other haunts in a while." Alex pulled another fiver from his wallet and put it on the counter with his hand over half of it. "Do you know if he's placed any bets here recently?"

The girl's eyes looked left, down the bulk of the room. She seemed satisfied that no one was paying her particular attention and she leaned in, putting her hand over the exposed half of the five dollar note.

"He's in here most days," she said. "Doesn't stay long, but he'll place a few bets."

"When does he come in?"

"Used to be late, around seven, but these days he's early."

Alex released his grip on the bill, and it vanished into a pocket in the girl's skirt.

"Now," she said, looking at the bills Alex had laid out previously, "what horses would you like to bet on?"

28

PONY UP

Alex sat reading the newspaper and sipping a passable tumbler of bourbon. He'd been in the betting parlor for over an hour and so far, no one that could be Benny Thorpe had made an appearance.

"Would you like another drink, Mr. Lockerby?" the chipper waitress asked. At first, Alex found her endearing, but she came around every five minutes and her perky interruptions were getting old.

"I'm fine, Delia," he said, not looking up from his paper.

As Delia headed over to the next table, Alex picked up his cigarette from the ashtray and puffed on it. Using the motion, he glanced around the room, making sure he hadn't missed someone coming in. Satisfied he hadn't, Alex returned to his paper, but before he could finish a story about the Nazi military buildup in western Europe, the door opened and a short, stooped man with horn-rimmed glasses stepped in.

That looks like a down on his luck alchemist, Alex thought, setting his paper aside. As the house manager moved to greet the new arrival, Alex stood and headed for the betting windows.

French, the front house manager held up the newcomer for a

moment and, as Alex passed, he heard the man call the newcomer, 'Benny.'

Alex stepped up to the second window, leaving the one closest to the door open. He made a pretense of looking for his betting slips, giving Benny a chance to reach the first window.

"Here we go," Alex said, passing the slips for two of the previous races over to the smiling girl.

"Well done, Mr. Lockerby," she said after she examined the tickets. "Two first place bets. Luck is definitely with you today."

Out of the corner of his eye, Alex saw Benny perk as he overheard the conversation.

"Oh, I don't know about that," Alex said, pulling three more tickets out of his pocket. "These were all losers."

"Well, I wish my luck was as good as yours," the girl said, stacking up Alex's winnings. He'd only wagered fifteen dollars on those two races, but one was a long shot, so his take came to a little more than a C-note.

"It's not luck," he said in a conspiratorial voice, "just a careful examination of the facts." He gave her a flirty wink, then pocketed his cash and headed back to his table. He'd barely resumed his paper when Benny approached the table and cleared his throat.

"Excuse me," he said as Alex lowered his paper again.

Now that Alex could see him up close, he noted how the man's shirt cuffs had water stains on them and his vest had spatter burns from some caustic substance. The real confirmation was the faint scent of alchemical base that accompanied the man's appearance.

"Yes?" he said, looking up into Benny's face. The man had a slight, off-kilter smile and weak, watery eyes behind his thick glasses.

"May I join you?"

Alex put out his foot and pushed a chair out from the table.

"Please," he said, then held out his hand. "Alex Lockerby."

"Benny," the other man said as he took the offered chair. "Benny Thorpe."

"Nice to meet you, Benny," Alex said, picking up his Bourbon. "You come here often?"

"Most days," Benny said. "I don't remember seeing you before."

"It's my first time," Alex said.

Benny started to say something, but Alex held up his hand as the drone of the race narration began a new race.

"This is one of mine," Alex said, leaning forward. He took out the betting slip and laid it down on the table. The name 'Summer Breeze' was listed to win at Aintree and Alex put it down in such a way that Benny could see it.

The two men sat in silence as the caller read out the tape, detailing the ins and outs of the mile and a quarter run. When he announced the winner, it was Summer Breeze.

"I couldn't help overhearing when you were up at the window," Benny said. "That makes three wins just today. How do you do it?"

"A lot of reading about horses," Alex said, "and a fair amount of gut feeling."

That clearly wasn't what Benny wanted to hear, although the truth was equally unbelievable. The reality of it was that Alex had Sherry circle the horse names she felt good about before he left the office. If he ever had to retire from the detective business, he and Sherry could make a fortune on the ponies.

As Benny searched for a way to keep the conversation going, Alex raised his hand and motioned to Delia.

"Bring my friend one of these," he said, holding up his bourbon, "and another for me."

"That's very generous of you, Mr. Lockerby," Benny said.

"Consider it a down payment," Alex said.

That got Benny's attention and he suddenly looked like a cornered animal.

"W-what to you mean?"

Alex took out his wad of winnings and put it on the table.

"I haven't been completely honest with you, Benny," Alex said. "I came in here looking for you."

Naked fear played over the alchemist's face, but he mastered himself quickly as his eyes snapped to the stack of cash.

"You a cop?" he asked, licking his lips.

"No," Alex said. "I'm a P.I. and I was told you know someone I'm looking for."

"Looking for why?" Benny said, gripping the table so hard his knuckles were white.

"Because he might be killing people with bombs," Alex said.

"The bomb at Matt's place," Benny hissed, his breathing suddenly coming in short gasps. "I can't be associated with that."

"Easy, Benny," Alex said, reaching across the table and grabbing the man's wrist to keep him from bolting. "I just need information. I know you weren't involved and if you tell me what you know, the cops never have to hear your name."

Benny stopped pulling against Alex's grasp and Alex withdrew his hand.

"You on the level?"

Alex reached into his pocket and pulled out the two remaining bets he'd placed on races that hadn't run yet, then he set them on the stack of cash.

"The man I need to find is Matthew McDermet's old partner," he said. "The one he forced out years ago, Sam Olsen."

"Sam Olsen," Benny scoffed. "Well, I know why you haven't been able to find him."

Alex raised an eyebrow.

"Why is that?"

"Because Sam isn't a he, he's a she," Benny said. "Samantha Olsen was Matt's old partner. She must have used Sam on the business license so the government wouldn't make waves."

It took Alex a moment to shift mental gears, but he managed.

"You know where I can find Samantha?" he asked as Delia brought their drinks.

"Nah," Benny shook his head. "She disappeared once Matt kicked her to the curb."

"Why did he push her out?"

Benny shrugged.

"Matt probably wanted to sell runes in his shop, but potions make more money and one alchemist can brew dozens of them at a time. Runes take time to write."

"Samantha was a runewright?" Alex asked, trying to keep his voice casual.

"Yeah," Benny said.

"What did she look like?"

"Short little scrub of a thing," he said. "She had short blonde hair, but I could tell it was a dye job."

"Anything else?" Alex asked.

Benny shrugged again.

"Not that I remember. She was really dedicated, though. Always in the shop working, and her runes were top notch. I told Matt he was a fool to get rid of her. He should have married her and kept her close, that way he could sell the runes whenever she got them done. Extra cash is extra cash after all."

"So she was pretty?" Alex asked. The fact that Benny suggested his friend marry Samantha suggested that he found her at least passingly attractive.

"Pretty enough," Benny said.

"Any idea where she might have gone after Matthew's place?"

"Someplace where she could use her runes," Benny suggested. "She was always excited about magic."

Alex finished his drink, then pushed the cash and the betting slips over to Benny.

"Thanks for your help, Benny," he said, dropping one of his business cards on the stack. "If you ever want to become a proper alchemist, give me a call."

Benny mumbled something, but Alex was too busy going over what he'd learned to hear it. Giving a nod to Harrison French, he headed back into the stairwell and up to the ice cream parlor. He had thought that the bomber hit the Office of Magical Oversight because he was investigating, but now he might know what it was meant to conceal. If Samantha Olsen wanted to go into business with Matthew McDermet, she would have had to register with the OMO. That bomb might have been meant to wipe out any traces of Samantha.

Now there were two missing women in this case, Anita Powell and Samantha Olsen.

"What if they're both the same person?" Alex asked himself.

It didn't seem likely that an old money kid like Anita would be slumming around with a cut-rate pharmacist like McDermet, but Alex had seen stranger bedfellows in his career. If nothing else it was a lead he would need to run down.

Alex went down the street to a general goods shop before stepping into a booth to use the phone. Closing the door behind him, he picked up the receiver and asked for the Central Office. He could have called from the ice cream shop, but that was a bit too close to the betting parlor for his liking.

"Detweiler," the lieutenant's voice greeted him once the Central Office operator connected the call.

"I talked with your boy, Benny," Alex said.

"Well," Detweiler replied, admiration in his voice, "you can move quickly when you want to. Did he know where we can find Sam Olsen."

"No," Alex admitted, "but he did have some useful information. Sam Olsen is actually Samantha Olsen."

Detweiler cursed.

"So Samantha put a name on the business license that people would assume was a man," he said.

"That's how I figure it."

"I'll have my boys go back through the records and see if we can find Samantha, but if there was a Samantha Olsen around this case, I suspect one of them would have brought it to me already."

"I'll see if I can find out more on this end," Alex said.

"Is that all Benny had?"

"Unfortunately," Alex answered. "It's been years, after all."

"All right," Detweiler said after a pause. "Get going on your end and see if you can dig up anything."

Alex agreed, then hung up.

During his afternoon at the betting parlor, Alex had tried to keep his drinking manageable, but he still felt a bit light-headed. To offset this, he stopped by an automat and grabbed a sandwich and some orange juice before heading back to his office.

"Billy wants to talk to you," Sherry reported once he stepped in from the hall and shut the door behind him.

Alex sighed.

"Of course he does. Anything interesting happen while I was out?"

"Holcombe Ward called," Sherry reported, "he wants to invite you and Sorsha to have dinner with him tonight at Delmonico's."

"He wants to pick my brain about the Leavitt case," Alex said. He wasn't excited about the prospect, but Sorsha might enjoy it. It had been some time since they'd eaten at Delmonico's. Sorsha liked to dance so they'd spent more time at clubs than in restaurants.

"I'm too busy for that," Alex decided. "Call Holcombe and tell him I can't meet him tonight, put him off for a few days. I'll go call Billy."

"Will do, boss," Sherry said. "There are some potential cases on your desk too."

Alex gave her a tired nod, then headed through the door.

"How did my picks for the ponies work?" she asked.

Before Alex could reply that they'd been perfectly accurate, the phone on her desk rang. Alex continued through the door, determined to let her handle whoever was looking for him this time. She'd bring him notes if she thought they were important.

When he reached his desk, Alex took some more aspirin. He knew going without his cane would be painful, but, surprisingly, it was going better than he'd expected. Lighting a cigarette, he sat staring at the stack of folders Sherry had left on his desk. The way his current cases were going, he was going to need some new work very soon. He toyed with the idea of going through the stacks now, but a glance at his clock told him it was half past four. By the time he'd read through the folders, it would be after five and Billy would be out of his office.

"At least this will be a quick call," he grumbled, reaching for his phone.

"Tell me you have something new," Billy said as soon as Alex greeted him.

"That bad?"

"I called up to Syracuse to talk to the mechanic that worked on Bess Hackett's car," Billy said, "the one Freddy crashed when he was drunk."

"Did you find him?" Alex asked.

"Yes, there aren't a lot of automobile mechanics in Syracuse. He remembered everything about the car and the work he did on it, but nothing about the Hackett family."

"Gotta love a man who loves his work," Alex chuckled.

"You should have heard him," Billy groused. "He went on and on about how he straightened out the body, sanded off the rust, and painted the car with twenty coats of hand rubbed lacquer."

"If I had a car, I'd want him to paint it," Alex agreed.

"You're my last hope," Billy said. "Did you learn anything new about Freddy?"

"Sorry," Alex had to admit. "I'm with you, I like Freddy for this, he had motive and opportunity. I just can't find any evidence to prove it."

"It would make it a solid case if we could prove Freddy was in proximity to Martin Pride's accident or Coach Page's killer sandwich."

That brought Alex up short. The police ruled that Coach Page had died of an accidental allergic reaction, but Iggy had told him that spiking the coach's salad wouldn't have been difficult.

"Where was Freddy when Coach Page died?" he asked.

There was a rustling of paper before Billy's voice returned.

"He was in Ithaca. He'd met with the Dean of Admissions at Cornell the day before."

"Pleading his case," Alex said, nodding to himself. "So, he was in town, and that means he could have poisoned Coach Page."

"Alex," Billy pleaded, "this guy's guilty, I'm sure of it."

"You publish that and he better be," Alex cautioned. "If he's got any exculpatory evidence, you'll be facing a libel suit."

"We get ten of those a week," Billy scoffed.

"The Hacketts have the money to back it up," Alex said.

Billy sighed.

"This is too good a story to abandon, Alex," he said. "A star athlete who murdered his way to the top. It's the biggest story in years."

"Well, so far all your evidence is circumstantial," Alex said.

"You think this is all just a big coincidence?"

"No," Alex said. "I think Freddy did it. I just can't prove it."

"Well, then what are we going to do?"

"Nothing I can do," Alex said. "Not until I get more information."

"And you're going to do that when?" Billy pressed.

Alex groaned.

"Holcombe Ward wanted to have dinner with me tonight," he said, "I was going to put him off, but I'll accept his offer. See if I can wheedle anything new out of him."

"So your plan is to let the president of the USLTA feed you?"

"It's a tough life," Alex said magnanimously, "but someone has to live it."

"How, exactly, does that help me?"

"Holcombe Ward knows everything that happens in the tennis world," Alex said. "Maybe he can shed some new light on what we already know."

"That's actually a good idea," Billy said after a moment's pause. "I knew I could count on you. I'll keep digging on this end; maybe there's something we missed."

Alex bid his enthusiastic friend farewell, then pulled out Holcombe's card from the back of his rune book.

"Holcombe," he said when the line connected. "It's Alex. Did my secretary get back to you yet?"

"No," he said. "I am glad to hear from you though. Dare I hope you and Miss Kincaid will join me tonight?"

"We'll be there," he said. "Thanks for the invite."

"It's the least I can do," Holcombe said. "Shall we say seven?"

Alex agreed, then hung up.

"Sherry?" he said, tapping the talk key on the intercom.

It took a moment for her to respond, so Alex assumed she was still on the phone.

"Yes, boss," she said.

"Forget calling Holcombe Ward, I already talked to him."

"Good," she said. "I just got off the phone with Sorsha and she said she wants to go."

"I'll call her," Alex said.

Sherry signed off and Alex sat looking at the phone. It had been a long day, he was tired, and he wanted nothing more than to sit in front of the library fire with a cigar and a book.

"It's a tough life," he repeated as he reached for the phone, "but someone's got to live it."

29

CHAMPAGNE NOTIONS

"You're sulking," Sorsha said as she took his hand to step out of the cab. She'd been delighted to hear that the famous and handsome Holcombe Ward had invited them to dinner, but Alex clearly wasn't excited.

Maybe he's jealous, she thought. Sorsha almost smirked at that, but she kept her face stoic. Alex could be surprisingly territorial at times and she didn't want to provoke him.

"Sorry," he grumbled as he paid the cabbie.

Sorsha decided she wasn't having any of that and leaned close, letting her magic rise so that her pale eyes began to glow.

"Do you know the last time I got invited out?" she said, her voice full of silky malice. "The word is out that we're a thing, and no one has invited me to dinner for months. I barely get invited to parties anymore."

That wasn't exactly true; Sorsha still got invited to parties, but thanks to Alex's schedule and having dinners with Dr. Bell, she had to turn most of those invitations down.

"We went to a party last month," Alex protested.

"I used to go to two parties a week," she hissed. "My social life is a mess thanks to you, so you're going to plaster a smile on your face, use your best manners, and at least pretend to have a fabulous evening with your beautiful fiancée."

Alex sighed, but he stood up straight and put on his most charming, boyish grin.

"That's better," Sorsha said, taking hold of his lapel and pulling him down to her level. Reaching up on her tip-toes, she planted a kiss on his cheek, leaving behind a quickly evaporating layer of frost in the shape of her lips.

There really wasn't a high class restaurant in Manhattan that Sorsha hadn't been to at least once, and Delmonico's was no exception. It had been years, though, and she was excited, not only to be out, but to be meeting Alex's famous client. She would never admit it to Alex, but she'd had quite the crush on Holcombe Ward back in his tennis days.

Sorsha didn't have to wait long as the man himself was waiting for them by the Host's podium. He looked much as Sorsha remembered, just a bit thinner and grayer.

"Miss Kincaid," he said, taking her hand and kissing the back, "I have so wanted to meet you."

"You're too kind," Sorsha said, blushing.

"I already have a table for us," he went on, turning to shake Alex's hand, "so follow me."

He led them through the entrance and into the dining room. The rumble of conversation was everywhere and groups of three, five, and more crowded around the tables. As far as Sorsha could tell, everyone seemed to be having a grand time.

Holcombe led them to the far side where a smaller table sat in a semi-private alcove. The tennis pro moved around the table to the rear-most chair and waited behind it while Alex pulled a chair out for her. Once Sorsha sat, the men joined her and a waiter in a bowtie and a maroon colored jacket appeared as if by magic. Normally, Sorsha would allow her date to order for her, to see if he knew anything about women and cuisine, but Alex knew her far too well for that, and of course he had the observational skills of a trained detective.

She listened politely as the waiter regaled them with the menu and ultimately ordered poached sea bass with new potatoes and a green salad.

Holcombe made small talk while they waited for their meal, never touching anything too serious. Sorsha asked about some of his more famous matches and the time he played at Wimbledon. For his part, Holcombe was happy to oblige, embellishing the stories with amusing little details.

When the waiter returned with their meal and another bottle of Champagne, Holcombe finally got down to business.

"I hate to talk business in front of you, Sorsha," he said, "but I am interested to know how Alex is getting on with my case."

"Oh, don't hesitate on my account," Sorsha said. "I enjoy hearing about Alex's cases. I used to be a consultant for the FBI regarding magical crimes, after all."

Both of them turned to look at Alex, who seemed to be busily cutting his steak.

"There isn't much to tell," he said at last. "I was looking into the two players that lost out to one of Ari's calls last year. Elizabeth Tisdale has an alibi for the night Ari was killed, as her mother was with her in her room."

"So that just leaves Freddy Hackett," Holcombe said, "and I doubt he's our man."

"Why?" Sorsha asked, genuinely curious.

"He accepted his loss with grace," Holcombe said, "even though everyone thought he lost on a bad call. I would think if he were angry enough to kill over a bad call, there would have been some outward sign."

"Or he would have griped to his friends at some point between then and the night of the party," Alex said.

Something about that bothered Sorsha.

"You said 'everyone' thought Freddy got a bad call," Sorsha said. "Who is 'everyone'?"

"The crowd," Holcombe said. "This was a championship match, the stands were full of celebrities, fans, family, friends."

"I don't imagine any of those people were at the party at the Dalton estate," Alex said.

"Maybe," Sorsha said, "but they are the kind of people to bet on tennis matches."

Alex gave a little nod as he considered the idea.

"Seems like a long time to wait for revenge," he said at last.

"Maybe the party was the first opportunity they got," Sorsha suggested. "I mean maybe your killer is another player."

Holcombe shook his head at that.

"If a player wanted to kill Ari, they would have had multiple chances during the tour."

Sorsha sighed and pouted a bit. It seemed like such a good idea, after all. A gambler who lost big taking revenge on the official who made a bad call, that was the kind of thing Dr. Bell would love in one of his penny dreadfuls.

"I bet a lot of last year's audience lives in the Hamptons," Alex suddenly said. "Maybe even one of Beals Dalton's neighbors."

"You think the party is what gave them opportunity?" Sorsha said.

"Danny said there was a fingerprint on the tainted bottle of vermouth that the police couldn't exclude. Maybe they should take a look at Beals' neighbors."

"You'll have to have more than an unknown print if you want the police to demand fingerprints from a resident of the Hamptons," Sorsha said. "Even the FBI treads carefully around the rich."

"That's Danny's problem," Alex said. "This could be a good lead. I'll call him as soon as I get home."

"What if that turns out to be a dead end too?" Holcombe asked, trepidation in his voice.

"Well," Alex said in his hedging voice, "I can keep looking, but at this point I'm afraid you'll only get diminishing returns."

"Do you mean to say that Ari's killer will get away with it?" he demanded, ire rising in his voice.

"Sometimes that happens," Sorsha said, reaching out and taking Holcombe's hand. "There's only so much Alex or the police can do."

Holcombe's eyebrows dropped low over his eyes, but after a moment he closed his eyes and sighed.

"I understand, of course," he said, "but I don't have to like it."

"Don't give up yet," Alex said, his tone surprisingly positive. "There are still a few leads to follow."

Sorsha looked at him, but nothing in his expression gave anything away.

"Shall we turn to more enjoyable topics?" she asked as Holcombe refilled everyone's glass.

Sorsha snuggled close to Alex as the cab bore them across town to the brownstone. She'd had a bit more than usual to drink and she was feeling warm and tired. Alex had his arm around her shoulders, but hadn't bothered to offer her his coat. He knew she didn't get cold and there was no reason for him to be cold just to satisfy the demands of chivalry.

Especially when it was a meaningless gesture.

That didn't let him off the hook for other things, however.

"So," she said, looking up at him as the cab made its way through midtown, "what did you figure out?"

"What?" Alex said, seeming not to have heard her.

Oh, he's definitely working on something, she thought.

"When I brought up gambling losses and those rich neighbors in the Hamptons," she reiterated. "You figured something out."

"No," he said, obviously lying. "I just never thought of someone having an outside motive to kill Ari Leavitt. I figured whoever killed him did it for personal reasons, not financial ones."

"You'll never get those Hamptonites to give you a fingerprint," she said, snuggling deeper into Alex's shoulder.

"It's not that hard to get a fingerprint if you really want one," he said, "but it is time consuming. You need to know who you're looking for before you start."

"And you know who that is?"

"Haven't got a clue," he responded.

Sorsha wanted to ask him more questions, but she was dozing and the thoughts just wouldn't solidify.

To avoid climbing the stairs at the brownstone, Alex carried Sorsha up to the landing, then used one of his vault runes to go directly inside. Once he shut the door behind him, he carried her to the bedroom inside the vault itself and set her down on the bed.

He'd never seen Sorsha drink to excess; she'd been tipsy around him in the past, but never to the point where she just passed out. Apparently she was making up for lost social occasions.

"You've got to take her out more," he said to himself.

Normally, he'd cover her up and go, but she was wearing a dress that had to cost five hundred dollars and she'd kill him if he let her sleep in it. A few minutes later, he had her out if it and wrapped up in a blanket. Thanks to her magic, she never really got cold, but Alex knew her habits well enough to know she liked the feel of a blanket.

After hanging up the dress in the closet, Alex headed back into the main part of his vault, shutting the bedroom door behind him. It was already after ten, but he headed for his drafting table anyway and picked up the phone on the side table.

"Pak," Danny's voice greeted him when the call connected.

"Am I disturbing you?" Alex asked.

"No, I was just going over some case files; do you have something?"

"Maybe," he hedged. "Did you ever find anyone that matched the fingerprint on the vermouth bottle?"

"No," Danny admitted. "You got someone you want me to try?"

"Not right away," Alex said, "we're going to have to do a little setup first."

"This is sounding sketchy."

"Don't worry," Alex assured him. "Here's what you need to do."

30

BLAST FROM THE PAST

The rhythm of the train car rocking on the track shifted slightly, but it was enough for Alex to detect. He finished the last few sentences of the article he'd been reading in the paper, then folded it closed and tucked it under his arm.

"Are we there?" Sorsha's sleepy voice came from the seat opposite him.

She had been lounging next to the window, reading a book while upstate New York rolled by outside.

"We're starting to slow down," Alex affirmed, holding his silver cigarette case out to her. "Palmyra is the next stop."

Sorsha slipped a cigarette between her painted lips and waited for Alex to produce his lighter.

"I still think you could have saved yourself this trip with a phone call," she said as he flicked his lighter to life.

"Not really," Alex said, lighting a cigarette of his own. "For something like this, I need to see how they'll react. That could tell me more than I could learn in an hour on the phone."

"What about Danny?" she asked as the train began to slow.

"It'll take a while for everything to get into motion on his end,"

Alex said with a shrug. "Thanks to my vault, we should be back in plenty of time for the festivities."

"And you're still not going to tell me what he's up to?" Sorsha asked, putting on her most convincing pout.

"No," Alex declared. "That would spoil all the fun."

"For you."

"Plus," Alex went on as if Sorsha hadn't spoken, "there's always the chance I'm wrong about all this. I wouldn't want to get your hopes up."

Sorsha narrowed her eyes at him.

"You are such a liar," she said.

Alex gave her a knowing smirk, then stood up as the train shuddered to a halt.

The home of Kernan and Hester Powell was a large brick house with at least four levels. It was situated on a grassy hill, giving it a commanding view of the surrounding lawn and the woods beyond. A long gravel drive led up to the place, ending in a small circle with a white portico, complete with Roman columns on the ends.

The cabbie Alex had tracked down at the rail station knew the place immediately, though he admitted to never having taken anyone there. As he drove Alex and Sorsha up the winding drive, he whistled at the elegance of the place. After he dropped off his fare, Alex could see the man watching the house in the mirror as he drove away.

"What makes you think anyone will let us in?" Sorsha asked as Alex led her to a massive, light colored door with gold painted accents. A small button had been installed next to the frame, and Alex pressed it, eliciting a chime from somewhere inside.

"That's why I brought you along, doll," he said with a smirk. "Most people would love to meet New York's only sorceress, and the rest of them would be afraid to say no."

Sorsha bumped him with her hip hard enough to make him shift his weight for balance.

"You are a cad," she said through a barely-concealed smile.

Before Alex could respond, the lock on the enormous door clicked.

Equal & Opposite

The door was opened a moment later by a severe-looking man in his fifties wearing an old-fashioned tuxedo. Despite the age of his attire, the seams were all straight and smooth and the garment had been recently pressed. In keeping with the tux, the man's bow tie was lustrous and perfectly tied, while his shoes shone with polish.

"May I help you?" he asked, revealing a slight New England accent. He had a long face with an equally long, snipe nose that pointed down and served as the anchor for a thick, impeccably waxed mustache. Alex got the impression the man took a good hour to get ready in the morning and none of that time was wasted.

"My name is Alex Lockerby," he said, handing over one of his business cards. "I'd like to speak to Mr. Powell, or Mrs. Powell if he isn't available."

The man at the door read the card, then looked absolutely aghast at such a suggestion. Before he could give voice to his outrage, however, Alex spoke again.

"And this is Miss Sorsha Kincaid."

That did the trick. The man's eyes snapped to Sorsha, as if he'd just noticed her, and went wide for a moment.

"May I inquire what the subject of this business is?" he asked.

"It's about Anita," Alex said.

That struck the man even more than Sorsha's identity had and he suddenly started sweating.

"Please come in, Mr. Lockerby, Miss Kincaid," he said. "I can't guarantee anyone will see you, but I will inquire." He stepped back, allowing Alex and Sorsha to enter the cavernous foyer of the estate. "If you'll wait there," he said, indicating an uncomfortable-looking couch along the left side of the space, "I'll go see about your request."

With that, the man turned and shut the door. Behind the door, a small table stood against the wall and the tuxedoed man picked up a silver tray from it, deposited Alex's card on it, then turned and disappeared down a side hallway. Alex could hear the tread of his heels on the marble floor as he went, echoing through the foyer.

"I do like the classical style," Sorsha said, looking around.

The entire foyer was covered in elaborate wallpaper that featured the French fleur-de-lis. The doors that exited off the room were some light-colored wood that had been whitewashed to match the marble floors. Diamonds of green marble had been set into the corners where the floor tiles came together and the furniture scattered throughout the space had green accents to match.

It was a bit ostentatious for Alex's tastes, but he had to admit, it did punctuate just how wealthy the Powells were.

"He's been gone a while," Sorsha added a few minutes later.

Alex just shrugged.

"Powell's probably trying to decide if he'd rather have me thrown out or meet you," he said.

After another few minutes, the man with the immaculate mustache returned, heralded by the rap of his shoes on the floor.

"The master is too busy to see you," he announced without preamble, "but the lady of the house will be only too delighted to receive you. My name is Pederson. If you'll follow me, I'll conduct you to the mistress of the house."

He offered them a small bow, then turned and headed off in an entirely different direction than the one from which he'd approached. Alex offered Sorsha his arm and together they followed Pederson across the long axis of the house and out into a southern facing room with large skylights in the ceiling.

The room had been set up in the style of a salon, with a round table in the center that held up several vases full of flowers, and couches and chairs that radiated out from that central point. Tall bookshelves lined one wall, with reading chairs situated where they could get the most light. An empty hearth was set into the back wall with a writing desk beside it, and the entire room gave off the feeling of quiet welcome.

In the center of the room, just beyond the round table, sat an older woman, in her sixties at least, dressed in comfortable-looking silk pajamas trimmed with some kind of dark fur. She had a pleasant face with dark hair, streaked with gray, and she appraised Alex and Sorsha with shrewd eyes as they crossed the room. At her elbow was an end table containing a tall champagne flute and an ashtray that held a smoldering cigarette.

"Mr. Lockerby and Miss Kincaid, ma'am," Pederson introduced

them with a bow, then he stepped back, withdrawing to the far side of the room.

"Well, well," Hester Powell said, eyeing them both up and down. "Detectives I've had before, but this is my first sorceress. Sit down and make yourselves comfortable."

Alex thanked her, then waited for Sorsha to sit before sitting himself.

"I suppose you'll tell me what this is all about now," she declared, reaching for her glass flute. "Your request was a bit vague, except for mentioning my daughter. I can tell you that if you're here looking for money for that girl, save your breath."

"No, ma'am," Alex said. "I'm afraid Anita might be in some trouble."

Hester Powell sighed, then drained her drink.

"Well, that's not surprising," she said. "I am surprised it took this long. What's she done?"

"Before I go into that, Mrs. Powell—," Alex began but she cut him off.

"Oh, please, call me Hester," she said. "My husband is the formal one."

"Before we talk about your daughter's present, Hester, I was wondering if I could ask you a few questions about Anita's past."

Hester raised an eyebrow at that, annoyance creeping into her countenance for the first time.

"It would be very helpful," Sorsha said, catching the shift in the woman's mood.

Hester nearly snorted with laughter at that, turning a shrewd eye on the sorceress.

"I see why your boy here brought you along," she said to Sorsha. "Figured you could smooth things over if an old goat like me got my back up."

"Nothing of the sort, I assure you," Sorsha lied, though she didn't seem to fool Hester.

"Oh, I'm sure," she said, with a chuckle. "Now what has my wayward daughter gotten up to that's brought you all the way out here. I'll have the truth of it or you can both show yourselves out."

Alex cleared his throat.

"You've convinced me," he said with his most affable smile. "You've no doubt read in the paper about the series of bombings in the city?"

The smile Hester gained winning her point vanished and Alex would have sworn she was about to curse.

"You think she's responsible for those?" Hester said, her voice quiet.

"There is reason to suspect her," Alex admitted. "She was, of course, engaged to Reggie Aspler, the first victim of the bomber."

Hester scoffed at that.

"Anyone who ever met that ruffian would want to kill him," she said. "I didn't blame Anita for running away from that."

"Why allow the engagement at all if you felt that way?" Sorsha asked.

"It was Kernan's idea," Hester said in a sad voice. "He's a brilliant businessman, my husband, but I fear he's got no head for human matters, only business. His mind is full of ledgers and deals, property and assets."

"And Anita was an asset," Alex surmised.

Hester didn't answer, but nodded.

"But she was a modern woman," Alex continued, "wasn't she? She wanted to go to college."

"Wanted?" Hester chuckled. "There was no wanting about it, she enrolled in New York University all on her own once she graduated high school."

"The School of Runic Constructs, to be specific," Alex added.

That got Hester's attention, and the old woman sat up straight.

"How did you know that?" she asked, staring at Alex as if she could see inside him.

"The man who was the dean of that college was the bomber's third victim, Brian Rodgers," Alex said. "Am I right in guessing that your husband paid him off to keep Anita out of college?"

Hester sighed and took a drag on her cigarette.

"I don't know Rodgers," she said at last, "but Kernan paid someone to reject her application. You could hear her screaming about it all the way across the lawn."

"And then your husband arranged for Anita to marry Reggie Aspler," Sorsha said.

"Yes," Hester admitted. "Reggie's shipping business is quite formidable. Kernan wanted those ships and railroad cars for his business."

"And he didn't care about what she wanted," Sorsha pressed.

"It wouldn't have mattered," Hester said. "Kernan is old fashioned that way. The idea of his daughter going to college, and to become a runewright, no less? Well, he simply couldn't permit his only daughter to become a lowly practitioner of hedge magic. No offense, Mr. Lockerby."

"None taken," he chuckled, "and call me Alex."

He was starting to like this spry old bird.

"The arranged marriage was the last straw for Anita," Hester continued, her voice heavy. "She was supposed to go into the city for a dress fitting two weeks before the wedding, but she...she just disappeared."

"And you haven't seen or spoken to her since?" Alex asked.

"No, Alex," Hester said. "She left a note with the dressmaker saying that she wouldn't allow anyone to control her life ever again, and that's the last time I heard from her."

"I'm sorry," Sorsha said.

"It doesn't hurt so much anymore," Hester said with a shrug. "Time heals all wounds, after all. That doesn't mean I like the idea that she's some kind of maniac."

That last was directed at Alex.

"Did Anita ever know someone called Samantha Olsen?" Alex asked.

"Not that I know of, why?"

"The second victim of the bomber was a man named Milton McDermet," Alex explained. "He ran a shady potion and runewright supply business that he started with Samantha, but then he forced her out."

"And you think this Samantha was actually Anita?"

"He does," Sorsha answered. "Whoever is making these bombs is an exceptionally intelligent and talented runewright."

"The kind of person who might want to go to college to better their skills," Alex added.

"And now she's killing the men who wronged her," Hester said, shaking her head. "Why now?"

"I don't know," Alex admitted. "I was hoping you'd heard from her, that maybe she'd said something to you that might explain it."

"She never had a quick temper," Hester said. "She'd build up, like a tea kettle with a stuck lid, until she would eventually explode."

"So she feels wronged," Sorsha said, "not just recently, but her whole life."

That made sense. Anita was a modern woman, but every time she tried to step up and make something of herself, she'd been denied. Professor Rodgers had taken a bribe to cancel her acceptance to a college for runewrights. Milton McDermet had forced her out of a business she'd helped start, and Reggie had wanted to keep her as some kind of ornament, locked away at his country estate while he chased women in the city.

Assuming that Anita Powell actually is Samantha Olsen, he reminded himself, though that seemed like a pretty solid guess.

"But if the bomber is Anita, what is it that set her off?" Sorsha asked.

Alex couldn't answer that, but before he could come up with a plausible solution, Hester spoke.

"Why hasn't she tried to kill her father?"

"Maybe she still has some feeling for him," Alex suggested.

Hester laughed at that.

"No," she said, "she hates her father worst of all, I suspect. If she's blaming men who wronged her, then Kernan shoulders the lion's share, at least in Anita's eyes."

Alex and Sorsha exchanged glances before Alex turned to look at the butler, Pederson. Or rather he would have if Pederson were still standing there.

"Where's your butler?" Alex asked.

Hester pulled a watch from her pocket and squinted at it.

"Probably went to get my husband his Spine Straightener," she said.

"Kernan is a night owl, so he usually sleeps late. Can't get going without a pick-me-up. Why do you need Pederson?"

"If you're right about Anita's relationship with her father, then your husband could be in danger," Alex said. "The bomber sends explosive runes to her victims disguised as regular mail, but they're always hand delivered. I suspect the rune is too volatile to be sent through the postal system."

"Do you know if the mail has been delivered yet?" Sorsha asked.

At that moment, the door opened and the butler entered.

"Pederson," Hester said, "has the mail arrived?"

"No, ma'am," he said, a bit surprised by the question. "The post usually doesn't arrive until mid-afternoon."

"Who gets it when it does arrive?" Alex asked.

"Anna, the downstairs maid," Pederson said. "She brings it in from the box and leaves it on the table by the front door. From there I take it to Mr. Powell's office and leave it on his desk."

"Does he go through it every day?" Sorsha asked.

"Yes, miss. The master is very diligent about that."

"It's possible that Ani—, uh, someone will try to send a magical bomb in the form of a letter," Alex said, standing up. "If you get a letter that was left in the box by hand, one without a stamp, leave it outside and call me immediately." Alex took out one of his cards and handed it to the butler.

"Ma'am?" Pederson said, looking around Alex at Hester.

"Do as he says," she said.

"Very well, sir," Pederson said, tucking the card into the pocket of his vest. "Will that be all?"

"There is one more thing," Alex said, turning back to Hester. "Do you have a photograph of Anita?"

"After we knew that Anita wasn't going to come home, Kernan got rid of every picture of her," Hester said, looking away.

Alex glanced at Sorsha, who had a look of absolute outrage on her face and her eyes were softly glowing. He still didn't know the specifics of her relationship with her own father, but clearly she saw a fellow traveler in Anita.

"Can you describe her?" Alex said, pulling his attention away from Sorsha.

Hester stood and turned toward the tall bookshelf. Moving to it, she selected a large book of etchings, opened it to the back, and removed a photograph.

"If Anita did the things you've said, I realize she'll have to answer for them," Hester said, holding the picture to her heart. "If I give you this, I want you to promise to protect her. Don't let anyone hurt her. She's still my daughter."

"Mrs. Powell," Alex said, keeping his voice even, "Hester, I will find Anita, and I will bring her in safe and sound."

Hester hesitated for a moment, then she walked to where Alex stood and handed him the photograph.

31

LONGSHOT

"Well, that was a waste of time," Sorsha said as Alex used the back side of the Powell's stone fence to draw a vault door.

He didn't want to admit it, but Alex suspected she was right. He'd known before coming that Anita had some kind of falling out with her family; if she hadn't then she would have returned home after ditching Reggie Aspler. The only potential saving grace was the photograph, but that turned out to be a dead end as well. The woman in the picture was thin and severe-looking with a narrow face and sunken eyes. She had long, blonde hair that was tied up in a braid that wound around the top of her head, which made it difficult for Alex to picture what she might look like with it down.

Not that it mattered.

He was positive he hadn't met anyone fitting Anita Powell's description.

"What if she is disguising herself as a man?" Alex asked as he stuck a vault rune to the middle of the chalk outline.

Sorsha reached out and closed her fingers, pulling the photograph of Anita into her hand from her magical storage. As Alex lit the rune, she looked at the picture at arm's length, turning it back and forth before looking at it through squinted eyes.

"I don't see it," she said as Alex unlocked the steel vault door with his key, "but it's possible, I suppose. Do you know any men who look like this?"

"No," Alex admitted. "Can't say that I do."

"Well, maybe this will come in handy at some point," Sorsha said, vanishing the photograph again.

Alex pushed the vault door open, then stepped back so Sorsha could go through first.

"We'll take the picture to Detweiler," Alex said, pushing the door closed behind them, "maybe his boys will remember her from their canvassing."

"Can that wait until after lunch?" Sorsha said. "Long train trips always make me hungry."

"I'm afraid you'll have to wait," Alex said, leading the way across the vault's great room and into the office hallway. "Danny is doing something you're going to want to see."

Sorsha gave him a penetrating look, but Alex just kept walking.

"All right," she said, following along, "color me intrigued, but let's at least get a sandwich on the way."

Alex rapped on the frame of Lieutenant Detweiler's open door. Inside, the man sat, slumped over his desk, reading the contents of a file. When he looked up, his expression shifted from exhausted to hopeful.

"Did you find something?" he asked, closing the file and sitting up straight.

"I've got a viable suspect," Alex said, stepping inside and laying Anita Powell's photograph on the table. "This is Anita Powell about fifteen years ago," he said. Alex went on and explained Anita's history and her possible connection to McDermet and his alchemy shop.

"So if you're right, and Samantha Olsen is actually Anita Powell, then all the bombings make sense," he said, picking up the photograph. "So how do we find Miss Powell?"

"Ask the men who did your canvassing," Alex said, "maybe one of them will remember seeing her."

"Long shot," Detweiler declared. "If you're right, Miss Powell could be doing this from anywhere."

"No, she'd have to be nearby to hand deliver the letters," Alex said.

"If you're right about the revenge plan," Detweiler said, "once she's done, she'll be in the wind."

Alex thought about that for a moment.

"The one bombing that doesn't fit the pattern is the one at the OMO," he said.

"And the one at your office," Detweiler reminded him. "Does Anita have something against you? Old lover or something?"

"No," Alex chuckled. "Nothing like that, besides, Anita seems to be getting revenge on people who wronged her. I was just in her way."

"So was I," Detweiler said.

"Yeah, but you're a cop," Alex said. "If she had sent a bomb here, there'd be a citywide manhunt, sorcerers would get involved...it would mess up her revenge."

"True," Detweiler admitted. "Do you still think she bombed the OMO to destroy her records?"

"I guess that depends on what's in her file," Alex said, rubbing his chin. "Of course, until now, we didn't know whose file we were looking for."

"Right," Detweiler said, catching on to Alex's train of thought. "I'll get a couple of uniforms over there and see how they're doing with the clean-up."

Alex wished him luck, then excused himself.

"What took you so long?" Sorsha said when he reached Danny's office. He'd left Sorsha on the couch while he went to talk to Detweiler. "And where is Danny?"

"He's down in interrogation," Alex said, offering her his hand. "I had him arrest Freddy Hackett."

Sorsha gave him a penetrating look, arching one of her makeup-blackened eyebrows.

"I thought you said you didn't have any solid evidence against him," she said.

"Technically speaking, I don't," Alex admitted. "Not yet, anyway."

"You're doing something clever," she accused.

Alex put his arm around her waist as they headed for the elevators.

"I'm sure we hope it's something clever," he said.

"You're not going to tell me," Sorsha accused, "are you?"

Alex gave her a shocked look.

"And spoil the surprise?" he said, aghast.

"Is Danny going to be hung out to dry if you're wrong?"

"It's a risk," Alex admitted, lowering his voice, "but Danny knows the risks and he's on board."

"Well," Sorsha said, pushing the elevator button, "let's hope you're actually as smart as you think you are."

A moment later they got off on the fourth floor. Normally it would have been easier to take the stairs, but the interrogation floor stairs were locked, leaving the elevator as the only way in.

"Hi-ya Alex," the policeman behind the desk greeted him.

"Milton," Alex acknowledged. "Lieutenant Pak is expecting us."

"Sign in," Milton said, indicating the visitor book, "I'll go get him."

Alex did as he was told and a few moments later, Danny emerged from the back hallway.

"Glad you're here," he said, shaking Alex's hand.

"How's it going?"

"You called it," Danny said, "he clammed up after an hour, demanded to see his lawyer."

"Is the lawyer here yet?"

"Got here half an hour ago, but he's not talking either."

"The lawyer isn't talking?" Sorsha scoffed. "I can't get mine to shut up. Is he a public defender?"

"No," Danny said. "Andrew Farnsworth."

"I've heard of him," Alex said. "Very expensive. If he's not talking, then he's waiting for something."

Danny nodded at that.

Equal & Opposite

"Freddy's parents are coming in from Syracuse," he said. "Should be here any time."

"Let's go, then," Alex said. "We wouldn't want to disrupt the party."

Danny took a deep breath, then nodded.

"Follow me."

He led them down the long hallway with interrogation rooms on either side, finally coming to a stop in front of a door marked, *Observation 8*.

"In here," Danny said.

Alex ushered Sorsha into the little room, then leaned over to Danny.

"Is everything ready?" he asked, keeping his voice low.

"Ready as it can be," Danny whispered back. "Assuming you're right about all this."

"Relax," Alex said, clapping his friend on the shoulder, then he stepped into the observation room.

Alex had been in police observation rooms before and they were mostly the same. Older rooms had a grating with mesh in it so the sounds from the interrogation room could be heard. The Central Office rooms were as modern as it got, with a sheet of one-way glass separating the rooms.

From where Alex stood next to Sorsha, he could see Freddy Hackett sitting at the little table in the room, leaning back in his chair with his hat over his face. Next to him was an older man with a grey mustache and an expensive suit, who sat reading a stack of papers.

"Freddy doesn't look worried," Sorsha said, keeping her voice low so as not to be overheard. "He just looks tired."

"He's been waiting a long time," Alex whispered back. "It's a long ride in from Syracuse."

As if on cue, Danny opened the interrogation room door and ushered in two people who could only be Freddy's parents. The man was short, but thin, with a little bit of a gut. A typical athlete gone soft. The woman was shorter still, with reddish brown hair and a pretty face that time hadn't diminished.

Freddy stood up as soon as they entered and the woman rushed to embrace him.

"Are you all right, dear?" she said, squeezing him tightly. "This is absurd, Andrew, tell them this is absurd."

"I'm afraid it's quite serious," Danny said, entering after the couple and closing the door. He went around to the opposite side of the table from Freddy and sat down, placing a thick folder on the table. "We have a lot of evidence against you, Freddy."

"A lot of circumstantial evidence," the lawyer said, flipping through his stack of papers. "I don't see how any of this implicates my client of being anything other than an innocent bystander."

"That's what we thought," Danny said, opening the folder on the table, "until we found this." He took a paper off the top and turned it around so Freddy and the lawyer could see it. "Ari Leavitt was poisoned," Danny started off. "His Manhattan cocktail was laced with strychnine, a poison that caused his muscles to lock up while he was swimming in Beals Dalton's indoor pool. As a result, he drowned."

"According to you," Andrew the lawyer said.

Danny took another paper from the folder and turned it around.

"Ari Leavitt's blood tested positive for strychnine," he said. "We have the glass Mr. Leavitt drank from, which also tested positive." Danny turned around another paper.

"And you think my client had something to do with that?" Andrew asked.

"I know it, Mr. Farnsworth," Danny said, turning around another paper. "We found a bottle of vermouth that had been spiked with strychnine." He turned over a picture of the bottle, adding it to the pile. "That means Ari's murder was premeditated."

"Still not seeing how that has anything to do with Freddy," the lawyer reiterated, sounding bored.

"To pull this off, the killer had to know Ari on a personal level," Danny said. "They had to know about his drink of choice. They had to know that he always went swimming after parties at Beals Dalton's house. That's a very small pool of potential killers."

"Small," Andrew Farnsworth said with a smile, "but larger than one. Do you have any specific evidence that implicates my client?"

"As clever as this plan was," Danny went on, "our murderer wasn't especially bright. After they made the deadly cocktail, they wiped off the bottle to remove their fingerprints."

"So?" Freddy spoke up, a confused look on his face.

"A smart man would have worn gloves," Danny said, turning over another page.

"Wouldn't that look suspicious?" Sorsha hissed, leaning close to Alex so no one in the interrogation room would hear her.

"Keep watching," Alex hissed back.

"We found a fingerprint on the bottom of the cork," Danny said, looking at Freddy. "Your fingerprint."

Freddy sat up straight, his eyes going wide.

"He's not doing himself any favors," Sorsha whispered. "He looks guilty."

"Doesn't he?" Alex replied.

"That print doesn't mean anything," Andrew the lawyer said, his voice still easy. "At best it proves that Freddy came into contact with the cork at some point."

"How?" Danny asked. "If he'd made himself a drink from that bottle, he'd be dead."

"You don't even know if that cork started off in the vermouth bottle," the attorney went on. "It could have come from anywhere and been accidentally put back in the tainted bottle by the real killer."

"That's for a jury to decide," Danny said, standing and gathering up the evidence files. "Officer Haynes."

The outer door opened and a young policeman with broad shoulders and a lantern jaw entered.

"Take Mr. Hackett down to booking and process him," Danny said.

"Andrew, do something," Freddy's mother implored, seizing the lawyer's sleeve.

"I can't do anything now," Andrew said, patting her gently on the arm. "Once the police finish with him, I'll go over to the courthouse and post Freddy's bail."

"But that will make him look like a criminal," she hissed. "It'll ruin his reputation."

"He can weather this storm," Freddy's father, Arnie, said. He stood and put a hand on his son's shoulder as Officer Haynes handcuffed Freddy.

His mother tried to grab Freddy, but Arnie held her back until Officer Haynes walked him out.

"Don't worry, Bess," Arnie said as Danny followed Freddy out. "We'll fight this, right, Andrew?"

"Of course we will," the lawyer said, "but I have to be honest with you, if that fingerprint is what that lieutenant says it is, it's going to be an uphill battle."

"He'll lose everything," Bess said, turning pale.

Before either of the men in the interrogation room could stop her, Bess darted through the open door and into the hallway. Alex and Sorsha couldn't see her, but her raised voice was easy to hear.

"Wait!" she called. "It was me. I killed Ari Leavitt."

"Bess!" Arnie and Andrew called at the same time.

"She didn't mean that," Andrew said, rushing to the door.

"It sounded like she did," Danny said, the sound of his heels on the floor coming closer. "But I think you're right, Mr. Farnsworth, it does sound like something a desperate mother would say to save her son."

"I did it," Bess insisted. "I killed that blind umpire before he had another chance to rob Freddy of the nationals."

"I think we'd better step back inside for a moment," Danny said.

Andrew Farnsworth stepped back, allowing Bess and Danny to return to the interrogation room.

Sorsha leaned over and whispered, "That story Danny told, about the fingerprint and the glass Ari Leavitt drank from, you two made that up, didn't you?" When Alex didn't answer, she turned to look up into his eyes. "Did you plan all this?"

Alex looked down at her with a sly smile.

"You knew she did it?" Sorsha demanded, quickly clapping her hand over her mouth as she realized she hadn't kept her voice down. "How could you have known that?" she continued in a whisper.

"Her car," Alex said, leaning close to her.

"What?"

"When Martin Pride was hit by a car while running, I suspected it was Freddy, trying to make room on his high school tennis team. Problem was, he didn't own a car and nobody brought their car to a repair shop with unexplained front end damage."

"Doesn't that mean that Freddy has an alibi?"

"It does, indeed," Alex said. "But Freddy did have an accident two years later in his mother's car. According to the police report, he was drunk."

Sorsha gave him a stern look.

"So he went back in time and hit Martin?" she said. "That must have been some very special booze."

"Nope," Alex said. "Billy Tasker was looking into the strange deaths and accidents that conveniently cleared the way for Freddy's career when he talked to the mechanic in Syracuse who fixed Bess' car after Freddy crashed it. He was very proud of the work he did, especially cleaning up the rust."

"Sounds like he did a good job," Sorsha said, impatience in her voice. "How does a good mechanic mean that Freddy's mother killed Ari Leavitt?"

"Because," Alex explained, "it takes time for rust to develop. A car that just hit a tree or whatever doesn't have rust where the metal buckled."

"Then why did the mechanic have to clean up rust?" Sorsha asked, her nose crinkling adorably.

"Why indeed?" Alex chuckled.

"It had older damage," Sorsha guessed. "Damage that hadn't been repaired for two years."

"Now why would a rich, important woman like Bess Hackett allow her personal car to stay damaged?"

"Because fixing it would raise questions," Sorsha hissed, an impressed smile spreading across her face. "But how did she hide the damage for two years?"

Alex shrugged.

"Probably parked it in a garage and just didn't drive it," he theorized. "It's not like she didn't have other means of getting around."

Sorsha looked like she wanted to argue, but couldn't find a place to start.

"Wait," she eventually whispered, "does that mean that she let her drunk son drive her car expecting him to wreck it?"

Alex shook his head.

"According to the police report, Freddy didn't remember driving at all and he supposedly ran into a tree just beyond their driveway."

"You think Bess drove the car, bumped it up against a tree, then walked back to her house and called the police on her son?"

Alex tapped the side of his nose and winked at her.

"But why call the cops at all?" Sorsha asked. "Wouldn't that get her precious boy in trouble?"

"Not with their money, but she needed the police report to explain the damage."

"That she could now get fixed without anyone asking questions," Sorsha said.

"Exactly," Alex said. "Once I figured that out, the rest was easy. Freddy was in Albany the night the tennis coach died from an allergic reaction to shellfish. He met with the principal the previous day, arguing that it was unfair for the coach to reject him because of a beef with his father."

"I'm going to guess that he didn't plead his case alone," Sorsha said.

"Mom was right there in the principal's office with him," Alex said, "and while Freddy has an alibi for that night, Bess doesn't. She also doesn't have an alibi for the night Ari was murdered."

"Did she know the owner of the home where the party was held?"

"Beals Dalton," Alex supplied, "and yes, she and Arnie had been there many times."

"So it wouldn't be hard for her to sneak in, impersonate a bartender long enough to poison Ari Leavitt, and then just leave."

"Not hard at all," Alex said.

On the other side of the glass, Danny stood up and headed out into the hall. Alex opened the door to the observation room, holding it for Sorsha, then followed.

"Well, it happened just like you figured," Danny said. "She confessed to the whole thing."

"She couldn't let her precious boy go through a trial," Alex said. "Not after everything she did to clear the road for his career."

"I thought I'd seen it all," Danny sighed.

"I guess Hell hath no fury like a woman whose precious boy is scorned," Sorsha said.

"Just make sure you get something ironclad," Alex warned.

Danny gave him an exasperated look.

"You don't get to be clever and tell me how to do my job," he said in an irritated voice. "Now get out of here and tell your reporter friend that I'd better not see anything about this in the paper until I give you the okay."

Alex nodded, then offered Sorsha his arm and headed for the elevators.

32

EVERY ACTION

Alex took Sorsha up to the fifth floor of the Central Office, then down the hall to the janitor's closet he used to open a vault door.

"You know," she said as he drew a door with his chalk, "we could have done this in the elevator if you were a bit faster."

"That might work," Alex admitted, "but I don't know what would happen if I opened a door into the wall of an elevator. They're usually moving, and I have no idea what that would do to the door. If the rune broke with the door open, it might explode...or worse."

"We should rig up something to test it," Sorsha suggested. "Go up somewhere high, put the rune on something and then drop it."

"What if it blows up my vault?" Alex said, opening a vault door inside the closet.

"Can you make another vault?"

"No," Alex said, "but we could use Mike's vault. He's only using it for storage right now."

"Sounds like fun," Sorsha said. "We should make an outing of it."

"Maybe when the weather warms up," Alex chuckled, escorting Sorsha inside his vault.

"Do you have any more visits to make?" Sorsha asked.

"Nothing until dinner tonight," Alex said.

"Good," Sorsha said, heading across the great room. "I need to go back to my office and make some calls."

"Pick you up at five?" Alex called after her.

"Six," she answered, then vanished through the door that connected to the bathroom in her office.

Alex shut the open door into the janitor's closet and it vanished, melting back into the featureless gray stone of his vault.

A minute later, Alex exited the back hallway of his office into the waiting area.

"I'm back," he announced to Sherry, who greeted him with a smile. "Does anything need my attention?"

"Billy called," she said, making a face. "Twice."

Alex sighed at that. Some other paper must have caught wind of Freddy's arrest. If they had any sources inside the Central Office, they might be putting enough of the pieces together to run a story, though it wouldn't be the right one.

"I'll call him," he said. "Anything else?"

Sherry shook her head.

"Mike took a few cases and I put a few on your desk, but that's it."

Alex thanked her and retreated to his office. The stack of folders on his desk was quite a bit higher than he remembered, but now that he'd wrapped up Holcombe's case, he'd have time to go through them.

Sitting behind his desk, Alex put his sore foot up and picked up the phone, giving the operator the exchange for the Midnight Sun.

"Alex," Billy's worried voice greeted him, "please tell me you've got something for me. Rumor has it that the Times is going to report on an important arrest your friend Danny made."

"That's probably true," Alex admitted, "but if they report any gossip, they're going to get the story wrong."

"Wrong or right, I've got to print something, Alex. You know how this game is played."

"I can't tell you anything until I get Danny's okay, but I'll call him and get it."

"What if you can't?" Billy demanded.

"This story is worth waiting for, Billy," Alex said. "Trust me."

Billy agreed to wait, though he wasn't enthusiastic about it, and Alex hung up. His next call was to Danny, but he was out so Alex had the operator take a message to call him.

Hanging up the phone, Alex called Holcombe Ward to give him the good news.

"I don't know what to say," he said once Alex told him the whole story. "It's almost unbelievable. Are the police certain of a conviction?"

"Freddy's mother confessed," Alex said.

"Could she change her story later? Try to weasel out?"

"I doubt it," Alex said, "she confessed to keep her son from facing a trial, after all."

"I suppose," Holcombe said. "I guess you did it, avenged my friend's murder. Send me your bill. As soon as the police announce the arrest, I'll get you paid."

Alex thanked him and hung up. He'd have to prepare a report for Holcombe to go along with the bill, but that wouldn't take too long.

"Might as well get started," he said to himself, picking up the case file.

Alex had just finished the report when his phone rang.

"Lockerby," he said once he picked up the receiver.

"I owe you a bottle of Scotch," Danny said. "Captain Callahan was thrilled with Bess Hackett's confession. I think if he could, he'd give me a medal."

"People murder other people all the time," Alex said. "What's so special about this one?"

"The papers are always accusing us of being too soft with the upper crust," Danny said. "This proves we aren't."

"Is it safe to assume the department is going to make a public statement?"

"Tomorrow morning," Danny said. "All the big papers will be here, so you'd better tell your muckraker in time to make the evening edition."

"Will do," Alex said, "and I'll hold you to that bottle of Scotch."

Hanging up, Alex picked up the receiver again and called Billy. As Alex predicted, he was over the moon with the story and promised Alex passes to the press box for any baseball game Alex wanted to see. He wasn't much of a baseball fan, but maybe Sorsha would want to go.

Checking his watch, Alex found that it was only four-thirty, so he pushed the phone away and reached for the pile of potential clients.

It was six on the dot when Alex knocked on the door to Sorsha's office. Normally his cover doors blocked out any sound, but since this one literally passed into the private bathroom of Sorsha's office, he'd made it differently.

When there was no answer, Alex tentatively opened the door and stepped inside. From the closed door that led from the bathroom to the office proper, Alex could hear Sorsha arguing with someone. Her usually cool demeanor was gone and her voice was raised quite a bit.

"Must be on the phone," Alex concluded. Most people were smart enough not to anger a sorceress in person.

A moment later, Alex heard the sound of a phone handset being slammed down into the cradle hard enough to ring the bell and Sorsha swore.

"Insufferable man," she growled.

"I hope you don't mean me," Alex said, opening the connecting door.

Sorsha jumped and looked up from her desk, blushing.

"Alex," she gasped, putting her hand over her heart. "You scared me. I...I was just—"

"I heard," Alex said with a grin, eliciting an even deeper blush from the sorceress. "Do I need to threaten someone for you," he said, making a fist and punching his left hand.

"You're not funny," Sorsha said, giving him a mock sneer. "And I can handle my own affairs, thank you very much."

"Can you handle dinner?" Alex asked, taking out his pocket watch and flipping it open. "It's after six."

"Thank the Lord," Sorsha said with a sigh. "If I have to deal with any more incompetents or surprises today, I'll start turning people into toads."

Alex felt his chest tighten at that, but he kept any sign of distress off his face. Today wasn't the time to surprise Sorsha, but it was too late to change course now.

"Some of Iggy's cooking will take the edge off," he said, offering his arm.

She smiled at him, seeming to return to her usual self, and followed him back to his vault.

"You're very quiet," she said when he led her through his brownstone bedroom and out onto the third floor landing.

"Am I?"

Sorsha squeezed his arm as her eyes narrowed.

"What are you up to?" she demanded.

"I do have a bit of a surprise for you," he admitted as they reached the foyer and turned toward the kitchen.

"Why do I get the feeling that I'm not going to like this surprise?" she asked.

Before Alex could answer, they exited the little hallway between the kitchen and the library. The table had been set with a linen tablecloth and Iggy had used the good china to set out four places. On the far side of the table stood a man in a well-made suit and Sorsha's grip on Alex's arm tightened even further.

"Hello, sis," Nils Eccles said. "It's good to see you."

"What are you doing here?" Sorsha demanded. She said it to Nils, but she looked at Alex.

"Your brother has a story to tell you," Alex said, looking Sorsha right in her softly glowing eyes. "I figured that stories go best with a good meal."

Sorsha looked like she was going to snap at him, but her grip on his arm relaxed and she stepped back so Alex could pull her chair out.

Iggy broke the tension by serving dinner. He'd gone all out with roast pheasant, potatoes and green beans with soft rolls. As they ate, Nils told the story of Roland's dying confession and the army payroll he'd stolen and then buried. In the story Alex had rehearsed, Nils had wanted to return the money, but knew Sorsha wouldn't believe him, so he came to Alex instead. Since the secret to the buried money was in Sorsha's music box, he'd tricked Alex into swapping it for the one belonging to Sorsha's sister, Mia.

Once he had the clue left by their father, he recovered the money and returned it to the government.

"That's very altruistic of you," Sorsha said, eyeing her brother coldly. "How uncharacteristic."

"People change, Kjir, uh, Sorsha," he said.

He was having trouble with his sister having a new name, but he managed the rest of the story well enough. When he was finished, Sorsha seemed to relax a bit, though she never really warmed up to Nils. When, at last, the meal was over, she walked him to the door and even gave him a quick hug before he left.

"That was your doing," she declared, turning to Alex as soon as the door was shut.

"I have no idea what you're talking about," Alex declared, turning back to the kitchen.

"Wait," Sorsha said, grabbing his coat. "I wanted to say thank you."

Alex gave her a quizzical look. She hadn't been very accepting of Nils during dinner, so Alex wasn't expecting any thanks.

"You wanted to connect with my family," she explained. "And I know you're the one who forced my brother to give the money back and settle for the reward."

"Oh, I just helped Nils make his plans," Alex said with a shrug, putting his arm around Sorsha.

"And I love you for that, even if I can't stand my brother."

"What happened between you and your family?"

Sorsha sighed and put her head against his shoulder.

"Maybe I'll tell you someday," she said, "but it's not good conversation after such an excellent meal."

"I imagine Iggy will have a cigar and a cognac while I do the dishes," Alex said. "He'll have some questions, no doubt."

"No doubt," Sorsha confirmed.

The next morning Alex was dragging his feet about returning to his office to go over cases. Once he was dressed, he headed into his vault, stopping at his drafting table rather than continuing to his office door. He ran his hand over the smooth surface, leaving a trail where his hand disrupted a fine layer of dust.

In the past the drafting table would never have had time to accumulate dust. Alex used it every day, sometimes for several hours. He'd crafted some of his most clever and inventive constructs right here, yet now the table just sat, gathering dust.

Sitting down in his chair, Alex reached into the inner pocket of his suit coat and pulled out his rune book. Thumbing through the pages, he found runes written by Mike and some of the more sophisticated and complex ones written by Iggy. He stopped at a major restoration rune that looked both familiar and foreign. As he looked at it, Alex realized it was one of his. He hadn't seen his own rune work in months.

Resisting the urge to crumple up the valuable rune, Alex flipped to the back of his rune book and pulled out two folded runes from the pocket under the cover. He'd had Mike make them but hadn't looked at them since.

"Are you keeping these because you're afraid to use them?" he asked himself. They were linking runes, made as a pair, and he'd wanted them for a crazy idea he'd come up with while he was hunting for Detweiler's bomber. He'd need to get a nice fountain pen to make it work, but that wouldn't be too hard. They might even have one in the terminal shop below his office.

He was about to get up and continue his trip to his office when the candlestick phone on his rollaway table rang.

"Lockerby," he said, picking it up.

"Oh, good," Sherry's voice greeted him. "I've got Lieutenant Detweiler on the line for you."

"I'm in my vault," Alex said. "I'll take it in here."

A moment later the irascible lieutenant joined the line.

"Any luck finding Anita Powell?" Alex asked.

"No," Detweiler growled. "The Office of Magical Oversight was closed yesterday on account of them only having one person there, that Clark fellow."

Alex remembered the officious man who was now the head of the Manhattan office of the OMO.

"That and the building people are still patching up the hole in the wall," Detweiler went on.

"What about the girl?" Alex asked, "Kim Carson? I figured she would have been released by the hospital by now."

"She was out a few days ago," Detweiler confirmed, "but the doctors wanted her to take it easy. She'll be back this morning, helping her boss clean up the records."

"Should I meet you over there?" Alex asked.

"I'm not going over there until they find Miss Powell's records," Detweiler said. "It's bound to take some time, that place was a wreck."

Alex had to agree there. The filing cabinets that held the OMO's records had been laid out along the side and back walls of the office. When the bomb that killed Hector Iverson had gone off it had thrown the cabinets on the left-hand wall across the room, spilling their contents all over the place.

Detweiler was saying something, but Alex didn't hear him.

Most filing systems were laid out like libraries, using the Dewey standard. That meant that the 'A's would start in the topmost file on the extreme left and run down and then to the right. The file cabinets that were damaged when Hector was killed would have been the ones containing the last names that began with the letters of the early alphabet.

"The records for Anita Powell would have been somewhere on the right-hand side," Alex said to himself.

"What?" Detweiler said in his ear. "Lockerby, are you even listening?"

"Sorry," Alex said, his mind snapping back to reality.

"Well?" Detweiler pressed. "What do you think?"

"I think we need to get over to the Office of Magical Oversight right now," Alex said.

"You want to tell me why I drove all the way over here first thing in the morning?" Detweiler demanded when Alex jumped out of a cab in front of the squat government building.

"Because Anita Powell changed her name to Kimberly Carson," Alex said, heading for the door. "She's been here the whole time."

He ran for an open elevator, ignoring his protesting foot, and held the door for Detweiler.

"Are you forgetting that Miss Carson was wounded in the blast?" the lieutenant said as the door rumbled shut.

"About that," Alex said, "she was only hit by the blast on her arm, her left arm."

"So?"

Alex held up his hand and suddenly moved it toward Detweiler's face as if he intended to hit him. The man might be pudgy and out of shape, but his reflexes were quick as he brought his hand up to block the blow.

"What was that?" he demanded when Alex's hand stopped a few inches short of his face.

"What hand did you block with?" Alex asked. "Your right," he continued before Detweiler could answer, "because you're right-handed."

"That doesn't mean Miss Carson is left handed," Detweiler protested. "She might just have had her left side to the blast."

"Then why was her arm the only part of her that got injured?" Alex asked. "There was barely a mark on the rest of her. It's like she was shielded by something heavy."

"Like a desk," Detweiler said, catching on.

"Exactly like," Alex said, "assuming I'm right."

"But why blow up her own office? If she wanted to destroy the records of Anita Powell, all she had to do was take them out of the file cabinet and throw them in the trash. No one would have questioned her pulling records, it's what she does."

"When Hector Iverson retired, who replaced him?" Alex asked, pulling open the inner cage door as the elevator came to a stop.

Detweiler's eyes went wide.

"Jeremy Clark," he said, "but he had seniority."

"What if that didn't matter?" Alex asked, heading down the hall toward the OMO. "From what I observed when I was there before the bombing, Kim and Ben, the young man who was killed, did most of the work. What if Kim thought that job should have rightfully been hers?"

"It explains Hector's murder," Detweiler said. "Wait."

This last was directed at Alex who had a hand on the new front door of the OMO office. He reached into his coat and pulled out a police .38 special. "Okay," he said, holding the gun down and behind his pant leg.

Alex pulled the door open and led the way inside. The broken desk that had belonged to the unfortunate Ben Moss had been replaced with a new one and most of the scattered paper and bits of debris had been cleaned up. Jeremy Clark sat behind the middle desk, just as Alex remembered, going through a large stack of papers. To the right was Kim's desk, but it was noticeably empty.

"Where's Miss Carson?" Detweiler demanded with all the subtlety of a sledgehammer.

"What?" Jeremy Clark asked, looking up with bloodshot eyes. "Uh, she went to use the ladies," he said as his mind caught up to the question. "She'll be back any time now."

"No," Alex sighed, standing by the absent woman's desk, "she won't."

"What do you mean?" Detweiler asked.

Alex reached down and picked up a heavy vellum envelope from the desk.

"Is that another bomb?" Detweiler said, his eyes going wide.

"I highly doubt it," Alex said, though he made no move to open the unsealed envelope. He did however turn it around so that the lieutenant could see what was written on the face.

A name had been written in neat, flowing script, along with two words below it.

Alex Lockerby. I'm sorry.

33

NOTES

Alex dozed as the cab made its way from the Central Office toward the brownstone. He'd spent the majority of the day with Lieutenant Detweiler trying to find Kim Carson, or rather, Anita Powell. They'd gone to her apartment, but there were signs of a hasty departure. From there, they'd gone to Alex's office so Mike could test the letter for explosive runes, but there weren't any. Now it was past three in the afternoon and Alex just wanted to sit in his reading chair and read anything other than the note from Anita.

As his exhausted brain began to slip into sleep, he felt the cab begin to slow as it pulled over to the curb outside the brownstone.

"That'll be three dollars, twenty," the cabbie said.

Alex handed him a fiver and got out, stretching once he hit the curb. The taxi had dropped him about twenty feet from the steps on account of there being a large black car already parked in front of the building. As he turned, Alex saw a tall, slender man in a glossy silk suit shaking Iggy's hand at the top of the stairs. He was distinguished looking with a handlebar mustache and iron gray hair.

As Alex approached, the man descended the stairs to the car, where he opened the passenger door and a moment later the car accelerated away from the curb.

"Who was that?" Alex asked, mounting the stairs up to the stoop.

"That was Phillip Faust," Iggy said, providing information that was no help at all. "What are you doing home so early?"

"It's already been a long day," Alex said. "I need a dram of Scotch, a good cigar, and maybe some music."

"If you think you can work an explanation in there, I'll pour the Scotch and turn on the radio," Iggy promised, opening the front door and stepping back for Alex to enter.

"Deal," Alex said.

He opened the inner vestibule door and turned into the library. After retrieving a pair of Iggy's cigars from the humidor, Alex flopped down in his reading chair.

"Must have been some day," Iggy observed, handing Alex the cigar cutter and heading for the liquor cabinet.

"I figured out who the bomber was and where she was hiding," Alex said, ignoring the cigar.

"She?" Iggy prodded.

"It was Anita Powell," Alex explained. "One of Reggie Aspler's former fiancées."

"Here," Iggy said, pushing a tumbler into Alex's hand. "Take a drink, then soak your cigar and tell me the story."

Alex did as he was told, running through the bomber case and the pieces he had eventually put together.

"Fascinating," Iggy said when he was done. "So she was seeking revenge from the men who took her too lightly."

Alex nodded, pulling his cigar out of the whisky and tapping it on the edge of the glass.

"When she lost the promotion at the Office of Magical Oversight she must have just snapped," he said. "She went after everyone who ever wronged her."

"Except her father," Iggy pointed out. "That seems like a telling oversight."

"You think she still loves him?"

"Perhaps," Iggy said, offering Alex a light for his cigar. "Either that or she was saving him for last so she could savor his demise."

As Alex puffed on the cigar, he was forced to agree with the latter.

Anita's father seemed to be quite the opinionated tyrant. Still, love, as the poet said, was blind. Unless a hand delivered letter showed up at the Powell residence in the next week or so, Alex doubted he'd ever find out.

"So now that you know where to find Miss Powell," Iggy said, taking his seat on the opposite side of the reading table, "is it safe to assume Lieutenant Detweiler has her in custody?"

"Nope," Alex said, blowing out a cloud of fragrant smoke. "We went to the Office of Magical Oversight but she wasn't there." He reached into his pocket and withdrew the letter addressed to him. "We found this on her desk," he said, handing it over.

Iggy took the letter and opened it.

"My, my," he said after only a few moments. "You made quite the impression on Miss Powell."

"I'm an inspiration wherever I go," Alex agreed, his voice flowing with sarcasm.

Iggy chuckled at that.

"If I didn't know any better, I'd say she was infatuated with you," he went on. "She says that she regrets her crimes and wishes she'd met you earlier so she could become your apprentice."

"I read it already," Alex growled, "you don't have to repeat it."

"You seem a bit touchy," Iggy said. "Is it possible you return some of her affections?"

Alex knew Iggy was goading him, but it had been a long, frustrating day.

"No," he insisted. "I'm sure she's a wonderful person, she just has the unfortunate habit of blowing up people who slight her."

"For every action, there's an equal and opposite reaction," Iggy said in his stoic voice. "I can't condone what she did, but I can understand the impulse. Especially in such a talented runewright."

"She is that," Alex agreed.

Iggy finished the letter and set it on the reading table.

"So she's sorry for her crimes, she knew you would discover the bomb she sent you and was just hoping to put you off, and she's leaving Manhattan," he summarized. "How are you going to catch her?"

"I'm not," Alex admitted. "Detweiler and I went by her apartment but it had been cleaned out. Only the furniture was left along with some cheap knick-knacks. Anita's too smart to leave anything behind that I could use to track her."

"What did she do," Iggy asked, "shove it all in her vault?"

"Yep," Alex said. "I found a chalk door on the wall of her bedroom."

"So that's it?" Iggy asked.

"The police will issue an alert, send her picture out to departments around the country, but that's not going to work. Anita has been hiding under various aliases for most of her life."

"What about you? You going to let it go?"

Alex turned and looked at his mentor.

"There's nothing else to do," he said. "I could spin my wheels for years looking for her, but unless she starts blowing people up with rune bombs again, there's no real chance of finding her."

"I'm afraid you're right," Iggy sighed.

"There's one other thing," Alex said. "When we searched the OMO building, I found a chalk door on the wall in the ladies room."

"You said she had gone to the ladies just before you got there," Iggy pointed out.

"But why did she open her vault?" Alex said.

"Maybe she donned a disguise so she could escape," Iggy suggested. "You said it yourself, she'd been hiding under aliases for most of her days."

"I suppose," Alex said, somewhat unconvinced.

"Is there another explanation?"

"I was just thinking that Anita is pretty smart," Alex said. "She figured out how to make a boom rune all on her own."

"And you're wondering if maybe she figured out how to open multiple doors into a vault," Iggy surmised.

"Bingo," Alex said. "That would explain how she cleaned out her apartment so fast."

"It sounds like Miss Anita Powell might be more dangerous than we first thought," Iggy admitted.

"It still doesn't matter," Alex said. "She's gone and she's not going to do something that would lead us to her. It's time to move on."

"I'm glad you came to that conclusion," Iggy said, finishing off his Scotch. "Tilting at windmills is best done from horseback, and there isn't room for a horse here in the brownstone."

Alex chuckled at that, a bit of the weight of the day lifting.

"To the one that got away," Iggy said, holding out his glass to Alex.

Alex clinked the glass and drank.

"To the one who got away," he confirmed. "So," he said, eager to change the subject, "who is Phillip Faust and what was he doing here?"

"Ah," Iggy said, standing and heading back to the liquor cabinet, "that is quite the story."

He retrieved the Scotch bottle and poured himself a dram before returning to do the same for Alex.

"Phillip is one of the high up muckity mucks at the local Masonic temple," Iggy said, causing Alex to sit up straight. "I thought that might get your attention."

"You asked about the vision stone?"

Iggy nodded, sipping from his glass.

"After our discussion the other day, I decided to go by and see what I could find out," he explained. "I was trying to be discrete, but apparently I said something that was some kind of passcode. The person I spoke to ran it up the chain after I left and that led to Phillip Faust paying me a visit today."

"Was he warning you off, or just trying to find out how much you know?" Alex asked.

Iggy gave him a sly smile and leaned close as if he were afraid of being overheard.

"Neither," he said in an excited voice. "Phillip said that they'd been waiting for someone to come and ask about the All Seeing Eye, calling it a vision stone."

"Waiting?" Alex said.

"For well over a century, apparently," Iggy said.

"That could only be possible if they had the eye," Alex said, sliding to the edge of his seat.

"Exactly what I figured," Iggy said.

"So what did Faust want?"

Iggy reached down and retrieved a heavy looking leather folio from the floor by his chair. It was covered in a coat of what looked like oil, probably to preserve the leather, and there was a large, purple wax seal on the front that bore the symbol of the All Seeing Eye.

"Faust said they'd been holding this since the late seventeen hundreds," Iggy said, "and they were to pass it on to whoever came to them with the pass phrase."

"Which is what you happened to say when you went to their temple looking for answers," Alex concluded. "So? What's inside?"

Iggy rolled his eyes and pointed to the still-intact wax seal.

"Sorry," Alex said, feeling a bit sheepish.

"As you saw, Faust had just left when you arrived," Iggy said. "Now that you're here, however, I think it's a perfect time to find out. Let's repair to the kitchen and I'll heat up a knife so we can cut this seal off. I'd like to preserve it if we can."

Alex thought that was a fantastic idea and followed Iggy to the kitchen. It only took a minute to heat up a sharp knife on the gas burners and once it was glowing slightly, Iggy handed the knife to Alex.

"You should do the honors, lad," he said.

Alex moved to the table, placing the knife against the edge of the purple seal and allowing the heat to melt the bottom edge of the wax. Moving steadily, Alex forced the blade along the leather, neatly separating the seal from the folio.

"I'll take that," Iggy said, retrieving the seal and placing it to the side.

"What now?" Alex asked. "Do we just open it?"

"I believe we do," Iggy said, peeling up the leather flap from where the seal had held it in place. He moved carefully, making sure the edges didn't stick to anything as it opened. Eventually, the flap came loose and Iggy opened it fully so the end laid on the table.

Inside, Alex could see stacks of paper, wrapped with a ribbon to keep them together. There appeared to be a box of some kind as well and other things that were too far down to reveal themselves.

"All right," Alex said, reaching for the papers. "Here we go."

THE END

You Know the Drill.

Thanks so much for reading my book, it really means a lot to me. This is the part where I ask you to please leave this book a review over on Amazon. It really helps me out since Amazon favors books with lots of reviews. That means I can share these books with more people, and that keeps me writing more books.

So leave a review by going to the Equal & Opposite book page on Amazon. It doesn't have to be anything fancy, just a quick note saying whether or not you liked the book.

Thanks so much. You Rock!

I love talking to my readers, so please drop me a line at dan@danwillisauthor.com — I read every one. Or join the discussion on the Arcane Casebook Facebook Group. Just search for Arcane Casebook and ask to join.

And Look for Alex's continuing adventures in "Gangster." Arcane Casebook #12 coming soon. You can preorder Gangster from the Arcane Casebook series page on Amazon.

ACKNOWLEDGMENTS

Special thanks to my amazing beta readers, they really helped take this book to the next level.

Lyn Adams
Bob Brown
Virginia Carper
RJ Carvalho
Cat
Mike Dunkle Sr.
Ann Engel
Pam Foye
Fiona Harford
Tan Ho
James Hodges
Mark

ALSO BY DAN WILLIS

Arcane Casebook Series:

Dead Letter - Prequel

Get Dead Letter free at www.danwillisauthor.com

Available on Amazon and Audible.

In Plain Sight - Book 1

Ghost of a Chance - Book 2

The Long Chain - Book 3

Mind Games - Book 4

Limelight - Book 5

Blood Relation - Book 6

Capital Murder - Book 7

Hostile Takeover - Book 8

Hidden Voices - Book 9

Pound of Flesh - Book 10

Arcane Irregulars Series:

Two companion volumes to the Arcane Casebook series. These books expand the AC universe and tie into the main story.

Curse of the Phoenix - Book 1 (Takes place after AC# 6)

Shadow of Anubis - Book 2 (Takes place after AC #8)

Dragons of the Confederacy Series:

A steampunk Civil War story with NYT Bestseller, Tracy Hickman.

Get the Dragons of the Confederacy books at Amazon.com.

Lincoln's Wizard

The Georgia Alchemist

Other books:

The Flux Engine

In a Steampunk Wild West, fifteen-year-old John Porter wants nothing more than to find his missing family. Unfortunately a legendary lawman, a talented thief, and a homicidal madman have other plans, and now John will need his wits, his pistol, and a lot of luck if he's going to survive.

Get The Flux Engine at Amazon.com.

ABOUT THE AUTHOR

Dan Willis wrote for the long-running DragonLance series. He is the author of the Arcane Casebook series and the Dragons of the Confederacy series.

For more information:
www.danwillisauthor.com
dan@danwillisauthor.com

facebook.com/danwillisauthor
tiktok.com/@danwillisauthor
x.com/WDanWillis
instagram.com/danwillisauthor